W9-CBP-599

OBSERVATIONS
BY GASLIGHT

OBSERVATIONS BY GASLIGHT

STORIES FROM THE WORLD OF
SHERLOCK HOLMES

LYNDSAY FAYE

THE MYSTERIOUS PRESS
NEW YORK

OBSERVATIONS BY GASLIGHT

Mysterious Press
An Imprint of Penzler Publishers
58 Warren Street
New York, N.Y. 10007

Copyright © 2021 by Lyndsay Faye

"The Gospel of Sheba" was previously published by The Mysterious Bookshop in the "Bibliomysteries" series, copyright © 2014 by Lyndsay Faye.

First edition

Interior design by Maria Fernandez

All rights reserved. No part of this book may be reproduced in whole or in part without written permission from the publisher, except by reviewers who may quote brief excerpts in connection with a review in a newspaper, magazine, or electronic publication; nor may any part of this book be reproduced, stored in a retrieval system, or transmitted in any form or by any means electronic, mechanical, photocopying, recording, or other, without written permission from the publisher.

Library of Congress Control Number: 2021917642

Cloth ISBN: 978-1-61316-261-3
eBook ISBN: 978-1-61316-262-0

10 9 8 7 6 5 4 3 2 1

Printed in the United States of America
Distributed by W. W. Norton & Company

This collection is dedicated to Otto Penzler,
who has been my hero throughout the process

CONTENTS

A NOTE FROM THE EDITOR

While it is well known that Dr. John Watson's accounts of Mr. Sherlock Holmes's exploits contain nothing save the utmost veracity in spirit, the recent discovery of these documents penned by the friends and colleagues of the Great Detective unfortunately lead to still greater confusion as regards the good doctor's chronology. That this occurrence is all too predictable does not make it any less confounding.

The letters and diary entries presented here were found collected in a long-abandoned safety deposit box by the linear descendant of a Baker Street Irregular. The lady has asked to remain anonymous, but she was the first of her clan to deduce the bank that housed the box that housed the papers that had been passed so faithfully down, as it were. As to why this volume was never published, who can say? Though it is possible that Sherlock Holmes himself, highly private during his years of retirement, forbade it for public consumption. One cannot very well doubt he would have been much moved by reading it with his friend Dr. Watson in a more private setting, however.

Dr. Watson's recorded dates having been for over a century the source of both fascination and hair-pulling mystification, I've ordered these stories in the way they seem most fitting as stories. Since they stand alone, having been penned by so many, this proved a simple enough—not to mention thoroughly enjoyable—task. They are themselves dated, however, in typically Watsonian helter-skelter fashion. Despite the fact there is much herein to debate as regards historical accuracy and its intersection with genuine calendar months (or even years), you will find nothing quite so maddening as the canonical Watson writing of Holmes solving crime in 1892, for instance, when the noble gentlemen was by most accounts dead at the bottom of a waterfall and by truer accounts fleeing for his life in various guises. While I'd hoped that this remarkable project would clear up some of the more thorny issues caused by Watson's biographies, I'm afraid all it did was muddy the waters further. And the sole wife mentioned is the tragically deceased Mary Morstan Watson, with whom we are already well acquainted from *The Sign of Four* and various short stories. Even Watson's matrimonial status, therefore, provides no valuable clue for the canny Sherlockian investigator.

As these tales in the purely temporal sense contradict not merely the canon as we know it, but *Strand Magazine* dates when Dr. Watson's manuscripts were published—and the stories even, in occasional cases as written here, battle with each other insofar as time is concerned—it is suggested that they be savored for their insight into the character of Sherlock Holmes rather than into his schedule. Should, however, playful arguments arise between scholars attempting to tinker with the queerly inconsistent clock which appears to be ticking, thereby making sense of the whole, the very best of luck and enjoyment is hereby wished to all participants.

Finally, it has been a heady privilege to be allowed to oversee this volume. Since all we definitely know of Sherlock Holmes has spilled from the pen of Watson—and, in two cases, Holmes himself, who can hardly be trusted on the subject of himself—this trove is sure to offer unique insights. I hope its readers derive as much joy from these words as I did.

Yours most sincerely,

Lyndsay Faye

INTRODUCTION

Dear Reader,

While this piece may seem eccentric to some for a practicing solicitor to produce, it has been one of the greatest joys of my existence to create it. The life and career of Sherlock Holmes, it is well known, have long held a fascination for me. He was my mentor. He is in fact rather revered. I dare say, even, he is my friend, which is an honour few can claim.

The current publisher of the *Strand Magazine*, therefore, desiring to publish more about Sherlock Holmes long after Dr. Watson retired from the practice of doing so, and after Sherlock Holmes took up beekeeping in Sussex, approached me as a man closer to the renowned figure than most. But sadly, unlike the wonderful doctor, I am no biographer. I would have no facility with such a project. I am not worthy of such a task alone.

Thus, I have taken it upon myself to collect other people's accounts of the man. Some of these were easy to come by. Others were not. The project in fact took years to complete. In each case, I asked for a favourite memory, a shared adventure, and for that person to consult any personal documents they retained and then tell the tale in their own way. This may seem like foisting my own assigned work onto others (though I, too, have made a humble contribution). But I instead think of it as expanding the full scope of the man, as he is seen from differing perspectives—his mind, his humanity. I congratulate myself on my approach, in fact. For when I asked these friends and acquaintances for their memories, none of them hesitated.

They all had plenty to say about Sherlock Holmes.

Most of these offerings regard events that happened long ago, and so appear in the form of diary entries and letters, the writers returning to the occasion wistfully upon remembering it, and then making the pieces much more expansive upon my explicit behest. Very few people would ever have written in their journals quite so effusively. I encouraged this technique, so that people might know that as outlandish as his life has been, that it was all true, and I am not a single witness, but rather part of the sea of people who remember Sherlock Holmes very well indeed following his retirement.

I deeply hope he will be beekeeping for several more decades, though I dread a bit to think what he will make of this project. It's just as well. Sherlock Holmes can be offended when you didn't notice a stray eyelash, let alone published an epistolary tribute to him.

The words in this volume are unedited save for small concerns to aid the eyes of the beholder. I added quotation marks, etc. But the rest is simply various authors' true stories regarding a great man who lived a great life and can now indulge himself in a little peace. Finding myself quite proud, I hope he shall not be angry over it. He deserves the acclaim ten times over.

From the Office of Mr. Henry Wiggins
Wiggins, Perry, and Tilton, Solicitors
4 Grosvenor Place, London

OBSERVATIONS
BY GASLIGHT

THE ADVENTURE OF THE STOPPED CLOCKS

(Irene Adler)

Entry in the personal journal and scrapbook of Mrs. Irene Norton, née *Adler, Thursday, May 31st, 1888:*

Goodness, I haven't had so much as a *second* to scratch down my thoughts!

We closed our concert's two-week run on Sunday 27th. To universal good notices, I add with a rousing huzzah! Here, I've my brush and paste at the ready, and this review of my performance is too sweet not to insert immediately—it's always better writing to the aroma of glue and newsprint anyhow:

> Den zutiefst berührenden Höhepunkt des Abends bescherte uns Kontraaltistin Irene Adler als Fidès mit ihrer fesselnden Interpretation von "O prêtres de Baal" im 5. Akt, welche den Zuhörern wohl noch Jahre im Gedächtnis bleiben wird.

Or, as it would be said in my native tongue:

> The deeply touching climax of the evening brought us con-tralto Irene Adler as Fides with her captivating interpretation

of "O prêtres de Baal" in the fifth act, which the audience will remember for years to come.

Isn't that darling? How could any singer not adore performing in Vienna, their being so deeply appreciative of our art? There was also a particularly nice sentence or two in *Deutsche Volksblatt*, but then again Meyerbeer always sits well with me.

Excellent accommodations, better programme, and the artistic company I kept best of all. And then chaos like a nest of hornets, and at my own instigation!

First the flurry of telegrams between Vienna and London on Monday. Then the wild packing, kissing my chuckling stage-fellows' cheeks at a farewell breakfast Tuesday before I dashed for the train, flinging myself upon Channel-chopped waters Wednesday, the glad reunion last night.

And now here sit I in this clean, featureless hotel bedroom.

Unsure of myself, after all.

◦—✦—◦

Well, it has been a year since I've seen London—nearly to the week. Anxiety is natural. And Godfrey, bless his beautiful heart, is anxious enough for ten people. (He's worth ten men, so that's hardly shocking.)

And all is quite as it should be! The empty shell of an egg in its porcelain cup at my elbow, my pen in hand. Silvered city light glinting over both. Carpets soft, pale blue velvet chairs plump, Godfrey returned to his former offices in the Temple.

Myself incognito, as needs must. Since Godfrey is so very anxious over my ever coming across a certain consulting detective hired by a certain Bohemian.

Perhaps the prospect of enduring my husband's brother this evening might account for my minor jitters? Or that I cannot freely be *myself*, swan about with my feathers agleam in St. James's Park? It cannot be fear of

Siggy, for he is long gone away home. And what a poor home the hereditary King of Bohemia's was, for all its riches!

I trace these irksome quivers to last night.

Champagne in bed at three-thirty in the morning may sound indecent to *some*, but Godfrey is not among their number. Our reunion deserved celebration. Anyway, what harm has decadence ever done anyone? In moderation, of course. He grinned at me from the headboard, snug in pyjamas and a shawl-collared robe. Its sable colour made his black hair blacker, mussed from where I'd mussed it. He gazed at me sitting Hindu-style in an emerald velvet dressing gown and silk shift, ensconced in about fifty pillows like the veriest Jezebel.

"There is to be champagne in the middle of the night upon every Wednesday last of the month henceforth, in perpetuity, to celebrate the month." Sipping, I savoured yeast and green pears.

"*Vox Regina, vox Dei.* You do look rather like a queen just now," he murmured.

"Mmm. Hearty thanks—we should buy me a sceptre. I've plentiful paste tiaras already, so that's not at issue. Ooooh, I should go fetch one."

"By George. It still troubles me on occasion." Godfrey's handsome face darkened.

"What does?"

"Your . . . situation. Oh, I comprehend full well what a cad the King was," he continued.

"Beg pardon?"

"Only . . . to think you might have been a monarch in truth once, and here you are, bride of a humble solici—"

"Bride of a king among men instead of in outmoded hereditary claptrap!" I exclaimed. "I'm a freeborn citizen of the United States of America, might I remind you. Don't tread on me! Live free or die!"

Godfrey scoffed charmingly.

My champagne splashed as I launched myself across the bed.

"No, no, listen to me! Not a wax effigy in a crown, to be revered and exalted. Not a figurehead on the prow of a ship, to inspire and—"

My spouse of just over a year stopped my protestations. Pleasantly, too.

"You must know by this time how I adore you," I breathed.

When I met his deep brown eyes, a smile appeared. "For heaven's sake, I ought to. You're the one outwitted all the king's horses and all the king's men to win my hand."

"I *did*, didn't I? Did I sweep you away on a white charger?"

"No, that should have been far too noticeable. It was a white steamer."

"How awfully clever of me. You helped, though, let's not forget."

"I haven't finished. To continue. Whisked us away to the continent, supposedly *never to return to London and Sherlock bloody*—"

I sat upright, indignant. "Is it my fault that my beloved has pressing business dealings in my favourite city?"

Godfrey frowned. I could write entire adagios for his frowns. "Is it my fault that my darling is wretchedly unsafe here following certain all-too-recent adventures? For heaven's sake, Irene, he could still want you *arrested* for *blackmail*. The man certainly tried his best."

"Well, is it *my* fault that you've a taste for women with a taste for *life*? While I don't regret my past . . . entanglements, I do detest the way this one hobbles us."

"Ha! The day I see you hobbled is the day Marianne Brandt outperforms you at 'Re dell'abiso.'"

"That'll never happen. But I *am* geographically hobbled, awfully so!"

"No, darling, you're right *here* actually, against all safety injunctions. In London. With me."

"How terribly vexing for you. You ought to have married a maiden in a tower," I sniffed.

"Should I desire such a dreadfully tedious wife, I've no doubt we can procure you a blonde wig and you can enact her for me."

Shaking out my chestnut hair, I tried to remain miffed. I failed.

Who could possibly *not* love such a man as Godfrey Norton? To reemphasise: it's *always* an honour to give a concert in Vienna, especially with my old pals from the Vienna Court Opera. But now I realise—no matter that Europe, improbably, was safer than England thanks to its lack of Sherlock

Holmes. No matter that Godfrey and I had travelled the Continent for eleven happy months.

He was called back to London Town. I was in Vienna.

And I *hated* it.

I was sick to death of the loneliness and the loveliness, wanted no more of clean grey Austrian streets and only good British mud, no more pillowy sausages and merely a bowl of buttered peas.

So I wired him. I'd paste the entire exchange here, but I was too frantic after the concert ended to save the initial telegrams. Most are irrecoverable, in my Austrian fireplace.

Prepare a parade in my honour, for I'm joining you quick as I can, I wrote.

You cannot return to England and you know it, he responded with undue urgency.

I'm going to though, so don't get rattled. I always sound more American when I'm very determined. *I'm not afraid of Sherlock Holmes.*

Please do not risk your safety on a whim.

You are no whim. You are the light that causes my soul to bloom.

This last response, though, I saved for posterity. Of course I did:

```
LONDON, ENGLAND to VIENNA, AUSTRIA,
Monday, May 28th marked URGENT:


IF YOU DON'T RUIN MY HEALTH WITH WORRY YOU'LL
RUIN IT TEARING MY HEARTSTRINGS STOP FOR
GOD'S SAKE TAKE A SHIP AND DON'T SWIM THE
CHANNEL STOP I LOVE YOU—GN
```

Anyhow, I hopped out of bed to refill our champagne glasses, I called, "What's got you so bothered over the whole business with Siggy tonight anyhow? Don't spare the scoundrel a thought. *I* rarely do, and then it's only to recollect that he had a nightdress with a white fox fur collar and laugh myself senseless."

Godfrey's face grew still more troubled.

"Godfrey!" Abandoning the glasses, I clasped both his hands. "You haven't moped over Siggy in . . . no, strike that, I don't figure you've ever moped in your life. This cannot be about Sherlock Holmes, I've already outwitted him. Spill it at once."

His lips brushed my wrist. "We must dine with Gilbert tomorrow."

"Haven't you finished your business with your horrid brother by this time?"

"No, more's the pity. And I've not the slightest capacity of giving you orders, but please darling, don't go running willy-nilly around London while I'm at the offices?"

"I, Irene Norton, swear not to run helter-skelter. And it isn't as if I'm a universally reviled figure, when people even do recognise me. I'm just a renowned opera singer. And Siggy poses no threat—the buffoon has all his socks monogrammed and is long married to an albino tadpole. He's long *gone* altogether."

Godfrey muttered something like *Sherlock bloody Holmes isn't.* I stroked a wave of his thick hair.

As I mentioned, I'm not afraid of Sherlock Holmes either.

Ever since I spent a week researching him, the man positively fascinates me. He invented a *definitive* test for identifying *bloodstains*—I'm no amateur scientist, but the journals do fascinate me.

"Irene, you attempted to blackmail the hereditary king of Bohemia."

"Nearly managed it, too, by golly."

"It was quite definitely illegal. Very, very punishable."

"It was *fun*. And necessary—who else would have taken that pompous oaf down a peg?"

"Do spare some pity for my nerves."

"Then spare some pity for mine! They'll be in shambles after an entire evening looking at your brother!"

He winced at that. "Irene, I flatter myself that you enjoy assisting me. Please help me to work out what the deuce is going on?"

"Oh, my *darling*. In a heartbeat," I soothed. "What's the trouble?"

"That's just it—I don't know. Gilbert wanted my help as a solicitor to rearrange some securities, sell others. But you shall hear all about it tomorrow, darling—never allow me to stand accused of ruining a topping bottle of champagne by discussing the Norton *finances.*"

I reined my temper, which was roused only on behalf of my noble husband rather than against him. *Of course* when he'd thought I looked queenly, he'd poked at a tender spot in his own heart. As if it isn't enough that his reprobate father lost half the Norton family fortune at the tables. As if it isn't enough that Gilbert is the eldest and cut from identical cloth, haemorrhaging money, and second son Gerald is in Sumatra overseeing a thriving peppercorn plantation.

Well, aces for Gilbert and Gerald. It left Godfrey, a half brother from a second marriage, with nothing save a sterling intellect and education, his character, and his determination to prevent his elder sibling from squandering the remainder of their assets. Gilbert insults me whenever he can, and Godfrey responds by—throwing me in his surly brother's face.

Oh! I should air the sapphire gown immediately; Godfrey will want me in finest fettle this evening!

I'm salivating to walk the streets again. I might have indicated to Godfrey that *Irene* Norton wouldn't be glimpsed today, but Irene Norton doesn't wear Paris-cut trousers and swallowtail coats.

Properly fried cod and chips are to be had nearby, and they aren't going to consume themselves.

Entry in the personal journal and scrapbook of Mrs. Irene Norton, née *Adler, Friday, June 1st, 1888:*

Speaking of fish, we are in a fine kettle of one.

Lord above, I cannot *bear* Gilbert Norton.

Gilbert greeted us in the front parlour of the townhouse, which is populated by the family collection of standing clocks. It is part museum, part showroom to dazzle visitors. The room was eerily quiet. He raked hazel eyes up and down as if I were some back-alley piece of flotsam instead of a headlining prima donna. He licked his lips.

Impudent *wretch.*

"Why, if it isn't my dear sister returned to haunt our hallways," he sneered, already three or four glasses of sherry ahead of us. "How was your triumphal European tour, then?"

My husband took my arm. "It was wildly successful—but had it been a series of decaying railway line inspections, I should still have been blissfully content."

Preening, I offered my hand. Gilbert had no choice save taking it, emitting a foul stench of snobbery. My spouse and I passed off the elopement as a sudden but necessary prelude to my emerging from retirement—when really we were married in a spectacular hurry to avoid a certain consulting detective and hadn't wanted anyone there—and I don't suppose Gilbert's ever forgiven me for snatching a free (and brilliant) solicitor from his clutches.

Happy thought!

As the brothers spoke, I took a turn around the receiving room visiting my favourite residents: the clocks. A stunning sky-blue Fryksdahl from Sweden shaped like a violin smiled down at me; a mahogany case clock with such a high polish it shone like tortoiseshell seemed to wink. Suddenly I realised why the atmosphere in the room was so strangely still.

"Gilbert, why are none of the clocks running?" I called.

He glowered. "They are all to be serviced and appraised to update the insurance policy. Whatever business is it of yours?"

Dinner passed predictably. Being half siblings, Gilbert is much lighter haired than Godfrey, going to fat where Godfrey is trim and broad-shouldered, with a tendency to stroke his side-whiskers when contemplating how next to snub me. This time it was "little music-hall melodramas" and "your sudden departure produced no . . . happy news for the family, then?"

Godfrey's mouth seemed carved of stone. Meanwhile I arched my shoulders like a hissing cat and drew my forefinger around my wine glass rim. Smiling all the while.

Yet . . . something more niggled. Sputtering and hissing between the siblings as I hadn't seen before. It all came out when the three of us retired back to the clocks parlour. Gilbert has neither wife nor real friends, so I joined the men as a trio. They couldn't exactly pack me off to the library to read Austen.

Godfrey gave me a subtle tilt of his eyebrow, his back to the grey marble fireplace, before volleying at his brother, "I say, Gilbert, you've never suggested letting go of the Peters-Carmichael stocks before now. I wondered for what possible reason? They're perfectly sound."

Gilbert, loose and louche in an armchair, curled his upper lip around his cigar. "I have it on excellent authority that they *won't* be sound in a few months' time, so don't fret over it."

"Are you in need of immediate funds?"

The question was posed coolly, but the elder brother spat, "It would behoove you to mind your own bloody business over what's *mine* by inheritance, Godfrey."

"All right. You've changed your opinion of peppercorns then?"

"Questions, questions, questions. Have you no family feeling? No, I know full well where your affections lie. With dance-hall girls and tavern keepers' daughters."

Godfrey badly wanted to strike him, but I interjected, "We can all hold multiple people in our hearts, my dear Gilbert. I'm sure Godfrey thinks of you exactly as he ever did."

Noticing the barb, Gilbert stuffed the cigar back between his teeth.

"Upon whose authority do you have it that Peters-Carmichael is unsound?" Godfrey persisted.

Gilbert slurred, "Oh won't you please shut your stickling head, Godfrey; the Baron tipped me. So I'm shuffling them off to Gerald in Sumatra. Does that satisfy you? Does it satisfy your *wife*?"

Wife, in this case, was spelled *courtesan*, and we could both hear it. We left five minutes later, Godfrey in a rage, Gilbert snoring.

So that's the trouble. The Baron. For all he twits Godfrey about his low company, Gilbert's moments of disgrace are spent banging his fists against gambling tables and other people's faces, while Godfrey's are spent—*used to be* spent—plying pretty chanteuses and actresses with hothouse roses and then doing their bookkeeping for them the morning after. All right, he was a bit of an adventurer, but so was I, wasn't I? And it's vastly better behavior to court an artist than it is to hush up scandals over beaten dogs and ponies. Servants, occasionally. Gilbert's footman once had the ghastliest black eye.

The Baron addresses these problems for Gilbert Norton. He cajoles, he bribes, he threatens. He fixes things, like a tinker in a toy shop. What are such men called? Well, anyhow, the Baron fixes whatever ails Gilbert.

He's a *fixer*, there, I've settled it!

Last night under the quilt, Godfrey said, "Forgive me, darling, for exposing you to that behavior. But you see why this vexes me? Why should Gilbert abandon something profitable to benefit a brother he doesn't give a whit about?"

"Nonsense, I've spread men saltier than your brother on toast and nibbled at them for breakfast. And of course I do. What have you tried so far?"

His shoulder shrugged beneath my head. "I can find nothing whatsoever wrong with the Peters-Carmichael holdings, nor with Gerald's dashed peppercorns neither. It's like selling a townhouse to purchase its exact copy across the street. The value is essentially identical. Gilbert never gave a fig over Sumatra, so why should he start?"

"Hmm."

"He never gave a fig for Gerald or me either," Godfrey continued with a yawn. "He always resented our striking out independently. He only hated it more when we proved competent."

"The stocks themselves are not what troubles you," I murmured.

"What does, then?"

"The Baron. Where the devil does he enter into it?"

"The back door, darling, I can promise you that much."

"And why should all your family clocks have been stopped?"

"It's been like that for days. I haven't the faintest idea," he sighed as he drifted into slumberland.

For my sleepless part, I recalled all I could about Dickie "Baron" Maupertuis, so-called because the scamp claims he's descended from French aristocrats who fled the guillotine's kiss. My left boot sole has bluer blood than does Dickie Maupertuis, and I have it on good authority his family is from Seven Dials. When his ugly head first reared up to fret Godfrey, I researched him thoroughly. And he fixes things for plenty of folks, not just Gilbert—gentlemen of leisure, yes, but also art collectors, banking magnates, very rich criminals, and two titled landowners. If you're wealthy and unscrupulous and have a problem, Dickie Maupertuis makes it *go away.*

Puzzling how to help my beloved, there in his arms, I came up with nil. Yes, I can pass as a man by night or with my hat low—but I can't conduct entire interviews with hooligans that way. Some women can turn masculine flawlessly, but my features are too delicate even using paint.

I like my ribs intact, and so does Godfrey. What I need is an *ally.*

Ooooh, I've the most *delicious* idea. It's so wonderfully funny that I just long to tell Godfrey about it—but he'd quash it like a bug.

Today I've a message to send while dear Godfrey is working down at the Temple. Oh, if I should pull this off! The finest haberdasher in Paris won't have a walloping enough feather for my cap. I won't be Irene anymore. I'll be Yankee Doodle and call the feather Macaroni.

As I drifted off, I couldn't help but reflect: what troubles my husband's repose and what troubles mine the most differ entirely. Obviously, the miasma of Dickie Maupertuis puts a right stink over the whole question of stock trading, especially when the transaction seems meaningless.

But why should all the grandfather clocks be stopped, even if they are to be serviced?

I've never heard of such a thing.

Entry in the personal journal and scrapbook of Mrs. Irene Norton, née *Adler, Friday, June 1st, 1888 (continued):*

He already said yes!

How my heart thrills at it! Huzzah! But *not* in the way it does when I glimpse Godfrey unexpectedly, that grasping glee that makes me want to cling to him like an ivy vine.

This is another thrill altogether. I loathe hurting animals, but I've galloped over fen and fencepost enough times to *know* what a huntress must feel like.

In a brown tweed suit and bowler hat, I crossed the river to send the wire. Giving away our location without due caution would have been unwise to say the least. My missive was so vague I was sure it would net him:

SOUTHWARK to MARYLEBONE, Friday, June 1st.:

OLD FRIEND REQUIRES AID **STOP** WORK MUST COME GRATIS BUT REPAID IN INFORMATION **STOP** WOULD ADD REPAID IN SENTIMENT BUT YOU ARE IMMUNE **STOP** APPLY THIS NAME AND POST OFFICE IMMEDIATELY IF FREE TOMORROW—NIGHTINGALE

And not forty minutes of pacing the tiles later, his reply:

MARYLEBONE to SOUTHWARK, Friday, June 1st.:

INTRIGUED NOT OVER OLD FRIEND BUT BECAUSE I HAVE NONE **STOP** AN ENEMY JUST AS DIVERTING SHOULD THIS BE A LURE, AS I'VE REALLY NO IDEA TO WHOM I'M TALKING **STOP** GLAD TO DISCUSS TOMORROW—SH

Now, to complete my planning!

It's difficult to separate one's life from one's work when one is lucky enough to be engaged in the *exact* vocation that best expresses her personality. I am that blessed by Fortune. So a certain amount of . . . well, *flash* . . . tends to be involved in my dealings, be they commonplace or outlandish.

My first official meeting with Sherlock Holmes requires proper staging. It's not as if I can simply turn up at Baker Street without Godfrey having kittens over it. Less hostile territory is called for, but a park bench or a tea shop would certainly not—

Oh my Lord. I *have it*, it's perfection itself! Farewell, dear journal, for I must disguise my writing and scribble two notes for hand-delivery.

One to Mr. Sherlock Holmes of Baker Street and one to the Cupid's Arrow Club.

Entry in the personal journal and scrapbook of Mrs. Irene Norton, née *Adler, Saturday, June 2nd, 1888:*

I've gone and done it, by God!

What a pleasant morning, and by pleasant I mean *thrilling*. But no, I'll write it quite pragmatically, so that in future readings of this journal I can savour it all the better. This may well beat out the occasion I saw Marietta Alboni give a secret post-retirement performance of Fidalma.

First, as to participants. I wanted to see Mr. Holmes sans his confederate, Dr. John Watson. For dual reasons: one, that we might converse freely, as I don't know quite how far their confidence extends (though assuredly as far as throwing smoke rockets); two, that I might concentrate all my own powers of observation on a single target.

Very good. Dr. Watson is in practice and married. I needed only demand a very early morning rendezvous to whisk him out of the picture. Decent men—and he does seem a decent sort, from my research—don't stand up a leisurely Saturday breakfast with their wives when the week is devoted to furthering their medical career.

My own spouse, at my behest, was engaged at our bank going over the accounts we could only access partially from abroad. At six-fifteen in the morning, I donned my nattiest opera-going attire of the masculine variety, a black suit and white cravat fit for Godfrey himself. I then pointed my boots towards the Cupid's Arrow Club.

Oh, what a sight it was nestled there in Tottenham Court Road!

My spirits leapt. The cobbles were strewn with manure and nutshells and violets, all smelling of rain and wet hay, and that sweet townhouse rose upwards like a beacon. I didn't know how badly I'd missed the London theatre district—the double masks of the club's door knocker almost moved me to tears.

A well-built stripling in white gloves greeted me. The staff are fresh as fields every hour of the twenty-four at the Cupid's Arrow.

I didn't bother hiding my face. What was the point when I'd come home?

"May I help you?"

"Is Aunt Cecilia feeling less poorly? I'd like to check in on her."

"She'll be delighted to see you." He smiled, stepping aside.

"Darling lad! I sent a note in advance. Is a room available for a private audience?"

"Indeed yes, it's quite ready."

"When a very tall, hawk-nosed gentleman arrives shortly, please tell him that the Nightingale will receive him. If he knows Aunt Cecilia, bully for him, and if he doesn't, show him up personally?"

So I found myself upstairs in one of the florid private sitting rooms. I'd seen that one before, but always by night. It was precious, though, by daylight—the mauve and green carpet didn't deserve the crimson drapes, the lucky Chinese hearth dragons growled at the Limoges mantelpiece cats, and the umbrella stand was actually an upturned post box. But it was perfection for an operatic star dressed as a dapper gentleman awaiting the world's only (so he claims, which I *highly* doubt) independent consulting detective.

I flicked on a tasseled amber lamp and moved beyond it. It never hurts to light introductions properly. And not a moment too soon, for I heard a quiet tread on the stair. Brisk knuckles tapped thrice.

"Do come in!" I slung my hands in my pockets, lowering my head to gaze sidelong under my silk hat brim.

It's difficult to convey the impression Sherlock Holmes imparts—a raven just landed, by turns flutters and freezing stares. Except the raven is one of Apollo's lot informing you that he's awfully sorry, but you've incurred the wrath of a deity. I'd only seen him dressed as himself in Baker Street by gaslight, so I studied him over. Paler and thinner even than previous. Pinstriped trousers; black jacket, waistcoat, and tie; tall hat not unlike mine; thin leather gloves. Immaculately polished boots. He was hard at work lately, then—weary enough to take a hansom the short but muddy distance between Baker Street and the Cupid's Arrow and prosperous enough not to mind the fare.

"Good morning, Mr. Sherlock Holmes."

As I looked up, I thought I might have overdone the drama. Then Mr. Holmes's head gave such a sudden tilt that it resembled a start, and his smile curled almost invisibly. Not from behind his lips, but from behind razor-grey eyes I'd only ever stared into when nursing an injured nonconformist clergyman.

Who was actually trying to rob me.

"You've been to the Cupid's Arrow before, Mr. Holmes," I remarked. "I never gave you the password, and the butler isn't with you. You aren't glancing around the room either. So you're already familiar with my choice of venue."

"Yes," he owned, drawing the tiny word out to extreme lengths.

"Oooooh, splendid! For work or pleasure?"

"I fear that would either disclose personal information about myself or my sources and clients. And the true question on the table," he replied, "is why did you guess I would know the place at all?"

"I didn't *guess*, I *reasoned*." It was a passable imitation, at least as Dr. Watson writes him, and I thought he exhaled in amusement. "The ink stain I observed upon the third finger of the nonconformist clergyman's left hand."

Black brows swept together. "There was no such ink stain, and even if—"

"That there's called a joke, where I come from."

The invisible smile intensified.

"So you've been here—you have the permanent password allowing you entrée. Maybe you were here for work. Still. I figured this place wouldn't discomfit you too terribly."

"It doesn't." As if recalling where he was, Mr. Holmes quietly shut the door. "One cannot help but note that you have staged this, however. I confess myself flattered."

"You should be. Sometimes folks interest me, and when folks interest me, I research 'em." I allowed the New Jersey accent to emerge for that single sentence, sweeping aside professional training, and his birdlike head found yet another angle. "The Cupid's Arrow is a particular haunt of artistic sorts of people. So I thought you might know of this place. You're as artistic as anything! The casework, the playacting, the *violin*."

His thin lips pursed. "That's hardly research—so much could be gleaned from my friend Dr. Watson's fairy tales alone."

"They could, but you don't know whether or not they *did*." I chummily leaned an elbow against the top of the nearest chair. "Speaking of the doc, I was stumped when you said you didn't have any old friends in your wire. He surely seems as staunch a friend as any."

"He is, thus my confusion as to the sender of your telegram, *Nightingale*," Mr. Holmes said flatly, dropping his walking stick in the umbrella stand. "Upon the instant I had skimmed your communique, I ascertained that he was well, as indeed I know at any given time anyhow. He was. Or there would be severest consequences."

Remarkable, how he pulled it off! Sherlock Holmes both confided in me and threatened me never to mishandle Dr. John Watson in a few brief sentences.

"Oh, but *do* you like this place?" I gushed, switching topics. "Truly, I mean, I'm just curious, because I love it to absolute bits—do you like it for itself?"

He smiled. "Indeed so."

"How shocking, sir."

"One cannot always rendezvous in palaces, madam."

Grinning, I answered, "A touch! But we seem to have skipped over the polite pleasantries altogether. How gauche."

The detective swept off his hat. "Mrs. Norton, what an unexpected pleasure."

I copied him. "Mr. Holmes! What a predictable one."

"In my defence, I can hardly help my arrival being so adroitly anticipated—you did invite me here. Still," he mused as his gloves came off, "apologies if I have disappointed you in any particular regarding the aesthetic value of my entrance."

"Oh, I should never *dream* of criticizing your theatricality, Mr. Holmes. Not when you fooled me once so thoroughly regarding who you really were."

"Twice."

"I . . . I beg your pardon? Oh, where are my manners, do sit down."

Mr. Holmes rounded the settee and sat with hat and gloves at his side, myself settling in the chintz armchair with its back to the light and my hat on my knee. The silhouetted effect still felt useful. He clearly relishes mysteries, and I mightily enjoy being one.

Let us never forego happy accidents! Words by which to live, says I.

Slinging one long leg over the other, Mr. Holmes flicked his eyes up and down my person with all the impassivity of a basking lizard (in the mirror opposite way my Godfrey does) and lifted a cigarette case questioningly. I nodded permission. He's not a bad-looking sort, and he's incredibly magnetic, he just carries everything a few notches too far, poor thing—the height, the gauntness, the pallor, the suavity, the tailoring. His tiniest gestures are both calculated and consummate. I'll be dashed if *he* doesn't believe they're real, these half-lidded expressions and clipped, cool tones. Well, they're about as real as the "horse" I used to "own" living with my parents, three sisters, and two brothers in a piddling New Jersey village where George Washington once headquartered and the pigs outnumber the humans.

Not to denigrate the place. They even added sewers when I was ten, in 1868. I miss it *ever* so much.

Anyhow, take it from a professional: I've never yet seen Mr. Sherlock Holmes in an unstudied exchange. I *ache* to know what it looks like. Happy interludes have passed imagining his face when he discovered my promotional photograph replacing the one of Siggy and me.

"Wedlock suits you." He took a pull from the cigarette. "You are looking very hale indeed, Mrs. Norton, and may I add that I am pleased to say so?"

"Well shoot, compliment how fit I am all you like and be as glad of it as you please."

"Then I observe that you have returned from the continent in haste and were spending your time there singing professionally, so it appears that further congratulations are in order."

"Expound."

Mr. Holmes nodded amiably. "While you have ever been immaculately careful of your dress in our brief acquaintance, white tie attire is notoriously arduous to achieve to perfection. Granted, the light may have been dim this morning. But I rather doubt you'd tolerate holing up anywhere which wasn't amenable to your tastes, as your Serpentine Mews lodgings were positively riddled with windows, and surely your chamber has lamps. Your cravat is white, your waistcoat very pale ecru. Doubtless you possess two matched sets, but your belongings have been disarranged, probably in packing your trunk, which combined with your presence . . . well, in my presence . . . suggests that you returned rather suddenly."

"Four matched sets. And the professional singing?"

He lifted one shoulder. "You'll laugh, I imagine. Lord knows I have. I've an uncanny knack for vocal tones, accents, and the like, though I humbly admit I failed to recognise yours when you so charmingly hailed me upon my doorstep. The context was entirely wrong—both your being there and your gender having altered, which led to that appalling gaffe. I've played women myself before, you know. Shocking that a logician should be so utterly trounced by setting. But I've heard the full range of your voice enough to perceive that it's in still better training now, meaning no offense whatsoever."

"None taken! It is, at that. How kind of you. Professionally, though? I could have been amusing myself."

The merriment drifted behind pale irises again. "I need hardly remind you that you *are* Irene Adler. If you're in full training, then surely you would not be so cruel as to deprive the world of hearing you sing?"

"Pish. Flattery is beneath you, Mr. Holmes."

"Dear me—I never flatter." He blew smoke at the ceiling. "It's a vice which benefits neither the speaker nor the listener. You may just as easily have assumed I was casting aspersions on your humility as paying you a compliment, you know."

"Ha! I grant you. But do explain fooled me *twice*. You were in disguise multiple times?"

Sherlock Holmes fiddled with his watch fob, a highly polished gold sovereign. "It was within the breadth of my job description to follow you, I regret to confess."

"Oooooh!" I smiled. "Did I do anything terribly untoward?"

"Not in the least."

"Were you a fishmonger? A little girl with a lolly? A cart horse?"

"As efficacious as those options sound, not as such."

"The cart itself then?"

He made a humming sound. "I shall tell you all about it sometime—well, I swear not to discount the *possibility* of telling you about it, at least. But first, pray inform me, are you in any trouble, madam?"

"It appears that I may be," I admitted.

The detective's long lashes drooped, both in calculation and dare I say even concern. It was *highly* gratifying. I always like to think I've left behind a favourable impression. Especially when I've soundly trounced somebody sporting. By all accounts, Sherlock Holmes is as sporting as anything—he's a member in excellent standing of the London Thames Fencing Club, and some of my seedier contacts even claim he goes at it Queensberry rules at least monthly in gambling dens, just for larks.

"Has the king sent further emissaries, then? I confess, I did not worry over such, as he assured me that your word was inviolate, and that the evidence you promised to destroy was as good as burnt. Has your husband perhaps caught wind of the scandal?"

Laughing, I exclaimed, "Godfrey? He knew all about it."

"Just a moment." Mr. Holmes raised a bemused hand. "Your husband . . . then fiancé, excuse me . . . was aware of the cabinet photograph featuring you and His Majesty as a couple?"

"Of course. We threw it in the Rhine together. We once discussed turning His Majesty's face into a Pierrot. I've always had a soft spot for commedia dell'arte."

"But Mr. Godfrey Norton didn't safeguard it for you last year."

"Why should he have done? The blasted thing was mine."

"And Mr. Norton is also apprised regarding the marginally more serious matter of attempted vengeful extortion?" One eyebrow snaked towards the ceiling.

"Extortion fiddlesticks! When did I ever ask him for a red cent? Self-protection was my aim, and if Siggy took it to mean his reputation with his fiancée was in danger, that was hardly *my* fault."

His lips twitched at *Siggy*. "You hinted at no such imminent peril?"

"Well, I *hinted* like the very dickens, didn't I, but give a girl some credit, I never broke the law. I'm not a simpleton."

"No, you are not," he drawled.

"You have hit upon a point of contention in our small household, however." I hesitated. "When you say vengeful extortion . . . well, that's not exactly legal, is it? Godfrey is in quite the tizzy over my being in London again."

"How so, now the photograph is destroyed and everything peaceably concluded?"

"Because of *your* being here, Mr. Holmes."

The poor fellow blinked, then grey eyes flew open as he understood me, and finally fell shut in dismay.

"You were the only person who knew what I'd done," I said gently. "Well, you and your doctor friend. I'm sure you've powerful allies amongst the coppers, and I have a very fine singing voice and a spectacular wardrobe. Who am I to challenge Sherlock Holmes should you think me some sort of low criminal who deserved to be brought to justice? Or should you be the vengeful sort, ready to toss me in the brig for the audacity of outwitting you? Far worse things have happened to women who trounce men, and in a very tangible way, I am in your power. My husband is deathly afraid of you."

I hadn't thought the poor fellow could get any paler. He could, bless him.

A sort of choking cough emerged. "Madam, I beg you, please do not imagine—"

"I didn't say *I'm* deathly afraid of you," I added, winking.

His shoulders relaxed a fraction.

"Anyway, as I mentioned, there was never any real extortion going on. I'm curious—did my erstwhile beau actually *show* you any of the correspondence between us? Did you ask to see any of the physical letters?"

Mr. Holmes wanted to flinch but wouldn't allow himself. "No."

"Well, then. And you wouldn't begrudge a wronged woman a bit of her own back?"

"No."

"Even though you acted as the king's agent last year?"

"Quite on the contrary, I assure you," he said with more heat than I'd yet heard from him.

"Then there you are! We neither of us disagree on any fundamental moral principles. Down to brass tacks, Mr. Holmes?"

A sad smile, quick as a river fish, made an appearance.

"Mrs. Norton, considering that you are facing difficulties, nothing could please me better."

The blithe tallow-haired boy arrived with coffee and brandies (and some lovely almond biscuits). I pulled up my armchair directly across from Mr. Holmes on the settee and unfolded my tale—well, not *all* of it. But broad strokes with a dot here and a line there of more delicate brushwork. The relative finances and characters of the brothers Norton, the oddly neutral exchange of securities, the sudden regard for Sumatra. Mr. Holmes sipped coffee, and I sipped coffee spiked with a nip of brandy; Mr. Holmes changed his mind despite the hour and followed suit. Throughout, he looked less and less pleased until he set his china down with audible frustration.

I saw this as an opportunity to take a biscuit. The detective sat back, tenting his fingers.

"Mrs. Norton, as whimsical as this transaction may seem to you, what the deuce have I to do with it? I know nothing whatsoever of finance and desire to remain in ignorance. Consult a banker. Or a solicitor. I'm reasonably certain you can lay your hands on one who is eager to please."

"Do you imagine Godfrey has not already pursued every avenue he could think of?"

"There still isn't any reason for me—"

"You're not here because Gilbert wants to exchange valuable securities for a large stake in his brother's Sumatra pepper concern."

"Then why the devil *am* I here, saving the pleasure of your company?"

I'll admit it: I fluffed up at that.

"You're here because the Norton family has an extensive standing case-clock collection, the pride of their forbears, and Gilbert has allowed each and every one of them to stop running."

Mr. Sherlock Holmes spread his full, considerable wingspan along the back of the settee. If anything, he appeared *less* awake than previous. But the eyes under the drooping lids had sharpened to shears.

"Tell me about it," he purred.

I did. There wasn't much to tell.

"And so, Mr. Holmes, I ask you: have you ever heard of stopping clocks so that they might be appraised?"

"If anything, the appraiser or the cleaner would stop them."

"Godfrey claims it's been days since they went silent. My hackles are altogether raised."

Mr. Holmes frowned, pouring both of us more coffee after splashing brandy in each cup.

"Then there's the matter of your fee," I continued. "We haven't . . . much money."

His active hands paused. "Madam, I assure you that I haven't the smallest qualm about waiving your fee."

"Bully for you. But I said I'd be willing to offer information instead. Have you ever heard of 'Baron' Dickie Maupertuis?"

"By Jove!" he exclaimed, sharp features lighting up. "Excellently played, Mrs. Norton."

"See, I thought you might have, and as Gilbert's . . . advisor of sorts . . . he's neck-deep in this business."

Sherlock Holmes, just as I'd hoped, relaxed into the cushions with an electric gleam in his eye. "Baron Maupertuis—five feet eight inches, dresses like a dandy, affects to royal origins, wears a monocle for God only knows what purpose unless half his eyesight doesn't match the other, has managed to at least *partially* eradicate his true accent, which is either Earlham Street or Monmouth Street, I can't decide. He still lives in Seven Dials, despite his hard-earned if also ill-gotten place in society. That lends a certain piquant quality. Not a particularly good pugilist, I'm afraid—I've watched him a number of times."

"At bouts in Seven Dials?" I exclaimed.

"Quite so. He leads with his neck, you understand, which rather telegraphs his intended blows. Where was I? Frequents high clubs where he's oddly welcome, low pubs where he decidedly isn't. I cannot seem to put my finger on the fellow—he is remarkably apt at squirming his way out of a fix."

"Yes, and squirming his clients out of them too. I myself have decided that he is to be termed a *fixer*. Specifically, he is Gilbert's fixer."

"Very apt," Mr. Holmes approved.

"He's the one who apparently instigated this queer stock transaction. And if you take on this case, you'll inevitably learn simply oodles about him. Which I imagine must be of use to you in the future. The man has nefarious ambitions."

"Without a doubt. And I always appreciate the opportunity to conduct, as you term it, *research*."

I added, suddenly anxious, "The good name of the Nortons teeters on a knife's point already. The matter is . . . it's of the *utmost* importance to me."

"I assure you that I shall treat it as such." His slender, chemical-scarred hand twitched in dismissal. "Mrs. Norton, I'm the most self-indulgent creature on the planet, only dealing with topics which hold my interest, eschewing all others. Ask poor Watson—it's ghastly for the fellow whenever he even attempts to tell me about a cricket match. I'm woefully incapable of feigning attention. My fee is, at present, languishing at the very bottom of any such list of my concerns. Somewhere around how many runs Bobby Abel has earned for Surrey this year."

"Who in blazes is Bobby Abel?"

"I haven't the slightest notion. A batsman, according to the doctor. You should be conferring an immense favour upon your humble servant by allowing me to look into this interesting little problem of yours."

"You're neither humble nor my servant, the very *idea*. And just why might that be? You're more eager than I anticipated. Fess up, please."

This was, I fear, a bald lie. He was exactly as eager as I'd anticipated.

Mr. Holmes's eyes slit again. "Because I already have an interest in Dickie Maupertuis." The sleuth overdid the French pronunciation of *Maupertuis* in such a comical way that I instantly knew he spoke the language fluently. I sing in it often enough.

"Oh?"

"Maupertuis does not work merely for Mr. Gilbert Norton."

"Ah," I said.

Of course, I've a complete roster of Dickie Maupertuis's employers. That's how I knew Mr. Holmes would snap at my bait. But there's no reason Mr. Holmes should realise it.

"You take my meaning, I see," the detective continued eagerly. "He is the most inveterate ruiner of pies."

It took me a moment. "What, sticks his fingers in them?"

"Precisely. Maupertuis has poked holes into so many baked goods that I cannot begin to list them for you. He is such a rogue that it's actually a wonder to me any of these noblemen trust him with their affairs, but then again . . . There is no vice so simple but assumes some mark of virtue on his outward parts."

"A favorite, as I played Portia not two years ago." I smiled.

"Of course you did," he returned with a twinkle in his eye. "Anyhow, I may be inventing connections where none exist. But I fear it may all be woven into a greater pattern, and to prove or disprove that hypothesis, I need all the data I can garner about the blasted villain. Fixer, as you say."

"Pie ruiner," I amended.

"Just so, Mrs. Norton," he agreed, standing. "Here is what I propose: you continue to investigate these mysteriously stopped clocks whilst I do some digging regarding Baron Maupertuis's most recent misdeeds. The stock securities are rather beyond my purview, but I can try to ascertain what the Baron has been up to. We shall reconvene the day after tomorrow to share our findings—here, say, at nine o'clock in the morning? Seven was a bit of a strain."

I likewise rose. "Mr. Holmes, I never supposed I'd say this. But I'm most grateful to you."

He executed possibly the smartest bend at the waist I've ever seen, once foot behind him in nearly a balletic posture, and then I *knew*. Knew it as I often know things, seeing them as if played on bare boards, lit by footlights in my mind's eye, the whole script of the thing mine to read.

"Ooooooh, you *perform!*" I cried. "Anonymously, of course. Probably in disguise. How awfully splendid!"

One eyebrow curved like the elegant contour of a violin. I knew he played, everyone did—is there a soul among us who *doesn't* read the *Strand Magazine*? But it was a treat to learn that he thought of the violin as he would a swordfight or a boxing match. Something to be savoured on occasion for purest pleasure.

"What in heaven's name can you mean? No, of course not." The hidden smile flickered.

"*That's* how you know this place! I'd lay it ten to one that you sneak into the Royal Opera House every six months and take over a violinist's chair. Which one? *Do* tell. First chair, so as to show off? Third chair, so as to blend in?"

"Dear me," he intoned as he donned his hat. "The woman is quite as fanciful as the rest of her sex after all. *Au revoir*, Mrs. Norton."

He gave a courtly nod and departed. Lack of sentiment: the reputation is not unearned.

One trivial point, however! Mr. Holmes claimed to be incapable of feigning interest in any dull subject. And he was all attention for the better part of an hour.

How *marvellous*.

Entry in the personal journal and scrapbook of Mrs. Irene Norton, née *Adler, Sunday, June 3rd, 1888:*

What a *day* this has been.

It's such a jumble of heady triumphs and ghastly mistakes on my part, my head is spinning. And here we are, barely teatime!

As to my failures, I have already fled to see Sherlock Holmes about them. And I plan to go out again this evening. I'll leave a note for Godfrey, but there's simply nothing else for it. Today proved that I still crash ahead with no regard for self-preservation, and I frankly see no end in sight. I'm in it to the neck now. Pray god I can swim to safety without any harm coming to me.

Without any harm coming to *Godfrey*.

The thought alone makes me shudder.

As to my successes, they again prove that I leap ahead of myself too often, too imprudently. Dearest Godfrey claimed once that he saw a huge display of Chinese fireworks years ago, on an exotic business trip to Hong Kong, all pinks and purples and golds exploding, and I remind him of that, and would I please occasionally allow him to rest.

I *thought* I needed Sherlock Holmes to aid me with tangible progress, not horrid as-yet undreamed-of blunders. But I've only gone and solved the mystery of the blasted clocks already, haven't I?

The remainder of Saturday after meeting Sherlock Holmes I spent secretly calling on old operatic friends, choruses of glad whoops ringing in my ears, because on Saturdays Gilbert's schedule is quite hodgepodge. Then this morning over tea, Godfrey reached for my hand.

"Irene, I'm grateful that you suggested I do some of our own banking yesterday. There certainly were a number of complex items needing my attention which touring the continent either rendered impossible or entirely invisible. Thank you."

"Well, you know me." I sipped my Darjeeling. "Practical to a fault, simply everyone says so."

He laughed, his head tilted, and my heart twanged like a Jersey fiddle.

"In fact," he continued as he set his napkin down, "I'm not nearly finished yet. Gilbert has had me so preoccupied with this securities nonsense I've given no thought to our own little family. The investments I've made, the quest for more funds. Forgive me?"

"Godfrey," I replied in some surprise, "of *course* not. Not when you've nothing to apologise for. I'll forgive you when you actually make a hash of something."

Godfrey gently tilted my head back where I sat, and he kissed me. I felt it in my slippers.

He went to slide into his frock coat. "I'll be at the Temple, Irene. I know it's Sunday, but I've locked the relevant paperwork in my office. You'll be able to occupy yourself again?"

"Oh, I'll think of something or other."

Our parting was brief and fond. Godfrey shut the door.

I tapped my fingers along the dining table in a simple little allegretto for a minute or two.

The mantel clock informed me that the day was young and the grass was growing under my feet. It likewise reminded me that other, more important clocks stood silent. I thought about what to do for another moment, finished my silent piano tune with a bright imaginary chord, and kicked my slippers off as I went for my boots. A quarter of an hour later, I was hailing a hansom to deposit me at the Norton family manse.

Of course I know Gilbert's daily schedule. He might be a drunk and a boor, but he still goes to his offices regularly, piddles about on Saturdays, and on Sundays, he idles at his club before eventually migrating to one of two gambling establishments. The Hunter and Hart if he wants slightly more civilised West End fun; Cleopatra's Necklace if he wants to cross the river and slum about.

I've researched him too, naturally. It wasn't any fun *at all*.

With a small thrill of apprehension, I knocked at the door. Gilbert's butler—a kindly, stooped old man with enormous side-whiskers—answered. His name is Glazier and he knows me well enough by sight.

"What ho, Glazier," I said affably. "Is the lord of the manor here?"

"Mrs. Norton," he wheezed. "I'm afraid not."

"Drat! Might I just pop in for a few minutes anyhow? I think I left my gloves here the other night, you see, and I don't like to part ways with them. You won't mind?"

"Not in the least, madam." He shuffled backwards. "Shall I help you to search?"

"No need!" I trilled over my shoulder, already off to the races. "I've a few ideas and can show myself about!"

So there I stood in the clock room, which now seemed more of a clock mausoleum, their souls having shuffled off the mortal coil as it were. Staring in frustration at what was now a very expensive assortment of highly complex statuary.

"What the *devil*, Gilbert?" I muttered.

Then I thought, *you aren't being very thorough, Irene, go on upstairs and sniff about.* So I went upstairs and sniffed about for exactly twenty-five seconds and had solved the whole matter.

Sometimes Sherlock Holmes calls himself the dreadfullest names when his judgement lapses, according to the doctor's stories. *Fool, brainless, simpleton.* I never quite believed those anecdotes because I am generally quite impressed with myself, and I thought Mr. Holmes was altogether in three-cheers-favour of himself too.

Well, I understand now. I am a dunce. All I had to do was go upstairs.

Having concretely solved the affair with nothing left to do save tell Godfrey and Mr. Holmes all about it—Lord knows I can't put the brakes on this by myself—left me frothing at the bit. And I *know* that Mr. Holmes ought to be taking the Dickie Maupertuis line, I dangled it in front of him myself as payment, but blast it, I was fired up from making the silent clocks deliver their secrets, my blood was high, and who was Mr. Holmes to have all the fun? Fun is *important.* It's an essential life force.

In moderation, naturally.

Well, I could make my own fun, and if that fun meant getting a clear picture of *why* Gilbert was doing what he was doing, that was just a happy dovetailing of labour and leisure.

What is it they say about idle hands?

I had an idea. A fairly sound one too, which made it all the more dangerous. Ideas are like that—they can become vast systems of Roman plumbing and ancient aqueducts, a *sight* better than the slop holes we had in New Jersey, or ideas can get your head snicked off. It didn't take long for me to have forgotten every vow of caution I'd made to my dearest Godfrey, because it was all *for him*, wasn't it, so it was justified?

Figs and fiddlesticks to that. It wasn't for him, it was for me to explode this feeling of being hidden away like a doll in a display case.

For a mad moment, I thought to change my clothes. But no, looking exactly who I was would suit perfectly. Godfrey was at the Temple, Gilbert was at his club, and Cleopatra's Needle—Gilbert's East End gambling den—would ostensibly be closed at this hour. But really the staff would be trading lurid stories and counting their earnings and eating breakfast.

I made certain I had enough coin of the realm and hailed a cab.

I am a county fair prize-winning horse's hindquarters.

Cleopatra's Needle was housed in a three-story brick rowhouse on the bank of the Thames, one of the small gaps left for residences amidst the more usual warehouses and docks. And when the cab clattered to a halt and I stepped out into the ripe air, I could see why Gilbert liked the place. Apart from the decidedly East End smells of lumber and creosote and river sewage, it was the sort of place that looked low and dirty but didn't make you *feel* low and dirty. The steps were clean. The windows were clean. No one let me in the locked entrance, but eventually a lanky stevedore came out, and he shrugged as I slipped through the gap.

There really is something to be said for East Enders. If it isn't their business, they don't make it their business to *make* it their business.

Cleopatra's Needle was up a flight of well-maintained stairs. The chatter of the sleepless staff drifted out of the open door alongside the pleasant aroma of a communal fry-up. I expected when I entered to find a huge tray laden with blood sausage and kippers and eggs and fried bread at the center of one of the gaming tables. I found exactly that, and then I realised I was ravenous.

"Miss?" One of the female servers noticed me first, a sharp-eyed blonde with a fae face and Cupid's cheeks. "Beggin' yer pardon, madam? Can we help?"

Heads swiveled. There's another point for the East End. They didn't pretend I was lost or coddle me in any fashion. I knew right where I was, and they didn't question it. The blonde spoke with an engagingly dockside accent, thick and expressive.

"I . . ." Pretending to falter, I gripped the nearest suitable surface, which happened to be the bar top. "I think my husband was here last night."

"Come 'ere often, does he?"

"No, I mean maybe . . . I think so."

They all nodded sagely, accepting my feigned uncertainty.

"Never made it home snug last night?" she ventured.

"He did, thankfully, he's . . . resting. Um. I had . . . would you mind answering a few questions?"

"Depends on what they is," she said reasonably.

"I don't want to know anything to do with your . . . your fine establishment," I assured them tremulously. "Or ask you to give away secrets. I *know* he was here last night."

Several employees went back to their breakfasts while still listening attentively.

"It's just that. Ooooooh, God help me. My husband is Gilbert Norton, and—"

"*Gilbert Norton?*"

"Well, saints 'ave mercy."

"Never thought I'd see the day!"

"*That* one with a pretty wife? S'pose there's an 'eart in the world fer every other 'eart after all."

"Except I never figured Gilbert Norton had a heart in the first place."

The blonde sprite who greeted me first said, "Oi you lot, shut it, she's a-standin' right there, in' she? Go on, Mrs. Norton," she coaxed.

"It's . . . humiliating, but I've no control over the, the finances you understand, and . . . And I only want to know what I'm facing. He's been acting even worse lately. Has he . . . done something? Have you heard anything? Not your secrets, you see, only Gilbert's . . . reputation. It ought to be easy to tell me, supposing you think so ill of him. I'm only trying to make ready for any disaster that might soon befall me. *Us*, of course."

The looks the staff exchanged weren't uneasy. But they were calculating, as if trying to determine a balance between helping me and protecting the privacy of one of their clients. No matter that he was a thoroughbred blackguard.

Thankfully, pure resentment won the day.

"What's yer fancy, Nicky?" She addressed a well-built ginger fellow of around twenty-five who sat quietly folding napkins. "Yer the one 'as yer finger on the pulse of it."

He shrugged, but when he looked at me his green eyes were sympathetic. "There's not much t' tell ye, Mrs. Norton." His accent was Irish, lush and lilting. "Gilbert Norton and 'is man, Dickie Maupertuis, been stirrin' the pot hard enough t' let it spill over lately."

I ventured shakily into the dining room, wringing my hands. Truly, having forgotten breakfast was nonsensical of me. "How so? Is there anything I can . . . should do?"

Nicky looked to the blonde. "Maeve, I din want t' get tangled up in this meself."

"No, right you are dearie."

"Tangled up in what?" I begged. "Am I . . . am I quite safe? Is my husband?"

"Nae," Nicky owned. "I din believe ye are."

It was no trick whatsoever to wobble in the open sea of floor. Not because I was frightened, but because I was hungry enough to turn that into swooning terror. Not all opera singers can remotely claim as much—but I am a superlative actress.

"Mrs. Norton!" Maeve exclaimed as a murmur rippled across the dining table. She was out of her seat instantly and leading me to the table with its booth, sliding me in. Then she perched at the outside with her hand still on my elbow. "Is there summat we can do? Fancy a little tea? Nip o' gin? Bite o' sausage?"

"I'm so ashamed of myself," I moaned. That was no great deception either—I was, at least a little. "Yes . . . yes, I haven't had anything at all today. It may help."

Quick as blinking, there was a plate of scramble and sausage before me, flanked by a steaming cup of tea strongly fortified with milk and sugar, next to a tumbler of unadorned gin. I availed myself of all three and swiftly did feel much better.

"There's some colour back in 'er cheeks," Maeve approved. "Nicky, best out with it. Waitin' fer the blow is worse than the blow itself."

Nicky nodded without looking up from his napkins. "I was bringin' a round of drinks t' the Baron and Mr. Norton nigh a month ago. Ye ken, Mrs. Norton, the sort o' ruckus those two cause?"

"Yes," I whispered, shamefaced.

"Well, tryin' t' cheat at cards when yer playin' nobles tryin' t' out-cheat ye back is one thing. So's gettin' in drunken brawls and the like. But the Baron, he does a lot o' dirty work for a lot o' filthy folk and I'm sorry t' say there your husband has been with his man, pallin' around like they're a set o' school chums. And 'tis gettin' much worse. Anyhow, a month ago, I was droppin' drinks at their table. Just the two o' them palaverin'. Yer husband was sayin' that somethin' or other would all blow over and the Baron was sayin' nae, the wrong toes were stepped on this time, *They* would be comin' after him. And yer husband too."

A cold thrill shot through me—I could hear the capital letter. "Who are *They*?"

Unspoken understanding ricocheted around the staff table. With glances, silent nods. From the eaters of eggs to the polishers of spoons to the smokers of pipes.

"Blast if *we* know."

"We don't, we don't pretend to."

"Only, s'queer days, innit? They didn't used to so many o' them be haquainted."

"Our well-off patrons, she means to say, the cream of the crop."

"They'd drink. Lay bets. Cheat. Squabble over hands. Change absurd sums o' coin."

"But now . . ."

"Remember when Walk Tall Ned were in trouble wi' the magistrate a fortnight ago?" Maeve mused. Nods all around. "Well, Walk Tall, 'e's a swell and a dandy all right, but that lad 'as razors 'idden behind his teeth, *frightful* dangerous, and suddenly along comes Sir Thomas Bluehill to tell the judge as Walk Tall were with *him* when that bookie got 'is arse kicked from 'ere to China and back. Walk Tall got off wi'out a scratch. Only one problem."

"Which was?" I asked breathlessly, eggs forgotten.

"Far as *we* knew," Nicky said, still endlessly folding, "Sir Thomas din even *know* Walk Tall Ned. They sure ne'er sat at the same tables. Walk Tall is the bastard son o'—well, I shan't say, I'll mind me manners, but 'e's powerful and rich and 'e gambles here. So does Sir Thomas. But over the past . . . would ye lot say two years?"

"Bit longer?"

"I'd only just started 'ere when it began."

"Same as me, luvvie, same as me, I'd say two and a half years."

"Just over two years sounds right."

"Slowly, slower'n treacle so's ye don't really notice, and think yerself a bit tetched if ye *do* notice . . ." Maeve continued.

"Seems as if they're all marchin' in their own directions," Nicky finished. "But . . . to the same drummer now. We can nae explain it and we din know who *They* are. We din want to."

"Hear, hear!"

"Sooner flirt wi' a live tiger."

"Amen to that."

"But if I were you, Mrs. Norton, I'd be *that* careful until this shakes out howe'er it's like to." Lift the white linen, fold, turn, fold twice more, add to the stack, on and on Nicky went. "Stands t' reason if these filthy rich lot are somehow *organised*, then crossin' them is piss poor luck. Go and stay wi' a friend maybe? Ye seem a good sort, and we din like t' see good sorts come t' harm. Folk 'ave disappeared."

"Disappeared?" I exclaimed, genuinely shocked.

"Aye," Maeve affirmed darkly. "Recall as when Sir Roger DeRose got 'imself mixed up in that group of shady art collectors? Started blabbin' about it sure sundown every night? Seemed like 'e'd flew hisself a bit too close t' the sun?"

"Went on 'oliday to Venice," Nicky supplied. His freckles stood out, oddly vulnerable, against delicate skin. "He ne'er came *back*, though. So Mrs. Norton, if I were you—"

Loud—ostentatiously loud—footsteps pounded up the stairs. All eyes swept to the door I'd left ajar. A silver-topped walking stick appeared first, rapping briskly against the doorframe.

Then its owner appeared. None other than "Baron" Dickie Maupertuis. Speak of the devil.

Heart hammering, I shrank behind Maeve. The table had a solid rectangular base, not unlike walls, or I'd have slid right under it. She sensed my distress instantly and somehow puffed herself into a larger shield as I slumped down into the shadows. I've met the Baron on a few occasions—charity auctions, garden parties, in Gilbert's company. Places where bottom feeders employed by the well-to-do mingle with other bottom feeders and well-to-do. The English employ a caste system Americans struggle to understand fully. But everyone comprehends money and access, and the Baron has fistfuls of both.

Dickie Maupertuis was, just as Sherlock Holmes described, five foot eight inches of a thick-shouldered, meat-fisted pugilist dressed like the parody of a gentleman of leisure in a melodrama. Not even a *good* melodrama. His brown sideburns were too thick, his waistcoat copper-threaded brocade, his top hat purple velvet, and his monocle just ludicrous. That being said, there are advantages to hiding in plain sight. If you peacock enough, loudly enough, often enough, eyes have a tendency to roll skyward and then slide right off of you.

I ought to know—I've done it frequently.

"My bosom friends!" he exclaimed with arms wide.

Tinny false smiles appeared. Even less sincere greetings sounded. *What ho, Baron* and *How're ye farin' then, Baron?*

"Ye can nae imagine we're open at this hour," Nicky said. He added a teasing wink, but it had a dagger behind it.

"Oh, no no no, I come with a request. I have need of all the holdings for my house account which are kept deposited in your safe, I regret to say."

"*All* o' your usual bank?" Maeve asked, incredulous. "Why, what the blazes, Baron?"

"On the double, if you please," the reprobate purred. "I shouldn't like to interrupt your breakfast any more than is necessary."

"But that's nearly—"

"I'm entirely aware of how much money it is, Maeve my dearest."

"Does that mean ye won't be a-comin' back to—"

"Too many questions," Maupertuis said with violence underlying his tone. "Quick march now, someone, and I shan't lose my temper over it, you've all been so hospitable in the past."

The Baron truly had done yeoman's work of eradicating his accent, but Mr. Holmes was right; you could still feel the sun glinting off the seven sundials monument marking the St. Giles junction where he was born and still lived.

A plump raven-haired beauty hiked her skirts, climbing over three coworkers to exit the booth. I was shocked to note she was in tears. Several Cleopatra's Needle employees heaved sighs of annoyance.

"Dickie," she sniffled, going to him with hands outstretched. He took them. "Dickie, what's this about? Aren't you coming back here, then? Please say you aren't . . . aren't deserting us," she finished.

Eyebrows around the table raised, quirked, or tilted in knowing confirmation.

"Nancy, my darling, please fetch the funds," the Baron repeated. "I'll send you word as soon as I can. Yes? Run along now."

She stumbled away, stifling sobs. The Baron started to whistle some skillfully trilled little public house ditty. Then his eyes drifted more fully over the table.

And caught sight of me.

"Mrs. Norton?" he exclaimed in some shock. "Whatever are you doing here?"

A single aspect of this worked in my favour: his calling me Mrs. Norton, albeit the *wrong* Mrs. Norton, failed to expose my fabricated identity. Absolutely nothing whatsoever else benefited me, however, and my heart pounded like a Wagnerian cataclysm.

"Mrs. Norton, do come with me," he said in a softer tone that was twice as sinister. "There's a private room for gamers just through here. I'd like a word."

Maeve stood to release me. I slipped out, following the Baron with my chin high. It doesn't do to let thugs notice they have you in a severely compromised position. He led me to a pretty chamber draped all in darkest crimson, containing a dozen or so tables and elegant velvet armchairs. Cigar smoke mingled with a fainter musk of men's toiletries. I willed my hands to stop trembling, longing for trouser pockets. Baron Maupertuis closed the door behind us with a sharp bang.

"Might I ask," he enquired, all smiling teeth and threatening posture, "what you think you're doing here, Mrs. Norton?"

"No, I don't think so." My voice didn't shake. My hands occasionally betray me—my voice never does.

"Come, now. It really would be best if you filled me in."

"I don't answer to the likes of you," I hissed. "I never *have* answered to anyone *resembling* the likes of you, Baron. I'm here on my own personal business, you don't dare to interfere with me, we both know it, and you can't intimidate me. It isn't as if you don't know me—both personally and by reputation. I'll be leaving now."

The Baron took several slow steps towards me. I didn't budge. He smelled of cheap tobacco and expensive cologne—just like the room itself only stronger, in a nauseating bouquet.

"All right," he replied in what was almost a whisper. "Let us part ways as friends. But first, I fear I must impart a final warning."

"Which is?" I snapped in a show of bravado I didn't feel.

"If you breathe so much as a word of my closing my account here . . . that I collected all my house funds and severed ties . . . I will spread the rumour throughout all of England that Godfrey Norton is cut from the identical cloth as Gilbert Norton. I'll trumpet to the skies that he's an underhanded criminal, and a liar, and perhaps either an extortionist or an embezzler. I haven't decided yet. And I assure you, that reputation would prove *much* more irksome for a humble solicitor who relies on implicit trust than it does for a man of independent means like Gilbert Norton. Do I make myself perfectly clear?"

He had.

And after gaping at the worm for several infinite seconds, I scowled at him, tossed my head, and positively *fled* Cleopatra's Needle, hurtling down the steep stairs so fast I might have broken my neck.

Finding a cab this time was much harder, but I managed. I gasped out directions. Fought to get my frantic breathing under control. What a positively *wretched* coincidence, and yet in another way a fortuitous one. Because not only had I solved the mystery of the stopped case-clocks—I had now accidentally worked out that Gilbert and the Baron were up to exactly the same thing. True, I didn't know *why* to a certainty. But I knew enough.

My brother-in-law and his cohort had made a cardinal mistake and offended *Them*. Whoever *They* were.

The door of 221 was answered by a tiny woman with snow white hair and bright blue eyes. Her half smile was warm in a way few people's outright laughter is. She gave the impression that once upon a time, she was just about the brightest pixie in the forest. I adore such specimens and aim to become one myself.

"Yes, how may I help you?"

"I'm working with Mr. Holmes. Please tell me he's in, oh please."

"My goodness, you're shaking—he certainly is. Do come in at once, dear. Do you want to send me up with a card?"

"No need," I called back, already on the staircase. "Thanks awfully."

I move quietly even in haste, and when I reached the landing and heard *two* male voices through the partially open door—and I realised I hadn't yet been detected—I paused. Insatiably curious.

"Well, well, it can't be helped now, can it?" came a concerned baritone. "We can only bide our time and try for him again."

"But the work!" exclaimed Mr. Holmes's brassy tenor. "It's maddening! Two months of tracking him, gathering evidence, stakeouts, let's not forget Lestrade getting *shot* at, to net Joe Baxby, and then to have the whole business botched by a trial lawyer so green one might mistake him for a spring salad!"

"That's hardly your fault, my dear fellow," in a soothing timbre.

"It is, it *is*, I ought to have seen it coming. They replaced a hoary veteran of the courts as prosecuting solicitor with the veriest infant, and with twelve hours' notice before the trial! Baxby is part of this elusive circle, and I ought to have been paying as much attention to the legal proceedings as I did the tossing him in a Black Maria portion of the process."

"Honestly, I rather want to thrash the blackguard." This in a low, fraught growl. "You're working yourself sick as it is already, Holmes, darting hither and thither scraping together hints and indications, arresting petty thieves who've the faintest connection to the pattern only you can see, and yet are somehow a peripheral part of it. Then in a triumphant pounce—"

"You make me sound like a jaguar, Watson."

"You arrest Baxby, whose ties are much more tangible . . . what is he, some sort of lieutenant?"

"If you want to put it in military terms, my dear fellow, I hypothesise so."

"And there was never a question of you *resting*, heaven forbid, but it was off on the next grueling quest for answers, sketching the edges of an invisible web, and now you're also meant to keep an eye on the Assizes? It's too much, Holmes."

"On the contrary, it isn't enough, not until I can take these scattered threads and work out the pattern of the tapestry. I'm well up in my British law, thank you, Doctor."

"Oh, in that case I don't see any problem." Dr. Watson didn't sound angry exactly, but he did sound mightily protective. "Since you're also well up in your lethal botanicals, why don't you write a definitive encyclopedia of natural poisons at the same time? Alongside your usual private cases for which you are actually paid, of course, and those of the Yard. You're going to do yourself an injury at this rate, my dear fellow, and yes, I would do my very utmost to patch you up and then you'd be off like a hare again, but what happens when your guard drops because you haven't slept for a week? Have some common sense, my dear fellow."

"I do not deal in *common* sense, Watson, I deal in rarified levels of sense, and while your concerns are more appreciated than you know, maintaining this velocity is infinitely simpler than stopping and then building momentum again. Don't you understand basic physics?"

"I do, thank you."

"I'm simply in a maelstrom at present, but that isn't *my* doing, it's the weather, and the weather will clear. It has happened before when there was a sudden flurry of activity in this web alongside my usual cases—as you said, both independent ones and those at the behest of our decidedly less competent professional counterparts. Baxby's trial was the flurry this time, but he has fled, and I have thirteen other problems of varying interest from which to choose. Dear chap, it's going to take *years* for me to even glimpse an end to this, and you act as if I'm in sight of the finish line."

This was all really none of my business. And yet it was, because I recollected Mr. Holmes saying he thought Dickie Maupertuis might be "woven into a greater pattern," and this sounded like the same topic as *Them*.

Still. I stomped my feet, coughed, and rapped at the cracked door.

"Yes?" Mr. Holmes called. "Who's there?"

When I opened it, I was privy to such a domestic scene I could scarce believe my eyes. There were two egg cups at separate place settings on the dining table, already dispatched, a teapot in a cozy, an empty toast rack, and a platter still containing stray rashers of bacon. Apparently Dr. Watson breakfasts twice on Sundays: once with the beautiful missus, and afterwards with the sable-haired stork.

Dr. John Watson rose from the settee to greet me and then allowed his square jaw to drop in astonishment. Mr. Holmes might be compellingly odd-looking, but Dr. Watson is a perfect mixture of seasoned soldier, capable medic, and someone you might find winning a friendly rugby scrum. He isn't to my tastes exactly—no one is compared to Godfrey—but I'll lay odds he's to nearly every other woman's taste on the planet. And I'm betting he hadn't let it go to waste as a bachelor. Dear Godfrey didn't either, the sweet rogue.

Mr. Holmes sat up straighter from where he was sprawled like a giant alley tom in his armchair. As much as I find I like him suave and starched, I might like him without a collar or cuffs, two buttons undone, in a voluminous grey dressing gown even better.

"Mrs. Norton! Are you all right? Is this about the clocks?"

"Clocks," Dr. Watson repeated, somehow both stunned and ironic in a single word.

"No, I solved the clocks earlier this morning. All I had to do was go upstairs, blast it."

"Holmes," said the doctor with exaggerated patience.

"Up . . ." Mr. Holmes blinked. "Oh, of *course*. It's perfectly obvious. How ridiculous of me not to have inferred such at once."

"Yes, well, that makes a pair of us then."

"It's peppercorn plantation insights, then?"

"Peppercorn plantation," and this time I think Dr. Watson's voice could have dried up some of the smaller offshoots of the Mighty Mississippi.

"That was everything to do with the clocks though, wasn't it?" I replied.

"By Jove, of course it was!" he approved.

"Yes, of course the clocks and the peppercorn plantation were inevitably deeply enmeshed clues, I should have seen it myself." Dr. Watson's moustache was twitching. "*Holmes*."

Mr. Holmes's dark brows parted ways, one for the ceiling and the other for the carpet. "Mrs. Norton, you've clearly been doing your own investigating, and not merely into the clocks. Please do sit down—you're obviously unwell. From the sound of your coin purse, you've been hailing multiple hansoms, and not in disguise either. Is that wisdom?"

"Absolutely not." I shut the sitting room door behind me. "It was a sam-fool notion and I ought to have tried chaining myself to the wardrobe first."

"Believe me, I quite understand that once the bit is between one's teeth, it can be difficult to get it out again. So the Sumatran securities—"

"*Holmes*," Dr. Watson somehow thundered without actually thundering. "Do you mind telling me what in heaven's name Irene Norton, née Adler, is doing in our—in your sitting room?"

Sherlock Holmes flinched—actually flinched—at the amendment from *our* to *your*. And my *heart*.

Oh, my heart.

Very nearly always, I get what I want. It's not luck, it's hard work and practice. I'd wanted to see an unstudied reaction from the unflappable Mr. Sherlock Holmes. And there was my wish all laid out for me, pretty as a present and topped with a bow, except I'd never wanted to witness anything so horrid as *that*. I don't suppose Mr. Holmes knew he did it. Dr. Watson didn't see the expression because he was looking, with much more bafflement than distress, at me. And I don't suppose many save myself and the doctor would have noted such a minute spasm from the sleuth at all.

But I saw it, that tiny terrible clench around the deep-sunk eye sockets, and I'll never be able to view that remarkable face again without remembering it.

Sherlock Holmes is a laughable excuse for an automaton. Oh, I don't doubt that he's nothing but happy for the doctor and his bride. He seems a staunch ally, one who truly wants his sole friend to be content. But I've been where he is before myself. In a freezing garret in Leipzig doing scales with three scarves around my throat just to keep from shredding my vocal cords. On an estate outside of Prague with a rakish viscount who was perfectly lovely at the outset and then wouldn't let me leave. In Bohemia, in a palace, wrapped in a fur with the curtains of the bed all pulled shut so that I had a nest in which I could sing softly and brush out my hair and pretend I was anywhere else.

Mr. Holmes had already gotten everything he ever wanted. Which wasn't much, all told, I think: someone liked and trusted, someone to talk to and laugh with, help with any smoke rockets, and two egg cups on the dining table instead of one. And since the doctor had married, he got half of it. Again, I don't for an instant think he was jealous. He wasn't, not a particle of him. Sherlock Holmes may be caustic and cold; Sherlock Holmes is not petty. But what's the use of being appealed to by everyone from dustmen to dukes if there's no audience to marvel at your magic tricks?

We're both performers, he and I. The difference between us is that *I* can content myself with a gaggle of clapping strangers, and *he* only wanted one set of eyes lit up with astonishment and gleefully calling *encore*.

Dr. Watson seemed eager to participate in the significant cases, the dangerous cases. To aid and protect. I don't suppose he'd have missed those for a king's ransom. But I highly doubt he could drop everything anymore to witness the Adventure of the Frayed Bootstring, no matter if it ultimately led to a sinister counterfeiters' gang, and still more do I doubt that Mr. Holmes would even have asked him to.

During those cases, by all accounts his favourites, he was alone again.

I wanted to march straight over and share that huge armchair with him—there would be ample space, I'm petite and he's lean—and run my fingers through his midnight swoop of hair. Such was my intensity of fellow-feeling. It was utter madness.

I still want to. I don't even know whether he'd like it.

It was a lucky thing, I thought, that Dr. Watson seemed the two-breakfast-of-a-Sunday sort of companion. He seemed about as likely to leave his friend to actually battle it out alone as he would insult the Queen.

"Mrs. Norton." Dr. Watson pinched the bridge of his nose and then showed me both his palms in supplication. "I've just made a scene, and a fool of myself. Welcome! Holmes and I were talking of something quite . . . different when you arrived, something which has me on edge, but that is no excuse. Please forgive my appalling manners, and do sit down."

"Never mind, Doctor, it was me doing the interrupting." I took the settee and Dr. Watson the chair across from Mr. Holmes. I had the impression that the detective considered it very much The Doctor's Chair. "I don't think we've ever quite, ah. Met."

"Forgive me again. Dr. John Watson, associate—"

"Friend," Mr. Holmes said exhaustedly, with his eyes closed and dark head tilted back.

"And sometimes assistant—"

"Colleague." With still less patience.

"Yes, I'm being quite foolishly self-deprecating, aren't I?" Dr. Watson agreed ruefully. "I always am after an apology, but I know perfectly well how you always introduce me. Mrs. Norton, I am Dr. John Watson, friend and colleague of Mr. Sherlock Holmes."

"Oh, *bravo*, Watson," the sleuth drawled, this time with an edge.

"Should I go on to tell her that she may speak as freely before me as before you, or is that enough to be getting on with? I can do the entire speech for you, if you like."

Mr. Holmes cracked an eye open as the invisible smile appeared.

Seconds later, they were chuckling as if there had never been any tension between the pair at all. By this time, I'm fond of Mr. Holmes. Tremendously. I hadn't been sure whether I'd cotton to the man in the bushes lobbing smoke rockets at me. But it turns out that I have.

"Mrs. Irene Norton, prima donna contralto," I supplied. "Pleased to make your acquaintance, Doctor."

"Heavens, I don't see why you would be."

"I don't either," I agreed cheerily. "It's a mad world, peopled with topsy-turvy citizens."

"Holmes, Mrs. Norton rather sounds like you," the doctor teased gently.

"I know," on a sigh. The detective ran his palm down his face. "I've noticed."

"And may I ask in what capacity we are graced with your presence here, Mrs. Norton?"

"Mrs. Norton is my client," Mr. Holmes supplied before I could get my mouth open.

"How oddly and marvellously fitting," Dr. Watson approved.

"In which capacity, Mrs. Norton, I ask again expecting an answer this time, are you all right? We were meant to meet at nine tomorrow morning. Are you here to report, or has something untoward happened?"

"Both, I'm afraid," I answered. "As to the report, as you've already inferred, the clocks are all stopped because Gilbert Norton is about to order them packed very carefully, doubtless by night, and whisk them away somewhere. An auction house? As insolvent as he may be, Gilbert's family pride being what it is, I hardly think so. Some museum storage facility or art warehouse he rented? Much more likely. I don't think he's mad enough to ship them where *he's* going."

"Sumatra does seem an unlikely place for a priceless standing clock collection," Mr. Holmes agreed.

"Yes, you have it to the letter: as soon as I bothered to go upstairs in the townhouse, everything was perfectly clear. I looked into the sitting rooms, the spare bedrooms. All the furnishings were draped in white fabric like a child's idea of a ghost. Everything shuttered. Gilbert took securities that were actually valuable, channeled them into brother Gerald's peppercorn plantation—perhaps under pretext of a reconciliation, perhaps as an outright bribe—and seems to be making a tidy escape from England. Hand in glove with his pie ruiner friend—"

"Do you know, I rather like 'fixer' better," said Mr. Holmes, but at least I'd made him smile, and a real one.

"—Baron Dickie Maupertuis, who probably whispered this whole scheme into Gilbert's ear in the first place. And who is fleeing London alongside him."

Relating the tale of Cleopatra's Needle and my being caught out by the Baron there took few words. The Baron's closure of his house account and the threat made against Godfrey still fewer. Dr. Watson looked outraged, Mr. Holmes icily vengeful.

"Why on *earth* would you risk visiting such a den, Mrs. Norton?" Dr. Watson questioned. "We would readily have escorted you."

"Oooooh, I risk going plenty of places where male escort locks lips. And I knew Gilbert was escaping to Sumatra already from the furniture covers and the stopped clocks. What I wanted to know is *why*. Other than the obvious, which I figured was that Gilbert's probably in hock up to his ears. Then at Cleopatra's Needle I learned the Baron was pulling up stakes himself, and the whole picture changed. For Gilbert, it makes sense to run like a coward and buy a big straw hat and a linen suit and make so-called amends to Gerald with a hefty infusion of stock purchases in exchange for brotherly sanctuary. But for Dickie Maupertuis? He's not only well-connected, he's richer than Croesus. So yes, I did some ill-advised investigating. I was keen to sniff out *motive*."

"I can speak to motive myself at least partially," Mr. Holmes mused, pausing in the act of lighting his pipe. "I've not been idle, you know—I began my campaign directly after exiting the Cupid's Arrow Club. The pair of them seem to stoke the flames of each other's worst impulses, and together they've been burning the candle at both ends. Not just your usual drunken debauches, mind. Real fights on the Baron's part, with real bruisers. High-stakes all-night gambling sessions on Gilbert Norton's, usually with the Baron present and egging him on. I am very gratified to state that there are at least five serious crimes of which I could solidly convict the Baron should I put my mind to it. The only question is whether now is the right time to put my mind to it."

I groaned. "How Gilbert is related to Godfrey *at all* is beyond my scope."

He nodded. "They've been careening out of control in tandem. I have it on good authority that Mr. Norton recently wagered a small but lucrative shipping warehouse in Southwark, owned by the family for decades, over whether he could name at least five varieties of penguin."

My face landed in my hands, my elbows on my knees. It wasn't ladylike; I couldn't help it. "I don't suppose he managed it?"

"Of course not." Mr. Holmes tossed a smirk to his friend. "Watson, care to give it a go?"

"Heavens, let me see." Dr. Watson's thoughtful frown was, I realised, artlessly charming. "Emperor is a favourite of mine. Galapagos penguin as a Darwinian nod. Um, royal penguin, Fiordland penguin. Just a moment, I'll manage this, it's always on the last hurdle that the brain tries to convince one it has given up."

I've no idea how Sherlock Holmes can look exasperated and fond at the same time. But he can.

"African penguin!" Dr. Watson exclaimed with boyish triumph. "There, I've done it."

"I'm partial to the chinstrap penguins," I put in, beginning to recover my sense of humour.

"Yes, of course!" Dr. Watson concurred. "They're altogether charming."

"They look like tiny hotel bellhops."

"Indeed. Or railway porters ready to whisk away your luggage and ask what time you'd care for a table in the dining car."

Sherlock Holmes appeared to be battling not to bubble over with mirth. "Or the palace guards of a number of nations. I might add Magellanic penguins, for the nonce."

Dr. Watson snapped his fingers. "Jolly good, Holmes. African?"

"South American surely given the name, my dear fellow."

"Forgive me, I ought to have known."

It was inevitable. I went first, scarce able to breathe and clutching my belly like a matronly tavern keeper, Dr. Watson fell like a domino, and Mr. Holmes held out for half a second before joining us. Finally, I wiped my eyes with my kerchief, and Dr. Watson likewise settled. Mr. Holmes gave a dignified cough before continuing.

"In any event," he said, "the pair of them all but lit their own reputations on fire while dousing them with kerosene. For a gentleman who lives solely off of existing material holdings like Gilbert Norton, that may not matter particularly, but for a professional fixer? It's potentially career-ending for the likes of Baron Maupertuis."

"That's not why they're fleeing to Sumatra, though," I noted as I got my breath back.

"Isn't it?" Sherlock Holmes cocked his head. "Then why are they making so clandestine a departure?"

I related everything I learned at Cleopatra's Needle about *Them*. Nicky's account of the Baron and Gilbert offending the wrong parties; the increasingly incestuous assistance rendered between the rich and unscrupulous.

The unshakable suspicion on the staff's part that some organizational force lay behind it all. Throughout my speech, Dr. Watson's expressive blue eyes widened into saucers as he shot increasingly urgent glances across the sitting room. Sherlock Holmes sat still as a carved Buddha, but I knew better already than to suppose his eyelids being at half-mast implied inattention.

"And so," I concluded, "it would seem that two fairly influential men would prefer to quit the British Isles than risk awaiting the wrath of *Them*. The whole thing's like a tall tale. Fanciful bogeymen and trolls lurking under bridges."

"Dear me. I fear it's rather more sophisticated than that," Mr. Holmes said, softly.

"Holmes, do you know what this means?" Dr. Watson sat forward. "You've had doubts before—doubts about your own mental faculties being so powerful that they fabricated conspiracy where there was none. My dear friend, you *aren't wrong*."

"I seldom am, Watson," Mr. Holmes replied, but the jest fell flat.

"So I take it you've caught wind of this before?" I ventured, having been shamelessly listening outside of doorways.

The sleuth wriggled long fingers. "Merest rumour for the most part. Our most solid culprit-cum-witness to date recently strolled out of the Assizes, more's the pity. We were discussing him when you arrived. Joe Baxby, one of the higher-ups. I'd frankly have suspected that the Baron was likewise integrated into the system. I'm surprised he isn't, but then again, he wouldn't like sudden orders falling out of the sky, nor would he care to be a cog in a larger machine. He's always been known to be ferociously prideful. He wears emerald spats, for heaven's sake."

"And I've just tossed that ferociously prideful man's marching orders in the nearest rubbish bin by coming here, and he plans to ruin my faultless husband for it." To my immense shame, I felt my eyes tearing at the prospect.

"My dear Mrs. Norton," Mr. Holmes said in a sweetly mesmerizing tone I'd not heard from him previous, "do you *really* imagine I would let that happen?"

And I realised—to my own shock—that I didn't.

"But considering that the clocks have been stopped for days now, and Dickie Maupertuis made his final withdrawal from his preferred gambling haunt just this morning, I haven't a moment to lose. This may in fact be a stroke of luck for us—supposing the Baron is at odds with this gang, *Them* being as good a moniker as any, he may be willing to give me information gratis and abandon any designs on your husband, in exchange for a favour."

"What favour?"

"My *not* messaging Joe Baxby, whose haunts are well known to me, that the Baron is fleeing for Sumatra," the detective answered with both the blinding sparkle and the warmth of a polar ice cap. "Even though Maupertuis isn't part of *Them*, he'll have apprised himself of their entire population and *not* merely the wealthy ones. He's neither stupid nor lacking enormous resources. You can be hurt as badly by a knife to your back as you can a well-placed word from an aristo, though the methods vastly differ. Excuse me. I must arrange a meeting with Maupertuis tonight. There isn't an instant to lose."

The doctor was already offering a sheaf of telegraph forms and a pen. A quicksilver glance of thanks passed between them before Mr. Holmes started scribbling.

"I'm going with you," Dr. Watson announced, crossing his arms.

"You aren't, my good man," Mr. Holmes supplied smoothly, without looking up.

"Why in heaven's name not, pray tell?"

"Dual reasons, my dear doctor. Firstly, because Dickie Maupertuis—whom I have met, and you have not—vastly prefers doing sensitive business with one individual at a time and grows positively fidgety when he feels outnumbered. And secondly, should something go awry, I should prefer *Mrs.* Watson not take her ire out on my hide. Why, I would be quite terrified at the prospect."

Dr. Watson examined the ceiling. "Holmes, do be serious. You and Mary get on tremendously."

"Pssh, naturally we do—she has all the instincts of an excellent investigator."

"My dear fellow, *is* something going to go awry?"

"Absolutely not, dear boy."

"Can you really assure me that is the case?"

Mr. Holmes draped a hand over his heart with an almost coquettish look of shock that was more amusing than it had any right to be. "Watson. Would I *lie* to you about such a thing?"

I left them ten minutes later, still affectionately bickering. They bid me take a very great deal more care, especially now. I returned to the hotel.

And I know what business I am going to be about tonight.

There's nothing for it—all my feminine intuition screams that Mr. Holmes should not engage Dickie Maupertuis alone. I can lurk in the shadows far better than can Dr. Watson, I believe, and I likewise aver that I can trail a chap better than the friendly medico. So this evening I shall don the clothes of a working man, leave a note for dear Godfrey about his brother and Sumatra and the clocks and my whereabouts (he'll be furious, but I'll make it up to him), wait across from 221, and see whether or not I am capable of trailing the world-renowned Mr. Sherlock Holmes of Baker Street undetected. It simply isn't fair for Mr. Holmes to take all the risk. Anyhow, my conscience won't allow it. And I follow my conscience.

To be frank, my sense of adventure won't either—I'm a woman who enjoys a challenge.

And *not* in moderation, either. The steeper the better.

Entry in the personal journal and scrapbook of Mrs. Irene Norton, née *Adler, Monday, June 4th, 1888:*

I shouldn't even be in the condition to write at all after yesterday.

By all traditions of the feminine, I ought to be curled up in bed with a glass of laudanum within my grasp and a vial of smelling salts should I require them. Well, thank goodness I have never been quite *entirely* feminine, and last night only serves to prove as much inarguably.

Begin where you left off, Irene!

Yesterday evening I dredged up the poorest of my mannish attire, the shabby tweeds and threadbare scarf and cloth cap that turn me into a hapless, slightly overgrown news hawker. I can't transform into an urchin exactly, but I'm easily small enough to pass for a lad who's about to be booted from the press and find work as a greengrocer's delivery boy. The night was unseasonably warm for London, breeze alive with fresh-budded trees and apple carts closing up shop for the day alongside the pervasive cart horse and coal smoke aromas. There wasn't much chance of a cab taking a shine to me, so I set off early and walked to Baker Street under an untamed wildfire June sunset.

Squaring my shoulders. Swinging my hips and taking up space. Enjoying it too.

As I travelled, I purchased four papers and some gin. In an alleyway in sight of Mr. Holmes's residence, I poured out most of the gin and settled the bottle on the papers, sitting on a crate with my head against the brick as if in too much of a stupor to finish selling the day's wares. My cheapest pocket watch informed me that the time was just after seven. Not a soul spared me more than a glance. I was as common as the cobbles and just as still and silent and dirty too.

There I waited. My eyes barely open.

At eight-thirty on the dot, Sherlock Holmes emerged, tripping down his front steps with nimble determination—dressed as, I was relieved to see, Sherlock Holmes. I could have followed him in disguise as well, but not nearly so easily. To my relief again, he did not hail a hansom, but set off on foot, swinging his walking stick high every other step like a gallant en route to court an heiress.

Just about the only person I've ever met who relishes their work as much as I do.

While I'm awfully deft at tracking people, I took extreme care in pursuit of this one. Retaining a single newspaper to flip open as a shield, I kept nearly a full block's distance. Thankfully, the gas lamps had been lit around eight, the neighbourhood was a brightly-illumined one, and Mr. Holmes himself is ungodly tall. We passed apothecaries, a spirits shop where I imagined him laying in brandy and claret supplies, and soon we were flanked to the right by trees and greenery. Turning to the left, away from Regent's Park, Mr. Holmes led me to Lodge Road heading west, next to the north again on Oak Tree Road.

Then he took a sharp dive into a darker corridor between buildings.

Pulling my flat cloth hat lower, I flicked up the newspaper, as it was still plausibly bright enough to read. I passed the alleyway in question, flicking my eyes over. Thankfully, Mr. Holmes was in the act of lighting a cigarette, but I flatter myself he wouldn't have noted me anyhow. Once I was clear of the gap, I stopped just out of sightlines, using the late edition of the *Pall Mall* as my barricade.

Ten minutes later, Dickie Maupertuis appeared in the same outlandish attire he'd worn that morning, complete with monocle for his perfectly healthy eye, jauntily whistling again. Something—an altogether superficial, vain something—about the Baron reminded me of Siggy, which made a smile flicker behind my newspaper. This I rather dramatically folded, tucking it under my arm as if setting off.

We passed one another. The Baron unawares, my eyes on the spats over his boots, which I'm horrified to report were not emerald today but rather purple velvet to match his hat.

It pains me to record such things. But artists, perversely, are devoted to the truth.

I glanced behind myself under a show of twisting to check my watch. But our prey didn't pay any note once his back was to me. When he followed Sherlock Holmes into the crack between the walls, I could not prevent my heart from clattering like a woodpecker. It had been stalwart enough thus far. But it beat a rapid tattoo regarding the thought of what danger I'd stupidly put Godfrey in, and what peril I myself was currently in, and what I could possibly do to salvage the matter should Sherlock Holmes fail. And the doughty chap *can* fail.

Living proof had just trailed him to a clandestine meeting.

My pulse wouldn't let up no matter what breathing tricks I employed, and I know *a great big whopping lot*. I feared the men might hear it, so loud it sounded in my own ears.

Creeping as close as I dared to the alley, I pulled out a pocket mirror to observe the proceedings.

"Mr. Holmes," blustered the Baron. "What a shock to the system your telegram was. Why, I don't believe I've hired the services of an . . . amateur private detective."

"Unofficial consulting detective." Mr. Holmes pulled at his cigarette, falling silent after this correction.

"Oh in that case, my *apologies*," the Baron sneered. It was even easier to tell that his accent was manufactured when in *contrapasso* with Mr. Holmes, as the sleuth's words were so effortlessly cultured.

Mr. Holmes took another pregnant pause before answering, "And I'm honoured to say that you are correct. My client is on a *very* different level to yourself."

And I thought, wonder of wonders. I can't even suspect he's flattering me. He has no idea I'm here.

Still Sherlock Holmes puffed away quietly as the Baron grew more agitated and then I saw his gambit. Silence is uncomfortable, grating. Especially if one is in a fit of nerves in the first place. Not only does it put people on the wrong foot.

It makes people *talk* to fill the void.

The Baron, as I expected, broke first. "Do you know, I've always wondered what you would be like. You have such an outrageous reputation that it seemed not to be believed."

Mr. Holmes smiled broadly but coldly. "Any verdicts?"

"I was right." Dickie Maupertuis adjusted his monocle fussily. "It wasn't to be believed. You're mere flesh and blood after all. An ordinary man. How disappointing. I have work to do, so if you'll excuse me—"

"I'm afraid that's not possible. I have some questions."

"Questions?" the Baron snorted. "Why should I answer any of *your* questions?"

"Because I know that you're leaving England, and I know why."

"Oh, that little minx!" The monocle popped out in his agitation. "That . . . that strumpet, I'll have her precious husband's head on a platter for this, you mark my words!"

As much as I quailed at the boldness of the game Mr. Holmes was playing, and shuddered at Maupertuis's threat, I had time to reflect that "strumpet" was rather hurtful.

"You won't." Sherlock Holmes crushed his finished cigarette against the wall before tossing it over his shoulder. It was pretty artful stage direction, I thought. "You would have been in Sumatra anyhow. Now, I want to know everything you have to tell me about a clandestine network of people—both rich and powerful as well as poor and ruthless—who are banded together to form a positive spiderweb of criminal activity, one that ensures wrongs go unpunished and illicit endeavors are successful."

Maupertuis's mouth worked like a fish's. I was lucky they were in profile to me and my pocket mirror, because it was belly-satisfying to watch.

"How—how did you know *Sumatra*?" the villain stammered.

Mr. Holmes lifted one shoulder. "I have my ways. Remember that. I suggest that you unburden yourself, Maupertuis. Who are *They*?"

"'They are the, the guardians of the dark.'" In almost a whisper. "'They owe fealty to one alone. They are without equal, without mercy, and they can haunt your nightmares or make your dreams come true.' That's what his truest followers are meant to learn."

"Interesting, but not very informative, is it? Who is this 'one alone'?"

Even from where I stood, I could see tremours running through the Baron. "I don't know."

"But you *do*, I can tell." Mr. Holmes smirked before his voice turned to iron. "I strongly dislike repeating myself, it's so very tedious. Who are *They*?"

"I don't know!" the pitiful creature cried. "I've only been able to glean a single fact about him."

"Then tell me that one, if you please."

"He's a professor of mathematics."

Sherlock Holmes's brows drew together in disbelief even as his entire body tensed like a leashed greyhound's. "A *mathematics professor*? Where does he teach?"

"I don't know, I don't know, stop tormenting me like this."

"What's his name?"

"I don't know, I told you. I've said all I have to say!"

"No, you haven't. You haven't come to Baker Street and given me the monikers of every member of this organization of whom you are aware. What did you do to upset this very interesting academic, by the by?"

"There was an, an exclusive garden party which doubled as an art sale." Maupertuis seemed practically in tears. "Norton and I had perhaps . . . overindulged. We got into a fight over something I can't even recall. Whether one of the ladies present was pretty, I think. It became a matter of defending her honour. I knocked Norton down and his elbow went straight through a canvas. How was I to realise it was a piece the professor had wanted especially for years?"

"And he would eliminate you both over this?" Mr. Holmes confirmed, brows raised.

"He would."

"We're going back to Baker Street." The tone brooked no argument. "And you're going to keep regaling me in this thoroughly diverting fashion."

"But I can't be seen *there*!"

"That's a pity, because if you don't indulge this little whim of mine, I'll tell Joe Baxby precisely where you are, and you won't last the night. You are familiar with the name, I think? Yes, yes, I see that you are. Let us begin an interlude of positively unforgettable—"

Mr. Holmes looked down to retrieve another cigarette from his case.

Which is when a panicked Baron whipped out a hidden knife from his waistcoat and pulled back for a mighty strike—leading, as the sleuth had said, with his neck.

"*Holmes!*" I shouted in warning.

He leapt back more economically than I've ever seen anyone save an acrobat born into a circus family move. So speedily that I nearly couldn't quite parse every nuance, Mr. Holmes blocked the villain's descending forearm, rotated it with his own until his left thumb was on the back of his attacker's fingers, for an instant clasped the knife hand in both of his as he forced his thumb down fiercely, and came away with the handle of the blade in his right hand. Slid neatly into his grasp through dexterity and pressure alone.

I could probably do that in a pinch, I thought, committing it quickly to memory.

"It ain't so easy as that to get away from me," Maupertuis spat in a thick Seven Dials accent.

"Isn't it?" Mr. Holmes mused, blandly surprised. "Dear me, and here I thought—"

With a rabid snarl, the wretch fell on him again, Mr. Holmes's body blocking his audience's view. For a deranged instant, I thought to assist him when I heard the knife clatter to the ground, and his assailant landed a serious body blow followed by a snapping jab to his stark jawline.

But where Godfrey *may* forgive my accidentally watching Mr. Holmes engage in a knife fight and fisticuffs, he'd draw the line at my leaping on a ruffian's back and attempting a chokehold. Besides, by that time I was honestly frightened. Not of watching a round of boxing (of which this was the lowest form, I grant), which I relish when the opponents are well-matched, but terrified that these men could possibly *be* evenly matched. Seemingly, I've fallen for Mr. Holmes's swagger as readily as the greenest chorus girl.

Guard against gullibility better in future, I charge myself: I've already proven the chap is not the demigod he pretends. No matter what adulations he himself might read in the *Strand*.

Shaking, I stood my ground, already in the mouth of the alleyway. I would not flinch back into the street. I wanted to, I admit it.

I do so adore danger—but in *moderation*.

Finally, just as I was about to tear off my manly cap and commence screaming my lungs out (an activity at which I'm adroit and for which my sex is noted), Mr. Holmes recovered from a vile strike to the ribs by hugging his assailant close to his body at the same instant he ducked his dark head into the junction of Maupertuis's neck and shoulder. Using momentum to upend them both entirely, he took a fistful of hair and knocked the brute's skull against the pavement as the pair went down.

Gravity did the rest of the work. And that was that.

I was left with Mr. Holmes on his knees, hatless, chest heaving, an unconscious thug, and a forgotten knife, which I duly retrieved. The detective's palm was bleeding, I noted. Doubtless from his assailant's attempt to wrestle back the weapon before it fell. Mr. Holmes checked the Baron's pulse, nodded to himself, and collapsed onto one thigh with his intact hand supporting him.

"Are you all right?" he enquired through great gasps.

"I think that's my line," I snapped. "Are *you* all right, you utterly ridiculous man?"

He offered a smile that was half post-battle drunkenness, half ironic. I ought to know what that euphoria feels like—I, too, have conducted discussions with my fists. In New Jersey, no less.

"Perfectly fine, thank you, although a trifle embarrassed. I've watched this slumbering lout prize-fight at Alison's rooms; however, it did not at first occur to me that he may actually have *improved* his boxing acumen during our halcyon period apart from each other. That was appalling hubris. Granted, I didn't suppose you'd be here, but I should never have forgiven myself if any harm had come to a lady over a lackadaisical mistake of mine."

"I'm hardly a lady currently."

"Be that as it may, Mrs. Norton. You may take your own best swing at me for that positively garish error—I shan't raise a single finger in self-defence."

"You want me to punch you for having failed to best the Baron quicker?"

"Unless there's a matter of more . . . personal import over which you'd still care to punch me?" He'd recovered his breath by this time and sounded, of all the incongruous things, regretful.

"What?"

"I wouldn't mind, you know. You were right. You were quite right about everything, Mrs. Norton, regarding last year." Sherlock Holmes's tone was as usual clipped and clinical, which made the content of his speech all the more shocking. "I didn't ask to see any of your physical correspondence, I didn't doubt what I was told by His Ma—"

"Siggy," I corrected him. "Please do call the wretch Siggy. All my friends do, you know."

It was dark, so I couldn't be sure. But at the suggestion we might be friends, I think Mr. Holmes may have flushed a little.

"I failed to question the account given me by my client," he continued. "It was, to be frank, quite unlike me. After doing the most cursory investigating into your background, career, and reputation, I simply donned a series of disguises—"

"A *series*?"

"I did tell you that I fooled you more than once, even though you had me at the finale."

"You really must tell me who the devil you were other than that blasted nonconformist clergyman."

"I'm not certain you would ever forgive me if I did. Then again, I'm not certain I deserve it. I spied, tailed, set up a street brawl, faked an injury, forced your unwitting confidence, and all on the word of a man who—"

"Has a seamstress who puts the royal crest on his undergarments."

"Yes, quite. I do not doubt it."

"Your point being?"

"I was the most appalling cad in Christendom."

Sherlock Holmes nearly looked meek. It was wholly, entirely wrong on him. Grotesque. Guilt can do very strange things to a person, I know this as well as the next adventuress who has truly *lived* in whatever capacity best suits her. I've done things for which I've felt guilty plentiful times, despite my boundless self-confidence. One cannot learn to thrive in the world, as opposed to merely inhabiting it, without making mistakes. It's the flagellating oneself over the mistakes that leads to wrack and ruin.

So I did the only thing possible under the circumstances.

I burst out laughing. Mr. Holmes readily chuckled in return, and then we roared with it, tears forming, positively howling with mirth. Every so often we'd stop. Meet each other's eyes and off we'd go again at a jolly clip. Sliding downward, I joined him on the ground when my ribs must have been aching nearly as badly as were my unlikely champion's. I hugged my knees to my chest. But the merriment had already driven away most of the tremours, and I was quite myself again.

"So it's 'Holmes' now, is it, Mrs. Norton?" the detective teased when we'd settled.

"Oooooh, good Lord, well. Expediency and all that, I didn't even notice I'd skipped your honorific."

"No, you were rather preoccupied with saving my life." The tone would have kept butter solid in August, but the cutting eyes were almost gentle.

"I don't know quite why I decided I ought to be here, but I *do* get a sixth sense about these matters. Call it women's intuition if you like. Besides, you were here in the first place because I asked you to be."

"I ought to severely take you to task for being here, and in all honesty it does quite offend not merely my sensibilities as a gentleman but my duties to my client."

"But I saved your life, remember? So you're just going to have to buck up about it."

Biting his lip, he ventured, "Shall we two call it *pax*, in that case?"

"Gracious! I truly thought we already had, but yes. As the very *Romana*."

He laughed again, this time silently and at the sky. Stilling he said, "Sweet mercy is nobility's true badge."

Heartwarming. I surmised, "I'm betting you have a Shakespearean verse for every occasion. Do you *mind* if I call you that?" I added gently.

The independent investigator blinked. "Excuse me?"

"Holmes. Would it bother you if I dropped your title? If we were friends?"

The poor chap froze. In a natural history museum in Warsaw, I once stared into the glass eyes of a taxidermied jungle cat. Dark as night, sleek and predatory, but forever seized in a quizzical posture.

This was similar.

"Madam, that would be a highly irregular—"

"And aren't those the words used to describe you more often than any others?" Sliding my knees down at last, I crossed my ankles. "'Highly irregular?'"

Emerging from the trance, he huffed. "Who am I to turn down the request of so eminent a personage?"

He was twitting me over the king, and that was when I knew we'd put that entire ridiculous business behind us. Needling your victim whilst still burdened by shame is painful, and never comes off so easily as did his teasing question.

"That's right. You're a lowly independent contractor, Holmes, and before you reposes the queen of all she surveys."

Brushing his right hand off on his trousers (thankfully it was the unbloodied appendage), he proffered it to me. "Dear me, I've nary a choice save to pledge my allegiance then, do I? Alongside another certain gracious lady, I need hardly add."

"Hardly. A dual fealty."

Briefly, I considered spitting in my palm before shaking—but there's such a thing as carrying a good idea altogether too far, and that's Holmes's purview, not mine. For he is *Holmes* now, and heartily glad I find myself too. Which is odd. But then, we are both of us queer individuals. And I do *so* want him to have more than one friend. I don't know how long Godfrey and I will be in London. But something about Holmes and myself is fundamentally the same. I've never felt like that before.

It's *wonderful*.

"A pleasure doing business with you, Norton," he declared as we shook.

"Oh, no!" Gripping his hand harder, I tucked one foot beneath me and allowed the still-seated Holmes to lever me to my feet. "No, no, no. Surely it ought to be Adler, for old time's sake. Now. Let's get out of this bedevilled place."

Holmes glanced ruefully at Maupertuis before pulling out a handkerchief and wrapping his palm. "First, I need you to run for a bobby, if you would be so accommodating, so we can toss this man in gaol. Then I can convict him of something or other, I hardly care which crime, and I can question him further. I'll guard the rascal in the meanwhile. If their boat is departing in the morning, Gilbert Norton shall be sailing unchaperoned, as it were."

"What if I do the guarding and you fetch a peeler?"

He pinched the bridge of his considerable nose. "You are nearly as amusing as my friend Watson, and I say 'nearly' because he doesn't alarm me remotely so much. Haste would be preferable at the moment, Adler, though I hate to rush you."

Glad to accomplish this task—since the Baron was essentially my new friend's consulting fee—I flitted away. It never takes very long to find a man in blue as they walk their rounds, in this case all of two minutes. The constable was a stout, ruddy chap who expressed little shock at an unconscious body splayed in an alley. Though he did allow himself a hint of surprise when it was Sherlock Holmes who handed over the knife, instructing him to take no chances of letting Dickie Maupertuis escape. Momentarily, the air was filled with shrill whistling and pounding footsteps approached.

Holmes paused. "One, two, three . . . a trio of able-bodied men ought to do it. Should you like to head directly home, in which case I'll find you a cab and pay the fare in advance with you in that attire, or would you prefer a celebratory brandy at Baker Street? I imagine Watson will be lying in wait, chafing. Which is fortuitous, since I need patching up and it's maddening to work on one's own hand."

"In for a penny, in for a pound."

After walking a little in search of a hansom, I mused, "I guess this makes us even, then. You worked for Siggy and then helped me out of a scrape to make up for it, but more than that."

"How so more?"

"Well, now we've both actually fooled one another with our disguises twice."

Holmes dipped his head back and let loose a laugh that rang across the cobbles.

"So now you'll tell me what the other one was?"

"Ah, one day, Adler." He was still smiling. "One day after rather more acquaintance I possibly shall."

"Fair enough."

Quiet only reigned for a minute or two.

"I don't suppose you're aware of it, but you're the most remarkable woman I've ever encountered," he stated with all the passion of a fencepost.

"Thankee kindly and you're not the first man to say so."

"What on earth can have produced such a unique specimen of humankind?"

"A decaying clapboard house in Hackensack, New Jersey, occupied by eight members of the same immediate family."

"'Pon my word."

"Yes, you wouldn't have liked it. There was scarcely any music *or* crime. I warbled hymns in the church choir until I was ten, when a retired soloist for the Teatro di San Carlo moved onto an idyllic countryside property nearby with her American husband and gave lessons out of purebred boredom. Mine were free. They may have saved my life, come to think of it."

"By Jove, I shouldn't wonder—the place sounds the stuff of nightmares."

"I didn't say *I* liked it either."

"No, you wouldn't, yet another point which heartily recommends you to me, Adler."

Dr. Watson was indeed pacing the sitting room when we tromped into 221B, and though his lips parted in chagrin when he saw me, he visibly held his tongue. He was under no such compunction when Holmes held up his palm, however, and executed a full *God give me strength* neckroll.

"Did I or did I not tell you to take me with you, Holmes?"

"You did, but matters wouldn't have progressed nearly so well if you had, my dear Doctor."

"That's very flattering. And you call this 'matters going well,' do you?"

"Let me see now. I've Baron Dickie Maupertuis in custody, where I plan for him to miss his boat, I've already learned valuable information, which I shall share with you in due time, and once he's convicted—which will actually happen, because he doesn't belong to *Them*, who are very real indeed—I shall extract from him every morsel I can until he is but bones. I'd trade it for a scratch on the palm any day. Though it would be best if you'd deign to look at it?"

The doctor shook his head and went for his medical bag. Holmes poured three brandies at the sideboard. I collapsed on the settee, the excitement catching up to me. Both Dr. Watson's return and the distribution of drinks were swift, and I couldn't help but smile as the medic shooed the sleuth into his chair and set to work disinfecting. The bowl of water and the towel he wielded were soon very much redder than I thought they'd be. Wincing in sympathy, I wondered how Holmes had stayed so utterly quiet on the subject all the way home.

"The human imagination can fix itself on unexpected subjects, don't you agree, Doctor? Adler?"

Dr. Watson, kneeling on the carpet with the wounded limb outstretched before him, stared up at Holmes in blank astonishment. His head whipped back to me. I raised my brandy glass to the estimable man. After all, it must have been a startling thing to hear. Slowly, he smiled and went back to his task.

"Certainly I agree, Holmes," I returned.

"As do I." Dr. Watson through his professional demeanour now appeared highly amused. "Are there specific instances that are immediately occurring to you?"

"Yes, I cannot stop thinking about how far from reality 'The Adventure of the Silent Clocks' will be when you write it up."

His friend snorted. "You know that for verisimilitude the only cases I write up are the ones where I was actually present."

"My dear fellow, if that's verisimilitude, then an algebraic equation and a Shakespearean sonnet are indistinguishable."

"Lads, though I know this is but banter, for God's sake don't write 'The Adventure of the Silent Clocks.'"

"Please don't trouble yourself over the matter, Mrs. Norton," the doctor protested over his shoulder. "Holmes and I have kept many confidences, not to say horrifically personal secrets. Upon my word, I swear never to even mention Baron Maupertuis or your good self—"

"Ooooh, but you can't do *that*!" I cried. "You silly man, don't you dare to finish that sentence. I featured *so* well in the other marvellous write-up of yours, you've really a flair you know, and this is coming from a consummate professional. I simply devour every word you pen, and I couldn't bear the thought of this adventure of ours going . . . well, unmarked. Just as I couldn't bear never to be mentioned again. Even supposing I end up postmortem or something equally outlandish."

"As to your untimely death, if you wish it, that is the slightest trouble of all," Holmes drawled. "I'm sure you could come up with something suitably fictional, couldn't you, my dear fellow?"

Dr. Watson's expression was that of a dog being taunted by a cat just outside its play yard—a bit maddened yet completely unconcerned, and well aware that the identical irritant would plague him tomorrow. "Supposing you think me such a fantasist, I'll glancingly refer to this entire matter by its proper opposite, as a question of high finance and political intrigue."

Clapping, I chuckled. "The very thing! But where do I figure into the affair of the scheming politician Baron Maupertuis, then? Do pay me the very highest of compliments you can think of, Doctor. All of them."

"You are of the feminine persuasion, my dear Adler." Holmes stiffened slightly as the first stitch went in. "As if the man could resist."

"Fine." Dr. Watson beamed at his friend. "In hinting at the story of Baron Maupertuis and his colossal schemes, I shall—without divulging its nature or the lady's identity—intimate that you have discovered an invaluable fresh weapon to aid in your lifelong battle against crime. Does it suit?"

Sherlock Holmes, I'd swear on the Good Book, almost choked on his brandy.

Dr. Watson accepted this reaction like a trophy. He looked as if he'd just won a round in an eternally played cricket match between them. Which, let us face facts, is true of all cricket matches.

My homecoming was not nearly as cheerful.

The instant the door squeaked Godfrey was crushing me in his arms. My nose was full of clove and ambergris. It would have been no great matter to stay there the rest of my life.

"What were you thinking, darling?" he demanded brokenly into my auburn hair, my cap having fallen to the ground. "What in the name of all that is right and good in this world could you have been *thinking*? I've been nearly sick, I—"

"I'm sorry," I gasped. "I'm so sorry, Godfrey. You did ask for my help, but this was perhaps . . . a trifle extreme."

"A *trifle?*" he cried. "God in Heaven, Irene! What happened?"

Briefly, I told him everything, with certain shall we say *theatrical* adjustments to lower his highly mistaken impression that I was nearly killed. It didn't help. The poor man collapsed into the nearest dining chair with his head in his hands and only emerged from the posture when I insinuated myself into his lap in a manner that brooked no refusal. He held on to me as if he'd found a handy log while drowning.

"I really am truly sorry," I murmured. "Not for trying to help you, my king, never that, but. For the rest of it."

He only sighed grimly.

"Tell me what happened after you got my note? What's become of your brother?"

Godfrey pressed his fingers into his eyes. "I rushed to the townhouse. When I arrived, all the clocks were gone."

"Oh, dear," I managed.

"I told him that I knew all, and I proved it. He begged, pleaded, cajoled with me to transfer the stocks. He claimed it was as much as his life was worth. Eventually I believed him. I've never seen Gilbert so cowed. When he told me that his fate was in my hands, I confess that the feeling of being the one in power for once was not . . . entirely disagreeable, though in retrospect I am ashamed of myself. In the end, I did the only thing I could do."

"I'm afraid I don't know what that might be, my love."

"I told him to bring the clocks back to where they belong," my husband whispered. "He agreed at once, the rascal. Then I in turn agreed to make the securities exchange. He departs for Sumatra tomorrow."

Making a humming sound, I laid my head on his broad chest. I wasn't surprised. Not where Godfrey was concerned. He may dislike his brother, even hate him, but in my spouse those feelings fall far short of fratricide.

"It isn't as if I'll miss him," Godfrey mused.

"Lord, no."

After an interlude of simply breathing, he continued, "Gilbert did do one thing rather unexpectedly."

"I shudder to think."

"He won't be needing the townhouse anymore, obviously."

"And he expects you to remain here and sell it. How charming."

Godfrey hesitated for longer than I expected. Finally, he drew a great breath. "He gave it to me."

"He *what did you say?*" I reared back.

"It's ours." A little half smile. "To sell or keep, just as we please."

"Godfrey," I gasped. "Godfrey, Godfrey, we aren't genteel poor any longer!"

"No," he agreed, allowing himself to laugh.

There were kisses, and embraces, and celebratory whoops. Then Godfrey said he had a lot of thinking to do about a number of things, and was still more than vexed with me, and that we'd talk further, but right now he needed a long walk to clear his head.

So he left, and I sat down to write. And despite our being so at odds, I can't help but feel an abundance of joy. Gilbert will needle me no more. The Baron is in custody. I solved the clocks. Holmes and I are friends. Godfrey is safe. And we have a townhouse at our disposal.

After all, I don't mind a little influx of wealth from time to time.

Always supposing it's in *moderation.*

Entry in the personal journal and scrapbook of Mrs. Irene Norton, née *Adler, Wednesday, June 6th, 1888:*

Godfrey knows all of my friends. I make a point of introducing him whenever the opportunity arises. In this case, the friend was Sherlock Holmes.

It usually goes better. I need a hot bath and a stiff drink.

Entry in the personal journal and scrapbook of Mrs. Irene Norton, née *Adler, Friday, June 8th, 1888:*

I've been stewing for *days* over the fact that I can barely manage to find a truly marvellous hat or get over a touch of ague or win money on a dog race without celebrating. Which meant I had unfinished business to see to, because there was something of actual *significance* to celebrate, but not yet any champagne between the pair of us. Myself and Sherlock Holmes, that is.

Why I kept dilly-dallying, I don't know. Probably because events had come so hard and fast and because my husband was so out of sorts.

Today I finally pulled the trigger.

> MAYFAIR to MARYLBONE, Friday, June 8th:
> YOUR PRESENCE REQUESTED AT SELF-CONGRATULATORY
> SUPPER **STOP** TOMORROW EIGHT CUPID'S ARROW **STOP**
> DO SAY YES—NIGHTINGALE

Soon enough, I had my reply.

> MARYLEBONE to MAYFAIR, Friday, June 8th:
> I NEVER FLOUT WISHES OF MONARCHY **STOP** NOT
> PINK ROOM GIVES ME HEADACHE **STOP** UNTIL
> TOMORROW—SH

Last night, after he'd made his weary way back from the Temple, I broached the subject with Godfrey over a simple repast of meats and cheeses. He looked so dashing sitting there, with the low gaslight playing off his inky hair, and I thought, *He had it all wrong.* I never really wanted to be a queen. I wanted to be the queen of someone's heart in truth instead of in fantasy, and I wanted that person to be the king of mine.

And that is exactly what we are, Godfrey and I. I do not mean to overly romanticise it; yes, I am a prima donna and he is a terribly capable solicitor. But I am also the girl from New Jersey who imagined herself in love half a dozen times and ended up wandering the grounds of an estate or the halls of a mansion with the heaviest ache of loneliness weighing her down. And he is the boy born the third son, by another mother, who made himself feel loved by plying beautiful performers with gifts and affections when he knew full well none of it was real.

Making them feel special made him happy.

I am Irene Adler and I do not like the idea of a hovel. I'm more amenable to palazzos, or a suite overlooking the Champs-Elysees. But to be with Godfrey, I would live in a cottage in a remote part of Wales.

"Darling, are you all right? You're looking at me very oddly and all I've done is taken another slice of *sopressata*."

Smiling, I said, "I was just admiring you."

"Oh." Godfrey smoothed his moustache with his napkin. "Well, do carry on in that case."

I laughed. The man delights me. "You are such a goose, Godfrey."

"Your goose, yes, Irene."

"Hmm. I love you."

"And I you. Are you sure you're all right?"

"Very, very sure."

The edges of his dark eyes crinkled as he smiled at me. He set his napkin on the table and when he passed me en route to hang his coat in the small wardrobe, he paused to kiss my hairline softly.

"I'm having a celebratory supper with Sherlock Holmes tomorrow," I told his back. "You won't mind, will you?"

He turned with his eyebrows raised. "Mind? Since when have I objected to your dining with friends? What a churlish notion."

"Yes, but I don't think you . . . like him."

"Admittedly that would be an issue if *I* were the one having dinner with him."

"That's rather a good point you make, dearest, but the whole notion of avoiding London was to avoid him. I expect you to tell me if my gadding about with him drives you spare."

Godfrey shrugged out of his shirtsleeves, and I openly treated myself to the sight of my husband in trousers and an undershirt in a tiny Mayfair hotel room.

"All right, Irene," he said with an air of high tragedy. "Confess, now. Do you plan to have a torrid romantic dalliance with Sherlock Holmes?"

He winked at me. That beautiful, impossible man of mine.

"Yes, I no longer like my swains modeled upon Prince Charming. Give me prickly and skeletal or nothing at all."

"Shall I become prickly and skeletal for you, then?"

"Ha, you won't do it half as well as *he* can, that much I can promise you."

"You are absolutely correct, darling, and I am undone. I cede the ground. I rend my garments and pour ashes over my head! My one true love has forsaken me because I could not compete at becoming the least likeable man in London!"

Laughing helplessly, I asked, "What don't you like about him?"

He pretended to think quite hard. "It may have something to do with the fact that he is arrogant, cold, calculating, snide, and attempted to rob you."

"Granted. Though he seems quite contrite about the last item."

"*That* man, contrite?"

"I'll own he doesn't wear it at all well."

"Ah, no, no he wouldn't."

"He really hasn't anyone," I mused, selecting an olive. "Only Dr. Watson and only when the doctor isn't otherwise engaged."

"And so?"

I shrugged. "I'll admit I'm awfully vain, but he does like me, I think. I've felt that way before even when I was in the middle of a love affair . . . an island unto myself. It's ghastly. I only thought I might provide him a little distraction."

Godfrey stared at me and slowly shook his head.

"What?" I straightened from where I was slumped with one elbow on the dining table. "Did I say something awful?"

He came back around and knelt in front of me, taking both of my hands. I was almost nervous, my spouse looked so earnest.

"Irene," Godfrey said clearly. "I didn't marry you because you're possibly the most beautiful woman to have lived since Helen of Troy. I didn't marry you because you're an endlessly talented opera chanteuse. I didn't even marry you because you're the cleverest person I've ever met, or the bravest. To my dismay, at times."

"Why did you marry me?" I whispered.

"This is why I married you," he told me. "It would only ever occur to *you* to show kindness to the likes of Sherlock Holmes. You don't pity him—the man isn't remotely pitiable—you're simply being kind to him because you can, you want to, and because that's the person you are. It's quite spellbinding, you know, and I plan to watch it for the rest of my life."

I kissed him. I may have had tears in my eyes, I can't remember.

If I did, they were happy ones.

The happiest ones I've ever had.

Entry in the personal journal and scrapbook of Mrs. Irene Norton, née Adler, Saturday, June 9th, 1888:

The weather is fine, the flowers in Mayfair are blooming riotously, and I find myself quite excited to celebrate besting the infamous Baron Maupertuis alongside the famous Sherlock Holmes. Though never a stated life goal, it's certainly a shining laurel leaf to add to my crown.

However, I confess myself at a complete loss in one single respect regarding this evening: what on *earth* do you wear to a celebratory supper with a man who looks at you as if you're an interesting specimen of tree frog?

Entry in the personal journal and scrapbook of Mrs. Irene Norton, née Adler, Sunday, June 10th, 1888:

Oh thank the heavens, that's a relief.

Dinner was a quietly smashing success.

We supped at the Cupid's Arrow in a small private room—the blue one, not the pink one—and I flatter myself had quite the convivial time. After the oysters, Holmes ordered a delicate fish preparation that was as close to not being a meal while still being an entrée as was possible. I ordered a steak, bloody, because the chef at the Cupid's Arrow is a delight and I maintain my grip on sanity better than does my detective friend.

Holmes picked at his fish. "Ah, I fear there you are quite mistaken, Adler. On the contrary."

I cut into my steak as if it had done personal harm to my mother. "So you *weren't* fast friends before Baker Street?"

"Dr. Watson and I had never so much as set eyes on each other."

"But trying to imagine you moving in with a stranger is next to impossible."

"I don't know whether to be flattered or insulted."

"No, no, that's not what I mean, you're just so . . ." I gestured helplessly.

"You may append whatever adjective you like and I'll have been called worse at school, even college. Well. Trevor was all right, but that fellow could have befriended an inflamed gorilla."

"Fine, Holmes." I took a sip of champagne. "But what was your impetus to take such measures?"

"Oh, come now! What is it for anyone? I was confoundedly poor."

"You?" I exclaimed.

"Why yes, it was getting worrisome. I was about to pawn my dress cravats."

"Do be serious. Not *too* serious. In moderation. Tell me the story, oh, I *adore* stories and you're shockingly good at them. Really, it's surprising for a man of your reticence just how good at them you are!"

The fine wrinkles at the edges of his metallic eyes rumpled in his Cheshire cat smile. "Very well. I was working at St. Bart's, where he went to school, and he had run into an old classmate. Stamford also happened to be one of my better sorts of acquaintances at the lab. We chatted occasionally on all manner of topics—whether or not lead poisoning was too slow to be used as a murder weapon was a memorably lively conversation, conducted over a passable bottle of claret at the restaurant down the street. He was intelligent, and friendly, and seemed a steady fellow. I even once daydreamed the mad notion of asking *him* to take rooms with me, since he seemed to be able to tolerate me well enough. Unfortunately, Stamford was perfectly financially solvent and I knew it, so I settled for telling him I was avidly looking. When he mentioned this to Watson, the good doctor turned out to be quite amenable to the notion even after Stamford warned him that he'd caught me beating the corpses in the dissection room."

"*Beating* the corpses?" I repeated. I set my fork down, giving it a minute before the outstanding steak would be palatable again.

"Well, yes," he answered mildly. "Exactly how else was I supposed to find out how far contusions would develop after the victim was already deceased?"

"Of course, of course, I should have guessed. That isn't the story, though."

Holmes swallowed a delicate bite of leek. "I was slaving over my chemical studies. How long had I been there, twenty-four hours? Longer, I believe. More like twenty-seven. I'd been obsessed with a single idea for months, mind. It was early afternoon, and I was nearly there. I *had* what I'd been searching for all that time at my very fingertips. If only I could grasp it. And then grasp it I did, and Watson walked through the door with Stamford at the same instant."

Setting his fork down, Holmes quirked a smile at me as he twirled his champagne stem. "In what could well have been an alarming incident which ruined everything, I ran towards them shrieking like a banshee that I had found it. I might as well have leapt naked out of a bathtub and been shouting 'Eureka!' at the top of my lungs. In retrospect, it wouldn't shock me if I'd started up an impromptu waltz with Stamford and they'd made hasty goodbyes and fled the room. In which case I'd have kept shouting, but out the open window to passersby."

Laughing freely, I was gratified to see that he wasn't offended, but chuckled as well. "I've never seen you in such a state!"

"Dear me, one hopes you never shall—it's extremely rare and quite uncontrollable, I fear."

I leaned forward conspiratorially. "What did you find?"

This time the smile was unfettered.

"I'd found an infallible test for bloodstains."

Thrilling at this confirmation of my earlier research, I gasped. "And how—what is it?"

Taking on a scientist's clinical air, he replied, "It is a re-agent. It reacts solely with haemoglobin and not with mud, or rust, or the juice of a ripe plum the victim had with his lunch. *Only* haemoglobin. It also has the advantages of being fairly simple to produce, and astonishingly cheap."

"Oooooh, you must have been so proud," I breathed. "What next?"

Holmes succumbed to a faraway expression. "Next I made the simple deduction that Watson had been in the Second Afghan War. He was very different back then, you understand. He was only recently returned, which is what made the inference so absurdly facile. He walked like a trained soldier, but the way he carried himself in the lab immediately suggested he knew medicine, thus I was meeting an army doctor. Watson's wrists were the colour his face is now, but back then his hands were very dark indeed. Not only did he stand as if at attention needlessly, he let his left arm hang—he doesn't do that very often anymore, thankfully—so he had been wounded in action. You can't imagine how thin and sickly he looked. It gives me no pleasure to think of it. Later he told me that after the wound nearly killed him, a secondary fever nearly did away with him again, which explained how unwell he still was. When I told Watson he'd been in Afghanistan, the *look* of surprise on his face. Most people I know would be startled or suspicious. He was rather . . . rapt."

As was I. I was hanging on his every word. The man truly is a good storyteller, to my endless surprise. "Then what happened?"

"I demonstrated my blood test. As much as I wanted to display it, I also wanted to see it again with my own eyes." Holmes gave a small groan, shaking his head. "Adler, Adler, I was *ridiculous*. Here was this perfect stranger to me, obviously suffering some sort of trauma, and I was so eager for him to witness my chemistry triumph that I *seized him* by the *coat sleeve* and dragged him over to it."

My jaw dropped, nearly to my plate. "Holmes. You did *not*."

"I can assure you that I did. I was there. It's rather alarming in retrospect."

Grinning, I raised my glass to him. "Carpe diem, my friend."

Holmes didn't so much roll his eyes as lift them swiftly then blink the expression away. "Watson says I looked like a child with a new toy. The worst of it is that I cannot even contradict him. I know perfectly well that he's right."

"And how did they react to your triumph?"

"They were not quite suitably impressed, but they were certainly attentive."

"What a shame. I'd like to see it *very* much. And then?"

"It was proposed we lodge together, since we were both in immediate need."

"Who proposed it?"

"Stamford, I think. And I said I'd my eye on a suite of rooms in Baker Street I thought would suit us down to the ground. I was right. I often am, you realise."

"I do. And then?"

"Then I commenced prattling off a list of my sins—I don't think I'd shed the *Eureka* mood yet. I told a complete and utter stranger what kind of tobacco I smoke, that I get trapped in my mind at times and go silent for days. All the things I do which might make a man prefer to take the next ship back to Afghanistan rather than remain in diggings with me. Well. *Nearly* all my vices, shall we say. Anyway, I went into shocking detail and I'd known him for about two and half minutes. I've never done such a thing. It was completely out of character."

"Once you'd found a comfortable situation, you didn't want to lose it too quickly because he hadn't known what to expect," I offered in a soft tone.

"Just so." Holmes took a sip of champagne and when he looked up, his grey eyes had regained their sharpness. "And Adler, Watson did the most surprising thing after I'd finished gushing out a litany of my worst qualities."

73

"Which was?"

Holmes gave me a real smile, bright and brief. "He told me a few of his own. And said yes anyway."

It's difficult to write how I felt in that moment. Holmes got up to bank the fire, and I allowed myself a moment to ponder the queer twists life's path can take us down. I am lucky enough to have many friends, nearly all of whom have been met through work. My vocation is one of the most social possible. Dozens upon dozens of singers call me *friend*, I am honoured to say. But I wouldn't even have met Siggy if I hadn't been singing in Bohemia, nor Godfrey for that matter if I hadn't been singing in London. My new friend Holmes's work is rather solitary.

Grinning, I poured more champagne. Or it *was*, and now it wasn't.

What a beautiful turn of events.

"What precisely is so amusing, Adler? Thank you," he said as I finished topping him off.

"So you were shouting 'I found it' because you thought you'd found an important thing that day?" I confirmed.

"Yes?" he agreed, puzzled.

"Well, you were wrong."

"But Adler, surely you can recognise the investigative value of—"

"You didn't find one important thing," I stated firmly.

"No?"

"No. You found two. What fortune-blessed day that was, to be sure."

The purse in his lips gradually stretched into a smile. "So it was."

Rising to my feet as I raised my champagne glass, I announced, "To our mutual success, which should be the stuff of *legend*."

Laughing, Holmes snatched his glass off the table and we toasted. "Hear, hear."

Dropping my voice, I continued, "And to finding things, whether we are looking for them or not."

He took a moment, but then Holmes returned in a hearty voice, "Hear, hear."

It was a lovely meal.

It was a marvellous adventure. I'm sure we'll share more of them, I just know it.

And I'd thought we were celebrating our success. We were. But I relish celebrating—especially for multiple reasons—and Sherlock Holmes now having more than one friend is also *undoubtedly* cause for champagne.

THE SONG OF A WANT

(Henry Wiggins)

From the Office of Mr. Henry Wiggins
Wiggins, Perry, and Tilton, Solicitors
4 Grosvenor Place, London

October 14th, 1904

My dear Mrs. R. Caine,

It is always gratifying to hear unexpectedly from an old friend, particularly one in whose career I can take such justifiable pride. Therefore, first: congratulations upon your I daresay meteoric rise in the ranks of feminine journalism! Your accolades have not gone unnoticed by your humble servant, and when I think of our earliest days as colleagues so long ago . . .

You know everything I have to say on that subject. There is too much in my heart for a young solicitor to express. It defies English.

Naturally, I received your letter of the eighth of last week with great interest. You are the best possible candidate to pen the article you described. A laudatory biography of Sherlock Holmes upon his withdrawal from public service . . . what could be more appropriate? Felicitations! Of course, on the occasion of a remarkable man's retirement, curiosity regarding his life and career—though I can't say we've ever seen public curiosity *wane* regarding Mr. Holmes—naturally increases. Questions regarding early life and influences arise. Origins take on the proportion of myths.

Are we myths, Mrs. Caine? Are we a part of something grown so huge that we are now fictional, nothing more than a carefully tapped out collection of two-dimensional letters on a page written by an equally famous medico? Have we been irrevocably flattened? Or do we still exist as flesh and blood, if only to ourselves?

The wind moans in the hearth I just stoked, and the mice at my small office whisper their secrets quite audibly tonight, and the thought of becoming a mere fable is unsettling. Not to mention ludicrously fanciful! So to the point: your project is a dear one. When I reflected on your queries, however, I came to realise that my own humble beginnings were very much tied up with the great man's *before* there was any such thing as the Baker Street Irregulars; and furthermore that I had never before sat down and done the tale justice with nib and foolscap.

It has taken me therefore some days to write this. I am penning it all out clean again now. But our mutual exposure to storytelling from a tender age drives me to give the full account—in a more complete manner, I daresay, than you bargained for when you asked such simple questions regarding my memories and his character. To my own surprise, I found myself losing some of the formal cadence of speech I worked so hard to acquire, and it happened more and more often as I progressed. A matter of phrasing here, of vocabulary there. But I made up my mind that the *me* I was as a child was no more inherently shameful than the *me* I am in a frock coat behind a desk. So I left some of them in, as you'll no doubt discover.

I have never previously revealed any of this, and now I ache—yes, I suffer, Mrs. Caine—for someone to know of the story. It writhes in my guts like a worm, so that whenever I am not composing this letter, I can think of nothing save what to write next. The plot was a right smasher. If admittedly dark, and dare I say at times even hopeless.

How hopeless were all our lives, back then? How hopeless would they have remained if not for him?

So. To commence! The first time I ever saw Sherlock Holmes, he was in a bad way and no mistake.

We destitute were all huddled about the fire barrels that night—in a horrid tight frozen corridor, a crack in London's face—near Shadwell Market. Wind sharp enough to freeze your blood to your bones, and every so often you'd catch a whiff of chestnuts roasting, or some lucky fellow's thermos of hot coffee. Something other than the stench of the sewer driftwood and the mudlark coal we were burning, and your belly would tie itself into a knot over something as insubstantial as a *smell*. But I don't need to explain that to you. You know the feeling all too well yourself, my dear Mrs. Caine.

January of 1878 wanted every man jack of us dead, is what. Though I think you're a bit too young to remember? When it wasn't snow, it was sleet, which was worse. Snow could freeze your finger-ends, but the sleet left you shaking like a flag in the wind, with a hard hurt in your bones that never quite went numb and made a gentle end of you.

That's how my best friend, Meggie, came to fall sick and vanish. And if it hadn't been for Mr. Holmes, the Lullaby Doctor might have gone on doing whatever he wanted with nobody the wiser. But it's best to begin stories at the beginning—we've all had that drilled into our pates, haven't we? And the beginning for me was January 21st, 1878, around those awful stinking fire barrels that kept the life clinging to our bodies like the muck on our boots.

Because that was the night we met Scott Williamson. Who wasn't Scott Williamson at all, of course, but Sherlock Holmes.

"Cold, innit?" said Meggie, appearing at my side out of the gloom.

"It must be. Your jokes are getting feeble, and they was bad enough at the start," I retorted, tucking a friendly arm about her. "Any luck?"

"Not I. Corner shop's boarded up, chophouse bins clean, and the chestnut men glaring at everyone what gets closer than ten paces, like they's regular peelers. It's more'n your liberty's worth to steal a bite tonight."

"So we won't try for it. Told you tonight would be a rum one, didn't I?"

"You did. But trying anyhow passes the time till the light's strong enough for us."

"So does standing here, you daft little thing."

"Aye, but I favor trying. Even if it comes to naught. Work is the best cure."

"For what?"

"Nighttime. Cold. Anything o' the sort what ails a girl."

"Freezing to death?"

She made no answer. Though already philosophical, Meggie was eight, scrawny as a sparrow, and I nine. Meggie's dad was a great kindly brute, Irish bred, a coal-whipper down at the dockside. I met him half a dozen or so times. Back when she was only a fire-headed lass of five, and he still coming home to their digs in the shadow of the bridge, with his eyes scarlet from the dust and his hands blacker than any gloves.

Then when Meggie was around six, he didn't come home one day. And he stayed away the next. And soon after that, you'll not be too staggered to learn, there wasn't a home anymore. Not for her.

Myself, I'd never known naught but the orphanage, and the work-house, and the streets. And the streets beat the other two by far. But it was lonesome out there, and what's more, dangerous without some sort of companion—an extra pair of eyes to watch the fire while you run for soup, an extra pair of ears to note distant police whistles. So when I found my mate Meggie curled up under a potato sack in Brick Lane, I took her in at once. As best I could do, you understand. Which was in the hold of a barge where I paid the lighterman tuppence a night to let me sleep behind the saltpetre bags and the bundles of whalebone, whatever the sad old sot was delivering that day. And whenever I had pennies.

By that night, we were thicker than thieves. Thicker than blood.

"Anyhow. Early start this morning would be best." Meggie clapped her hands to warm them. Tossed red curls.

"Don't I know it. Beat the rest of 'em to the shoreline and set to."

We'd slept rough in the shadow of a carpenter's barrow for the first half of the night. But that was risky on account of the peelers as soon as dawn crept over the garbage-choked river, and the sooner Meggie could clamber up my shoulders between the barges and knock some coal onto the shoreline, the sooner we could sell it and eat something. Anyway, it had grown far too cold to risk sleeping any longer—unless we had our sights set on doing it forever and being dumped unceremoniously into paupers' graves. It wasn't just hearsay that had so many strangers huddled around the fire barrel, either. Everyone present had a grim tale of their own to tell about London winters. I'd once tripped on what I thought was a discarded sack of rubbish and was decidedly *no* such thing.

"Give us a tune, luv." The voice came from the other side of the fire, where a toothless crone with a rotting straw bonnet stood dribbling down her own chin. "Pretty please? Just a ditty or two. For luck, like."

Meggie drew her shawl closer. "My luck or yours?"

"It's all one, dearie. I ain't partial. Any fair fortune is better than none, says I. It's like sunshine. Where's the harm?"

"What tune d'you fancy, then?"

"Give us 'The Song of a Want,' luv. That always warms the blood, doesn't it?"

Smiling, Meggie started to sing, in that peculiar piercing child's lilt she had, as if you were listening to a wind chime or a silver spoon struck against crystal. It sent icicles down your neck. She started with a rouser, one to whip up sluggish blood and make the night shine. But in her voice, it came out high and queer and prickling. Pleasantly eerie, like watching a candle snuffed without any draft, or a door creak open with nary a soul to push it. And of course, the subject was drear despite the jolly, jouncing melody.

We didn't know any other songs.

> *Now, gentlemen, be you all merry,*
> *I'll sing you the song of a Want;*
> *I'll make you as merry as may be,*
> *Though money begins to grow scant.*
> *A woman without e'er a tongue,*
> *She never can scold very loud;*
> *'Tis just such another great want*
> *When the fiddler wants his crowd.*

The old witch cackled with glee as Meggie reached the chorus, and anyone with strength in their lungs croaked and wheezed and howled it out along with her. It must have sounded like a dust-up in Bedlam. But for a small sweep of the second hand, we were in a pub with a roaring hearth and a frothing pint.

Not battling freezing to death in Stepney.

> *Good people, I tell unto you,*
> *These lines are absolute new;*
> *For I hate and despise the telling of lies—*
> *This ditty is merry and true.*

Cracked shoes and flapping boot soles tapped. Our own hardened bare feet jigged on frozen dirt. The meager blazes spat and fizzled, the wind shrieked against the suffocating smell, and there were worse ways to speed along the sunrise. Meggie quickly warmed her voice if not her fingers, and it rang out sharp as a knife in the back despite her youth.

> *A bell without e'er a clapper,*
> *Will make but a sorrowful sound;*
> *And he that has no land of his own,*
> *May work on another man's ground.*

We had just finished another chorus when a strange voice—one that could pronounce the letter *H* and had vowels as smooth as a lady's silks—exclaimed, "Well done indeed. Brava!"

We peered into the dim, startled. A very tall, thin fellow hove into view.

That was our first glimpse of Sherlock Holmes. You'd think that trumpets would have sounded or fireworks would have blazed. Such was his later influence, the angel Gabriel ought to have heralded his arrival. But no—the world kept turning as it always did. I wonder often what my life would have been and how long it would have lasted if Meggie hadn't been singing. And if Sherlock Holmes hadn't heard her. Or hadn't given a fig about a little street girl's queer tunefulness.

"Young lady, that's a fine instrument in your throat," the intruder continued. "But it should serve you far better in Tottenham Court Road, supposing you wish to profit by your innate musicality. And I don't see why you shouldn't."

"Who in blazes are you, then, what wants me to be taken up for begging and like as not packed off to the reformatory?" Meggie scoffed.

"Mr. Scott Williamson," said Sherlock Holmes. Even in the darkness the man's pale eyes glittered, his words came fast as bullets, and he'd a violin case tucked under one arm. "Lately of Cambridge, but the victim of unfortunate circumstances. At least until my fiddle here can earn me back my proper clothing, and I can visit the employment offices, and then all will be right again."

Meggie and I exchanged a look. It held, puzzled.

Because this Scott Williamson fellow was lying.

Murky as the night was, it might have worked; I might've taken Scott Williamson for a Distressed Scholar type—which is what he was playacting—except that his togs were too grand. They didn't even resemble what he wears as his actual self, mind. But they were good enough for our suspicions to be roused. The regular dodge of the beggar who makes his way shamming to be an unlucky academic is simple: compose a letter of recommendation with dollops of Latin and wave it about, and claim you only need get your proper gear out of hock. Then ask for what you will—railway fare back to school, generally. Again, and again, and again. But this fellow wore valuable workingman's clothes. They were mended, but they were never *cheap*, so the fabric alone he could sell to a jerry shop (which is where I imagine he obtained them in the first place). He wasn't a beggar, therefore, who'd have been unabashedly in rags. And I didn't think him a true street musician either—not at three-thirty in the morning two blocks from the Thames. Not on a night like that one.

No, this chap was off his kilter. He had long fingers, like a conductor's, and was waving them as if he didn't know he was doing so. Mr. Williamson's voice was rapid. But the energy with which he spoke seemed leashed by only the flimsiest of leads. It bucked and reared. I could equally imagine the man bursting into a pool of scattered starlight or taking flight like a bird.

"Well then, Mr. Williamson, this here's Henry Wiggins, and I'm Meggie Hart," my friend offered.

"Never mind all that, I've a marvellous idea." He unsnapped the case and tucked the violin under his neck, as if he'd never been so keen to do anything in his life. "Oh, come, I'm accounted better than decent. I'll bring no shame to your esteemed concert. On my honour. Nothing, really? Here, I'll lead us in!"

The man rattled like an express train. An instant later, notes poured out of his instrument. Crazed ones, quicker than Meggie's tempo had been and twice the number, dancing around the melody like demons poking at a lost soul.

Meggie's eyes turned saucers. Then she laughed and struck up the next verse.

> *A blacksmith without his bellows,*
> *He need not rise very soon;*
> *And he that has no clothes to put on,*
> *May lie in his bed till noon.*
> *An innkeeper lacking in custom,*
> *Will never get great store of wealth;*
> *And if he has ne'er a sign to hang up,*
> *He may e'en go hang up himself.*

The dregs of London bellowed their accompaniment and the fires hissed their approval. The world changed, as if a great curtain had been swept aside. This was a genuine performance. The flaming barrels were footlights, and Mr. Williamson swayed to the music while Meggie sang words about empty spaces that would never be filled.

I wish I could better describe to you what happened next, or how he did it—but one second we were hunched around the barrels, and the next we were edging out of the alley behind Mr. Williamson, inching towards the awakening street. He was our Pied Piper, leading us off into some godless horizon. Sherlock Holmes's ability to do such things no longer shocks me. But that doesn't make them any the less impressive.

At the mouth of the corridor, he stopped. And we behind him, framed as if by a genuine proscenium, lights dancing behind us. I've no doubt that it made for a ragged, ugly scene; but every time I think back on it from the perspective of the street, I cannot help but picture the tableau utterly beautiful.

He took us right up to the edge, where the alleyway ended. That was when coins began to hit the straw and the stones, flung carelessly at us by early rising or late-retiring passersby huddled into their mufflers. We could barely see them for the smoke, but they could *hear* us sure enough, it was clear. *Plink clink plink clink* all around, like the beginning of a thunderstorm, the starving folk squealing and diving at the mud. And me not being simple, well, I looked to Meggie and whipped off my cap to hold out, and she stepped up brazen as you please next to Scott Williamson, and he arched his back like a great black cat's and the metal rain fell harder.

> *A warren without e'er a coney,*
> *Is barren, and so much the worse;*
> *And he that is quite without money,*
> *Can have no great need of a purse.*

Fingernails tore as our neighbours scrabbled for ha'pennies and my hat filled. Minutes passed. Meggie doubled back on the verses for a second time as she watched the coins rain. The stranger smiled as he played, a melancholy moonstruck look, and his fingers flashed faster as we hurtled towards the final chorus.

> *Good people, I tell unto you,*
> *These lines are absolute new;*
> *For I hate and despise the telling of lies—*
> *This ditty is merry and true.*

The song concluded with a flourish on his part and a high note on my friend's. Wild applause erupted from both the street and the crevice alike. We were in a jungle, and Meggie and Mr. Williamson our idols. Cheers went up likewise from the open doors of two public houses opposite, and several windows high above.

I clutched my hat to my chest as Meggie grinned at me with sweet, crooked teeth.

"What did I tell you?" Scott Williamson gasped, sweat beading along his gaunt temples despite the arctic temperature. He staggered, lithe back hitting the bricks, and swished his bow at the pair of us. "If you're blessed with a talent, why not earn a few quid by it, is what I say? You can whistle while you work, but if you can be paid for merely the whistling, then so much the better! Supposing the whistling is superior to everyone else's. There's no call for meadowlarks to go to away to war, or for angels to dig ditches. The very fabric of the universe frowns upon such degradations, don't you agree?"

We couldn't, not having the faintest idea what he was saying. His head drooped. He slumped down to the rough stones gracelessly, though careful of his instrument—he cradled it, and the bow he likewise guarded in his lap as he hung his head over his knees. Sherlock Holmes loves few things as much as he loves his Stradivarius to this day, and back then it was especially true. He clutched it as if it were the only thing he had.

We shifted our feet.

"What in bloody hell is wrong with this 'un?" Meggie wondered.

"Gives me the morbs, he does," the crone rasped. "Knows things as no man should. You can see it in his eyes. Too pale. They's like moonlight, they is, and the moon sees anything she cares to. No secret's safe from the moon, luv. Best to steer clear."

"Knows things he shouldn't or not, he made us half a crown," I whispered urgently to my friend. "We can't just leave him for the bobbies to pick up."

"Mr. Williamson." Meggie stooped, touching his shoulder. "Sir? Do you know whereabouts you are?"

"Hell." Shuddering, he raked an unsteady hand through his hair and regarded the blank skies. His hat had long ago been knocked away, and he didn't seem concerned over retrieving it. "Specifically, Stepney. But I know of a worse one. This isn't the lowest by far."

Clip clop clip clop rattle rattle scrape.

A carriage slowed to a halt before us. Briefly, I thought of nothing save running, with our coins clutched against my chest and Meggie's frail hand in mine—the newcomer could herald the onset of police. But it was a toff's two-wheeler, with peeling paint and dirty windows but matched sorrel horses. The driver stared unseeing over his drooping whip.

Then the owner swung the door open and stepped down, and the sour iron taste of fear rose in my throat.

"Not him again," Meggie murmured, crossing herself.

The Lullaby Doctor, or so we all called him, stepped down from his derelict conveyance with a lit bullseye lantern. Using it to pierce the gloom of the fissure we occupied made him all but invisible. But I'd spied him some half a dozen times before. He was a spindly-legged man with a distended belly, like a ruined woman's, which he patted continually as they often do. His face was clean-shaven and I couldn't imagine hair growing on it, so childlike and smooth was his skin. Watery blue eyes, a curiously cocked head, blond hair he wore in lank curls to his shoulders, and a weak mouth completed this picture of warped innocence. One which made every last one of us want to make tracks whenever we saw him.

"My name is Dr. Manvers," he called in a soft squeak. "Some of you know of me, I daresay, yes, yes, yes, and some do not. I am here to ascertain whether any child present among you is seriously ill, one who might qualify to be treated *pro bono* at my practice? I provide free services for the young and the destitute."

He walked down the alley—bending over a quaking heap of rags here, touching the face of a lice-ridden street urchin there, murmuring questions. Everyone shrank from him. But no one ran. There was our coal fire to consider.

"Now, *that* one," Meggie breathed, wrinkling her nose. "That one gives *me* the morbs."

"Who the devil is he?" Mr. Williamson enquired, glaring in disgust—insomuch as he could focus at all.

"That there's the Lullaby Doctor," I said. "Comes round every few months, sometimes Stepney, sometimes yonder on the Rotherhithe side. Finds the sickest, he does, and takes 'em off the streets. Doctors 'em. Them as come back can't remember much save being warm and kept in good vittles and treated well. They don't always pull through once they're set loose again, mind."

"Not worth it," Meggie muttered.

"Why would you say such a thing?" Mr. Williamson's eyes slit like a feral tom's. "It's a life, it isn't a handkerchief. There's no coming by another. Isn't any chance better than none, mathematically speaking?"

"It's on account of her hair," I explained.

"Beg pardon?"

"He takes it away." Meggie shivered. "That's the price. When they come back, it's gone."

Brushing my friend's copper tangle off her shoulder, I pressed rough fingers against her neck, meaning only comfort. It spilled to her waist, Meggie's hair—corkscrews, matted in places, a crown worn by a wild animal. There was outrageously much of it for a child her age, and she was famous for that as much as for her voice. Meggie was practical about most things: work, food, shelter, all the daily dozens of tiny pragmatic considerations that kept us alive. Whether to buy a cone of fried fish from the chap who might easily sicken you, and still have a space on the barge that night, or whether to spend all on a fresh kidney pie and walk the waterfront till the stars retreated. She was no mewling kidlet.

But about her hair, she was as vain as a duchess. Meggie would comb it with fork tines, scrub it with ash and rinse it in rain barrels, steal grease from the dockyard mechanics' tubs to make it glisten. Next to me, and maybe roast chicken, Meggie loved her hair.

"Takes it?" Mr. Williamson seemed sharper, all his angles jutting. You know well enough the expression Mr. Holmes gets when his teeth are in the bit. It hasn't changed a whit in all the decades I've known him. And even in his condition, it was no less cutting in that instant.

"Aye," Meggie assured him. "Cross my heart. Doesn't hurt, shouldn't matter, but it does to me."

"Just a moment. Workhouses shave hair as a hygienic measure against parasitic infestation, prisons and madhouses for that and a number of other reasons, including discipline and dare I say even deliberate cruelty. Why should a doctor of medicine require a child's hair?"

"Says it's part of the therapy—ain't said how," I replied.

"He's a rotter, that one," the haggard old woman interjected. She had retreated behind a barrel, and we could see the glints of sickly light off her own locks but little else. "Thank our Savior I'm old as dust, and he wants none of me. Small mercies. They're like luck. Take any as come along, is what I say. Hurts no one."

"Why do you call him the Lullaby Doctor?" Mr. Williamson wanted to know.

"When any o' the ones what he takes pull through, they says it was all like a soft, warm dream," Meggie answered. "And sometimes . . ."

"Yes?"

"Some of 'em have said they saw others of us. Still there, like. Where he lives. But they can't have done." Peering into the polluted mist, I gritted my teeth.

"And why is that?" Mr. Williamson persisted.

"Because the ones as they saw were dead and buried already."

Mr. Williamson pressed twitching fingers to either side of his face, lips pressed into a line as if he might be ill. "I shouldn't have asked. Not in this state."

"Been wondering what state this is, guv," I admitted.

"Oh, a touch of this, a dram of that, all meticulously prepared to the exact specifications I required to test a theory. Not to worry! It's a perfectly safe compound. Although I'll admit that it isn't one I've ever tried, nor am at all likely to try again. I seem to have had an adverse reaction. This . . . I was testing something." He dropped his hands. "It's an experiment. I dabble in chemistry."

"Looks like you do more than dabble."

"Sir," Meggie attempted again, "are you—"

"Well, well, well, and how are you faring this morning, my dear?" a sickly sweet voice interrupted.

My belly slid towards my bare feet. Dr. Manvers wouldn't have loomed over us if we two hadn't been underfed children, and Mr. Williamson hadn't still sat on the frozen ground with his wrists draped over his knees. But as it was, I shrank back, drawing Meggie with me.

"Hale enough, sir, and with promise o' better," she replied, tossing her head.

"That is excellent news! I am very glad to hear it."

"Thank'ee."

He leaned down and whispered in her ear. Meggie made a face, but did not turn away.

"Plenty of tea when you can come by it, and no gin yet for one so young, I hope? Ah. Try not to overindulge, then? You will remember, I trust, that should you ever find yourself in direr circumstances, I am your friend? Good, good, good."

A flash of light seared my eyes. I shouted something, hand before my face. It was as if the sun had risen all at once. When I could see again, I realised that it had been the sweep of the bullseye, which Dr. Manvers had been aiming low, and furthermore that it was now held in the tenuous grip of the now-standing Sherlock Holmes. His attention was as fixed as the Pole Star and pinned to the Lullaby Doctor before him—brightly illuminated now, every follicle and crease on display.

Glancing down, I saw with watering eyes that the violin and its bow had been placed carefully behind a few disintegrating bricks.

"What is the meaning of this?" Dr. Manvers exclaimed. Now the full light shone on him, I saw that his complexion was a gelid grey, and that his suit was mottled with stains. "Who are you, sir?"

"No, that's—that isn't," Mr. Williamson attempted. "Not remotely. The point, I mean. Not at all, you see. You aren't even close. Who are *you*?"

"I have already explained," the medico snapped, arms akimbo. "I am Dr. Vincent Manvers, and in addition to my regular researches, I do charitable work amongst the street urchins of the London docks. Return my dark lantern at once!"

Mr. Williamson was shaking his head urgently. "You had better go."

"Go?"

"Yes, and quickly too. Something might befall you in one of these wretched alleys, something you wouldn't like."

"And what might that be?" the repellent man questioned, quailing.

"Well, I might knock you down, you know." Mr. Williamson teetered again, then righted himself against the wall. "I've knocked other chaps down, quite a few, at Alison's rooms, and none of them liked it. I need hardly add that they were much bigger than you. They were much bigger than *me* might I add, and it hardly made any difference. Here, quite right, I've no wish to rob you—just take your lantern back and be on your way. These are dangerous streets. Particularly for men who aren't themselves, I ought to know it, and you're about as far a cry from you as . . . from anything else I can think of. It's all far too much to explain at present, don't ask it of me, I fear I cannot oblige. Go! I shall give you ten seconds."

Most of our companions of the night had scented danger and slunk further into the shadows by this time. The few remaining, the crone included, leered at the scene with reddish gleams in their pupils, awaiting the crowning of the victor.

Mr. Manvers snatched his bullseye back, stepping away, and again we were lit and he a black cutout.

"Very well. You, sir, must not excite yourself to violence before innocents. Seeing none who require my professional services, thank God, and pugilism being against my principles as a doctor, I shall withdraw," he said. "You will not try to impede a philanthropical physician again, however. No, no, no. Consider yourself warned!"

I could hear the ripple of fear in his voice, like spying an eel slithering through calm water. You recall as well as I do the effect Mr. Holmes could attain when he liked.

"Oh, thank heaven you're going, you were making me dizzy," Mr. Williamson moaned. "Everything about you. Whatever you are—I frankly don't know. And I'm a trifle indisposed at present. If you'd wanted to scrap with me, you might accidentally have landed a blow or two, and I should never have forgiven myself. Disgraceful."

"You dare too much, sir, you really do!" Dr. Manvers squealed.

"I disagree. We certainly needn't trouble over violence in front of innocents, for instance. If that lot there are innocents, then I'm an itinerant Cambridge tutor. This is *Stepney*. May you have every bit as good a morning as you deserve, and not a whit better."

The violinist's lids fell shut. His breath came shallowly. Sliding back to the stones, he tented his fingertips before his prominent nose. With a sound between the snarl of a terrier and its whimper, Dr. Manvers turned on his heel. The steady percussion of the horses' hooves fell immediately after his slamming the door.

I knelt before our baffling new acquaintance, riveted. Sherlock Holmes always had that effect, of course. Even when in disguise and even when in what were—apparently accidentally induced, of course—absolute staggering altitudes.

"What did you mean just now, sir?" Meggie appeared at my side with the violin case. "About him not being himself?"

"Dr. Manvers, if that is his name? He wasn't." Mr. Williamson managed a spasm of a smirk. "Neither am I, to be fair, though *I* meant no harm, only to earn you lot some income, which worked out precisely to my satisfaction thank you very much, despite the fact that this particular chemistry foray isn't working out precisely how I expected it to, nor is it to my liking. And *that* scoundrel could have meant anything. Steer well clear of him, promise me that you will?"

"Why?"

"Detectives know things, it's my business to know things, I cannot help but know things, it's my sole raison d'être. God knows I haven't any other." Opening his eyes, Mr. Williamson rolled his skull against the brick and then tapped it backwards in frustration. He gently returned the violin and bow to his lap. "What the devil are you imps staring at? You've chink enough now—go and spend it. There are shoes to be bought, dare I say even stockings, and as you can see, I'm fatigued."

"I've ne'er seen a detective before, only peelers. It's interesting. And y'can't sleep here!" Meggie, for all her vast knot of hair and blackened toes, looked scandalised. "You'll freeze to death for sure. Sure as this girl's talking sense at you."

Blinking, he rubbed at the crook of his left elbow as if it both pained and pleased him. "Dear me, that sounds rather dire. Are you sure? How long would that take, I wonder? It'll be an experiment. I'll write it up for the *Scientific Review*."

"Sir!"

"Hush now, hush, I'm only joking. I didn't mean to frighten you. Anyway, I can hardly write any more articles for the *Scientific Review* once I have departed this vale of tears, can I, and that would be a genuine shame since I'm halfway through no less than three of them. I wasn't *entirely* lying about being a scholar, you know. Any fabrication based in truth stands a much greater chance of being believed. Everything will be fine in a moment, when I get my bearings and my wits about me."

By this time, I had all our precious new coins secreted in three separate hidden pockets, and I slung my cap back on with loyalty to our bizarre guest renewed. "Bollocks. Up you get, Mr. Williamson, and we'll see you safe home. It's the least we could do. Whereabouts do you live?"

"In Bloomsbury. Montague Street, twenty-six, flat D."

"Well, off to Montague Street, then!"

"No!" His eyes, which had struggled against closing, flew open. Mr. Williamson buried his face in his hands. "I can't go back there, I can't."

"Don't be daft, that's your—"

"Please. Anywhere but there."

I think it was the entreaty that caught our notice. You could touch it, sure as you could have reached out and touched his face. And do you know, my friend, the oddest thing about it? I've never heard Sherlock Holmes beg for a single thing since that night. It may have been one of the dark slumps we all know he slides into taking hold, and it may have been the "experiment" he was conducting. (I recall reading *A Study in Scarlet* for the first time when I was able to do so and coming to Stamford's suggestion that he'd happily give himself a pinch of the latest vegetable alkaloid poison just to measure its effects without bothering to find a willing volunteer for such a mad action, and not knowing quite whether to nod grimly or burst out laughing.) But there he was, begging not to go back to his own lodgings.

"But—" Meggie attempted.

"It's four walls. Do you understand?" Mr. Williamson pushed his hand over his mouth as if stifling a smile. "You couldn't possibly, could you? No. You'd love four walls, saying such a thing was inexcusable. I apologise for that. It was very thoughtless of me. But by Jove, only four walls, and nothing else of consequence, and they're shrinking. Every day. Sometimes I am almost tempted to measure it. Then I'd have some empirical proof. If you could only see them, getting smaller. It's like being Alice without the company. In Montague Street it's only me and the walls. I can't, not tonight. Not until this wears off, which it certainly will within the hour. I did very precise calculations, you've no idea, and despite the admitted fact I am not who I said I was, I'm very good at formulae. Then I'll be off to Bloomsbury and *you* will have funds for tea and shepherd's pie and oyster sandwiches—do *not* spend it on gin, I positively forbid the idea—and this will have been an altogether delightful and informative evening. I'll write it all up in my research journal."

"Ain't evening though, is it, mister?" Meggie prodded. "It's blackest night. And it'll be dawn breaking soon enough. Evening's long passed."

"I told you." The old woman, bones creaking, made her way past us, shaking her head. Her stooped silhouette continued towards the mouth of the alley and the subtle hint of sunrise. "Knows too much, he does. Things as he shouldn't. Haven't you noticed the colour of his eyes? Never saw more moonlight in my life. Leave him to sleep, luv. The devils are at that one, something fierce. It'll be kinder in the end."

"There are no such things as devils," Mr. Holmes whispered. He smiled at one side of his mouth. "Yes, go on with you, I'll be right as rain soon. I always am, you see, I never haven't been. Otherwise I wouldn't be here. That's only logical. Isn't it? I think it is. You needn't worry—I always come out fit as my fiddle in the end." He caressed it with fingertips white from the cold. "Look at me, *I'm* not worried. I only need to rest a moment, as I'm feeling deucedly sleepy. It's terrible, those four walls. I never get any rest at all. Afterwards, I'll feel much better."

His lips were turning blue as Meggie's eyes. The trembling had stopped. His body was quite still. Sherlock Holmes was lax and listless and nearly unconscious in an abandoned Stepney alleyway in January, our fire was swift dying out, and I knew what happened next supposing he didn't take shelter or keep moving.

Meggie looked at me, and I looked at Meggie, and we made a decision. You've already guessed what it was.

My friend gently took the violin and bow. It's a testament to the fact he was near to leaving this world that he let her. We got Mr. Williamson to his feet and started off towards the barge we called a shelter if not a home. After a feeble protest, he went like a lamb. He was monstrously tall, and tense as a whippet—but we could make a slow progress tucked up under his arms, steering him like a dandy who'd been all night at the lush. He didn't smell of spirits though, and he kept muttering nonsense when a drunk would have been long asleep—thank Heaven he stayed somewhat awake, or we'd never have made it the quarter mile to our dock as the sun all at once slashed the sky's throat in a thick band of crimson.

When we stumbled onto the deck, the lighterman proved to be snoring great whiskey clouds in the pilot's cabin. No morning deliveries, then. We could pay him when next we saw him conscious, or when he kicked us awake.

"We can sleep," Meggie sighed happily. She steadied her grip on the violin. The bow she had endearingly shoved into her hair, where it rested quite safely.

"We can all sleep," I agreed, worn to a nubbin.

The stairs were problematic and Mr. Williamson nearly squashed us twice. Below deck, the air was always foul. But we'd last transported tallow and coffee, so that morning it smelled strangely of bitter roasted fat, which was better than most days by leagues. The pile of tarpaulin where we slept lay blessedly near the engines. We deposited Scott Williamson on the outside, violin and bow between us, and my friend and I curled up together with our backs to the hull, our skin burning as the nerves sparked back into life, all thought of food forgot in our weariness.

"What did the Lullaby Doctor say to you?" I enquired.

"How to contact the blighter. Fat chance o' that, says this girl."

Mr. Williamson convulsed gently, winced, buried one hand in oil-dark hair, and held on as if for his life. He'd never got around to finding his hat and we'd quite forgot it.

"Do you suppose he's this barking when he's sober?" I mused.

"I don't figure as he's barking, Henry," Meggie whispered. "Just alone."

She began to sing softly and slowly, and Scott Williamson settled into fitful oblivion after a few more seizures of muscle, and I fell asleep thinking of wants.

A peddler without e'er a stock
It makes him look pitiful blue;
A shepherd without e'er a flock,
Has little or nothing to do.

When we woke after a few hours, as you can imagine, there were only two of us. But as I sat up, reflexively checking our lucre was safe in my pockets, I saw by the sulphurous light that Mr. Williamson had left us a message. Crawling to the edge of the tarp, I laughed.

"What d'you have to wake an honest girl for?" Meggie mumbled.

"Cheer up, my lass, and think over what color ribbons you fancy. We're rich, that's what!"

She laughed in her turn. We couldn't read, of course—I had my numbers and name and anything else was a right head scratcher, and Meggie signed her mark with an X—but the communication was perfectly clear. It was a middling quantity of odd coins piled next to a chalk drawing. Two neatly sketched pairs of boots, surprisingly three-dimensional, surrounded by three arrows and underlined for emphasis. I would have wondered where he came by the chalk, but there was a tin of the stuff in the barge's hold for marking inventory, and Sherlock Holmes is nothing if not resourceful.

"Guess Mr. Williamson wants us to scare up two pair o' secondhand bats somewhereabouts." Meggie yawned. "Lord save us! We'd never have charged him so dear for a night's stay. This must've been everything he had on him, poor blighter."

"He ain't as poor as all that," I reminded her. "He's a 'tec. The Distressed Scholar dodge were just for show. Cor, been so long since I had boots, I've like as not lost the knack of it. Let's spend it on summat else?"

"Yes, please," she agreed, blue eyes flashing. "What first? Chops or a bloody great kidney pie? Or a proper fry-up with runny eggs? D'you reckon it's still morning? Or luncheon by now?"

Squinting at the quality of light, I answered, "Eleven, thereabouts."

"Luncheon *or* breakfast! Hip hip hooray!"

Chops proved the readiest to hand, with onion gravy, and we stuffed our faces till our ears stuck out. But as for the rest of our money—it went to neither boots nor ribbons. About a fortnight later, Meggie began to cough.

Just a bit, at first, the sort of wheeze everyone acquires from sleeping on a boat floating on pure coke sludge, and from climbing up my shoulders to knock coal off barges for a living. She refused to let us survive off our savings after a few nights. So we went back to the mudlarking. Fearing I'd be robbed if anyone had heard rumour of that fateful night, we kept our precious treasure hidden onboard behind the fuel storage—the plank I'd loosened unmarked, in full shadow, and discernible only by counting five grooves to the left of starboard.

Though I will not dwell on that time in detail, we'd need every penny.

After a month of coughing, Meggie started to shrivel. The money dwindled. The ailment worsened. I paid a nurse to visit, and she left ingredients for mustard poultices and told me to pray. It got bad enough that Meggie would stay abed, and after I'd paid the grumbling lighterman, I'd race to a new apothecary. Sometimes I found the barge where I'd left it; sometimes I'd catch it in Rotherhithe after sprinting over a bridge; sometimes I'd meet her upriver. I didn't dare to take her to a workhouse, lest she be trapped there, nor to take her to a proper doctor, lest she be turned away and have wasted her strength.

"That makes rubber," Meggie announced one night. We were playing cards on the barge in the early evening, and though I'd wrapped her in potato sacks and bought her a boy's secondhand woolen jumper, she still crouched like our friend the old crone. "Have y'any explanation for losing three hands o' whist in a row when I'm this poorly?"

"You cheat," I accused gamely.

My heart wasn't in it. It only beat for my friend.

A brief fit stole Meggie's breath, and then she smiled. "If you've naught better to do, you could fetch a girl some soup? I think I could eat today, if we've the coin, and supposing y'keep losing at whist so as to keep me cheerful, like."

When I arrived back half an hour later with a little pail of pea soup and a spoon to share between us, provided I returned both to the market stall, she was gone.

You had best believe, Mrs. Caine, that I searched high and low. A stale rain fell, filling the cracks between cobbles until my naked feet threatened to slip and I could no longer gauge the depths of puddles that aspired to be lakes. She wasn't in any of the saloons that granted us custom, any of our usual haunts.

"Henry! Henry, luv, over here!"

I skidded at the sound of my name. The ancient woman stood under the archway of a door on Upper Shadwell, her rags draped shapelessly about her and her face half-hid by a muffler. I stopped, panting.

"Your friend went with him," she rasped, both hands resting on the stout stick she used for a cane.

"With who?"

"With the Lullaby Doctor."

At first I stood there, stunned speechless. But she knew his address, I realised—he had whispered it to her the night we met Mr. Williamson. Though too ill to walk far out of our own neighbourhood, she could have sent for him via courier. Obviously Meggie couldn't write, but she had plentiful friends who could if she needed writing done. Sending a note with a plea for help and a rendezvous would have been simplicity itself for her. The courier would only need to have been instructed to ask for payment from Dr. Manvers, which solved the question of funds. And she'd hardly been in my sight every moment, foraging for river coal to keep us tenants of the barge same as I'd been doing. We'd only a shilling left of the strange violinist's money. It was still there, untouched. I'd checked.

"She was afraid of him," I protested. "No, it ain't sensible."

"Always clawing for life, that one was, always trying, never believed that giving up can make for a softer end."

"Well, you're still here!" I snapped.

The old woman only sighed. "I'm sorry for you, luv. But there's about as much hope in the Lullaby Doctor as blood in a brick."

"How do—"

"I saw wee Meggie get into a cab with him." She shook her head, spittle from her pendulous lower lip trailing a cobweb to her scarf. "No telling where. If she comes back, give her a kiss for me, would you? She brought an old woman comfort. And comfort's like sunshine, you know."

"Is it?"

"Yes, it is. Take it as it comes. Whenever it comes. It can't do nobody no harm."

The lovely hag wandered off, leaving a terrified boy of nine with chest heaving and throat thick with terror. I had to find Meggie. I had, at least, to try, and succeed or fail.

And if I failed—well, then my heart would be broken, and how anyone could live with a broken heart I didn't know. It seemed to me a vital organ, one that if injured would ruin the whole mechanism, like a train with a shattered engine. But Meggie always tried. Work could cure anything, she said.

So work I must, I determined, but how?

It took me five minutes to recall that I knew a detective. A real one. *26D Montague Street.*

It took me an hour, hopping on the back rails of hackneys until I was angrily forced off them, to reach Bloomsbury. But never having been there, and not a soul wanting to speak to me, it took me an hour more to locate the address of Mr. Scott Williamson, Detective. He had a landlady, then as later, only this one was a shrew, with a staring circle of a mole above her left brow and an expression sour enough to turn your milk into cheese.

"What's your business?" she asked when I knocked, frantically banging.

"I need to see Mr. Scott Williamson," I answered, trying to look as if I was straightening a jacket I wasn't actually wearing.

"Do you take me for dense? There's no such person as lives here."

My only hope was slammed in my face. But I knew she was wrong—he'd been too far past sense to be prevaricating, and he rattled off the address rapidly and in tones of profound distaste. He really did live in Montague Street.

So I tried.

I banged and I banged and I banged on that door. I had dishwater thrown out at me, and dodged most of it. She threatened me with an (it turned out) imaginary dog. Then the police. Never once did I think of giving up, because it was for Meggie, but just when I was ready to start sniveling, the door flew open and there he was, holding a silver-topped cane. Tall as a scarecrow, perfectly brushed tails, snowy collar, and his prominent chin dropping in surprise. As immaculate as we think of him now.

"By Jove!" His voice was as clipped as I remembered the scholar's being, but much more piercing today, and his strange eyes were as clear and calm as ice blocks in the daylight.

"Thank the Lord above us," I breathed. "Mr. Williamson. You ain't forgot me, have you? It's Henry Wiggins, from Stepney. You remember?"

"Yes, yes, of course I do, I've an exceptionally keen memory. Even during experiments gone sadly awry. But what in the name of the devil can you be doing on my doorstep?"

"Looking for you."

"Oh, no!" He held a palm up, one steady as a painted signboard, and young though he was, you'll believe me when I say I almost flinched. When I do the maths quickly, he was only twenty-four. "There will be absolutely none of that, if you please. It simply won't work."

"What won't?" I asked, dazed.

"Look here, my dirty little chap," he continued, "if you think you can somehow find out my address and extort payment from me over the regrettably botched experiment I was performing on the night we met, you needn't bother."

"But I ain't of no mind to—"

"I am on my way to complete a particularly complex branch of my studies at the British Museum, and I won't be detained. Not even when admittedly we shared a rather . . . memorable night. My humble thanks, I already left you a token of my gratitude, may fortune shine on your every endeavour. Now, if you will be so good as to excuse me."

"Mr. Williamson—"

"'Tention!" he barked, pointing with the cane. "March straight along, young rascal, you aren't wanted."

"You've the wrong end, I tell you, I—"

"Fine, yes, very well, here is . . . let me see, three shillings." He fished coins out of his waistcoat pocket. "Go and buy yourself a pie. Or half a dozen of them. And some soap, while you're at it, you are in dire need of the substance. *Not* gin, I told you before and I'll repeat it for emphasis. If you attempt to blackmail me again, you shan't enjoy the results, and if you attempt to blackmail my family, he'll have you transported. He is well aware of my peculiar . . . scientific studies, and should you threaten me, he would think nothing of snapping his fingers, and then where would you be? Shanghai. Good afternoon."

"Please," I begged, ashamed the tears were starting. "It's Meggie, she's gone. I think she went to the Lullaby Doctor, the one as you said ain't right."

Mr. Williamson's face changed—first to a complete blank, you know the look well—and then a mark appeared between his dark eyebrows and he pulled his lips between his teeth.

"Dear me. You had better come in." Whirling, he held the door for me.

I don't know what I expected to find as we trotted up three flights of stairs and he whipped out the key to his flat. But so far as I was concerned, the space was a princely one. Over there under the window was room for a bed on the floor for a renter like me, and over there, too, under the desk, and past the chemistry set, and over there if a body were to move several stacks of imposing-looking books out of the way.

There was nothing else, though. Only space. Oh, I don't mean precisely *nothing*. It had impersonal furnishings rather the worse for wear, a Persian slipper tacked to the mantelpiece, dark red carpeting, and there was the familiar violin in a place of pride tucked up in the bow window against some pillows. Its case rested open beside it. The walls were papered in faded blue damask, and the gas was laid on, so there were simple sconces which I imagined gave off a pleasant enough glow in the evenings.

But I could see what he had meant about the walls closing in. The desperate cubbyhole under the tarpaulin where Meggie and I spent our nights seemed almost welcoming by comparison.

"She got sick and run off yesterday and I ain't seen her since," I reported as Mr. Williamson threw newspapers into a corner seemingly devoted to that purpose. "It's not like her. And one of our folk said she got in a cab with the Lullaby Doctor, Mr. Williamson."

He sighed as he tossed his hat aside. "It is always so very, very awkward dealing with the inevitable aftermath of an alias, and had I not needed one to fully imagine the Distressed Scholar character, I certainly wouldn't have employed it. Allow me to introduce myself. My name is Sherlock Holmes."

"Sherlock Holmes?"

He offered what seemed like a cordial hand, and we shook.

"Yes, young Henry Wiggins, Sherlock Holmes. From the beginning, please," Mr. Holmes begged.

He lit a small pipe, placed me in a chair, and eccentrically crossed his legs on the floor. You could have knocked me over with a swift puff. I was that staggered. I'd never seen anyone who actually *had* furniture refrain from using it. Then I recalled that our mutual friend was a very strange individual. And absolutely detested the place.

You are speculating, my dear Mrs. Caine, that our great affection for his subsequent address makes my recollection biased against his Montague

Street rooms; but apart from serving to keep the rain off his head, I reiterate that they were quite barren. I studied them in further detail. A lone brandy decanter with a pair of snifters rested on the sideboard. The single grime-streaked window looked out on a crumbling back area. His intricate chemistry set—frankly quite costly in appearance, and the same one with which you are acquainted yourself—rested on the dining table, rather precluding any dinner parties, scores of books were neatly arranged on the plain shelves in addition to the stacks I'd noted on the floor, and smaller end tables with little painted porcelain lamps flanked both chairs, which faced one another.

But it seemed from the oppressively solitary feeling that only one of the snifters and one of the chairs was ever put to much use.

"Do be still, you're fidgeting as if you're covered in ants as well as coal," Sherlock Holmes ordered. "Let us put our heads together and try to puzzle it out between us. Oh, where are my manners? What do I have in, heavens, there's . . . yes, we shall have a *little* brandy and water, with more *water* than brandy for you of course, but enough to be fortifying, and here's some cheese left from my supper last night, yes, very good, and just enough bread to suit it. Now. When did young Miss Meggie go missing?"

As he bustled about gathering refreshments, I told him everything. About Meggie's ailment, and the Lullaby Doctor's personal interest in her, which was long-standing and persistent, and the gentle witch's report that Meggie had gone off with the repulsive fellow in a cab.

"You're quite sure she said cab? Not a carriage?" Mr. Holmes, having deposited a small hunk of Stilton and the heel of a bread loaf on a plate with a knife, folded himself into the opposite chair this time, with one knee drawn up under his angular jaw.

"Certain sure," I avowed. "Though I can't vouch for her eyes, mind."

"Oh, she had excellent vision, she dove for any shillings that came within a yard of her, and with admirable accuracy in such poor light. As well as two ha'pennies. I was mainly looking streetward, naturally, but it suddenly came upon me that I was depriving the natives of feeling included and turned around." Mr. Holmes linked spidery fingers around his shin. "I suspected that wasn't Dr. Manvers's carriage, and this confirms it."

"It does?" I asked, swallowing the rude luncheon gratefully.

"Beyond the shadow of a doubt. I haven't any carriage or matched horses either, as you can see I don't. But if I did, I would take enough pride in them to personalise my conveyance, as indeed most do. Additionally, if some unruly young street musician stole my bullseye and threatened to knock me down, I should expect my driver to at least do me the courtesy of looking alarmed, if not rush to my aid. The Lullaby Doctor's coachman was a complete stranger to him."

"But you said as he weren't a doctor."

"He wasn't." Mr. Holmes pressed at his left brow. "He didn't make a whit of sense, nothing about him. I'd . . . well, as you know, I was not quite myself that night."

Glancing over my shoulder and around the chair arm at the chemistry set, I nodded for the sake of peace. I thought he'd been very *much* himself, nakedly so. Brilliant, riveting, gregarious, assured, and underneath that . . . absolutely storm-tossed hidden waters.

"But the data were altogether bizarre. Sometimes the act of detailing observations aloud can be quite useful, and since you're here, I may as well try it—one wearies of talking to a Stradivarius. Let me see," he mused, shutting his eyes. "Medical men are shabby occasionally, but they are seldom *unclean*, as it goes against their training, and he sported a rather astonishing variety of marks, which I was able to see when I turned the dark lantern on him. I'm glad I had the presence to do that or we'd have almost nothing to go on. Wax in both liquid drop form and in hardened shavings on his sleeves. Clay, or what I thought must be dried clay because of the dusty patina, on his fingernails. Plaster stains on his trousers. The residue of what appeared to be an oil-based paint on his shirt cuffs. It was an embarrassment of clues. I've never witnessed anything of the kind before."

"And you . . . that's the sort of thing you notice, then?" I confirmed, destroying the last of the bread. "As a 'tec? And that's why you done warned Meggie off?"

"Yes, for all the good it did," he replied with visible pique. "The detail of the missing hair from his 'patients' is likewise alarming. A wigmaker perhaps? No, no not with that much detritus on his coat. Confound it! If I could deduce his profession, we could gamble that he employed his real name due to complacency among the impoverished and lack of imagination and then cross reference it, considering the fact he lives in Rotherhithe."

"Does he?"

"Yes, you mentioned you'd encountered him on both sides of the Thames, but on foot in Rotherhithe and in a carriage in Stepney. When he journeys further afield, he rides in style. Look here, my unwashed young acquaintance, would you do me the favour of not speaking for as much as perhaps half an hour?" Unfolding himself, he went to the Persian slipper and packed tobacco into his pipe. "I need to smoke. And ruminate over the highly distressing number of substances this man comes into contact with. And then we'll see that Meggie comes to no harm. All right? Yes, yes, very well, another splash of brandy for you, but that is the end of it. I haven't the means to keep street urchins in their cups."

As it happened, it wasn't half an hour at all—he sat still as a bust for fifteen minutes, emitted a noise like a gasp, and covered his mouth with his hand.

"What?" I cried. "What's the matter, then?"

"I beg your pardon, I—it's possible that I'm wrong. And even if I'm right, it might not mean anything. Answers come to me like oncoming trains sometimes, don't be startled by it." Sherlock Holmes flung himself out of his armchair and pulled down one of the impressive directories from his bookshelves. "Manvers . . . no, no, excellent, no . . . ah."

I could see him calculating as he raised his eyes, staring into the middle distance as if it contained the solutions to the deepest mysteries of the human soul.

"My dear, dirty young fellow, I imagine you should like to accompany me," he said softly.

"Bet your life," I confirmed. "But where?"

"An artisan's workshop in Rotherhithe. You'll be quite safe, I assure you, I wasn't exaggerating when I claimed to have something of a talent for fisticuffs. I have an impressive talent for fisticuffs, with all due modesty.

Admittedly, at times I wish for nothing more than a comrade with a serviceable weapon and aim—but on this occasion I've confidence in our powers, and anyway it doesn't do to indulge in the fantastical."

We left Bloomsbury in a cab hailed by Mr. Holmes. It occurred to me belatedly that I would have to pay for these services, but not knowing how, I kept my mouth shut. So long as Meggie was all right, I could face debtor's prison, the workhouse, anything. When we pulled up to a shop front surrounded by warehouses and dockyards, with peeling grey paint and heavily curtained windows, I fought the urge to be sick on the cobbles, so tense was the set of Mr. Holmes's face.

"Allow me to handle this, if you please," he instructed, stepping down. "I do not believe us to be in any physical danger from this Dr. Manvers, and pray God Meggie isn't either—there, there, Wiggins, I don't think that she is—but if I am right, this could be touch and go. Do nothing rash."

There was a sign next to the door: MR. VICTOR MANVERS'S RESTORATIONS, FIGURINES, AND CURIOSITIES. Mr. Holmes strode in that headlong way he has to the entrance and rapped with his stick. When no answer came, he pounded with it, sending staccato booms down the windswept street. I heard commotion within, and then Dr. Manvers himself opened the door, and as little as I knew of society, I knew that was wrong. A maid ought to have greeted us, not the master of the house.

"Ah," Sherlock Holmes said. "I thought as much."

"Heaven save me!" Dr. Manvers gasped. "I had half convinced myself you were a nightmare, and here you are upon my doorstep dressed as a gentleman, and with a child from the same hellish morning. What are these clothes you are wearing? What dark business were you about before? I shall cry for a policeman!"

"Dr. Manvers, or rather Mr. Manvers, for you are no doctor, by all means summon a policeman." Steel had threaded its way into Mr. Holmes's tone. "Where is Meggie?"

Mr. Manvers's lank blond hair was tied back in a queue, his pasty complexion bright with sweat—he had looked unhealthy, but respectable, until the detective uttered that query. He shrank back as if from a hooded serpent. His lips grew white. He patted his belly in a soothing motion.

It frightened me.

"Yes, go on," Mr. Holmes commanded. "Lead us to her. If we find her unharmed, I may yet have mercy on you."

Mr. Manvers bowed his head. He turned away. The wallpaper was stained with sooty rain from cracks in the ceiling, the carpeting dotted with mold. All along the entry hall were installed glass cases. Scores of pairs of unseeing eyes stared back at me, glittering as coldly as jewels, and the unliving skin painted with blush, brow, and lip stain reminded me of the single occasion I saw a corpse dressed for a formal burial. These undead creatures wore immaculate clothing, their lips parted as if about to speak, their tiny hands reaching for me. Never having seen anything like them, I shrank back in terror.

"Wiggins. Steady on, lad. It's merely a display," Mr. Holmes said quietly. "They're the children of his profession—Mr. Manvers is a dollmaker. Wax molding, plaster casts, clay modeling, and finally paint. I don't know why I didn't see it at once, I was unforgivably slow. Come along, Wiggins. Bear up. Let us take Meggie home."

Fighting the urge to cower behind his coattails, I obeyed. We ascended a staircase, each step groaning like a tormented ghost. When we reached the first floor, Mr. Manvers gestured to an open bedroom, and Mr. Holmes hastily ducked inside.

Meggie lay on a bed with a threadbare but thick quilt covering her depleted form. Her eyes opened only a crack—but upon seeing me, she gasped, and attempted to pull her arms from the bedclothes.

I could see freckles on her scalp, tiny new constellations I'd never had cause to witness before, because her head was entirely shorn.

"Henry!" she rasped. "What in the name of all that's holy are y'doing here? And with Mr. Williamson?"

"Removing you from this establishment." Mr. Holmes delicately lifted the tonic bottle resting on the bedside table. "Only simple laudanum. Ah, and a jug of water, I see. Diluted, then. Better than I had feared, as we might have been dealing with ether or chloral. If we *had* been dealing with ether or chloral, I should have been quite put out of my temper. Very good. Mr. Manvers, you will now show me your collection. As Miss Meggie gathers herself, young Wiggins here will accompany us. I require an eyewitness of the correct age to spread news of this back to the urchins of Stepney. Who will, I hope, share the same information with the youth of Rotherhithe. In order to ensure that nothing of the sort ever happens again."

Mr. Manvers already boasted a juvenile face, a cringing demeanour, and a repulsive aura. But at this edict, he collapsed still further into himself as he clutched his strangely round belly, strings of hay-like hair drooping in front of his eyes.

"You . . . you know about the collection?" he whimpered. "But how? How could you possibly?"

"It is my profession to unearth what others cannot manage to discover. Or at least, I sincerely hope that it will one day be my profession as well as my preoccupation. Currently it is only occasionally my profession, but that is neither here nor there. Lead the way, sir. I mean to remove your latest victim from your premises with all speed—but first, you will show my friend Wiggins here what you have been about."

We followed his hunched back down the hallway, then up another staircase. A peculiar aroma drifted down to meet us, one reminding me of tallow candles and the more astringent smell of turpentine.

"I can take 'em as they comes generally, Mr. Holmes," I whispered. "But I don't understand. I ain't—"

"He is a dollmaker," Sherlock Holmes said without inflection. "As both a profession and a hobby, I believe. The items downstairs you saw displayed were commonplace. I suspect these won't be, so steel your resolve, all right, my unwashed young friend? Specifically, he molds wax figures, which require the use of paraffin, plaster, and paint. All of which I observed on his clothing. His public occupation need not concern us, as it's perfectly legal. Regarding what I suspect to be his private collection, however, you and I are going to put a stop to it. Whether it's perfectly legal or not."

When we reached the attic level, Mr. Manvers withdrew another set of keys from his pocket, jangling them like a church bell at high noon, his hand trembled so badly. I felt sorry for him.

Then he opened the door, and I could never feel sorry for him again.

I cannot dwell upon that chamber. Not even to describe it to you. Dozens of children, some of whom I had known or still knew, stared back at me from that wretched room. Their waxen faces may have been blank, granted. And their glass eyes fixed. But they were perfectly, even immaculately rendered, life-sized, and some grotesque part of me was able to marvel at it. In a corner beneath a window, a new mannequin stood with her new face drying, a matted but genuine head of red hair meticulously attached to the scalp. Given a few more seconds, I discerned that all the false children had real hair, and then I knew as much as did Mr. Holmes.

"When they're sick, you feed them laudanum, and . . . and then you copy them? With their real hair?" I stammered.

Mr. Manvers said nothing. But he sank fully upon the floorboards, scarcely breathing.

"God in heaven," Mr. Holmes marvelled. "I cannot . . . this is unspeakable. You may well have justified it by telling yourself that they needed warmth and drugs more than they needed their hair, but to pretend to be a physician and return them to the streets without it . . . it's monstrous!"

"I never, never, never meant any harm!" Mr. Manvers protested, clasping his hands prayerfully. "And I didn't *do* any harm. I'll never do anything of the like again. I swear it, I'll swear it on a Bible. Only I'll keep these, and be finished for all time. I never hurt Miss Meggie, only took what I needed. I fed her good strong soup, with beef. Please. Ruin my reputation even, but don't take these away. They're all I have."

Mr. Holmes took half a step back in disbelief. Maybe even horror. "No. God no, they cannot be all you have. You're a respected dollmaker, with a profession aside from this hideous hobby. I found you quite easily in my latest directory. There's a roof over your head and food on your plate and customers at your door. You've an *occupation*. That must mean something."

"Not as much as they do," Mr. Manvers whispered.

"No, there must be a line somewhere!" Mr. Holmes cried. "You took a little girl and you took two dozen other children and you lied to them, they call you the Lullaby Doctor, and it may not be a crime precisely, it may even be considered a charity in some idiot circles, and you may have fed and warmed them and kept their illness at bay briefly, but it's *wrong*. These must be destroyed."

"I can't," Mr. Manvers claimed, his lips trembling.

"You haven't any choice!"

"Yes, I do!"

"I'm not giving you one!"

"Please!"

In the act of standing up, Mr. Manvers accidentally kicked over the lantern. Its glass shattered. Before anything had even really happened, he screamed. When the first lick of flame sprouted, he leapt backwards.

"Dear God in heaven," Mr. Holmes gasped. "Mr. Manvers, have you anything to put this out? Smother it? Water won't work. A tarp, something to contain it—clay! Wet clay, pour wet clay on it. Mr. Manvers, are you *listening* to me, do something!"

The smaller man stood frozen in shock. Sherlock Holmes flew about the room in search of a makeshift extinguisher, constantly glancing back at the conflagration.

It reached the wax figures and the Lullaby Doctor shrieked again even louder. Spreading from one to another rapidly as the wax melted, the voracious fire followed along to its next target. Like dominoes, countless hours of the dollmaker's work sank into the floorboards.

"It was going to happen anyway!" Mr. Holmes cried. "I would have seen to that. I would have made it my *utmost* priority. Mr. Manvers, help me! I don't know where you keep your supplies."

The pleas were well intended. But that workplace floor was also dry as tinder, the greedy fire was surrounded by fuel, and I honestly don't think anything could have been done.

All at once, as if it had happened instantly, the shocked Lullaby Doctor was trapped behind a wall of flame. His shrieking, rather than intensifying, stopped as he fainted dead away.

The reek of kerosene flooded the small chamber. Mr. Holmes shouted, and dove for the man, but the spilt fuel quickly ate its way through the outer perimeter of carefully dressed waxen figures, ignited against the paint and the plaster, until within seconds the attic space was a conflagration and Mr. Manvers could not have been reached by the most adroit of firefighters.

The now-stifling chamber had begun to reek not merely of smoke and kerosene, but of burnt human hair.

Mr. Holmes tucked my underfed nine-year-old body under his surprisingly strong arm and fled for our lives.

On the instant I was out of the room, he began flinging doors open in search of something useful. He found nothing save more flammables—paint, fabric, cotton batting for stuffing, turpentine. He cursed under his breath.

"Meggie," I coughed. "We have to . . ."

"Yes, of course." Taking my hand, Mr. Holmes shook himself. "Run with me. On the double. I'll carry her, and you lead the way."

We did precisely that.

When we emerged from that terrible building, Meggie still wrapped in the quilt in Mr. Holmes's arms and I holding his walking stick, shivering not from cold but from terror, we all turned to look behind us. The house was beginning to bellow smoke from the upper windows, and neighbours were shouting, running to fetch help.

"Her figure looked newest to me," Mr. Holmes said numbly. "I don't think we need worry about anyone else trapped inside, and he answered the door on his own. That's probably where all the filth comes from. Imagine keeping servants in such a house, no matter how many locks you put on that room. Or on his ghastly false infirmary."

"Who would do such a thing?" I demanded, digging my nails into my palms.

Sherlock Holmes thought about it, visibly disturbed. "I cannot tell you. It was revolting. But I think it was the song of a want. In a way. In a terribly wrong way."

We stayed until the fire was mostly extinguished, or at least until the firemen had it under control. Then we three made our way to a charitable hospital Mr. Holmes knew of, where Meggie was made warm and comfortable. They were most kind to my friend. I would have been forever grateful to him for that alone. It would have been a lifelong debt.

Even had he not sent me to school. Even were I not today a successful solicitor.

Meggie passed into God's care only a short while later, because as false as the Lullaby Doctor had been, her ailment was not. My heart was indeed broken. It was as though the world had ended. No activity held any appeal to me. Certainly not gathering coal, which was something Meggie and I did *together*, always together. To my surprise, my body kept going despite the barest of upkeep. When I could not stop weeping and I ran out of any scant coin I had, I went back to Montague Street, knowing of nowhere else to turn. Even the ratlike landlady when she opened the door proved herself capable of pity when she took in my emaciated, red-eyed condition.

Heaving a sigh, she said, "You'll be wanting His Lordship, I suppose?"

"Is Mr. Holmes here?" I rasped.

"As it so happens. Go on, show yourself up! I don't suppose I'll be carrying up your card."

Barely seeing them, I staggered up the stairs. I don't recall rapping on Mr. Holmes's door, but I must have done. When it swung wide, his grey eyes flew open in dismay. He was wearing shirtsleeves and a dressing gown, and the room was thick with pipe smoke.

"Wiggins, what on . . . oh, dear. Come in, my boy, come in."

Wordlessly, he installed me in one of the chairs. After assuring me he'd be right back, he vanished for a few minutes and returned with a small glass of claret, a hunk of bread not unlike the last time, and half a dozen thick slices of cured meat. I shook my head despairingly. I didn't want them.

"I suffer many flaws in those few with whom I keep company, Wiggins, but being utterly ridiculous is not one of them." He thrust the food out more insistently. "I hardly ever partake more than once a day, as it wreaks havoc on the intellectual properties. Eat it. You obviously haven't been indulging in the practice, and it's more than recreational for the likes of you. Lord knows *I* needn't get any taller than I already am, but I think you would be disappointed to stop now."

I took the items, which were doubtless his own meal.

Curling my hand into a fist, I thumped it against my chest where the pain was most piercing.

"I have the song of a want now."

Lowering himself Hindu-style to the carpet in one smooth movement, he nodded silently.

"The barge," I whispered. "I know when you woke up it must have seemed *that* horrible, to a gentleman 'tec like you what lives *here*. But it were home when she was with me, and now it's just . . ."

"Four walls?" he asked softly.

"Four walls." A few tears spilled.

Mr. Holmes passed me his handkerchief.

"Will it ever go away?" I whispered.

"I am no expert and possibly the last person to ask such a question." He paused. "But from what I understand, the want gets . . . smaller. Bearable. Less. This is just hearsay, of course. As for myself, I prefer complete detachment to finding out definitively, a rare instance in which my chosen profession would actually *suffer* from research of any sort rather than benefit from it. Such unwieldy emotions could well cripple my faculties entirely, and then I should have to take up furniture making, or perhaps dog breeding. Emotions wreak shocking havoc upon the well-ordered mind. Still. Despite my lack of firsthand experience, I am confident that you will indeed recover."

"How?" I sniffled. I couldn't imagine it.

Mr. Holmes shook his head. "There you have me, my unbathed friend. Maybe the want will always be with you, and you'll simply have made a home for it somewhere safe. Maybe it will slowly dissolve until it is more . . . evenly distributed. Who can say quite how it works? Perhaps it's unique to every individual. But I cannot imagine that the heart is fundamentally different than other aspects of the human body, though I confess I know nothing about it and am speaking only as a scholar. And when other parts are wounded, sometimes even gravely, they heal, Wiggins. Scars may be left, but they still heal. Look—I just took the plaster off this one last night. *Some* scarring is to be expected by the end of your life, you know, as unfortunate and uncomfortable as that may be, or else you never really lived at all."

I stared at the still-crimson chemical burn on the back of his pale left hand. I was a friendless, grieving street urchin of nine, who from the orphanage to the workhouse to the streets in that short period had only ever been told by adults to be quiet, move along, and do as I was told or face the painful consequences.

Is it any wonder I would have followed him anywhere, after that?

For the next three nights, he insisted that I sleep on his sofa. He did take the precaution of soaping and wetting a large cloth and scrubbing anything which might have attached itself to said sofa off me, which in retrospect was wisdom. I don't think I was ever so clean in my life. We shared his meals, and he laid in an extra supply of coarse bread. Thankfully, his landlady back then was a bit of a drunkard, for when one morning I perceived rising voices in the hallway and crept closer to the door to eavesdrop, I heard Mr. Holmes silkily saying that I'd left around eleven P.M. the day I arrived and seen myself out, hadn't she heard me going?

"Thank you, sir," I said with cap in hand on the day of my departure. We were in his back alleyway, where he was quietly sneaking me off the premises. "I'll never forget—"

"Have a care with yourself, my dear Wiggins," he interrupted, sliding out from under the thanks. "Oh, and Wiggins?"

I turned back. "Mr. Holmes?"

"*Do* find an actual bath somewhere. Even the sight of you makes me itch. I'd have drawn one myself, but I shudder to think of the departing bathwater should it have been observed."

Sherlock Holmes shut the gate, and for the first time in a long time, I laughed.

I returned to the outdoors a new man. Well, a new vagrant child. I was not healed, not by far, but I was much restored.

Afterwards, he once said to me, when I'd for some time been acting as the lieutenant of the Baker Street Irregulars even though there wasn't much to do yet and only four of us to do it, "God forgive me for it, but I thought you were lucky."

I of course demanded to know what he meant.

Mr. Holmes still lived in Montague Street at the time. So he said, "I thought you were lucky because you would have done anything for her. No one will ever feel that way about me."

He was mistaken.

He employed more children. Others followed, my dear Mrs. Caine, which of course is the reason I may confide in you, since you were one of them and would guard Sherlock Holmes's secrets as closely as do I despite the article. Yourself, in 1885, and what an asset you proved at the ripe age of seven! I was in school by that time, but I knew all of you very well indeed, for Mr. Holmes turned me into a trainer of sorts when I outgrew my lieutenant role. Lucky, three months later. George, Lizzie, Gunn, Hollins, and Lacy in 1886. Jack Tilton, who did more with one leg than most any chap I've ever met could do with two. Bessie, who was lost to us so young, and who not even the good doctor could manage to save.

Though there is much that is questionable, and perhaps even mightily embarrassing to a man who has reached his great stature, there is nothing *wrong* with any of Mr. Holmes's actions in the narrative I relate. On the contrary. Nevertheless, I beg that you will burn this letter after culling what respectable matter you will from it. My anticipation of your forthcoming article could not be more keen, and may I presume upon your kindness so far as to request that you will inscribe a copy to an old friend?

For at the end of every man's long, lingering twilight, what have we of more value than old friends? It gives me great joy that we are yet young, and that many more decades of mutual admiration lie before us.

I remain, my dear Mrs. Caine,
Very sincerely yours,
Mr. Henry Wiggins, Solicitor

OUR COMMON CORRESPONDENT

(Geoffrey Lestrade)

Entry in the diary of Inspector Geoffrey Lestrade, Sunday, January 6th, 1889:

I must have stared at this confounded page for half an hour. The wretched thing was still blank up to a moment ago. If I weren't such a practical fellow, I'd have vowed it was laughing at me. The journal's spine, a pair of empty pages, the silent mocking of a pale paper mouth.

How can I be expected to write down so much as a banking slip on January the sixth?

My tea's gone cold. The snowstorm that this afternoon played hide-and-go-seek with the chimney ash pounds at my windows like a plague of white locusts. It'll be a foot if it's an inch by morning. Then turned to soot stew by the time I've trudged to the Yard. And me with the left ankle already kicking up a fuss. Not that I pay it any mind. If I start to limp, people take notice. Jonas takes notice—that tyke's eyes are as sharp as his mind.

So I don't limp, and that's that.

Jonas. He'll be back at school next week. Did my best to lend a bit of cheer to his winter holiday, oranges and firecrackers and the like. But it frets me to see how solitary a little chap he is still. Always cadging the cook for hot cider, then pestering Dad for another book. Joining Mum with her knitting and pulling out his sketches before the fire. Last night when I paid them a call after my shift he showed me a dragon he'd drawn, a whopping big brute roaring great plumes of flame. Of course I praised it, quick as winking. What kind of an uncle would I be if I hadn't done? I didn't even have to lie. It was good, very good indeed.

"Jonas," said I, "that's just about the snarlingest dragon I ever did see."

His sombre hazel eyes lit up. I smiled.

Never mind that the entire forest he'd sketched for background was blazing like Christmas trees, with a castle all in flames. Stick folk running with fire lapping at their heels. ~~Thoroughgoing tyke like Jonas, mustn't forget to make a thorough hellscape of it, eh?~~

There, I've done it again, and I'm putting a stop to it. This dry pessimism will not stand. Last week, I looked through old journal entries trying to cheer myself. But there was scarce any cheer to be found. Complaints, dark musings, and criticisms? Yes. In spades. Happy memories? Golden-lit evenings? Not so much. Therefore whenever I am getting too glum or too grumbling in this little book, as well as any subsequent ones, I have resolved to strike the sentence from the page. It is all very well to brood to oneself, but we must not grow *dour*.

A quick line of my pen through such dark thoughts will help to excise them. A training exercise of sorts.

January the sixth is a hard nut to crack though.

Yes, it's been a decade to this very dot. And yes, Jonas is twelve now. But he remembers what happened, for all that he was two and a half. He can't snap his fingers and undo it any better than I can, for all my efforts and his paints.

Every morning it haunts me still. Sometimes it'll fade, the way newsprint does when it's hung up to patch a window. Marriages, assaults, deaths, and every sunrise more facts slowly vanishing. Details erased as the article gives up the ghost. Today, though, I've hardly focused on aught else. All those hours—weeks, months, bloody years—and for what? Blisters on my feet as a roundsman, needling my way into crime scenes. Finally earning my plainclothes, hanging up the blue wool and the brass buttons, hearing folk call out *detective* when I was wanted, the very same year she was lost for good, ~~and so for what, in the end?~~

Stop this, Geoffrey.

To solve other people's crimes, is for what. Giving them a bit of justice, a scrap of peace. Being a bobby is honest work—or at least, to you it is. So you'd like some of the same redress for yourself, some for Hannah and Jonas?

~~It's times like these I wonder why I ever started a bloody journal in the first place.~~

No, I know why. It was my police reports. Always the sense when I'd finished writing one up of a case closed, like ringing down a curtain. No more of the nagging what-ifs or maybes or on-the-other-hands or perhaps. Puts a period to the sentence, lets me know I can rest. Tells me I'm finished.

I'm a fool. Ten years gone in a blink.

Ten years, and I'll never be finished.

Entry in the diary of Inspector Geoffrey Lestrade, Monday, January 7th, 1889:

Just once—just *once*, for the love of queen and country and heaven and all its saints—just once, I'd like for Mr. Sherlock Holmes to arrange an appointment with me.

Or send a wire.

Or call out a view halloa. So I can hide in the filing room.

Just once, instead of interrupting me when I'm deep in thought over a possible crime. And yes, I am capable of being very deep in thought indeed, thank you, Mr. Holmes.

Good Lord. It's like I can hear him in my head sometimes, and I'd not wish that on the lowest rascal in St. Giles. ~~Or even on Inspector Gregson.~~ *That's* how much Mr. Holmes wormed his way under my skin this afternoon when I was busy cogitating over a fresh case.

The account itself was . . . well, the account was odd. It bears setting down in my personal journal, since there wasn't nearly enough to merit a police report. But something queer may well be afoot. I've been twelve years on the Force now, I should be able to sniff out when the fish has turned.

I hadn't any time to puzzle over it, though. Because Sherlock bloody Holmes arrived. My office door flew open with the testy grunt it always gives as it scrapes the flooring.

"No, there's absolutely no way round it." The amateur removed his shining hat and flicked his muffler from his long neck. "What cannot be avoided 'twere childish weakness to lament or fear."

"Afternoon, Mr. Holmes. Please take a—"

He sat before I'd finished inviting him to. Folding himself into the chair like some monstrously massive, spindly jack-in-the-box.

Sherlock Holmes studied me. Some folk at the Yard are plenty put off by his scrutiny, unnerving as it is. It isn't as if he looks *at* you when he studies you, oh no. Feels more like he's peering at the wall behind you, or at what your opinion of the current Parliament is, or at last Tuesday.

I returned his stare. It's a talent of mine.

A flicker of a smirk twitched his lips.

Next he took a cursory glance round. There wasn't much to give away any hints, I thought with satisfaction. My directories were neatly shelved, my map of London free of any telling pins or notes, my desk clear. I'd dined on cock-a-leekie at The Black Sheep down the road, so he couldn't even sniff out what I'd brought with me for lunch (as if it mattered). The *clump-clump* of the constables outside and the soft crackling of the coals were the only sounds. And if Mr. Holmes can tell anything about a bloke from his recently polished boots, then I was ready to eat one of those boots myself.

"Well," I coughed, "if the unavoidable you're referring to is a case we're working on, you've lost me. I've just settled a drunken assault dispute—it certainly didn't call for Shakespeare."

One eyebrow snaked inward. "You know the speech?"

"I'm fond of the Henries, yes."

"Ah, naturally—I ought to have guessed so. Plentiful derring-do and ribald jokes."

"I'm not the one who quoted it, Mr. Holmes."

Mr. Holmes grinned.

Sherlock Holmes is a menace to peace and to good humour, but I'll say this for the man: he never fails to own up when you've scored a point. It's not generally so easy, but then Mr. Holmes doesn't usually barge into my office with a nick in his jaw from shaving and a smear of pomade on his left ear. That was odd enough to be almost alarming.

"Somebody's been burning the candle at both ends," I remarked.

"Dear God, please don't tell me that the faculty of deductive reasoning is contagious. I'll have to seek out another field of expertise altogether—most likely falling within the sciences, but then again, I've always possessed something of a yen to run off and join a travelling carnival. What do you think?"

I think that would serve me for the next ten Christmases.

"Cigar?"

"Please," he exhaled, pulling his fingers down that pale beak of a nose. "The solace of tobacco will soon be all that is left to me in this vale of tears. How did you determine I was rather the worse for wear, by the by?"

"You seem unwell, is all."

Yes, it would be fair play to explain to Mr. Holmes how I work things out, when I work things out. God knows he peacocks every chance he gets. But it's considerably more fun to let him assume I made a lucky guess. It gets me a little of my own back, knowing he's dead wrong about someone—even if the someone is me.

And he really did look a fright. Skin more oyster-ish than pearly, and his foot below the pinstriped trouser leg twitching back and forth like a metronome. Not that he was any the less eerie looking for the messiness. He's enough to give your average chap the creeps even when dead asleep.

He doesn't fool me, though. Most of the Force think he's off-putting because he doesn't give a fig what people think of him. That's a right laugh. Sherlock Holmes cares so much what Yarders think of him that he swans about like he's the star of his own panto, and I've worked alongside the ridiculous man probably twice as much as any of the other inspectors. Strange enough, he singles me out for the punishment of his company. I passed him a cigar to pep him up and took another for myself. He pulled vestas out of his black frock coat, I did the same out of my desk, and for a minute or so, we sat in silence.

"All right," I sighed. "How can I assist, Mr. Holmes? You might not think so by appearances, but I'm busy."

"Dear me! Has PC McGettigan's cat sallied forth to conquer unknown lands again and missed its breakfast?"

I nearly laughed. "No, Socks is accounted for and sleeps in his cellar now."

"You cannot possibly understand how relieved I am to hear you say so."

"That was *quite* the ruckus over a cat," I admitted, referring to McGettigan's near hysteria a fortnight prior when his feline friend had gone a-wandering.

"I very nearly called in my young Irregulars for a citywide sweep at my own expense."

"Well, never mind. She's back. She apparently brought in some half a dozen mice last week, presented as trophies."

"Half a dozen? What a remarkable undertaking."

"Socks is no loafer. When she sets her eyes on her prey, she flushes it out and carries it home."

"Every detective, one and all of us, should be so lucky."

This time I did laugh. Couldn't help myself—Mr. Holmes does own a wit as well as a brain, and he has a trick of drawing you into his small circle when he chooses. Generally when he wants something, or is planning on wanting something later, or notices that you just did something he wanted. He took a pull of the cigar, weary lines creasing his high forehead.

"If I didn't know you better, I'd say you got cockeyed last night," I realised.

Instead of contradicting me, Mr. Holmes made a sound like a calf in distress.

"By George, so you did!" I exclaimed, dropping my fist to my knee. "Ha! Oh, that's rich. The world's most famous amateur detective—"

"Independent consulting detective." His eyes as he glared at me were bloodshot beyond the clear, queer circles of steel.

"He of the keen insight and the massive intellect, potted."

"Don't be ridiculous, Inspector."

"Oh, I wouldn't dream of it!" I chuckled, making my way to the cupboard in the corner. "Last night, you were swilled to the gills, I'd bet my pension on it."

"How many ghastly slang synonyms for immoderate intoxication am I meant to endure?"

I poured a single whiskey for me and a double for the sufferer. "As many as I like, taking into account that yesterday you managed to get stewed as a hare."

"If you are possessed of the smallest drop of the milk of human kindness, pray desist."

His face was buried in his hands now as he tapped the unlit cigar end against his temple. ~~It was the best time I've had in months~~. Nudging his knuckle with one of the tumblers, I cleared my throat meaningfully.

"Drink this."

Head lifting, his trout-like complexion shifted from grey to green. "What the devil for?"

"Because it'll help. And I happen to know that not twelve hours ago, you were as swizzled as a stevedore. Go on."

I pushed the drink into his hand and clinked mine against it. Pupils boring into me, Mr. Holmes downed half at one go. With a grimace I ~~heartily enjoyed~~ almost pitied, he did so again and set the glass heavily on my desk.

"If you recount so much as a word of this to Gregson," he enunciated carefully, "I shall see to it that the next ten cases you're assigned have to do with tax evasion."

I propped myself against the front of my desk. The world seems that much more reasonable when Sherlock Holmes is sitting slumped onto his knees, and I'm standing upright.

"That's impossible. Even for you."

"Improbable," he corrected balefully. "And try me. I've government contacts so lofty that you couldn't spot them with a telescope. Anyway, this is all Watson's fault, confound the fellow."

I drew back, surprised. "Dr. Watson is the last chap I'd suspect of dark designs."

"Of course you needn't suspect him of dark designs, the man is incapable of *designs*," Mr. Holmes scoffed, affronted. "January the sixth is my birthday."

When I burst into peals of laughter, he gave me a sheepish, lopsided smile. It wasn't a look I'd ever seen on Sherlock Holmes. I rather liked it.

"Oh, Lord that's rich," I gasped. "All these years I've known you, never let a personal detail slip, and then Dr. Watson gets a little free with the libations on your day of birth and suddenly you're Whitaker's Almanac! How old?"

"Neither old nor young, but at the crossroads." Mr. Holmes glowered at his empty tumbler. "Five and thirty. The precise middle, taking stock of all of life's many fruits and many poisons, the sweet and the bitter, the gales and the doldrums, and questioning which events land in the one or the other column."

"Heaven save us!" Pouring more liquor, I raised my arm. "You're still sack-sopped—best to keep ahead of it until you can catch forty winks, or your head will split like a melon. Waxing philosophical isn't your style, Mr. Holmes."

"You would be surprised, perhaps," he returned coolly, sitting up straighter. "Thank you, but no, I had better not have any more."

"As you like. And no offence meant. You natter philosophy as well as any, I suppose."

"And you speak with admirable aplomb regarding techniques by which to avoid a sore cranium after a night of barbarous hedonism."

"I was a roundsman once, same as the rest. I've seen plenty of good sorts deep in their cups—bad sorts too."

An image flashed before me of Hannah. Her mirth muffled behind her hand, pretty pink cheeks wan excepting the occasional lurid streak of purple. Like a paint smear, or a streak of rot on a fruit. It wasn't until well over four years of it that she started into the lush with as much gusto as he. But I know how to cure a woolen mouth all right.

Mr. Holmes needn't know about any of that. Ever. Just how Mr. Holmes needn't know that I'm well aware he has a stronger taste for needles than he does for toddies. Not nearly so often these eight years Dr. Watson has been with us. Sometimes, though. Sometimes his spiderlike fingers dance absently and sometimes the smile he flashes could have been carved on a jack-o'-lantern.

"Are you ever going to tell me what you're doing here?"

Mr. Holmes tugged a book from within his frock coat and shoved it against my ribs.

Mystified, I examined the title. *The Matrimonial Guide for Bachelors: A Textbook of Courtship and Marriage.* Published in America and written by a chap named Mr. H. William Snooker.

"I don't follow," I admitted.

"Off to our traditional start, then! Capital. If you'd understood every-thing, I'd have been all at sea."

"Are you tying the knot, or maybe taking the cloth?"

"I've about as much intimacy with God as I do with the female of our species, so congratulations on a pair of spectacularly wrong guesses. Both are utterly inscrutable, lamentably capricious, and ultimately unfathomable. Anyhow, I'm only positive that women actually exist."

"For heaven's sake, Mr. Holmes, out with it! I'm a working man. What's so vexing that you can't even say what it is?"

He frowned. "Miss Mary Morstan's employer—I say employer, but her dearest friend in a matronly fashion—has inherited a moderate sum and wishes to take a European tour with her family, never having previously experienced the wonders of Italian sculpture or the miracles of French cuisine. In short, Miss Morstan will be cordially sacked in a fortnight."

"Aha," I ventured.

"The estimable lady is engaged to the good doctor."

"Yes, he told me. And so?"

"So instead of waiting for spring's soothing climes, they are to chain themselves together body and soul in a fortnight in Lower Camberwell!" he exclaimed, stabbing the air with his cigar.

I took a draught of my own, savouring the taste. I set my drink down. The familiar tinkle of a constable's keys jangled past. The fire, I thought, needs a bit more coal. My brain had hit one of those irksome walls which seem to crop up so often when near Mr. Holmes, because Mr. Holmes doesn't believe in bridging the gap between one fact and an unrelated one. Oh, no. He simply points at the chasm and crosses his arms expectantly over the pile of bricks he's left for you.

"All right . . . Dr. Watson and Miss Morstan are speeding up the wedding date. What has this book to do with anything? And what has any of it to do with me?"

Sherlock Holmes looked so disappointed that I swear he'd have thwacked me with a ruler if he could.

Then it dawned on me.

"Don't tell me he asked you to be his best man?" I cried, not hiding my dismay.

For that matter, neither did Mr. Holmes. "He did! Last night of all occasions, confound the fellow, after he'd plied me with enough brandy to get Goliath himself owl-eyed, as you would no doubt so eloquently phrase it!"

Whistling, I shook my head.

"I know, isn't it horrendous?" Mr. Holmes fluttered his hands. "It has only been three days since we solved the murder of Sheik Yousef Al Sharqi, Inspector Blakesley has me attempting to trap a cracksman who jauntily leaves a wax seal on his plundered safes, and I've barely begun to look into this matter of Colonel Merridew Fitzpatrick giving away his keenest hunting dog, which may well be of international import."

"Just a moment." We'd skipped a key point. "You actually said *yes*?"

"Naturally I did," he snapped. "Watson's nerves when first he arrived here disinclined him to forge many new acquaintances. Why, I myself only met him through an old schoolmate. He'd never have taken up residence with me at all if not for the merest whim of fair fortune. Since that time, whether thanks to disinterest or laziness or bloody-mindedness, he has managed to pass eight years living in the greatest city on this remarkable planet, and the one most fully stocked with upstanding folk to boot, with no better options for a best man than the humble fellow you see before you."

If you are humble, then I am the King of Zululand.

"You've attended weddings previously, yes?" he urged.

I nodded. I'd worn tails to Hannah Lestrade's wedding to Verle Cullen, a handsome and ambitious gentleman who'd wanted to make his mark on the tea securities market. When that didn't work out, he made other marks. Mainly on my sister's person.

"Then you simply must assist me, because this book—I imagined one penned by an American would surely be franker—is *rubbish.*"

Mr. Holmes looked so tragic that, had it not been for yesterday's significant anniversary, I would have smiled.

"I've conducted extensive researches ever since the British Library opened its doors this morning," he fretted. "Are you aware that the origins of this charming tradition were rooted in the Germanic Goths, and that it was the best man's happy task to help kidnap a presumably unwilling maiden? The Huns took this honoured role rather further, by arming the best man lest the groom be attacked by the bride's vengeful family. The Vandals likewise readily equipped the poor fellows with spears. As I've no intention of clubbing Miss Morstan—who is very quick and clever and might well prevent me—nor of fending off her male relations, as they are deceased, I am mystified. In brief, I'd defend Watson with a spear without an instant's hesitation, and yet the possibility of him requiring such aid appears remote."

"Have you even been to bed yet?"

"No, why do you ask?"

"Never mind." Rolling my eyes, I enquired, "But just where do I come into it?"

"What am I to *do*? I already served as unwitting matchmaker and lost half the rent by it, not to mention a constant sounding board and a man who can always see his way safe to the end of a fracas." His rail-thin arms spread like bats' wings, an expression of genuine helplessness on his drawn face, mixed with something deeper I couldn't begin to parse. "What role, if any, do I play now?"

"You actually want to make a good job of this," I realised, gaping.

"Of course I do!" he cried. "You're talking of a soldier, a sturdy comrade, a chap who doesn't shirk or slink or shy away—not from Ghazis, nor poisonous snakes, nor even the Ku Klux Klan, for God's sake."

"The good doctor deserves all you say, but it's not very like you to care about such a thing, is it?"

"Naturally I care, as personal self-respect likewise enters the picture. I'd prefer to make a good job at *everything*." His thin upper lip curled in disgust. "After visiting the Library proved sterile, I went to my usual bookseller just now; the man has never once failed me previously, until he gave me that steaming pile of printed tripe."

"Really all that bad, is it?"

With an actual snarl, and the weird quickness so odd for a man of his height, he planted his cigar between his teeth for safekeeping, sprang forward, and snatched it from me. Mr. Holmes quickly found a page. Then he stalked to the fireplace and threw the cigar in it as if it had offended his honour.

"Mr. Holmes, they aren't exquisite, but they aren't free either."

"Should you like to clean your floor after I defile it, Inspector, or will you have one of the more irritating constables do it? Because I'm certainly not volunteering."

"All right, fair enough."

He scowled at the book as he read to me. "'The consideration of whom to take for your wife is of utmost import,'" he sneered in an uncanny nasal American drawl. "'Imagine that she hides within her bosom the empty soul of a heartless termagant? Picture yourself sitting meekly listening to her prattle; or caring for your progeny with your own hands, while she goes to the woman's rights convention; or arriving home from a long day of toil with no promise of a kiss, or a caress; or seating yourself for the sacred tradition of familial supper, choking down dry, sour bread and burnt coffee?'"

He made three long strides back to my little stove and threw the book onto the coals alongside the offending cigar.

"It's the most invidious fiddle-faddle I've ever read." Mr. Holmes loomed over me with that hungry cat's expression he gets. Poised to bite, or scratch, or hiss at the very least. "Since when does the *woman* pose the *man* any risk whatsoever in the state of holy wedlock? She loses her property, her holdings, her freedoms, sometimes her very *life*, and for what? When a man marries, his last rational thought leaves his head; when a woman marries, she never had any in the first place."

"Excuse me?" said I, coldly.

He didn't notice. He's like that sometimes, a cannonade, and all you can do is duck. Pacing, he made a few sweeping turns.

"Listen, I grant that women can be powerfully conniving creatures, but Watson need fear no such thing from Miss Morstan. Believe me, I made certain of *that*. She's quite unimpeachable. But a woman can be scorned, railed at, imprisoned, abused, ignored, even horsewhipped, and so long as it's done by her beloved helpmeet, it's all perfectly legal. Any woman would have to be insane to enter into such an arrangement, or else pitiably slow."

"That's not the case," I growled, feeling my much smaller shoulders bristle. "Some do it for money or title, I suppose, but others do it for love."

"Love," he snorted. "An outmoded evolutionary drive homologised by the Church, or simply a crude commercial transaction cloaked in a fairy tale? Oh, never mind." He sighed. "I can't imagine why I came to you in the first place. The very idea that a bachelor peeler could know the first thing about the matrimonial state must be evidence I'm still intoxicated."

"Get out."

"Hmm?"

He'd pursed his mouth into a question. I hadn't realised I'd been whispering.

"I said *get out*."

Mr. Holmes huffed a breath, surprised for once. And glad I am for that too. God knows he had it coming to him. I stood there, fair shaking with rage, while he peered down from on high.

He cocked his head like a bird. Not regretful, just puzzled.

"By the Lord Harry, get out!" Suddenly he'd a lit cigar being waved in his face. I must have looked like a bantam fixing to fight a jaguar. I didn't care. "If you're not gone in under ten seconds, I'll tell Gregson who really hid the Countess of Bessborough's body in those catacombs. Because we both know full well that it *wasn't* her son. I agreed with you—the real guilty party had been punished more than enough, and I didn't say peep. But make yourself scarce double quick or I'll tell the man probably next in line for chief inspector that Sherlock Holmes regularly lies to the Yard."

The detective's palms were up in what was meant to be a gesture of peace. I'd have none of it. His mouth was actually open.

It was the only remotely satisfying thing about his visit.

"Not another word from you," I hissed, pointing at the door. "Get out."

When he'd escaped me, I sat down at my desk and set my own cigar in an empty teacup. Just shaking. Not even really thinking, not anymore. Not even about Hannah.

If Sherlock Holmes so much as comes within ten feet of me at a crime scene again, he'll have to watch out for a fist in his face. I tried to breathe slowly, focus on the case I'd been approached with.

Of course I couldn't, though. So I threw on my bowler and ulster and walked home. Past the corner where the Italian beggar sets up the tightropes for his trained mice in better weather. Past alleys that were decked with fresh snow this morning, all stained brown and black again. Past the chestnut vendors blowing on their fingers and the acrid, velvety fumes from the ironworks and the pale feet of the gutter children glowing like grubworms. Not really feeling the cold myself. Not feeling anything but an emptiness where an ache should have been.

Because I'd thought back on what Mr. Holmes had really been saying, if you take away the insults, and he wasn't far wrong. I'd been in agreement with half of what he was spewing. It wasn't until I'd already knocked the sludge from my boots that I realised I'd been limping horribly all the way here.

Before bed, though, I'll write down Millie Sparks's tale while it's yet reasonably fresh. Two hours before Mr. Holmes arrived, Miss Millie

Sparks walked into my office bright as a new penny, sat herself down, gave her name, and listed her occupation. Under-housemaid, 17 Somerleyton Road, Brixton.

I stopped writing then, her not being an under-housemaid. Some folk have it hard, and women have it harder, and some women even harder than others. And I'd never be so churlish as to assume a woman was no better than she should be simply because she was poor. But under-housemaids have more muscle than draft horses. Downcast eyes, for the most part. And hands cracked like cobblestones from all the lye and the vinegar and the lead-black and whatnot it takes to keep the ton feeling like they've the cleanest house in the row.

This woman's serge dress was cheap but not somber, forest green, cheered by scraps of mismatched ribbon and lace. It was also cut low enough to bar her from entering public museums, let's say. Her arms were thin but not strong. Her honey-coloured hair was frizzled with cheap curls, her wide froggy mouth turned down with worry and smeared with lip rouge. Blue eyes active as a sparrow's, and bold as a tomcat's. And her hands were perfectly normal.

So she wasn't an under-housemaid. I'll put it that way.

"It's on account o' me sister. That would be Miss Willie Sparks, spinster." She scooted forward in her chair. "Ain't ye going to make a note to keep us straight? Mam done birthed her first, christened her Wilhemina Sparks, and then I come after, and Mam already takin' such a shine to the sound of it, named me Milhemina Sparks, but them bein' our Sunday names if ye like, and fer the rest o' the week just plain Willie and Millie."

Trying not to smile, I dutifully wrote it down. "So, the elder Miss Wilhemina Sparks, spinster, and the younger Miss Milhemina Sparks . . ."

"Under-housemaid," she affirmed, nodding.

"What's happened, Miss Sparks?"

She inched so close I feared she'd fall off the chair. "Only that me dear, sweet sister Wilhemina done been snuffed, Inspector."

I blinked.

"Croaked," she obliged.

"No, I already know what it—"

"Though she mightn't ha' laid down the old knife and fork just yet, pray God." Tears stood out in Miss Sparks's eyes. "I only know as she done been *spirited away*, like. By *snatchers*. They're everywhereabouts, and me sister Wille was 'napped, and I beg ye to find her afore it's too late. Though it may be already, by now. Who knows?"

"If you suspect your sister was kidnapped or, ah, snuffed, Miss Sparks, who do you imagine would do such a thing?"

"I done told ye, *snatchers*. But ye never wrote it down, so ye fergot. Better write it now, to be safe."

"I mean to say do you suspect she might have been taken to a particular location?"

"Who could know any such thing?" Miss Millie Sparks tilted her eyes at the ceiling. "But lemme give it a think, like. Folk what done get napped could end up in all sort o' dreadful scrapes. . . . Maybe Bethnal Green? Shoreditch. As far off as Newcastle? If they done made it to the Thames and took a boat, though, could be any foul place. Africa? Canada, maybe. I hear tell what there's the dreadfullest scallywags there, who'd skin ye as soon as look at ye, sell yer 'ide fer a pelt, and then roast the guts fer supper. I hope to Christ 'tisn't Canada, Inspector, I most devoutly pray so."

My head was spinning. Dropping my pen, I rubbed my eyes.

"When did your sister—"

"Miss Wilhemina Sparks, spinster."

"Yes. When did she go missing?"

"Who could say, sir? Coulda been six in the morn. Coulda been just as the church bells tolled noon. But when I done went to her crib, and up the stairs to her bedroom, *she weren't there*."

I'll admit, I was ready to throw her out on her ear. But when I tried, she gripped the arms of her chair as she delivered her story. And I'll be hanged if it wasn't just odd enough to be true.

Miss Millie Sparks had been estranged from her sister Miss Willie Sparks for some ten years (she being twenty-five years of age now, and her elder sibling twenty-nine). She claimed this was thanks to a difference in temperament, and a squabble over inheritance when their mother died, and a beau, and a mysterious betrayal (I suspected it had rather more to do with Miss Millie's choice of vocation). One day though, as Miss Millie was out "taking a constitutional like what I does every afternoon," she chanced upon an old friend of the family and begged to know how her sister was faring, as their parents were both long departed.

The family friend told Miss Millie that her sister was very unwell indeed. A recluse, in fact. Shut in, renting a single furnished room. Relying on the widowed proprietress to cook and clean and go to the shops. Apparently, after their mother and father passed, Miss Willie fell in love. She met a man at a pub and they courted. Exchanged gifts and tokens and letters. He vanished six months later along with a goodly percentage of the family's inheritance, having known the whereabouts of certain valuable securities. Miss Willie had been the sole keeper of this sum, Miss Millie "not needin' handouts, thank ye" (having spent hers, I took it). Understandably, following these tragedies and betrayals, Miss Willie got in the dumps.

Miss Millie did not allow grass to grow under her feet upon hearing this news. After discovering her sister's address in South Lambeth, she marched there, banged on the door, and barged in.

"And weren't she a sight fer sore eyes!" Miss Millie gushed, dabbing away tears. "Me own dearest Willie, brought low and without a chum in the world and ready to let bygones be bygones. 'Twere something to see, Inspector. *Forgiveness*. There could have been a sermon done writ about us, though it beats me which of us were the prodigal!"

Afterwards, Miss Millie took to visiting Miss Willie every day; and Miss Willie always received her, since after all she never went out, and by this time was far enough gone to be stubborn over staying that way. Until the previous afternoon, that is—the landlady opened the door, reported that Miss Willie had gone off to be married, and then shooed Miss Millie away like she was chasing a rat out of the larder.

"It fair broke me heart it did, sir." By now my visitor was sobbing. "To have me sister back, and then, then live to see her *snatched*, that's what, by *fiends*, and who could tell in this great world the names o' the culprits? John?

Sam? Jim? I can't. So I done run up to a bluebottle trudging his circle, and he laughed at me, and he said *run along*, and when I wouldn't, he said *be off*, and threatened to have me shut up in a cell if I wouldn't scarper. Please get me sister back, Inspector? She's the only kin left to me in the world, she is."

Knowing something about sisters, I asked a few more questions. Her sister's landlady's name and address. How I could reach Miss Millie (she primly gave the name of a pub owned by a "cousin what can track me down right quick"). When I sent her on her way, she was calmer, but bereft. I know the look.

There's nothing else I know about the matter, though. How does a body find a friendless woman who went off with a strange man? There are needles in haystacks that would be easier to trace.

Two things I'm convinced of, though. Women deserve someone to fight for them, no matter their lot or their station. And every word regarding her sister Miss Millie Sparks told me, however ridiculous, was true.

Entry in the diary of Inspector Geoffrey Lestrade, Tuesday, January 8th, 1889:

Nobody wants to consider himself an unsociable fellow. We all hope that when the lads down at the pub take that first bittersweet sip of froth, they're wondering what could be keeping you. We're all downcast at the news of having missed a special celebration, if the persons involved were the good sort. Right up to this morning, I'd thought that was gospel.

It isn't. It's absolute rubbish, is what.

Every so often, the higher-ups at Great Scotland Yard decide to shake the trees; I've been through department secretarial supply audits, demands to know how much in fines we garnered as roundsmen, even the barmy request that we "add together all the days spent in incarceration by those whom you have assisted in apprehending." I'd forgotten all about it, I suppose, or pushed it aside as too humiliating to be credited. But this morning I was charged with making a brief account of every unsolved case I'd ever had.

In other words, a guided tour of personal shortcoming.

So when Dr. Watson arrived, preceded by a cheery knock, he found me thus: papers scattered on my desk like October leaves, my tie off and collar undone, my hair like a hedgehog's from scraping my nails through it, an empty coffee jug beside me, and my brow slumped on my fist.

"Good heavens!" he exclaimed.

"Don't worry, Doctor," said I, dourly. "It's much worse than it looks."

Dr. Watson made as if to put his hat and coat on the rack but hesitated. Then he turned back towards the door.

"Where are you going?" I exclaimed.

"Please don't bother over me, Inspector—your mind appears to be all too fully occupied. Forget I was here!"

"No, come in, do come in and then have a drink with me," I groaned. "If I keep at this one second longer, the lot of it is going out that window. Just a moment, though. Is, er, does Mr. Holmes—"

"I'm here entirely on my own recognisance, Inspector."

"Then by all means sit down and I'll pour some much-needed fortifications."

He approached with rueful caution. "I do believe I know that look. I wore it every day in 1878."

"Which was?"

"My final year of medical school at the University of London."

"Ah, well then it can't have been *this* look, because I happen to know you didn't fail medical school."

"Exacting work, is it?"

"No, demoralising."

"Oh, well I certainly won't ask you another word about it then. To your good health, Inspector Lestrade!"

We toasted. When Dr. Watson finished, he set the glass neatly on my desk, his bowler on his left knee and his gloves in his right hand, smiling at me in commiseration.

For all I'm still fit to be tied over Mr. Holmes and his remarks, I shouldn't have supposed he'd be as callous over the doctor's feelings as he would, say for example, mine. No gentleman would go so far against his conscience as to abuse Dr. Watson, because Dr. Watson is just about the warmest, steadiest fellow you could hope to meet. And whatever else Mr. Holmes is, I'll admit that's he's a gentleman. The doctor looked worn—but in a happy, comfortable vein. Worn like a woodland path or worn like a favorite shirt. The desert had almost ruined him when first we met. Little shivers, sharp glances, dark skin creased and sagging like discarded packing paper. In a morose humour, I'd given him a year in London before fleeing for some coastal village. And a month before Mr. Holmes lost interest in the poor devil. Neither, happily, came true.

Some folk do get justice after all. And in Dr. Watson's case, I was thoroughly glad of it.

"You must be wondering why I'm barging in like this." Dr. Watson's moustache twitched with amusement.

"Did His Eminence send you, or did he just hint as much until you imagined you'd got the idea all by your lonesome?"

Dr. Watson laughed readily. "Actually, I came here to deliver this in person, so I might learn your response."

He passed me a card—formal design, a warm eggshell colour edged with a blue border. At first, I imagined that Mr. Holmes had ordered his friend to deliver evidence to me. When I saw what it was, though, I think I flushed.

I hope I didn't. But I think I did.

"I'm a touch staggered, Doctor, but . . . yes, of course I'll come."

His square, open face lit up. "Wonderful! It's short notice, but Mary has had a change of circumstances, and since neither of us possess any family to vex with a sudden change of plans, why delay what we both want?"

"Can't think of a reason in the world. Same as I can't think of a reason why you'd want a detective inspector at your wedding," I added, smiling.

Dr. Watson's eyes didn't darken exactly. But a wisp of cloud did pass over clear blue. "I don't want to make any implication whatsoever that I wouldn't invite you no matter the circumstances. However, Mary and I are quite alone in the world as regards kin. Thankfully, we've some of the best kith we could possibly ask for, so it's only natural that we should want them at our ceremony."

Nodding, I took a sip of spirits. The Lestrade clan is neither sprawling nor dwindling. Aside from my parents and my nephew, there are aunts, cousins, Mad Uncle Charlie, etc. I could equally turn up at my Aunt Annette's suite in Chelsea for hot crumpets with bitter marmalade, or at my cousin Roger's dairy farm in Shropshire for tea cakes with strawberries and cream. We're not in danger of extinction. . . . But there's a hole in the fabric. And I've been trying to mend it for so long, to so little avail, at the expense of any activities that might be considered sociable, that I almost was cheap enough to envy Dr. Watson his friends. Right up till I reminded myself that he considered me one.

"You appear perplexed, Inspector—have I caused any offence?"

"God, no. You surprised me, that's all. Last I saw you, Mr. Holmes was shouting at me about removing that poor woman's clothing before the autopsy. How he imagines we should have done an autopsy with her corset and stays intact is beyond me."

Dr. Watson's laugh, unlike Mr. Holmes's, makes a chap join in before he's knows what he's about.

"I suppose it might appear odd to some that our nuptials will be populated with so many who have been introduced to us by means of work instead of leisure." Lifting one shoulder, Dr. Watson shrugged pleasantly. "Apart from a few mates from my club, and one or two friends from Mary's days at boarding school, everyone there will have something to do with industry or endeavor. My new neighbor Charles Anstruther from the medical practice I purchased, Michael Stamford from my St. Bart's days . . ."

"Sherlock Holmes," I found myself muttering.

"Here, now." Dr. Watson set his elbows on his knees, copying his friend's recent posture in a much more easy manner than a sleuth with a sore head and sour stomach. "I'm well aware that you and Holmes don't get on from time to time, but may I ask whether anything's troubling you specifically? This . . . seems worse than usual. Would you believe me if I confided to you he was distressed?"

It was right there in front of me. The offer, fresh and generous and honest as anything, like a perfectly baked steak and kidney pie. The doctor wouldn't have minded me grousing. Probably would have taken Mr. Holmes to task over what had happened if he knew the whole story to boot. But I didn't need Dr. Watson miffed at his own best man. ~~And for all that I've precious few folk to talk to now Hannah's gone, I don't need pity over the fact.~~ So I kept mum.

"No, and I'm sorry I'm in a foul humour today. The truth is I'm meant to write down every unsolved case that's ever passed through my docket. It's distressing."

"My word." Dr. Watson frowned. "While potentially practical, that sounds . . . unnecessarily demeaning."

"Such is the life of the regulars. Mr. Holmes should thank his stars he has no one to hold him accountable for a thing."

"I wouldn't quite say that." Dr. Watson coughed demurely. "But I don't envy you, and I'll leave you to it, so it can be over that much sooner."

"Much obliged, Doctor. I'll be at your wedding with a spring in my step."

He was halfway to the door before I realised he was limping a little. He always does in the winter, though it isn't nearly as noticeable as it used to be. So do I. Too many memories came crowding in, scattered and terrible, and before I knew what I was about, I blurted, "Have you ever lost a patient, Dr. Watson, one that . . . one that stayed with you?"

The doctor stopped with his hand on the doorknob. "We all have."

"Does it get any better?"

He bit his bottom lip with a slight shake of his head. "Inspector, I cannot claim that it does. May I be of service to you in any way?"

"No," I said quietly. "Apologies, Doctor. I don't think anyone can. It's been some ten years. But I'll manage, never fear, and these reports are nearly finished. I'll be right as rain tomorrow."

After a cordial goodbye, Dr. Watson left. He isn't one to force a confidence. And he understands, God knows he does, what it means to be haunted. There used to be screams in his ears and sand in his teeth—we all saw it plain as daylight in the desert. And I was glad enough to be invited to such a decent bloke's wedding that I nearly picked up my chin and squared my shoulders to finish my ludicrous assignment in a better mood.

But then I thought of Mr. Holmes again. That smile of his that's almost a snigger, his refusal to acknowledge anyone's choices as valid if they aren't the exact ones he would have made.

This camaraderie business is hogwash. Oh, I've a nice warm feeling at the prospect of seeing Dr. Watson happily wed. But once you're friends with someone, not to mention colleagues, you have to be friendly with *their* friends in order to be thought civilised. And Sherlock Holmes will have to give an actual speech of some kind. With a captive audience too. He'll be unsufferable.

At the thought of being trapped in a room with Sherlock Holmes, I wonder whether I'd prefer to swim naked through the Thames or catch some gruesome, incurable disease.

Entry in the diary of Inspector Geoffrey Lestrade, Wednesday, January 9th, 1889:

PC Noll and PC Holloway were foolish enough to leave their galoshes where PC Zordan could get at them when the trio checked in from their rounds today, and the former two kept asking as they left the Yard why everything smelled of raspberry preserves. Their boots will be sticky as anything, supposed they aren't glued to their overshoes entirely. Nobody said peep, either, though they all howled when the poor chaps were clear of headquarters. I'd run PC Zordan down over such a prank under normal circumstances, but I can't find it in me to care. Anyway, preserves never hurt anyone.

Stopped by Miss Wilhemina Sparks's residence for a chat with the proprietress. Paradise Road turns out to be a considerable exaggeration if not an outright lie. And Mrs. Bray is a dour old thing, skinny as a plucked hen, with her hair in such a tight bun it's a wonder she can move her eyebrows. She can, though. She can lower them right quick at a fellow.

"I haven't the slightest where Miss Willie's gallivanted off to," she sniffed. "And now I know that her sister's no better than she should be, and that it never even occurred to Miss Willie to show her a Bible and show her the door, I don't care either. She had a carpetbag packed, and claimed she'd been corresponding with a man, that she was off to be wed, and that she would reach Miss Millie by letter in a few days."

"What sort of a man, Mrs. Bray? Can you describe him in more detail, please?"

"Certainly *not*. I never snoop in my boarders' business, and once they aren't my boarders anymore, well all the better reason to keep my nose out of it. Never once met the fellow."

I hesitated. "Despite their being engaged?"

"Well, it's hardly *my* affair, is it?"

"Might I conduct a quick—"

"No, you may not search Miss Willie's former room, and I don't see what cause you might have to request such an extraordinary thing."

"Miss Willie's sister, Miss Millie Sparks, thinks she may have met with some misadventure."

"Miss Millie Sparks," Mrs. Bray intoned with a truly religious zest for suffering, "doubtless encounters so much misadventure, as you put it, that she fancies it surrounds her at all times. And I've just finished having the suite cleaned—young Mary has already been at it all morning. Spick and span and ready for my next tenant, may God speed them on their journey. Is there anything else I can help you with, Inspector Lestrade?"

There wasn't. So I left. Gnawing the end of my pencil and wondering, as I pulled my peacoat collar over my neck, why a spinster who'd once been taken in by a charlatan would risk everything all over again on a man she clearly barely knew in person. If at all. I don't pretend to understand the way passion works. I do hope to someday. But I do know how commonsense works. And women tend to have no lack of the stuff. On that point more than any other, I think, Mr. Holmes and I land at the opposite ends of the Pole.

Entry in the diary of Inspector Geoffrey Lestrade, Thursday, January 10th, 1889:

Colour me staggered.

It's not often I'll admit I've been dead in the wrong, because it doesn't often happen. That's not hubris—I weigh options, I consider. I calculate probabilities. Mr. Holmes loves to say that I was born without an imagination. Well, imagination is dandy, but I'm a detective inspector, not some brilliant scarecrow who's consulted over only the daftest crimes and solves them by practicing alchemy and making the world spin backwards. Most of the time, the plain explanation is the right one. So most of the time, I'm correct.

But today I had the stick by altogether the wrong end. Not about the case, mind. The case, a Bedlamite could have solved. Blindfolded, with his hands tied behind his back. I was quite correct about the case, to my dismay.

No. I made an obvious assumption and was proven mistaken. I was wrong about the character of Mr. Sherlock Holmes.

The crime scene presented the sort of miserable, wretched outcome we all hope never to encounter again, but crops up every year or so anyhow. I stood at the corner of Greencoat Row and Francis Street, watching as two PCs carted away the body of Mrs. Jane Gibbs, wife of Mr. Merripeth Gibbs, City banker. The wind was a scalpel against exposed skin, and soon the coroner would be wielding the same. But neither cold nor pain would trouble Mrs. Gibbs any longer. Tucking my neck into my muffler, I watched my breath smoke like a funeral pyre.

"Here now, take care!" I snapped as the nearer constable banged a corner of the stretcher against the door of the police wagon. "You'd not want your mum to be carted off to the dead house like a sack of potatoes."

He flushed. But Mrs. Jane Gibbs deserved what respect the police could offer her. She'd already encountered us regularly, when her husband took it into his head to tenderise her flesh and then lock her out of their sedate grey townhouse, which had no grounds and was facing the road. So she'd been discovered with bits of her face bloodied, coatless and shivering, before she'd time to scurry off to a discreet refuge, on multiple occasions. She always claimed that she'd been terribly silly and fallen in the park. Or on the stairs. And that the servants were all taking a half day, and that she'd forgot her key, and that her husband was working late. That didn't even work on us the first time, the bastard.

Let alone after some half a dozen.

Scribbling in my notebook, I ignored the bustle that sudden death always produces. Not just from us police. From the neighbours, and the street urchins, and the press, and the servants, and probably the fleas on the kitchen cats. I've never understood tragedy as a spectator sport. I saw a hanging at Newgate once and didn't sleep for a fortnight without waking up to visions of a hooded body spasming like a drowning fish. It was disgusting. Knowing I send people there doesn't make it any easier, either.

"Everything secured?" I called to PC McGettigan. I'd already questioned the butler and housekeeper, who assured me that the entire staff lived in utter terror of the master of the house. And I knew the history of that sad, sorry place. And I'd found the cause of death. All I needed was the coroner's opinion.

And I would write up a viciously damning police report.

"Aye, sir!" McGettigan rubbed at his ruddy side whiskers. "Servants have all been seen to, the bedroom locked and marked fer a crime scene, and her brother wired. He's a Leeds man, so he'll arrive on the morrow."

"Good. Let's start to clear out then. And get those yellow journalists off the corner! I don't care if you have to use your truncheon."

Spitting with significance, McGettigan trudged off. I turned to the street. Several of the reporters kicked up a fuss at being ousted, but one twitch of the beefy Irishman's hand in the direction of his club and they slunk off, muttering. So I glanced in the other direction down Greencoat Row to make certain there weren't any other riffraff to send packing.

Only to discover that there was indeed an undesirable leaning against a wrought iron rail and smoking a cigarette, and his name was Sherlock Holmes. And he was staring with eyes like steel-tipped arrows square at me.

"Oh, no you don't," I growled to myself.

"Sir?" The unknown constable had reappeared.

"Right." I shoved my hands in my coat pockets. "The prisoner is secured?"

"Snug as a sardine, Inspector Lestrade. Cold too, I'd bet."

"Excellent. Go on and take out the rubbish, then. Don't take the good roads to Newgate. That blackguard ought to feel every bump and scrape on the way to the last home he'll ever know. If anyone needs me, I'll be at headquarters signing his death warrant."

If the greenhorn roundsmen were put off by my enthusiasm, I suppose I'll find out later. I put my head down and marched hell for leather away from that twisted townhouse and the world's only (thank God) independent consulting detective.

Thinking he would expect me to make straight for the Yard, I hurried in the opposite direction. Down Francis Street, then Thirleby Road. Once I made it as far as the wide fairway of Victoria Street, I could cut north along Whitehall to sneak in through the rear of the building. A gaslighter nodded while skirting my trajectory, using his long staff to ignite the city's beacons as the stars began winking to life. The streets in that part of London are quieter than some, and the pubs snug and cheery. I was tempted to warm my bones before a fireplace with a mug of ale in my hand before my fingers closed around the little bottle of cyanide labeled ELIMINATES ALL PERNICIOUS PESTS that I'd stored in my pocket for safekeeping. I'd found it in Mr. Gibbs's *fireplace* of all the idiotic places to hide a murder weapon. No, that report needed writing and it needed writing without delay.

An effective murder weapon if ever there was one—and a stupid one, to boot. Thank God. There would be no trouble with the Assizes. I quickened my pace. A bearded fellow with a placard and a rheumy, electric gaze shrieked that the world was ending, and that we must all repent or be cast forever into the pit.

"Pits are as may be," I intoned under my breath, "and Mr. Merripeth Gibbs is headed to one if I have anything to say about it."

It was a pleasing thought. For about thirty seconds, I was actually comforted. But just as I reached the end of Thirleby Road, the smell of frying onions and sizzling mutton seeping from drafty kitchen windows, I turned the corner which would land me safe in the melee of Victoria Street and nearly trod on the toes of Mr. Sherlock Holmes.

"Good evening, Inspector Lestrade," he said evenly. The cigarette he'd been smoking was spent, and he crushed the butt under his sole.

"I . . . how the *devil*," I spluttered.

"Come now, you really can't be as surprised as all that! You were clearly leaving the scene of a crime that mattered to you; therefore, you would not have wasted precious minutes over writing it up. You are a dogged man, and a thorough one. When you spied me, you made the snap decision to take a circuitous route to Scotland Yard in spite of this relentless weather—I traversed the opposite semicircle by way of Parliament Street with the intention of cutting you off, which as you can see was gratifyingly successful. For an instant I nearly deluded myself into thinking you might choose Great Peter Street—but not only is it less anonymous than Victoria Street, they are tearing up the pavement between Chadwick Street and Monck Street, and when I considered how badly you've been limping of late—"

"You aren't wanted!" I all but shouted.

Heartsick, exhausted, and furious at once might have allowed me to keep my temper . . . but add the pain from my shattered ankle into the equation, and I was ready to rip the amateur's head clean off his swan's neck.

"Damn it, Mrs. Gibbs's murder is *already solved*. I unraveled it within two minutes and proved it in twenty more."

"I can see that for myself," he replied, unflappable. "May I offer my heartiest con—"

"You may not. Want to know how I solved it?"

"Of course, professional discourse with you is al—"

"Mr. Merripeth Gibbs is a notorious drunkard and vicious egomaniac who threatened to sack his entire household without a character should they ever say peep when he was amusing himself attacking his wife. Or tossing her out on the streets. It was her fortune he used to invest in a number of securities when they married. He did well enough to impress a City bank. But he was always badgering her to sell the land she brought to the union so that he could speculate with bigger sums. She objected because her grandparents were buried on the grounds."

"Ah, your train of thought is very clear. Mr. Gibbs considered his wife a financial obstacle rather than a helpmeet. An obvious motive and a superb starting point for an investi—"

"It's more than just *motive*, blast you. The butler saw him skulking about the tool shed used to maintain the rear courtyard three days ago, the housekeeper informed me that he asked to be given privacy with his wife after dinner, and the upstairs maid said he uncharacteristically followed the missus into her bedroom, in a 'flirtatious' vein. We were called in by the housekeeper when Mrs. Gibbs failed to appear at breakfast, then at luncheon, and the husband had decimated an entire decanter of fifty-year-old Scotch by midafternoon."

"What more did you find, Lestrade?" he pressed in a quiet, sober tone.

"What *didn't* I find? Her bed is covered with blood and vomit, it reeks of bitter almonds, I unearthed the cyanide bottle that's currently in my pocket at the back of Merripeth Gibbs's study fireplace, and the murderer is raving blootered in the back of a Black Maria, calling his late wife every foul name imaginable and rolling about on the floor en route to Newgate. The man is sharp enough with finances and a sadistic dunce about every other facet of human relations. There's *no reason* for you to be here. So if you please—"

"Ah, but not for the first time, nor the last, you are on the wrong track." Mr. Holmes's eyes creased with something I might have mistaken for kindness in another man. He removed the black leather glove from his right hand. "I've excellent reason to be here and shall prove it at once. The reason only happens to be a personal and not a professional one. That is where you went astray. I owe you my sincerest regrets; I've waylaid you with no object in mind other than delivering such an uncommon statement face to face. I apologise for having so upset you day before yesterday. It was most uncivil of me, and I beg your pardon."

He thrust his hand out. I gawked at it.

"Apologise?" I repeated stupidly.

"Yes, an enterprise I infrequently practice but nevertheless am capable of enacting," he huffed. "It's confoundedly cold out here. My fingers are going to fall off. Shake my hand and let us bury the hatchet, as our American cousins put it. I always quite liked that phrase—it smacks of zest, and honour, and the rugged wilderness."

Dumbly, I pumped his hand. I may as well have been shaking the hand of an orangutan who'd just shown me a card trick. I was that bowled over. When I made no move afterwards, just stood there knocked for six, Mr. Holmes clucked behind his teeth and took me by the arm.

And here's where it all gets hazy. This was some five hours ago and I can't for the life of me recall which pub we sheltered in. All I can say is that for some small stretch of time I was freezing and wretchedly morose. And then I was warm as could be in a shabby armchair with bald patches worn in the velvet arms, and a snifter of something sustaining was in my hand. A woman cackled in a gentle rasp. The dog toasting itself by the hearth raised a leg to scratch behind its curly-haired ear. Off in the thicker patches of cigar smoke, a man was singing "Oh Mother, Take the Wheel Away" very badly.

> *Oh Mother, take the wheel away, and put it out of sight*
> *For I am heavy-hearted and I cannot spin tonight.*
> *Come nearer, nearer yet; I have a story for your ear*
> *So come and sit beside me*
> *Come and listen, Mother dear.*
>
> *You heard the village bells tonight—his wedding bells they were*
> *And Mabel is his happy wife, and I am lonely here . . .*

"When was the last time you apologised, then?" My brandy glass empty, I set it on a worn deal table. Mr. Holmes made some obscure flicking gesture and before I could blink, it was topped up again.

"Dear me!" His eyes twinkled. "I imagine it must have been some three months ago. There was a marvellous murder case in Market Harborough, Leicestershire—remind me to tell you about it sometime—and Watson and I were staying at the village inn. The place was lacking in superfluous frills, you understand, quite pastoral, and it was of the very utmost importance that I determine the effect of combustion on button boots. The proprietor could think of nowhere between his robustly Spartan establishment and Nottingham where I could purchase such a fashionable commodity. Luckily, while I happened to be wearing a Balmoral boot during said investigation, the good doctor had recently purchased the increasingly popular button variety, and in a thinner leather that more closely matched the deceased's footwear."

"You apologised because you set Dr. Watson's new boots on fire."

"Of course not, don't be absurd—I apologised because I didn't think to purchase him another pair first."

I laughed, not even caring that it was Mr. Holmes who made me laugh. Laughed till fat tears welled in my eyes. And then I wasn't laughing. And Mr. Holmes's chair was closer, his long fingers were wrapped around my wrist, warmer to the touch than they looked, and my mouth opened and the words came spilling out.

"I'm sorry. This isn't like me. God, I was going positively spare, I was that angry with you for calling them witless, but you were right enough about the rest of it. A woman all but takes her life in her hands when she marries."

"To which particular woman do you refer?" he asked almost gently.

"I had a sister." I shook my head at the tinplate ceiling. "A younger sister by two years, Hannah Lestrade, and we were close as peas, and when she first took up with Verle Cullen, I didn't see anything amiss with the blackguard. I'll never forgive myself for that. He was well situated—a manager at a coffee importation company—and if he had a few drops too many at holidays, well who could blame him for a little frivolity? I was such a fool. And by the time they'd married . . . Hannah lied about the bruises, and when I wouldn't let her lie anymore, she said he didn't mean it cruelly. That she *loved* him. That it wouldn't happen again."

Nodding, Mr. Holmes studied his shirt cuffs. His hand hadn't moved, but mine had clenched into a fist.

"I begged her to leave. Go with me to France and stay with our *arrière-grand-mère*. Hannah only listened to me once—and once was more than enough. Cullen turned up at my lodgings. I wouldn't hear of her leaving with him, but he won her over in the end. The next morning, a group of roughs set on me. Dragged me into a corridor, beat me until their arms gave out. One of them had a fire iron. I've never walked straight since."

Mr. Holmes's eyes glowed weirdly molten in the firelight. He patted the back of my balled hand before tenting his fingertips. "What did you do?"

Barking a laugh, I passed my wrist over my eyes. "I joined the police force. I knew it was Cullen behind the attack but could never prove anything. Figured that the next time he threatened me, or hurt Hannah, I would know what to do. I'm every bit as prize an idiot as you claim, Mr. Holmes."

"It's possible that I exaggerate for effect, my dear Inspector."

"Be that as it may. Nobody ever taught me a damn thing about what to do, and eventually Hannah took to the bottle just to make it through her days."

"Did she? I quite understand, believe it or not." Mr. Holmes's mouth twitched oddly. "The slow passage of days, I mean."

I nodded. "Yes. I never blamed her either. And she never did leave him. First their son Jonas came along, which tied Hannah to that bastard all the more close, and then Cullen converted her savings account to his name, claiming she'd been 'unstable' since giving birth. She was a drunkard by that time herself, just to erase her day to day suffering a little, so. It wasn't difficult for him to prove this 'instability.' The drink led to screaming, weeping fits, hurling breakables. Strong spirits made him violent and made her wildly hysterical. When I finally made detective inspector, it was too late. That was ten years ago—ten years on your birthday, as it happens. The bastard still lives in London, investing in tea futures."

"God in heaven." Mr. Holmes sat back, narrowing his eyes. "Lestrade, when you say it was too late . . ."

"He needed money," I confirmed hoarsely. "He somehow arranged for their house to burn down so he could collect the insurance. I *know* he did, but there was never enough proof to charge him. Hannah was inside, and their son was with my parents. I don't know if Cullen drugged her first, locked her in. I don't know if he was aware she was still inside at all. I don't know anything. And I never will, not after a decade, and never a single clue. My nephew Jonas lives with my mum and dad. He draws wildfires. Hellish things. Keeping Cullen away from him is the best I've ever managed to do. My own sister burned to death and I've spent these ten years solving other people's crimes."

That's not the whole scope of what I don't know. Not by a long shot. But it's the most painful by far.

I don't know why I told Mr. Holmes about the worst thing that ever happened to me.

I don't know why he sat there, collected and yet somehow simmering beneath his composure. Like a kettle before it whistles. Then, like a gas lamp being turned up, Mr. Holmes brightened. Another pair of full snifters had arrived without my noticing. When I lifted mine, my unlikely companion extended his glass in tribute.

"To your late sister," he stated with none of the glibness that always rubs my nerves raw. "To peace and to justice for all, not excepting ourselves."

And after we drank, I don't know why I stayed there with him. Impossible, maddening, arrogant Sherlock Holmes. Talking of cases. He told me about an investigation an unnamed earl had set him on, to discover why some score of invaluable books in his library had been gutted and stuffed with blank foolscap, ruining them inexplicably. I told him about Miss Millie Sparks (not an under-housemaid, he agreed with a wry smile) and the unfortunate Miss Willie Sparks. The amateur was mightily intrigued. He ordered us a mountain of fried oysters and insisted I eat something, and listened with rapt attention, and soon enough the lancing ache in my ribcage had faded back to the dull throb that never lets me be. And never will, I suppose.

It's gone one in the morning now, and poor poisoned Mrs. Jane Gibbs's paperwork not yet filed. But nevertheless, I feel unmistakably better. I've an eleven o'clock meeting to plan our strategy in finding Miss Willie Sparks with none other than Mr. Sherlock Holmes of Baker Street.

So I'm glad to admit that in his case, regarding the man himself, I was very wrong indeed.

Entry in the diary of Inspector Geoffrey Lestrade, Friday, January 11th, 1889:

If there's a single man on this sad planet who cannot resist melodrama, that man is Sherlock ~~bloody~~ Holmes.

After writing up Mrs. Gibbs's case and drinking about a quart of coffee, I eradicated anything that might tempt Mr. Holmes into irksome deductions (the cold compress I'd used at dawn, for example) and sat down with fresh copies of the *Globe* and *Echo*. When he was five minutes behind his time, I chalked it up to carelessness. When he was a quarter of an hour late, I supposed it vanity. When a full forty-one minutes had passed since eleven o'clock chimed, I slapped my exhausted newspapers into the rubbish bin, concluding that Mr. Holmes hadn't actually given a damn. About any of the events of last night.

I was sliding my arms into my peacoat, eager for the hearty meal that would banish the last twinges of brandy from my skull, when my door flew open. A beggar dressed all in mufflers and scarves like a tattered Pied Piper, perhaps eight or ten of them, stumbled into my office. The sweet reek of cheap spirits radiating from him lodged in my throat.

"What the devil do you think you're doing, sir?" I cried.

Gripping the back of the chair to halt his forward momentum, the wretch nodded vigorously. "I've a complaint to make. With a soo-perior, like. Done in a jiff, and I'll be on my way again, Captain."

"This isn't a ship. And I am not the smallest bit interested in any complaint that has managed to sprout and take root within your cranium," I snapped. "Now kindly—"

"Hoo my word, gently now. Gently. Ye'll be glad o' this hintelligence soon enough, aye, so ye will. Why, I'd not be surprised if ye kissed me square on the gob once ye've 'eard me tell o' the *disorders* and *corruptions* a-going on right under yer very nose, Captain!"

"Detective inspector. I'll give you five seconds, and then I'll have you in a cold, draughty cell, sweating it out. One . . . two . . ."

A hand fluttered mothlike to his concave chest. "Me in the lockup! And these old bones past three score year wi' nary a stain on me good character!

Remember that me poor sainted mam yet lives, a hunnert and two and ever so tetchy over *shocks* and *squalls*."

"Three . . . four . . ."

"Begging yer mercy, Captain, take pity on a bloke what spies on the peelers when *they* figure they's spying on *me*. I'm come to give a full-fleshed reporting as regards yer division, from the wobbly-kneed gaffer down to the greenest o' the green!"

"Five. Come with—"

The ancient mendicant tugged his own greasy hair off his head.

I groaned. Both inwardly and audibly.

"My most abject regrets over my tardiness, Inspector." Sherlock Holmes commenced making a neat pile of drunken beggar man on the chair seat. "Granted, it is terribly frigid today, but may I prevail upon your good nature so far as to grant us a little fresh air? I suspect that your nose will thank me for it in spite of the chill."

Dourly, I unlatched my window. When Mr. Holmes deposited a set of eyebrows, a wig, ten or so mufflers, a disintegrating greatcoat, torn leather overshoes, and a pair of side whiskers into a fraying cloth bundle, I blinked. When he pulled his grey jacket out of the same, I understood that he was dressed quite normally underneath the ragpicker's gear, and thus able to revert to his natural state in seconds. I suppressed a mournful sigh.

"As to the intelligence I promised regarding your roundsmen just now, I'd never dream of keeping secrets from you, Lestrade." Mr. Holmes combed his fingers through his hair, buttoned his suit, and tugged on a cloth cap which could not be crushed in his sack to complete the transformation. "PC McGettigan has had another row with his mother, probably over what Socks may or may not consume for breakfast—his hat is never properly brushed unless she sees to it. PC Allen is strongly considering investing a modest sum in his brother-in-law's pub venture—he has been agonizing over it for days and this morning packed a sack lunch, which is highly out of character. Finally, PC Zordan badly requires corrective spectacles and ought to be subjected to an eye examination posthaste, which I shall explain forthwith."

I waited. ~~Not very patiently, as he was already on my last nerve and needed some courtesy slapped into him~~. Mr. Holmes stalked to the open window, threw the cotton bag outside for the countless street urchins to paw through, and collapsed into the chair, lighting a cigarette. The cloud of liquor began at once to dissipate with the disposal of the costume, so I shut the window with a *bang*, shivering.

"Do me an immense favour and don't brag a word about how you knew any of that tripe. I don't need you to play parlour tricks with my constables as subjects. And I'm sure these theatrics will all be of enormous help with the case we were going to discuss," I barked. "Miss Milhemina Sparks will be deeply comforted when she calls on me this afternoon."

"I should hope so," Mr. Holmes drawled, spinning the lit cigarette in his fingertips as if he were a card sharp. ~~Which he probably is, may the devil take the man. Let's be honest~~. "When she learns that I spent the latter half of the night in her missing sibling's former suite, and that I made some significant progress in our joint—or so I think of it now, if you'll pardon me, Lestrade—investigation, she ought to be heartily gladdened indeed."

My jaw dropped. I shut it again. "How did—"

Interrupting me peevishly, Mr. Holmes explained. After we parted last night, he darted off to the nearest of the small chambers he rents for a pittance in various districts of London. He donned fresh linens, covering these gentlemanly togs with scrap fabric. He altered his posture. He glued on facial accessories, painted on dirt, and pinned on his wig. Doused himself in spirits. Transformation complete, sack over his shoulder like an indigent Saint Nick, he shuffled off on foot to South Lambeth—no cabs being eager to offer him their hospitality—and made straight for Paradise Road.

"As unprepossessing as that stretch of dingy boardinghouses may be, Mrs. Bray's did possess certain features which endeared it to me. It boasted an empty barrel not far adjacent to an exquisite drainage pipe, for example, and the gutters were sturdy, and a few hard tugs with a wrench were enough to get the better of Miss Willie Sparks's erstwhile window latch. I was ready to turn tail if any member of the household proved a light sleeper, or if a canine ally enquired as to my motives, but they all slept like lambs.

A scrape on the wrist as I crawled over the ledge—here, you see—was a modest price to pay for a carte blanche midnight tour of the premises."

Mr. Holmes had with him a dark lantern, which he set in a corner and lit by slow degrees. Mrs. Bray was telling me the truth when she claimed to have emptied and cleaned her guest room. But her housekeeping standards proved to be lackluster. My colleague was able to eke some information from the threadbare rug and the secondhand furnishings.

"Miss Willie Sparks had a fondness for lemon biscuits," he reported dryly, "which I know because Mrs. Bray is deeply in need of a housemaid who sweeps *under* the settee. Miss Sparks was an avid reader; the chair was angled for the best light from the southward facing window, its pillow was pressed nearly flat, and the carpet was more worn, as if she had got up a number of times for tea, and then returned to her book and her perusal of lives which were wider far than her own."

"That's balderdash. How can you know that she wasn't sewing or embroidering? She could have craved the comfort—maybe even the money, under the circumstances."

"A housemaid who overlooks lemon biscuit crumbs isn't likely to check beneath cushions she hasn't even plumped, and every seamstress no matter how meticulous leaves snippets of thread behind in the cracks of the upholstery seams. There were none. Ergo, she was a great admirer of the written word."

Rubbing at my eyes, I settled on the other side of the desk. "Right. Fine. What else?"

The hearth informed Mr. Holmes that Mrs. Bray was stingy with her coal supplies, for the shards and pebbles were all carefully swept into the center of the grate. The curtains informed him that Miss Willie Sparks still retained her curiosity about the world beyond her fishbowl, for a slight discoloration remained just where a woman's fingers would smudge the pale material in pulling it aside to peer out. Apart from that, he concluded with a lackadaisical shrug, he could only tell me that our missing spinster left in a very great hurry, and that while her departure had been sudden, it was not entirely unexpected, and that the dairy farmer who whisked her away lodged in a village called Lynchmere in the district of Chicester, West Sussex.

"Mr. Holmes, you can either cease this useless parading of fabrications or you can go to the devil," I snarled. "I should have thought that our conversation of yesternight proved how very serious a business it is for me!"

"Yes, quite." He yawned, tugging a sheaf of letters out of his inner pocket. These were tied with a red string, obviously well taken care of. "I beg your pardon, Inspector, but the night I passed was a sleepless one. As I was about to elucidate, when I had drawn what superficial conclusions I could regarding Miss Sparks's narrow habits, I performed a cursory check of the floorboards after my boot produced an unlikely creak. One of the slats was indeed loose, and upon prying it up, I unearthed this small cache of correspondence. A man by the name of Mr. Richard Boxall, who claims to be a dairy farmer in the hamlet of Lynchmere from a family of many generations' standing, has been penning love notes to our missing sister—and doubtless Miss Willie Sparks left in a hurry, too taken with the sight of the chap in the flesh to worry over retrieving her billets-doux."

"Good Lord, you might have said so in the first place!" I exclaimed. "Here, hand them over! You really are the most maddening fellow I've ever come across—you're aware of that, aren't you?"

"My good Lestrade," he intoned darkly as he obeyed, "not a soul on this planet is more aware, as you phrase it, than I. More's the pity."

I'll not attempt anything so daft as reproducing the letters in my own journal. Yet I soon saw what Mr. Holmes meant by saying that Mr. Boxall "claimed" to be the latest edition of a long line of dairymen. His penmanship was perfectly legible but blocky and unpracticed. Like a child drawing its mother, with a circular head and triangular skirts. As for the prose, however, . . . it was uncannily elegant. I've not made any great strides with the fair sex personally, having long been preoccupied by darker matters. But if I'd wanted to woo some cheery, buxom lass, I'd have patted myself on the back for these rudely penned sentiments. One passage impressed me particularly:

While I know that we have never met in person, we have each separately met with Our Common Correspondent, and her descriptions invest me with such affection for you that I find myself smiling upon the instant I spy one of your envelopes. How quickly can the mind come to associate mundane objects with special joys! My thoughts wander as I fret over the price fresh cheese will bring—what exact shade of blue are your eyes? What would your laugh sound like? Could I hope to produce such a lovely sound?

Then as the sun sets over my lonesome corner of the world, I fear that my happy imaginings are all unfounded. That I must not wish for too much, that surely Our Common Correspondent cannot have described me in such glowing terms to you as she did in the reverse. That I must content myself with the sight of your envelopes—and I could almost be content with such a small portion, so glad is my heart whensoever I read news of you.

"Yes, that page struck me as well."

Glancing up, I found Mr. Holmes staring as he so often did at nothing, or at a quarter to midnight, or at the bush tracking techniques of the aboriginal Australians.

"What, some singular clue struck you, embedded in this page?" I asked.

"Not at all. The author employed a very effective metaphor for tenderness, however—the sight of the envelope. One grows accustomed to the physical traces of those for whom one has an affinity, which is a scientifically sound instinct as regards natural selection; I have of late been making a small study of the phenomenon. Even the most customary objects—nay, especially those—can be imbued with the comfort of the wolf pack's cave. It's stamped in our bloodline and there's no avoiding the urge no matter how passionate one's love of the unprecedented. A scatter of papers on a desk, a bowler hung on a peg, the scent of familiar tobacco . . . anything may serve to trigger this Darwinian appetite for humdrum detritus. Mr. Boxall is simply more poetic about it than most."

When this extraordinary speech had run its course, Mr. Holmes gave no sign of having made it. He just crossed his legs and blinked at his bootlaces.

I pretended to flip through more of the letters. "Did you notice anything else?"

"Of course I did. What's more, I imagine you have too."

Pursing my lips, I held up a page. "There's something devilish odd about these, yes."

"Oh, well done," he murmured. "Describe this oddity a trifle more *specifically*, if you please, as carefully as you can."

I scratched the back of my neck. "It isn't easy to put into words. Certainly nothing a jury would give weight to. And I'd expect these blockish letters from a dairy farmer, maybe one whose father passed on untimely. One forced to quit schooling altogether. But like you said, Mr. Holmes, the writing itself is first rate. Why should that be? I'd surmise that this fellow was a great reader of romances, perhaps. And surmise that his life revolved around them, mentally speaking. And surmise that he was introduced to Miss Sparks via this 'Common Correspondent,' who saw two equally solitary folk and decided to kindle a rapport between them."

"Your surmises are merely that—surmises," he mused, scraping his thumbnail over his temple as the cigarette quietly fumed along with its owner. "Dairy farmers, especially on a scale as small as he claims, do not often expend candle wax on hobbies as frivolous as reading romantic fiction. However, I concur with your impression that something concrete is amiss. I merely hesitate to leap to any specific conclusions. Currently we stand hip-deep in a morass, our suspicions based almost entirely upon common *types* of people, if you will, rather than more uncommon examples of Homo sapiens, the study of which I have in essence made my livelihood."

"Meaning?"

"Meaning that the unusual does not always connote the sinister."

"It only usually does."

Mr. Holmes almost smiled.

"So we're not really any further along than we were before," I sighed.

"On the contrary, Lestrade. We have been gifted with something remarkable—it is the unremarkable crime that always proves the most arduous to solve, because anyone may have committed it."

Mr. Holmes in a lecturing mood generally makes me want to stuff his throat with his perfectly knotted cravat. This time, though, there wasn't any joy in it on his part. Which took the wind clean out of my sails. It's good sport to picture sticking it to Mr. Holmes when he's puffing himself like a prima donna. But his eyes were leaden, and his tone was weary. I almost longed for a few of the more extravagant hand gestures.

Almost.

"This man's letters, then, are idiosyncratic because they are both articulate and crude at once," Mr. Holmes explained vacantly. "Our subject's word choice is vivid, precise; but his handwriting suggests the mental acuity of a man better used to the ploughshare than the ink nib. This, however, is only a generalization—manifestly, there exist aristocrats with infantile penmanship, and ironworkers well up in their Aristophanes. As the Grecian satirist put it, youth ages, immaturity is outgrown, ignorance can be educated, and drunkenness sobered, but stupidity endures."

"All right. Sounds like a toff, writes like a farmer. Which could simply be for a medical reason—a stroke, perhaps, or an affliction of his hand from birth, or an injury involving some farming apparatus. Though it remains unusual for a dairyman to be so expressive."

"Admirably expressed. Now, there exist large estates upon which cattle play a key economic role, and those landed gentry are schooled by private tutors prior to public boarding schools—then there are dairy farmers. Supposing our man the latter, his education was either extraordinary or he enjoys a noteworthy acumen. In both cases, I should expect his longhand to reflect as much."

"It doesn't. Which means he's either the oddest chap in the British Isles, or he's two chaps."

Mr. Holmes opened his mouth to speak, but nothing emerged. Instead he commenced smoking rapidly. Not enjoying the cigarette in the least. Just sort of inhaling. For almost half a minute, I thought a string of minutiae was about to spill from his throat like a magician producing a string of pearls. Paper weight and manufacturer, chemical composition of the ink, the name of the clerk who sold the stationery, the peculiar shape of a capital *W*, followed by a description of what the absent Miss Willie Sparks would be taking with her tea in a few hours.

He shrugged and commenced a survey of my floor.

"All right, out with it," I demanded.

Mr. Holmes looked as if he'd just caught a whiff from a local tannery. "Excuse me, Detective Inspector?"

Linking my hands into a single fist, I continued, "You, Mr. Holmes, are . . . how shall I put this? Glum."

"Glum?" he repeated, impossibly giving the word several syllables.

"Blue, or perhaps even dispirited."

"Dear me, this is shaping up to be as painful as your tour of every English euphemism for overdone frivolity," he replied coldly.

"That wasn't all the terminology I know for being whiffled, not even by half."

"Heaven save us."

"But now you know the reason I'm so versed, you're going to be civil about it in future, and that's not negotiable."

A puff of air resembling a laugh escaped his lips. I confess, I was surprised at myself as much as he was. I'm not an impressive chap—not physically, not like Mr. Holmes. But I'd never tried putting my foot down or digging my heels in with him previous. I'd tried ignoring him, being civil to him, losing my temper at him, and walking away from him. Nothing had worked. He doesn't seem to be going anyplace, however. The confounded man keeps cropping up. ~~I'm stuck with the wretch~~.

And for all his faults, he really is a brilliant investigator, if he'd only stop looking for unicorns in stable yards.

"All right," he demurred. "Far be it from me refuse to incorporate fresh data. You can trust me not to rib you over your extensive knowledge of the subject."

A thrill passed from my hair to my feet.

You're going to try this ordering Mr. Holmes about again. Just don't overdo it, or he'll lose interest in the novelty.

"Good. So what's wrong? It's much easier for you to lie to Gregson than to me, you know. You pester me too frequently."

"You flatter yourself immensely if you consider yourself worth prevaricating to."

"Then tell me what the trouble is."

"Leave it, Lestrade," he hissed.

Then it came to me.

I'd admittedly been as slow as a blister-heeled Yard trainee. Trying to make sense of suppressed sighs and rants about Darwin. Right up until I realised that he'd unwittingly listed scattered papers, a bowler hat, and the aroma of familiar tobacco right after introducing the subject of *home*.

Mr. Holmes had every right to be melancholy. Who save Dr. John Watson would ever remain in his orbit long enough to learn to tolerate such a comprehensive ass?

"Dr. Watson found something he was looking for," I mused. "And once you've found something that was missing, well . . . the mystery is solved, isn't it? No more need for a sleuth."

Mr. Holmes's entire body tensed. "I don't know what the devil you're blithering about."

"He's not going to forget you," I offered.

"He . . . what did you say?"

"You have excellent ears. Anyway, you boast about them often enough."

"Lestrade, do make your meaning clear," Mr. Holmes growled. "I may well be manifestly brighter than you are—don't look so piqued, I'm brighter than most everyone—but I have never affected to possess psychic powers."

"Dr. Watson isn't going to forget you," I repeated. "And we'll still have the work. Stop gawking at me like that, it's unnatural on you. I had a sister once, and she had me, she had me right to my marrow, and I dare say that Dr. Watson is like a brother to you by this time. He won't forget you. And for as long as the world is cruel, we'll have the work."

An ant could have started a trek across my office and we'd both have flinched. Everything was that still.

"Yes." I fancied he must have been catching a chill and regretted the open window, for a rasp had crept into his throat. "Yes, the work must be enough. Mustn't it?"

As I wrote before, I have misjudged Sherlock Holmes entirely. The rogue is endlessly clever and in possession of a malleable conscience when it comes to fibbing. If he had wanted Dr. Watson to remain a bachelor, he could easily have accomplished such. A lesser man than he would have done so. So would a self-professed calculating machine in an effort to retain a valued asset. But I don't think the notion of interfering with the happiness of John Watson so much as crossed his capacious mind.

"What are we to do, then?" I asked when Mr. Holmes said nothing. "Assuming Miss Willie Sparks went to rendezvous with this Mr. Boxall of her own accord, then no crime has been committed."

"And therefore, we need not investigate any further. I was speaking with perfect candour, however, when I mentioned to you that PC Zordan's vision requires, if you'll pardon my use of the phrase, looking into. It was coming upon dawn this morning when I realised that the empty barrel I'd employed for my ascent had been rolled away in the night. The drop was a daunting one in this morning's downpour, I could barely see the drainpipe, and it seemed easier to soak my togs with the last of the rotgut in my satchel and pretend to be a drunk seeking shelter in—I admit—a *highly* improbable sanctuary. Mary the under-housemaid shrieked to wake the dead when she discovered me asleep in the armchair. It was PC Zordan arrested me, and my picking the derbies with a hairpin ought to have been detectable for such a sharp lad. I gave him the slip within a block of his dragging me out the front door."

By then I was laughing so desperately that I was hardly minding him. Mr. Holmes weighed being irritated versus being pleased and ended by saying, "Well, what with the chamber being unoccupied, I got two hours' sleep out of it without interruption in the lockup, which you must concede—"

The door flew open. For the second time, a marauding personage invaded my sanctum at the wrong time, for she was not due until one. Miss Milhemina Sparks stood before us, ample chest heaving. Mr. Holmes responded first, springing out of the only chair save mine as if caught on Queen Victoria's throne. He whirled, bowed, and extended a languorous hand all in one motion.

"Our esteemed client, I presume! Do please sit down. We were just discussing your case in detail—there have been developments Inspector Lestrade and I are eager to share with you. My name is Sherlock Holmes, I am the world's only independent consulting detective, and I am also very much at your service."

"Gorblimey," she breathed. "Are ye a gentleman 'tec then, engaged special fer me? I knew as I'd come to the right crusher, Detective Lestrade 'ere bein' known fer his willingness to stand up fer the fair sex, like, and come to find 'e's already called in the cavalry! Met plenty o' bluebottles in me time, stiff-necked and walking round and round like ponies at a fair, but never a real live *toff* sniffer, what knows how to treat a lady, and don't mind if I do sit down, beggin' yer pardon supposing yer fagged after chasing down any cold-blooded ruffians."

"Is that how you imagine I passed my morning?" the amateur enquired with an odd mixture of disdain and satisfaction.

"Who's to say what ye've been about this fine morn, Mr. 'Olmes? It's quite beyond *me*, says I, seeing as in a great 'ousehold, a servant's life is that protected, sir, coddled as we are and shielded from the harsh gusts o' misfortune and foul play. Ye could ha' been recoverin' a chest o' diamonds at the bottom o' the Thames or happrehending a bloodthirsty 'ighwayman what knifed throats fer sport and drank the blood after. Still warm, even. Oh! Where is me manners at, Mr. 'Olmes? Miss Milhemina Sparks, under-housemaid, pleased to meet you. I'll wait if yer keen to write it down."

Sherlock Holmes's grey eyes met mine.

I gave a small nod.

Yes, she is always like this.

Slowly, Mr. Holmes beamed. It was the delight of a connoisseur of the bizarre, a veritable collector of human oddities. I was almost charmed by it.

"What brings you here before your time, Miss Sparks?" I asked. Mightily fearing the answer.

"Only I'm so worried about Willie." Miss Sparks's voice was a whine, her hair was a hay bale, her blue eyes wide and clear as undiscovered lakes. But her sincerity was unmistakable. It even affected Mr. Holmes, for he leaned against my desk with his ankles and arms crossed, attending with care. "Snatchers underfoot 'round every corner, and me own sister in their filthy grip! It's enough to turn a girl's stomach, Inspector. Me dear Willie still ain't written, nor sent word through a street boy, nor hadvertised, nor—"

"You mean to say the elder Miss Sparks has failed to extend any communique whatsoever thus far, regardless of medium," Mr. Holmes interjected silkily.

"I'll be 'anged if I don't mean just that!" she exclaimed. "But when you says it, it comes out all polished and primped, like . . . like ye were reading it right off a page, by jingo! Fess up now, Mr. 'Olmes—*did* ye make a note o' that phrasing, and trot it out to impress a poor, lowly under-housemaid? Or did it spring up natural, straight from yer brain?"

"I conjured it on the spur of the moment," my colleague admitted.

"Saints alive," she marvelled. "It's like summat out o' Shakespeare. Or a hadvertisement fer Lyle's Golden Syrup, even."

We brought Miss Millie Sparks up to date as quickly as possible. Which wasn't very fast, all told, and Mr. Holmes appeared too fascinated by her bubbling, blubbering candour to object. She gushed over his escapade the night previous and confirmed that when Miss Willie Sparks was low, she turned to books about romance and distant frontiers for succor. But Miss Millie Sparks knew nothing at all about any male correspondent, although she eagerly reported that in hindsight, her sister had occasionally seemed on the verge of confiding a secret of some kind.

"Figured it was summat about our dear departed mum, or maybe . . . maybe even that now we was reconciled, we ought to kip together someplace warm, far from London's stink. Brighton, maybe. Portsmouth? Hastings.

And now I'll never again know the sound o' me sweet Willie's voice." Her broad mouth wrenched almost as hard as she was twisting Mr. Holmes's handkerchief. "And who's to say what cause she had to take up with anyone from West Sussex? It's beyond my scope, gents, and that's the gospel truth. Were it an old flame? A scallywag, bent on me only kin's complete ruination? A mate o' some friend she made in the CCC? It's a sight too much fer *this* under-housemaid to puzzle out, and that's past remedy."

"Beg pardon—what is the CCC?" I questioned.

The CCC, Miss Milhemina Sparks explained, was a club her sister joined when she cut herself off from public life. It was an organization of respectable female letter writers of limited social scope. Unmarried, childless, often friendless, seldom well-situated. Upon filling out a brief personal application and providing some details regarding favourite hobbies, members of the CCC wrote to one another after being "matched" with like-minded women. The fee for this service was nominal, simply to reimburse the coordinator for the postage she spent. After the introduction, the women were free to converse as often or as sparsely as they liked.

"It sounds an admirable association." Mr. Holmes deposited the end of his cigarette in my ashtray with a neat twist. His face had regained some of its—well, I won't say colour, but he looked livelier anyhow. "How long had your sister been a member?"

"Oh, I couldn't tell ye, Mr. Holmes. Since her beau done dropped her and she lost her way. When I think o' Willie sufferin' without me . . ." Miss Millie Sparks glanced up, twin pools overflowing. "Clean breaks me 'eart I weren't there to give a bit o' comfort. I were only fifteen when Mum took ill, and . . . I liked to have a laugh with the lads down at the pub now and again, and then she passed, and I might ha' carried it all a wee bit far? A touch wild in me ways, ye understand, not meanin' any harm by it, but—"

"But you left home to become an under-housemaid and thereafter your opportunity to commune with your sister was regrettably truncated," Mr. Holmes supplied.

Blushing hotly, Miss Sparks nodded. "Yes, aye."

"We quite understand. Do you know how your sister came to learn of this club?"

"I sure enough do, fer 'twas the first thing I asked!" she affirmed triumphantly. "Mum always called me naturally curious. It were hadvertised in the *Ladies' Society Journal* agony columns."

"The *Ladies' Society Journal*—minor weekly publication, annual subscriptions holding steady at around five thousand, main consumers understimulated spinsters and bored housewives, focusing on light news, moral politics, original poetry, society gossip, and fashionable trends," Mr. Holmes rattled off. "I stopped perusing it two years ago when *The Queen Lady's Newspaper and Court Chronicle* proved to cast a wider net. I shall have to re-evaluate my position, it seems. Do you know what the CCC stands for, perchance, Miss Sparks?"

She blew her nose—fruitfully, it sounded—into Sherlock Holmes's handkerchief. "The leader, who's a most reticent lady, calls it the Common Correspondents' Club, and herself the chief Common Correspondent. Always struck me as pretty sounding. A touch daft, mind. But pretty. Could it help ye find me lost sister, and capture the snatchers what took her away?"

And there we have it. So much data and still not enough for me to write up an actual police report. Aggravating in the extreme. We asked whether our guest knew the names of any of her sister's letter-writing acquaintances. She replied tearfully and in the negative. Miss Sparks left soon after, curtseying to each of us when we took her hand. Mr. Holmes said something about needing to assist Dr. Watson regarding the price of the wedding ring, and a pawnbroker who owed the detective his life following a false murder charge. I was only half listening. I called to him that we each ought to pursue the case further along our own lines and meet the day after tomorrow at Baker Street to share our findings. He agreed.

One thing is certain: Sherlock Holmes is every bit as intrigued as I am about this matter of the Sparks sisters. Me, having lost a sibling, wanting her back. Miss Millie Sparks, having found a sister, not wanting to lose her twice. Mr. Holmes, about to lose a brother of sorts, wanting to return her sister to her.

Or maybe something about the tale of Miss Willie Sparks frightens me. To have her fortune and her heart spirited away by a blackguard, then to vanish with a near stranger. Where would she turn if she were in peril? To whom? Where would I, if I were her?

If I were her.

What an absurd and yet crucial thought that is. What if I'd been born a woman? I'd still live with Dad and Mum. Be raising Jonas. Unmarried, probably, and the clock ticking faster every day, until what used to be a waterwheel spun like a carriage spoke. What if Mr. Holmes, too, had arrived on Earth in a different skin? Of course, being women, our interests and talents would differ, I suppose. We'd not need to be as active. Might even appreciate peace and quiet. Still.

How would it feel, not to be allowed to set sail and make your own way in the world?

Entry in the diary of Inspector Geoffrey Lestrade, Saturday, January 12th, 1889:

I don't know what to say anymore.

I don't know how to write of it, or where to begin.

My half day began with ordering PC Zordan to the optometrist. He groused, poor fellow. When I handed him a late morning edition of the *Star* and asked him to read me the petty theft report, he sulked for a bit, and then shuffled off to comply. Lord knows why he's dragging his feet over it. The man is bald as a billiard cue, florid, nearly as short as I am, and with a voice like an asthmatic terrier. A pair of spectacles might lend the unfortunate creature some gravitas. They can't possibly *hurt* matters, anyhow.

When I arrived at the small but impeccably neat offices of the *Ladies' Society Journal*, I was greeted by a clerk with a damp, fussy manner and a waxed moustache. He introduced himself as Mr. Pemberry and enquired with nose wrinkling why a policeman should be interested in their publication.

"Oh, I am not, sir." Shrugging, I tapped my fingers on the countertop. "But a number of your writers must be female, yes? Arrive here in person to drop off their manuscripts, I imagine, and to collect their cheques? It's only that I've heard rumour of this street growing more dangerous. I'd hate to have to post a pair of constables at your front door. That might give the more sensitive ladies an unfair impression of the place . . ."

Teeth visible in his smile, Mr. Pemberry urged me to ask anything I might wish.

"You keep accurate records of your advertising revenue?" I began.

"Of course, Mr.—I do beg your pardon, *Inspector* Lestrade. Our books are quite pristine."

"I need to know everything you can tell me about the Common Correspondents Club."

"Everything?" His eyelashes fluttered.

"Unless you want PC MacGregor for a new entryway statue. The man's hairy as a bear and dead tired of walking rounds. Ready chap with a truncheon, too. I'm sure the womenfolk will feel much safer with him greeting them all—"

"Why don't you accompany me to my private office, Inspector?" Mr. Pemberry turned, radiating displeasure. "I'm sure that I have *nothing* better to do than to gossip with you about one of our most loyal clients."

When we'd reached a cramped, windowless box with a plain pine desk and every wall covered in filing cabinetry, Mr. Pemberry became marginally more agreeable. Either because he detested being put upon in front of the other staff, or because he wanted to be rid of me more expediently. Pulling a folder from a drawer, he invited me to peruse the documents.

"All related to the Common Correspondents Club—receipts monthly and annually, etc. Miss Mullinax is a *longtime* patron of the publication, Inspector. Our costs are not exorbitant by any means, but Miss Mullinax requires a weekly guarantee, prominent placement, and ample space, all of which we are happy to provide."

"And what can you tell me about this Miss Mullinax?"

The waxed ends of the appalling moustache quivered. "Miss Hope Mullinax, yes. She is a most *distinguished* woman, I assure you. On the occasions when she comes herself, we are always happy to see her, that fine profile held high, dressed all in grey. To tell the truth, Inspector, when we first viewed her in the flesh, we all imagined she must be a widow, for she is unmistakably a *very* handsome woman. But she never married, she says, and now in her later years takes what joy she can in brightening the monotony of other's lives."

"Very admirable. I take it that she advertises regarding her rather peculiar club, and you forward to her any replies, so as to keep her private address from being published in a weekly journal?"

"Precisely so, sir. Miss Mullinax is not in the business of running an agony column. Her preferences regarding clientele are stated quite clearly, as you may see for yourself."

He pulled a fresh edition from a pile of papers and opened it to an elegantly lettered page of personal columns.

~ THE COMMON CORRESPONDENTS' CLUB ~
FOR THE PRICE OF A SINGLE SHILLING TO DEFER COSTS, LADIES OF
RESPECTABLE CHARACTER AND IMPECCABLE BREEDING
WITH AN AFFINITY FOR LETTER WRITING
ARE INVITED TO SUBMIT THEIR APPLICATIONS TO BE
MATCHED WITH OTHER
DISCREET AND LIKE-MINDED INDIVIDUALS
SINGLE LADIES WITHOUT SURVIVING RELATIONS
STRONGLY PREFERRED
APPLY TO MISS HOPE MULLINAX, OUR CHIEF COMMON
CORRESPONDENT
LISTING INTERESTS, HOBBIES, AFFILIATIONS, AND DIVERTISSE-
MENTS, CARE OF THIS PUBLICATION.

It was, to put matters mildly, a head-scratcher.

"Well, if that's everything?" Mr. Pemberry made rather a spectacle of checking his pocket watch. "As you can see, it is a singularly edifying entertainment, and Miss Mullinax a benefactor of the friendless woman of educated background—"

"Just a moment." Tapping my pencil against my lips in thought, I produced my notebook. "I'll have the address of this Miss Mullinax, if you please."

"Really, sir!" Mr. Pemberry exclaimed. "Out of the question!"

"It's nothing of the kind. Hand it over."

"You go *very* far, sir!" he huffed, jotting a note and passing it to me disdainfully. "The entire point of her advertising through us is to maintain a modicum of privacy."

"How exactly does this arrangement work?" I pressed. "How popular would you say this club has become, and who passes the applications on to Miss Mullinax?"

Mr. Pemberry, with severely ill grace, explained that women who expressed an interest in the organization were then sent a questionnaire. Completed questionnaires were then collected—five to ten a month, at his estimation—and collected by Miss Mullinax at the *Ladies' Society Journal*, in person, every fortnight.

"That's what the nominal shilling fee goes towards, I take it?" I asked shrewdly. "You charge Miss Mullinax to advertise, and then on top on that, a processing fee?"

He spluttered, moustache quivering. "I am a man of business! I've every right—"

"Yes, yes, I'm sure you do. Tell me everything you can about Miss Hope Mullinax, at once."

Miss Mullinax was, as Mr. Pemberry described to me gushingly, a very prepossessing individual, with deep chestnut locks streaked with silver, and pale blue eyes. She was the picture of refinement—and to some extent, of hopes left to wither on the vine. She had ample means, but no family of any kind, and there was some rumour of a love lost when she was young and impressionable. A woman of deep sensitivity and chronic poor health, she had never passed out of half mourning. But one happy day, frustrated by her struggles whiling away the weary hours when too indisposed for social calls or charitable work, she realised that she could hardly be the only woman with a similar set of woes. She founded the Common Correspondents Club at once and took out an advertisement.

"Are you aware that a woman has gone missing?" I pressed when he fell stubbornly silent. "A woman who took part in the Common Correspondents Club?"

"Certainly not! And I don't know what you think you're implying. I've important connections within the press, Inspector Lestrade, and if you think you can bully me into admitting any impropriety whatsoever—"

"Her name is Miss Wilhemina Sparks. I've every reason to suspect that something unpleasant has become of her."

"It's none of my affair what you suspect, you impertinent little man! I've nothing to do with the wretched matter."

My heart pounded angrily against my ribs. "When you collect these applications for Miss Mullinax, where do you keep them?"

"What the devil can that have to do with anything?"

"They're placed in a strongbox or a safe of some kind, yes? I'm sure a chap of your thoroughness and professionalism wouldn't leave such sensitive materials lying about for anyone to rummage through? Belonging as they do to such an assailable group of women?"

Mr. Pemberry gaped at me like an upended beetle. Then he sat down. "I keep them in a stack, in that filing cabinet."

"It doesn't have a lock, does it?"

"No," he whispered, paling. "Why should our advertising records—"

I didn't wait for him to finish. I didn't even say goodbye. I snatched up the copy of the *Ladies' Society Journal* he'd shown me and hurtled out into the street shouting for a cab.

I don't recall how long it took me to get to Baker Street. The gaslights leered at me as they passed in a blur, fizzing and spitting. The driver encountered an upturned dray at the corner of Marylebone Road; I stumbled out, not heeding as he shrieked at me, my boots sloshing in the snow. If he wanted to call for a constable, I'd happily agree that I'd shirked the fare. I've arrived at that blasted doorstep more times that I can count, and I've never seen Mrs. Hudson's hand at her throat as I abused her doorbell, never ignored her startled remonstrations, never been gladdened at the strident whine of a violin.

When I crashed into their familiar sitting room, Mr. Holmes was lounging in a purple dressing gown on the settee while somehow bowing at his fiddle (though no one in his right mind could have mistaken it for music), and Dr. Watson was in the act of gripping their fireplace poker in alarm.

"Good heavens!" the doctor exclaimed. "Are you all right, Inspector?"

"I need you," I gasped to the detective.

To his credit, he was already on his feet, violin abandoned, rushing into his bedroom. Upon return, dressing gown shed, he was worming his way into his frock coat. "Speak of the devil! Watson will inform you that I sent you a wire mere seconds ago. I'm just these twenty minutes back from the National Gallery—there was an urgent little matter of an Anthony Van Dyck portrait that could not be put off, and—"

Slapping the *Ladies' Society Journal* into his lean chest, I tried to get my wind back. "The editor collects these applications on behalf of a Miss Hope Mullinax. He keeps them in an unlocked filing cabinet."

Mr. Holmes took all of four seconds to grasp the significance of the advertisement before his eyes flew to mine in alarm.

Dr. Watson had by now dropped the fire iron and stood with his hand on his friend's back, reading over his shoulder. "My dear fellow, is this the case you were telling me about over breakfast? Miss Sparks, was it, and her missing sister?"

"The listing is meant explicitly to connect ladies without family or friends of their own!" I cried, pacing. "This idiotic Mr. Pemberry kept all their information in a *box*, in a *drawer*. Any employee of the *Ladies' Society Journal* could have rifled through it, stolen a questionnaire, stolen half a dozen of them for God's sake, and then who knows what dark machinations could have followed? I don't even know how to begin to narrow such a thing down! One of the journalists? A clerk with a twisted mind? The cleaning staff, a guard, and even if he'd been pilfering these documents in secret for years, how am I to prove it?"

"You think that some ruffian has been forging letters to defenceless spinsters?" the doctor clarified.

"I have not a doubt of it!"

"Let's be off at once, then." Dr. Watson smoothed his hair back, donned his hat, and wrapped a muffler about his thick neck. "Holmes! Surely you can find some indication after we've questioned everyone with access to these files? There may even be some physical clue Lestrade failed to—I beg your pardon, Inspector, I never meant to insinuate—"

"No, no, I only pray there was something I missed! I hardly knew where to look at all. Are you coming back to the offices with me?" I demanded when Mr. Holmes remained motionless.

The detective pressed his lips into a line. He carefully folded the paper. The simplest way you can tell that Sherlock Holmes is deeply distressed about something is that he stops performing. You aren't an audience member any longer. He stops flicking sly looks, tossing his head, minute finger gestures he knows are eye-catching simply because they're so subtle. When something has upset him, you stop seeing Sherlock Holmes the genius. You can see Sherlock Holmes the person.

~~It's what I've wanted to glimpse for years. And it turns out to be terrifying. And I hate it.~~

Dr. Watson leaned with both hands against the back of their sofa. Saying nothing, but clearly having witnessed this before. I wondered what it would mean for Sherlock Holmes to lose a friend like that. And I concluded that nothing, not hell or fire or flood, would keep me away from the doctor's wedding.

"My dear Lestrade, we aren't going to the offices," Mr. Holmes said softly.

My heart was in my throat. "You think it's already too late?"

"I don't know." With a grim expression, he allowed Dr. Watson to pass him his overcoat. "I only wonder. I wonder why any woman, no matter how naïve or sheltered or well-intentioned, would create such a dangerous advertisement. I wonder why she might wish to disguise her own address, and to create such a careful system for the screening of applicants. I wonder at the fact we both noticed that Miss Wilhemina Sparks's love letters owned a distinctly romantic—not to say feminine—turn of phrase. I wonder why any such correspondent would purport to be a dairy farmer. Not the sort of life that an actual workingman would think to brag about, mind, the manure and the sweat and the callouses—but perhaps the sort of biography that would appeal to an avid reader of pastoral fiction. And I wonder very much, Lestrade, why I imagined that blockish handwriting implied a lack of education. I've been a great fool. You'd be well within your rights to toss me in a gaol cell as a warning to the arrogant."

"I don't understand," I pleaded. Though I was beginning to.

"Call us a cab, my dear fellow." Dr. Watson nodded, ducking down the stairs as Sherlock Holmes took me by the elbow. "Lestrade, we are going to ascertain the reason why Miss Hope Mullinax entered into a disguised exchange of love letters with Miss Wilhemina Sparks. Because I very much fear that it cannot possibly be for anyone's good."

Entry in the diary of Inspector Geoffrey Lestrade, Saturday, January 12th, 1889 (continued):

I must have drifted off before my fire. It's gone cold.

My eyes ache something terrible. Dr. Watson mixed me some sort of powder before I left, begging me to get some rest.

I don't know how I'll ever rest again.

Miss Hope Mullinax is every bit as elegant as Mr. Pemberry indicated. Noble jaw, porcelain skin. Streaks of grey in all that dark hair, shining like sheet metal. Like knives. And eggshell blue eyes with a fan of wrinkles at their edges. She stood there in the drawing room of that beautiful townhouse, lips quizzical, mystified at having been knocked up at such an hour. Sweet as an angel she looked, offering us drinks. Urging us to sit down. Wondering what she could do for us.

Mad as a hatter, of course. Stark, smiling mad.

Mr. Holmes did the talking. Asked her all about the Common Correspondents Club. How it came to be. He was gentle in that way he can affect, his voice all honey, no trace of a sting. He said that we had a friend, a maiden aunt. She was lonesome and desperate and had taken to laudanum.

Could Miss Mullinax offer any hope of a recovery? Of having something to look forward to in the post every week?

"I was orphaned when I was very young and raised by heaven knows how many relations." Miss Mullinax sipped the tea for which she'd rang. "They were quite cold, Mr. Holmes. Well-intentioned, lord knows, but I lacked for the affection that having a kindred spirit can provide. Or even a motherly figure to help guide my first steps into society. For a time, I took what comfort I could from travel, from various causes, but none of it ever touched me the way exchanging letters did. It was a bit like having a novel all my own—one which I could help shape, and affect, and guide even as I savoured the words. I could relate to people whose lives were quite different, feel that I shared in their adventures, tell them of mine, and all from many miles away. Sometimes sharing an adventure can be more thrilling than having one, don't you find?"

"I entirely understand." A shard of ice had slipped into his tone. "What I cannot conceive is what purpose it could possibly serve to prey on gullible women and convince them you were their suitor. Were you always playing the role of paramour, or did you expand your repertoire? Invalid grandmother, perhaps? Exotic heiress? Long-lost uncle?"

Her jaw spasmed. A hint of stone in the soft exterior. Something that had hardened a very long time ago.

Then she shrugged. "I don't have the slightest idea what you're talking about, Mr. Holmes. But now you have been sitting with me for a little while, I believe I recognise you. You're some sort of would-be sleuth for hire, is that it? I imagine that my Common Correspondents Club is peculiar enough to sound strange to a self-made man of the world. But I have certainly never preyed on anyone, nor has anyone accused me of such an outrageous thing."

"Yes, you made certain of that," I growled. "Hence the outrageous selection process—only the isolated, you made sure of that, probably rejected dozens of applicants, and Miss Wilhemina Sparks would have been just another jilted woman, except she had an estranged sister, and that sister returned. What in hell have you done with Miss Willie Sparks, Miss Mullinax?"

She laughed—a pretty peal of a sound.

"Don't be ridiculous, Inspector. I haven't done a thing with her. Willie was a sweet enough diversion at first, but let's just say that the game escalated too quickly for my liking. Constant demands to meet in person, increasingly lurid prose. I couldn't possibly have let it continue, could I? She went to meet . . . oh yes, Richard Boxall was the name, and he lived in a village called Lynchmere, I believe. Dear Willie ought to be back any day now. It isn't as if there's anyone waiting for her. She'll forget all about him, and her sister will be greatly relieved, and I can't imagine how you could prove any of it."

Seconds passed in silence.

"Then allow me to enlighten you. Handwriting analysis," Mr. Holmes ticked off on his fingers, seething. "Paper type, ink chemistry, pen nib, postal forwarding to disguise your actual London address, the offices and employees of the *Ladies' Society Journal*—that's just to begin with, before I set my mind to it."

"Perhaps." Miss Mullinax stood gracefully. "But why bother? Anyway, what is there to prove? I wrote a lonely woman letters. Her life was really brightened considerably thanks to me, if you stop to consider. No crime has been committed, no money exchanged, either mine or theirs. Only words. It was at worst a few harmless pranks, and at best a service to my sisters in solitude."

It's not that I've never heard of such a thing. Cads inventing tales of land and titles to ensnare rich heiresses, all the brutal possibilities Mr. Holmes railed about when he barged into my office with that ridiculous little book about marriage.

But for *no* reason? Other than amusement?

"That's the cruelest thing I've ever heard, Miss Mullinax," Dr. Watson bit out. His hand gripped his knee fiercely.

"No," Miss Mullinax corrected him, "the cruelest thing you've ever heard is that I once had a beau, when I was young. I turned down six separate offers of marriage while waiting for him to start a life for us in Philadelphia. Years passed. Hundreds of letters. Eventually his sister wired me to say she had found all my heartfelt missives in a drawer, and she thought I deserved to know that his young wife was pregnant with their second child. Goodnight, gentlemen. I trust you can find your own way out."

Supposing I live long enough, maybe I can manage to forget the look in her eyes when she said those words. Or the stricken expression on Dr. Watson's face when he heard them.

One thing, in all this mess, is for certain.

This is the sort of case that could only ever have involved Sherlock bloody Holmes.

Entry in the diary of Inspector Geoffrey Lestrade, Sunday, January 13th, 1889:

Passed my day of rest with Jonas and Mum and Dad. Lamb stew with carrots and turnips and a good bottle of burgundy. Jonas seems happier the longer it gets from January 6th, and I imagine I'll soon feel the same way about this wretched case. Mr. Holmes said he'd "arrange everything" with the Sparks sisters right before he and the doctor shared a cab back to Baker Street. No idea what that could possibly mean, but Miss Mullinax had a point: I don't know what in hell I'd arrest her for. And Mr. Holmes wired me to say Miss Willie Sparks and Miss Millie Sparks were enjoying a tearful reunion while I was busy abusing Mr. Pemberry and tearing around London.

I'm through with writing. For the moment. What I need is rest, and quiet. There will be more cases tomorrow. ~~Maybe even ones with better solutions.~~

~~Who can say? But I very much doubt it.~~

Entry in the diary of Inspector Geoffrey Lestrade, Monday, January 14th, 1889:

My life as I've counted on it for these long years is through.

I thought I knew when determination was what was needed of me. Persistence, some courage, enough sheer grit to stick it out.

I also thought I knew when things were hopeless. Could be laid in the ground at last, left to decompose and then slowly heal over.

I thought I knew the limits of what Sherlock bloody Holmes is capable of.

One thing about Sherlock Holmes, though: you'll never get his limits.

I suppose I'm just going to have to learn to appreciate that about him.

This morning, I was bone-weary enough not to expect anyone barging into my office. Foolish, in retrospect. Altogether amateurish. I didn't bother tidying up the last orange peel from the holiday basket my parents gave me, loosened my shirt collar when I sat down to work, opened a case file I wanted another look at and didn't bother to put it away when I was done. Or to rewrite it all out clean because I'd splashed coffee on the corner.

"Good morning, Lestrade!" Sherlock Holmes exclaimed when he barged into my sanctum. "Ah, I see you've been savouring the last remaining bounties of Christmas cheer—you'll have to tell me sometime where your mother locates such fine specimens of *Citrus sinensis*, as Dr. Watson is likewise partial. One can atone for nearly any sin with that fellow provided one makes a friend of the greengrocer. Dear me! Please don't tell me we need to bother over the Lake Mayne matter again. Athelney Jones is very seldom right about anything, but when it involves monied aristocracy attempting to tip the scales of justice at the Assizes, particularly in the Chester Circuit, I cannot help but chime in my hearty agreement. Shall I ring for more coffee? You appear rather in need of it."

"Get out." My face was buried in my palms.

Sitting down, Mr. Holmes fussed with a cuff link. "My dear Lestrade, you appear to be somewhat under the weather."

Opening my hands, I spread them. "I am begging you. No oranges. No reading paperwork upside-down. No noting coffee splashes. No deductions. This is me, pleading, humbling myself before the superior detective. I'll say anything you like. I'll *do* anything you like. Please for God's sake just—"

"I thought you might like to know that Verle Cullen, your late sister's husband, is currently in police custody and will shortly be awaiting trial."

I stared at him.

And stared.

"Lestrade, do please take a breath, there's a good fellow." Mr. Holmes looked almost sheepish.

Then he poured me more coffee, and thought better of it and poured me a large brandy, then thought better of that and threw open the window, slapping me twice on the back for good measure.

"All right, all right!" I choked. "What have you . . . how . . ."

I trailed off, staring up at the gangly chap in dumbfoundment.

He shut the window. Shoving his hands in his pockets as if he didn't know what to do with them, Mr. Holmes returned to his side of the desk. "Are you sure you're all right? I've shocked you, and following a difficult case to boot, and if you need another moment—"

"*Mr. Holmes!*"

He coughed, nodded, and levered himself back into the chair.

"Well, you see, there was never anything remarkable about it. I quite trust your judgement in professional matters, as you know, and your word was enough to convince me that Mr. Cullen was a blight on the face of London. You told me that he worked in tea import speculation, so there was my starting point. Obviously, if a man of your passion and commitment to seeing the arson case through couldn't find sufficient evidence to lead to a conviction, then some ten years later, what could I possibly unearth? However, when one is dealing with a brute polluted with his lusts, stain'd with the guiltless blood of innocents, corrupt and tainted with a thousand vices—"

"Enough of Henry the Sixth, please!" I cried.

"Quite." Mr. Holmes's cheeks dusted with actual colour. It was the most impossible thing I've ever seen him do. "Yes, what I meant to say was that most men who abuse women in such fashion are unrepentant blackguards. I've friends in high places, key government positions, and I did a little digging. Verle Cullen, in addition to murder and arson, is guilty of gross embezzlement and securities fraud. Surely this is the *least* surprising thing about the wretch. So you see it was all absurdly simple. I weighed the balance of probability, deduced that he had continued his life of crime, and exposed him. I imagine you should have preferred to witness his murder trial, but . . . I can see to it that he never leaves off breaking rocks in Australia, if you like."

Mr. Holmes gave me an unreadable expression, biting his lower lip.

There was never any choice apart from diving out from behind my desk and pumping his hand so hard, I think I must have bruised the absurd creature. His eyes flew open in shock.

"I don't know what to say to this. I never expected, I never . . . bless you! God bless you, Sherlock bloody Holmes. Thank you. I can never repay you for such a gift."

"Dear God!" He was physically backing away in apparent terror as my tears began to fall, extricating himself from my frenzied grip. "It was nothing, it was—"

"It was the maddest, kindest thing I've ever heard."

The detective practically threw his handkerchief at me. "Lestrade, please calm yourself!"

"I'll do no such thing!"

"Sit down this instant. Get a grip on yourself, man! It was only a matter of—"

"You are incredible." Laughing hysterically, I wiped the tears streaming down my cheeks. "A wonder, you are. The eighth wonder of the bloody—"

"Look at the time!" Sherlock Holmes exclaimed, genuinely panicked. He hadn't even bothered to glance at his pocket watch, the absurd creature. "I'm ah, most inexcusably late! You are most heartily welcome, and—no, no, please keep the handkerchief, and—I've some business with Bradstreet that won't keep, and the Sparks sisters are quite well and sharing new rooms, and Miss Hope Mullinax is presently the subject of a *very* large cautionary advertisement I myself took out in the *Ladies' Society Journal*, so I will bid you good morning, and I assure you that we need never discuss the, ah, the other matter ever again, as between friends. Farewell!"

With that, he fled the premises. My friend, Mr. Sherlock bloody Holmes of Baker Street, to whom I now owe a debt of honour that can never be repaid.

Tonight, as soon as I've finished recording this miracle in my journal, I'll pay a call on my parents and Jonas. I've picked up champagne. And more oranges. And I've already stopped by Hannah's grave.

It isn't enough. It can never be what she truly deserved. But it's a bit of justice done. And I can live my life for that—the work. The work has to be enough. Even if it's never truly finished.

And now at the very least, I know exactly how to send Sherlock Holmes flying hell for leather out of my office.

THE RIVER OF SILENCE

(Stanley Hopkins)

Letter sent from Inspector Stanley Michael Hopkins to Mrs. Leticia Elizabeth Hopkins, Saturday, April 28th, 1894:

Dearest Mum,

Thank you for the new scarf and fingerless gloves—you're dead right to suppose a promotion calls for a fellow to look smart, and right to consider that I should have my hands free to boot. You worried over the colour, but it's just the ticket. A nice, dignified navy will do very well with my brown ulster.

How strange and freeing it is to be out of blue livery and stalking the shadowed streets in neat tweeds! The lads from H Division ribbed my plainclothes at first, saying I looked a smug breed of pigeon, but there was no malice in it and they toasted me plentiful times calling out, "Three cheers for our own Inspector Hopkins!" down at the Bull's Head last week. (I didn't myself join in enough to mar the solemnity of my new station, I promise you.)

My musty cubby at the Yard is well outfitted now, with maps and reference volumes, plentiful ink and paper, and a flask of brandy should any females be forced to consult me in a state of distress—you understand I'd never hope for such a thing, but we live in a dark city, and I mean to shed some light on it. My resolve has impossibly redoubled since the news came down I was to shed my uniform, and when I've already thought of nothing else for just over five years now.

Enough dark reflections. Probably you've read of this, but Sherlock Holmes himself has returned as if by miracle from the dead and is to practice independently again in London. What a weird and wonderful world! Before I'd any inkling of joining the Yard, I admired his brilliant methods ("idolised" Dad used to tease, remember?) and now to make inspector during the very week of his triumphant return from the depths . . . what an absolute corker. I can't but think it providential, Mum, truly.

On that note—dare I surmise that the gloves and muffler suggest you're at peace with my occupation, and your disappointment over my not becoming a clergyman, as Dad was, have faded?

Trusting I interpret your kindly gifts aright, as I'm now to become a professional at reading the subtlest clues, I remain,

Your Stanley

Letter sent from Inspector Stanley Michael Hopkins to Mrs. Leticia Elizabeth Hopkins, Tuesday, May 1st, 1894:

Dearest Mum,

I'm sorry for thinking the muffler and gloves suggested you had come round to the notion of my being a policeman. Rest assured that I'll prove you needn't simply make the best of a bad business and can instead feel as proud as you would if I were delivering sermons (a task at which I've many times told you I'd be dismal). Remember all the occasions when Sherlock Holmes's exploits led to God's justice being served?

Thank you for the dried sausages—they arrived quite safe, and I wrapped them against mice just as you said. Must beg pardon for brevity, as a strange teak box was just dredged from the Thames with something terrible in it. The other inspectors seem not to want to touch the business—dare I hope that I might have the chance to test my mettle, and so soon?

In haste,

Your Stanley

Telegram from GREAT SCOTLAND YARD, WHITEHALL to BEXLEY Tuesday, May 1st, 1894:

CONTENTS OF TEAK BOX MOST DISTRESSING **STOP** THANKFULLY CASE ASSIGNED TO ME **STOP** WILL FULLY APPRISE YOU AS SOON AS POSSIBLE **STOP** DUTY CALLS **STOP** YES I WILL BE CAREFUL—STANLEY

Entry in the diary of Stanley Michael Hopkins, Tuesday, May 1st, 1894:

Too much has happened to set it on paper—but I must put my thoughts in proper order, no matter if I'm grasping at snowflakes only to watch them dissolve. Here at Great Scotland Yard I feel as if I'm starting my career afresh, and in a sense I am, and a warm glow lodges at the base of my spine whenever I'm reminded of my new responsibilities. But lord, it would be something fine to have one of my trusty H Division boys to natter with. Here the inspectors call out obscure jokes to one another I can't begin to savvy, and their eyes slide off the newly promoted when we pass in the crowded corridors. I don't blame them. They're overworked, and soon so shall I be. Headquarters smells of wearied sighs tinged with whiskey, shirt collars too long worn over interrogations and filling out of forms.

And I've no one to consult with over this confounded box.

But I mustn't pity myself, for that isn't quite true—Inspector Lestrade visited me in one of the evidence lockers as I went through the contents and, though I know him to have been ensuring that a raw detective wouldn't botch the matter, I was thoroughly grateful.

I realise that this is only a diary entry. But I wonder if, supposing I incorporate dialogue into my accounts, I can make them sound even the slightest bit like the *Strand Magazine*? Ha, what a fanciful notion. But it's not as if anyone reads my personal journals or likely ever will. It would only be for my own amusement and no one the wiser. I shall take a crack at it, by Jove!

"All right, Inspector . . . Hopkins, I think it was." Lestrade said in greeting. "What have you got yourself into on your first day that has everyone buzzing like an upturned hive?"

Sweeping off his bowler, Inspector Lestrade frowned at me. I think he frowns to impart his words with weight rather than signal displeasure, though, and he needs all the gravitas he can muster. The little fellow can't weigh more than eleven stone. He has brown hair and eyes, both several shades darker than mine, and I tried not to seem to be looking down at him even though I couldn't help it—hardly anyone could.

Clearing my throat nervously, I began to answer.

"But you're already through writing it up, I see. Just pass that over and I'll check your form is correct."

I obeyed. Lestrade stood in full view of the peculiar—not to say ghastly—contents of the box, both objects resting upon the thick plank table, but he'd every right to supervise my paperwork on my first go of it. The other sight seemed not to disturb him, as indeed it couldn't by this time shake me either.

A grunt emerged as my senior inspector scanned my handwriting, reading:

Item: one large carved box
 —teak wood (foreign origin)
 —decorated with stylised lotus flowers (suggests Chinese import)

Contents: one severed forearm with hand, human, female
 —white flesh, decomposition not yet set in (recently amputated, not an outdoor worker)

—mild swelling and discolouration (indicating submersion in river water for not more than five hours)
—clean nail beds (respectable, not a labourer)
—nails thin and cracked (poor health or nutrition)
—no sign of ever having worn a ring (unmarried)

Lestrade raised his eyebrows, seemed about to speak, and frowned instead.

"Something wrong, sir?"

"On the contrary. Not bad for a greenhand." He returned my report. Lestrade has a very fastidious, almost affected way of speaking that I actually find quite soothing. I suspect it may be another way of making up for his size. "Don't forget to sign and date everything. And I can tell you that although the brass latch is equipped with a lock, it wasn't used—merely fastened. I opened it myself without a key."

Hastily, I bent to record this fact.

Lestrade rubbed at one temple fretfully. The arm looked much more poignant adrift on the sea of the large table than it had cradled in the ornate box. "You came to us from H Division, I hear."

"I did."

"Well, we don't want any repeats of that business."

"No, sir." If it sounded like a vow and not a mere reply, there was nothing to be done.

"So this must be solved as quickly as possible. What are your plans?" He tapped his foot awaiting my answer.

Straightening, I rubbed my palms together. "Obviously, first we must ensure it's not some wretchedly coarse jest, and I've already dispatched wires to all major hospitals asking after autopsies during the last twenty-four hours. I'll circulate word for dockside police to look out for any similar objects, God forbid. Next I'll canvass businesses that import Chinese goods, particularly small furnishings such as this box, down Stepney way. If that fails, I'll scour both Yard files and the papers for missing persons, as well as for recently executed females at Newgate to see whether she might have been the victim of a grave robbery. That ought to hold me for a day or two."

Lestrade's bright brown eyes narrowed suddenly in comprehension.

"How old were you when you joined the Yard, Hopkins?"

"Twenty-five. I'm only thirty now, sir."

"Eighteen eighty-nine, then. You read the *Strand Magazine*, don't you?" He crossed his arms, tapping a brusque finger against his sleeve.

"I, that is . . . yes," I stammered.

"Can't be helped, I suppose."

"No, sir."

"Inspired you, I shouldn't wonder, or some such rubbish."

"I confess so. This matter at hand . . . you mentioned H Division yourself, inspector, and spoke of not wanting another catastrophe. Bearing in mind the severed limb, I . . . I wonder whether Mr. Holmes would be interested?"

A bona fide snort quashed my fondest hope. "Mr. Holmes goes in for the grotesque, not the gruesome."

"That doesn't surprise me, considering the stories. They're marvellous. I've read every single one." I was an upturned pitcher with no notion how to shut the flow of words off. "Is he just as Dr. Watson says he is? Impossibly tall, impossibly brilliant, all of it?"

"Impossibly irritating? Yes. Everything about Sherlock bloody Holmes is impossible," Lestrade huffed.

"You arrested Colonel Moran, you must have seen him again—so the roundsmen are gossiping. Is he much changed? I mean—not that you didn't solve Adair's murder yourself, Inspector, I only—"

Lestrade made a motion as if shooing a gnat. "It's all true. He's alive, he collared the colonel, he's even more impossible than previous, and he'll be back to his mad antics, I shouldn't wonder, with me left to tidy up the shrapnel."

"You must be so pleased he's miraculously safe home."

I blurted this knowing it was true, not only from the fact they'd worked extensively together but from the half-rueful, half-wistful smile hovering over Lestrade's features. They warped in surprise, but then he shrugged.

"Of course I am. He's good for the city, and it's the city I serve. And I missed being driven half out of my wits on a regular basis. Well, I must be—"

"Dashed if I can think of anything on earth I want more than the chance to work with him."

"Take that back," Lestrade advised with a sour grimace, returning his hat to his head.

"Why?"

"Because working with Mr. Holmes means *you* failed." A shadow from the open door sliced across his face.

And then he was gone, and I alone again, wondering how a mere mortal could trace a box with a poor and (presumably) dead girl's limb in it. I've every confidence of filling my hours meaningfully upon the morrow, and yet . . . it is difficult to be optimistic.

Everything is difficult, under the circumstances. Lilla's letters are still in the drawer of my night table. Every day I try to move them to my battered trunk of keepsakes, and every day I fail, and check the post with fingers crossed and heart equally as twisted, the same weird curling feeling inside as I sort through mail never finding her name as I'd used to, and always hoping against sense a new missive may appear.

One must dwell upon the positive, however. What fun it was to set down our conversation in addition to the events themselves! I flatter myself I didn't do too bad a job of it either. I shall endeavour in these pages to become the next Dr. John H. Watson, man of action and man of letters. It can hurt no one and cheered my spirits immeasurably.

Letter sent from Inspector Stanley Michael Hopkins to Mrs. Leticia Elizabeth Hopkins, Thursday, May 3rd, 1894:

Dearest Mum,

No amount of cajoling will budge me—it's impossible for me to pen you details of an open investigation. For open it still is, and I'm nigh ready to start up banging my pate against my desk. The trail grows colder every instant whilst I tilt at windmill after windmill. When I solve the case, for I will solve it yet, you can scold me for bragging. Meanwhile, my nose must be to the grindstone and not hovering over correspondence, and I hope you'll forgive me.

I'd not thought of the question before you asked, but under these glad circumstances, I'll be dashed if there aren't more *Strand* stories to come, now you mention it! How could Dr. Watson resist? I certainly could not. The mince pie you mailed arrived only the slightest bit crushed, and I'm leaving it in my desk to have with my tea.

Still in haste,

Your Stanley

Entry in the diary of Stanley Michael Hopkins, Friday, May 4th, 1894:

And now I know what Inspector Lestrade meant by warning me against working with Mr. Sherlock Holmes. Today was simultaneously the best day of my life since 1889, and the worst to boot. If someone asked after the whereabouts of the sky, I'd hardly know which way to point.

No warning was given for his appearance. I don't suppose there ever is—do God's angels send cards announcing their arrival, or do they simply appear, frightening shepherds (to say nothing of sheep) out of their wits? One moment I was writing up futile reports at my desk—*no indication of desecrated graves, no missing persons providing leads, no similar Chinese boxes sold in Stepney discovered*, etc.—and the next moment I heard Lestrade say, "Oh, what luck he's right where he's wanted. Mr. Sherlock Holmes and Dr. John Watson, meet our newest detective, Inspector Stanley Hopkins."

Whirling in my chair, I fished for words and caught none. Maybe I shall find them in these pages, for I am going to continue this delightful attempt at recording dialogue. It's just possible, it has occurred to me, that the practice I am getting at setting down spoken conversation will even hone my skill at questioning witnesses! Wouldn't that be a lucky coincidence!

Sherlock Holmes is both identical to and nothing like the man in the magazine. Every physical characteristic is correct (frightfully tall, sinewy, and so forth), but his bearing and movements defy description. The vast intellect in his grey eyes is hooded behind affected languor, like a sheathed sword, and dying must take its toll on a fellow, for plentiful cats' whisker lines fanned from their edges I did not expect to find. And there I was, first week as a proper detective and my first case at that, already a failure, goggling at him as if he were the risen Christ. (Wouldn't Mum and dear departed Dad pitch a fit if they ever read *that* comparison.)

Dr. Watson (a handsome, sturdy gentleman with a soldierly bearing and moustache) thrust his hand out after I'd sufficiently embarrassed myself. The act galvanised me and I sprang to my feet. The doctor had pulled a drowning man back onto the deck of the boat. But then, he always comes across as truly kind spirited on the page.

"An honour, Dr. Watson, an absolute honour."

"Likewise," he affirmed warmly. "Congratulations on your promotion."

"I've followed your biographies very closely indeed. You might even say I've made, well, something of a study of them. And the celebrated Mr. Sherlock Holmes—your international reputation now extends to the underworld itself, I take it. I hardly know what to say. What does a chap say when Orpheus is standing in his office? I, that is . . . hang it. The world is thankful for your safe return. Welcome back to London, sir."

Lestrade half-turned to cover a sneeze I suspected was not a sneeze at all. Dr. Watson merely smiled and rocked onto his heels and back again, tilting his head to see what reply his friend would make. Mr. Holmes examined my hand for an instant too long before gripping it.

"France is hardly Hades," he demurred—but I know the look of a man who has seen prolonged hardship and danger, and it was the look he wore. Come to that, the doctor likewise appeared a touch left of center, eyes continually darting at his friend as if to ensure he was really there. "Inspector Hopkins, I believe you've something unpleasant to show me."

"Growing more unpleasant every hour. But Lestrade, I thought—"

"Another limb washed up this morning. A leg," he interjected tersely. "Left one, to be specific, decayed about as much as you'd expect it if was set adrift with the arm. I mentioned the last box wasn't locked—seems there may have been another, and it popped open."

"What the devil!" I cried in dismay. "I must see it, I must—"

"So you shall, Hopkins, but Mr. Holmes here already has, and it's more urgent that he have all the facts in his hands. He did more than his part during the dark times, much more I ought to say, and agreed to come down when I wired. Follow me, gentlemen."

Swallowing my shock, I nodded as they turned away. I knew this already, knew everything about his involvement that could be gleaned from the gutter press, though I also knew better than to trust so much as a word written by a yellow journalist. But the H Division lads had confirmed Mr. Holmes was in the thick of it when I joined their ranks, would mutter *'twas its own special hell and not another word I'll speak on the subject.* After snatching up my paperwork, I hurried after the trio.

Mr. Holmes visited the arm, which had been preserved as best we could in glycerin, but pronounced there was little to see, glancing at Dr. Watson to determine whether his medical companion agreed. Then we strode in his long-legged wake towards the evidence lockers and I located the box, watching as the great detective circled the table like a panther. Suddenly he froze. Somehow his stillness appeared more electric than his motion.

"I'd hardly any hope of being able to assist when you wired me so unforgivably late, inspector," he admitted, glancing up at Lestrade. "Happily, I was guilty of rash pessimism. Your box, Hopkins, will be of immense help to us."

This surprised Lestrade, and Dr. Watson likewise blinked. Staggered as I was, my pleasure took precedence. "I'm glad you think so, sir. Here is my initial report."

Mr. Holmes took the paper with a bored air, but his eyes flicked back to the page almost instantly. A faint dusting of colour had appeared on his wan face. When through, he passed the page to Dr. Watson and quirked a brow at Lestrade.

"Hopkins here reads the *Strand*, you see," Lestrade pronounced with an air of martyrdom.

"Good heavens! He certainly does," Dr. Watson exclaimed.

"And provided me with clues I should have lost otherwise due to the arm's inevitable decay." Mr. Holmes's tenor remained clipped, but an icicle twinkle appeared in his eyes.

"Did I really?" I cried, overjoyed. "Which ones, sir? Do please tell me."

The consulting detective's eyebrows went akimbo, I think with amusement, but I was past caring.

"It's all to do with the nails. You set down that the nail beds were clean underneath, but the nails were weak and cracked, which I am no longer able to tell with them sitting in glycerine for so long. Anyone's would have begun to deteriorate. Malnutrition is the probable cause, I quite agree, but the malnourished seldom refrain from work, in my experience, preferring food to idleness. Therefore we are looking at skilled labour of the indoor variety, most probably some type of artisan or craftsperson. Sadly, the list of possibilities is endless. But it does *eliminate* anyone performing manual tasks which involve grime on the hands."

"Fantastic!" I exclaimed. "I'm so glad I could prove useful!"

Mr. Holmes huffed a breath when the doctor glanced at him in undisguised glee.

"It's going to be utterly intolerable around here from now on," Lestrade sighed. "I'm requesting a transfer to Wales."

"Best pack earmuffs, in that case," Dr. Watson suggested, biting his lower lip valiantly.

This elicited a soundless laugh from Sherlock Holmes. "Come, Lestrade, you needn't despair. He's missed absolutely everything to do with the box. So have you, but we can hardly be shocked over that occurrence."

Lestrade ignored this jab. "By Jove, splendid! You've really found something?"

"What have I missed?" I protested. "The teak wood and lotus flowers strongly suggest foreign origin, likely Chinese I thought, Lestrade informed me that the lock was not used, the hinges are quite normal, and . . . and I don't see anything else."

"Wrong again, I'm afraid. You do not *observe* anything else." Mr. Holmes flipped the box onto its side with long fingers. They are uncannily agile and mottled with old burn scars. "What is this?" he asked, pointing.

"A chip in a lotus petal, sir." Mentally cuffing myself, I moved to examine it.

"Why should that have happened, I wonder?"

"The box must have been subjected to violence in the Thames. A boat or a piece of lumber struck it."

"That may well be true, but it is not remotely what I meant."

"What did you mean?" I questioned, mesmerised.

"What do you conjecture I meant?"

"I can think of no other answer."

"If you give up so quickly on your first case, I shudder to think what will daunt you six months from now. Astrological impediments? The state of Parliament, perhaps?" When I flinched, he continued in the same ironical tone, "What do you know about teak wood?"

"Very little," I admitted, my face heating.

"Teak has an average weight of forty-one pounds per square cube, rendering it extremely hard, and thus resistant to stress and age. It also contains a high level of silica, which often causes instruments used on it to lose their sharpness. A direct blow to this box while in the river could cause this chip, but not without cracking considerably more of the body. Thankfully, this is not *Tectona grandis*, however. This is *Alnus glutinosa*, which is remarkably helpful and ought to narrow our search considerably."

"Beg pardon, Mr. Holmes?"

"Dear me, I've considered writing a monograph regarding the fifty or so commonest woods hereabouts, and I see I've been sorely remiss in delaying the project."

His air of self-recrimination was just melodramatic enough to indicate that he was teasing me. I didn't know whether to be mortified or honoured. It was a very confusing feeling. I'm still confused over it, in fact.

"Inspector Hopkins, this is European alder, indigenous to our fair isle and might I add a fairly soft wood," Mr. Holmes expounded, gesturing delicately. "Observe the scratches covering the surface—this vessel was knocked about by flotsam, but as you noted, Hopkins, the limb was not waterlogged enough to have been very long in the Thames, and teak could never have suffered such myriad injuries in so short a period. It would simply have cracked apart, whereas these are indentations. It is stained in the expected dark reddish manner, and there its resemblance to the Chinese product ends. This is a sham," he concluded, pressing a small pocketknife into the wood. A faint but clear mark resulted.

"Thank god. You think it a hoax made by some perverse anatomist?" Dr. Watson ventured. "Meant to look like a depraved murderer is afoot?"

"You misunderstand me, my dear fellow. Deteriorated as the limbs we just viewed were, the cuts severing them were never made with any medical precision—you must have determined as much yourself."

"Certainly. I would hazard our suspect used either a small axe or a large hatchet in both cases."

"I concur. An anatomist would have done a better job of it." Mr. Holmes had produced a notebook and pencil and made short work of recording something. "No, the arm is quite as real as the leg. They are from the same body, by the way. The proportions as well as the physical similarities between the toes and the phalanges assure us of that."

"Yes, I thought so as well."

"Of course you did, Watson, I never doubted it. The conveyance is the sham, and we must be grateful for its abnormality."

"Hacked-apart remains ought to be abnormal enough," Lestrade muttered.

"Would that were true, but this serves our purposes better." Sherlock Holmes's eyes glinted with enthusiasm despite our sobering mission. "What sort of person would create a false Chinese box?"

I couldn't answer. None of us could. But when Mr. Holmes spun on his heel and glided through the door, we understood that we were about to find out.

As it happened, the sort of man who would create a false Chinese box was a skilled wood carver who lacked access to the high-quality lumber of his homeland and yet wished to ply his trade, or so Mr. Holmes deduced most convincingly as we four hastened from the slate monochrome of Great Scotland Yard into the colour and chaos of London's busiest thoroughfares. I'd been sniffing about the wrong neighbourhood, though I was as close to the mark as was possible without having the faintest notion of what I sought, the sleuth claimed (this seemed to be meant as neither censure nor condolence). I apparently didn't want the gritty straw-strewn byways of Stepney, with its deafening markets and echoing warehouses and mountains of imports.

"You wanted Limehouse, my good Inspector," Mr. Holmes finished, clapping me on the shoulder as he stepped down last from the four-wheeler. "The single neighbourhood hereabouts where Chinese culture thrives in corporeal rather than merely imported form."

Air thick as soup filled our nostrils, the tarry odour of the docks combined with roasting meats, simmering vegetables, and unfathomable spices. Beneath all skulked the reek of strangely foreign refuse—for whatever they were discarding, it wasn't potato peels and apple cores. Chinese pedestrians with glossy queues teemed along the sidewalks, and intermingling with them loitered grizzled career seamen and leather-skinned stevedores making deliveries. Lestrade flipped up his coat collar against the chill breeze.

"Are we to communicate what we're looking for through pantomime, or spend a few minutes learning Mandarin?" he asked dourly.

Mr. Holmes smirked, flipping open his notebook to reveal three Chinese characters. "I rather think the signature of the maker might be of greater immediate use."

"Capital, my dear fellow," Dr. Watson approved, grinning.

"How the devil did you find that out?" I cried.

"It was a positive tour de force of inferential reasoning," Mr. Holmes drawled. "When I flipped the box over, I discovered the mark had been scratched very subtly into the base."

Dr. Watson had the decency to study a stray cur worrying at an oxtail as my face flamed, but Lestrade gave a low whistle.

"Oh, come, none of that." Embarrased as I felt, I was grateful that Sherlock Holmes sounded impatient rather than pitying. "*Ut desint vires, tamen est laudanda voluntas.* You mistook the characters for more ill-use visited by the Thames—resolve to do better during your second case or I shall despair. Now. I'm acquainted with one or two nearby apothecaries in this warren, and I'd wager a fiver my friend Wi Cheun will do right by us. Do wait here, for the poor fellow suffers from a tremendous sensitivity to strange Englishmen."

"I really don't see why he tolerates you, in that case," Lestrade quipped.

"Do you know, I don't either," Mr. Holmes agreed cheerfully. "Some mysteries were never destined to be solved."

We watched his gleaming black hat bob away in the throng of men fully a foot shorter than he. Or I did, while Lestrade and Dr. Watson complacently lit cigarettes under a mud-spattered gaslight, as if they had waited for Sherlock Holmes to consult Chinese apothecaries some dozens of times. Which they probably had. Decades seemed to pass. I'll be dashed if glaciers didn't dissolve.

"I feel such a fool," I confessed as my cheeks faded to their normal colour.

"That was nothing," Lestrade scoffed. "Wait till you really bungle something. He'll verbally roast you on a spit."

"It wasn't nothing! My father was a clergyman—I do have some Latin, enough for Ovid anyhow."

"What did he say, then?" Lestrade asked idly.

"Roughly, 'the spirit is willing, but the flesh is weak.'" Dr. Watson supplied.

"Aha. So our young Hopkins here had the intention of finding a Chinese maker's mark, but not the skill."

"Precisely so."

"Pretty tame for him, Hopkins, I warn you."

"I suppose it's too much to hope he'll forget about it?" I asked with what must have been outrageous optimism.

The men continued smoking. I forced my jaw not to clench in dismay.

"Never mind, Inspector Hopkins," Dr. Watson offered along with a genuine smile. "If everyone were Sherlock Holmes—"

Lestrade mock shuddered, and the doctor chuckled gamely.

"I say, if everyone were Sherlock Holmes—"

"Then my career would be ruined," the man himself finished, vibrating with energy as he materialised in our midst. "I've traced the box, and we've a brief trudge. I'll tell you on the way that I dislike extremely Wi Cheun's account for the hypothesis it suggests to my mind, and yet—well, we refuse to draw conclusions before the evidence is scrutinised. Quick march!"

We set off briskly towards the Limehouse basin and soon were crossing its dingy footbridge under the octagonal hydraulic tower, surrounded by the clatter, shouts, and bangs of the lifeboat manufactory. As we walked, Mr. Holmes shared what he had learned.

Five years previous (according to Mr. Holmes's druggist acquaintance) the mark, which read "Wu Jinhai," would have designated Wu Jinhai himself, an immigrant from the outskirts of Shanghai who had once made his living carving teak. Upon arriving in London, he discovered that he could procure a few shillings by foraging driftwood along the riverbank, creating landscapes and animal menageries and the like on the flotsam's surface, and staining the piece to a high sheen. In time, he earned enough not merely to buy wood and commence crafting boxes, for which there was a perennial demand, but to marry a beautiful young Chinese woman and set up both shop and household in Gold Street near to Shadwell Market.

"A single domestic canker blighted this idyllic scene," Mr. Holmes explained. "Wu Jinhai and his wife were childless, and no amount of visits to either the local physicians or the temples could banish their infertility."

So distraught were they over their lack of progeny that one day, when Mrs. Wu was scattering wood chips and sawdust over the slippery ice in the back alley and spied a pair of white children on the brink of starvation, she did not chase them away as most would have done with street rats, especially those of another race—she invited them in for soup.

"In Chinese society, benevolence can be a way to reach across social boundaries and forge acquaintances that would otherwise be impossible," Mr. Holmes continued. "In this case, however, there was a catch which manifested almost immediately."

Mrs. Wu by this time spoke good English and discovered over empty bowls of dumpling soup that the children were mudlarks—the most wretched of the destitute, scouring the riverbanks for scraps of rag or coin or metal or coal, as her own husband had once been forced to scrounge for wood. Far worse, the girl suffered from a spinal deformity—possibly brought on by polio, Wi Cheun had theorised to Mr. Holmes—and the boy, though a few years older, was simple, only speaking in monosyllables and even then mainly gibberish. The girl revealed that they were siblings escaped from the cruelties of a nearby orphanage, and neither knew who their parents had been nor where they had lived before the bleak institution.

"The Wus took them in," reported the detective. The intersections we now crossed, though no less cramped or refuse-strewn, were populated with as many Italians and Jews as Chinese, though queerly picturesque Oriental writing remained slashed across many ashen shop placards. "As employees at first—or so Mrs. Wu presented them—but later, apparently they were indistinguishable from her children save for their skin. The sister, Liza, worked on accounts and answered supply orders after learning her sums and letters from a paid neighbour. She also proved capable of delightfully delicate carving work, and her adopted father made a tidy profit from staining and selling the wood scraps he provided her. Landscapes, seascapes, swallows in flight. Arlie, the brother, never learned eloquence, or common sense come to that, but he too showed an immense aptitude for carving once Wu Jinhai taught him technique. Though he suffered from a fearfully combustible temper and occasionally alarmed the neighbourhood with onsets of inexplicable but highly vocal anguish, the strange family was nevertheless well thought of once."

"What happened five years ago?" I enquired breathlessly, for our pace had been set by the man with the longest stride.

"Five years ago," he reflected with a darkly introspective look. "Yes, five years ago Mr. and Mrs. Wu passed away from an influenza outbreak, leaving Arlie and Liza alone to run the business as best they were able. And that, gentlemen, is the part I do not like, though I decline to make inferences in advance of tangible data."

A chill stroked my spine, and my companions' faces froze, for we had all seen Mr. Holmes's mind. A doltish and sporadically distraught brother, a defenceless sister who might have been thought a burden, a leg without a body, a frail white arm consigned to the Thames. None of us wanted to contemplate such a thing, and I'll be dashed if the world-famous problem solver did either.

"You're right, Mr. Holmes. We know too little as yet to condemn anyone," I declared.

The sleuth's steely jaw twitched. "Are you being fawning or optimistic? Neither serves an inspector very well, you know."

"I'm being charitable, or attempting it. I was meant to become a clergyman like my father," I said wryly.

"Disinclined to resemble the patriarch?"

"On the contrary, I admired him more than anyone I've ever known. Didn't share any of his talents, more's the pity. Always stammering my way through catechisms with no poise, no elegance. Dreadful. He passed some eight years ago and Mum thought I'd finally see the light, but all I saw was the noose in the prison yard. When my cousin took the cloth, I gave him Dad's Bible with heartiest blessings and a helping of good riddance."

Dr. Watson nodded sympathetically as Lestrade sniffed in mild amusement. A flicker of a smile ghosted across Mr. Holmes's lips and vanished.

Then we had arrived, and I'll never forget it as long as I live. The crooked house in the middle of the block, runoff trickling down Gold Street, rivulets sparkling despite their leaden colour. The Wu residence's steps had not been cleaned since the last snowfall melted, streaks of soot painting black waterfalls down them, and one of the windows was patched with four or five layers of rotting newsprint.

Mr. Holmes and Dr. Watson approached with the bearing of men who've looked into the abyss and lived to tell about it, Lestrade close at their heels. Trailing only slightly though my nerves hummed and sparked, I watched as the independent detective whipped out his pocketknife and bent to one knee at the top of the steps.

"We haven't any warrant, Mr. Holmes!" Lestrade hissed.

"You directed my notice to a trail old enough to be considered positively historical, and now you're quibbling about warrants?" the detective snapped in return, fiddling with the lock and producing a sharp *snick*. "Supposing we find anything, claim you investigated because the door had been forced. It would even be true."

Lestrade struck his palm against the rusted iron rail but made no further protest. Indeed, we were all about to burst into the room when Mr. Holmes flung his arms out, causing Lestrade to stumble and Dr. Watson to catch his friend's shoulder.

"Enter, and then don't move a muscle," Sherlock Holmes ordered. "I must read the floor."

We crowded inside, and my senior edged the door closed. It was a murky room, lit only by the undamaged windows, with a thin haze of wood dust tickling our throats. Stack after stack of carved boxes filled the chamber, only interrupted by a deal table with an unlit lamp resting upon it, next to a bowl of soup with dried broth staining its lip. Mr. Holmes tiptoed along the walls, hands hovering in midair, reading the sawdust.

"All right, come in." Mr. Holmes's brows had swept towards his hawklike nose. "There's been traffic within the past day or two, but—"

He cut himself off and stalked across the room, staring down at a row of boxes piled six and eight high. While a layer of dust blanketed the stacks, it was plain to see that a single column had recently vanished, for its rectangular outline was printed clearly on the hardwood.

"Dear God," Dr. Watson breathed.

The trio sprang into action, opening doors and cupboards, urgently seeking more evidence. My efforts to assist soon bore morbid fruit when I took the corridor leading to the back area and discovered a bloodied hatchet lying on the ground.

"Mr. Holmes!" I shouted (though I ought to have called for Lestrade). "In the rear yard!"

Both men were there in seconds, gathering around my hunched form. Mr. Holmes's eyes darted hither and thither over the cornsilk-hued grass but, seeing nothing he deemed important, he sank to his haunches next to me, peering at the dull blade with its encrustation of gore.

"What do you see?" he asked. Lestrade opened his mouth. "No, no, my dear fellow, let us test his mettle a bit further. Inspector Hopkins, tell me what you observe."

A needle of panic shot through my breast, but I soon rallied. "The blood is not more than five days old, which fits our timeline—it rained on the twenty-eighth, which would have washed much of this away, and the arm was found on the first, quite fresh. Additionally, there is not a large amount of it. While it coats the edge of the hatchet, the dead grass beneath is spotted, not soaked."

"Meaning?"

"The body was moved."

"Or?"

This required thought, but I soon had it. "The body had been dead for long enough for the blood to begin to coagulate."

"Top marks." Mr. Holmes stood. "This is manifestly the scene of the crime, and it would do to call in—"

"Holmes!" Dr. Watson's face appeared in the door, his pleasant features somber and still. "You had better see the bedchamber."

Not twenty seconds later, we were standing in the queerest room I'd ever encountered.

Two beds nestled against opposite corners, indifferently dressed in stale bedclothes. The single round table hosted dirtied teacups and several amber bottles which the doctor shifted to study.

The rest of us gazed in astonishment at the walls, which were entirely covered with maps. Maps of the world, maps of Great Britain, maps of our dozens of colonies. Maps of America and its southern neighbours, maps of Arabia and Brazil and the Sahara, maps of Japan and the Bering Sea, maps showing entire constellations of islands I'd never heard of before. Stuck into these scores of maps were pins of every colour, some with notes—"*Tropical, parrots and pineapple trees!*"—and some without, creating a dizzying spectacle of a smashed globe spread out flat and fixed to the plaster.

"By Jove, someone's taken an interest in geography," Lestrade muttered.

"This was recently a sickroom," Dr. Watson reported. "Here is a willow bark tonic, elderberry syrup, yarrow extract, ginger . . . whoever was being treated had a severe fever."

"By George, Liza was taken ill then," I realised. "And only her brother left to care for her. Supposing we have indeed identified the body. But did he speed it along, or—"

"Hsst!" Mr. Holmes lifted his palm.

I heard nothing, and from their faces neither did the others. But an instant later, dashed if Sherlock Holmes wasn't out of the room and already halfway up the staircase. Quick as we ran, he had the advantage of us both in start and size, and when we reached the upper floor (which housed a single combined workshop and lumber room) a guttural moan reached our ears.

"Stop! Slowly, now," Mr. Holmes said in a calm, clear voice, and we proceeded at a more measured pace. "Watson, I need you."

Mr. Holmes was half-kneeling with his forearm resting on his upraised thigh, looking for all the world as if he'd happened upon a friend in a quiet lane on a summer's day. The lad cowering behind a stack of alder planks before him looked to be around eighteen years old, his face streaked with tears and sawdust, his sandy hair matted into a squirrel's nest, his blue eyes round and anguished. His lip bled where he gnawed at it, and the boy was thin enough to be a wraith. Lestrade cursed as we stood aside for the doctor to pass.

"Your name is Arlie, I think," Mr. Holmes said with a voice like warm syrup. "I am Mr. Sherlock Holmes, and this is my friend, Dr. Watson."

"She don't need a doctor no more," the boy replied, almost too thickly to be understood.

"I know she doesn't, but do you think that you might?" Mr. Holmes continued. Dr. Watson sat unobtrusively on a crate to Arlie's left, smiling at him. "We'd be grateful if you allowed my friend to take your pulse. He's a very good sort and would never dream of harming you."

"Hello there," Dr. Watson said softly. "I want to help you, all right? Just keep calm, I'm going to touch you now. Only for a few seconds."

Arlie was too far gone to protest when Dr. Watson slipped his fingers around the lad's wrist. Tears continued to stream from his eyes, his wasted body shaking.

"He's dehydrated, in shock, and in considerable need of food, but otherwise healthy." Pulling a brandy flask from his coat pocket, the doctor offered it. "Take a sip, if you please. That's right! Good man—you'll feel calmer in a moment. You say that your sister needed a doctor but doesn't anymore?" he added, casting a tense glance at Mr. Holmes.

Arlie nodded, choked on more tears, and swallowed them back. "All she wanted were to see more'n that back room. For a long spell we managed on our own, but a week ago my sister done showed signs o' the sickness, and when the boxes didn't sell fast enough I tried hiring meself out to buy the medicines and tonics. No one would take me, for all I'm plenty strong. It weren't *fair*. Then the doctor stopped coming, right after he shook his head. It weren't good when he shook his head. It meant she'd *leave* me. It were too soon for her to be ill, too soon by far. She didn't want to stay in London, in that room, not *forever*."

"Do you mean to say your sister was too weak to leave the house?" Mr. Holmes prodded softly.

"Aye." The boy winced. "These ten years she has been, for all the cures the Wus tried. Me, I done brung all such maps as I could find, and she'd tell me what it were like there, in other lands. Dragons and beasties and tigers ten foot tall. She wanted to see 'em with 'er own eyes. Liza said as the Thames don't look like much, but the Thames can take you anywhere in the world, *anywhere*, and one day we'd sail down it together and see something other than Limehouse. But she stopped sipping the broth I brung, and then she stopped breathing. For *hours*." Racking sobs did violence to the boy's lungs. "I done sent her off to the islands and the deserts like she wanted, the ones as she called a Paradise, for we never did believe in Heaven. Down the Thames, she said. She always said as that were the way to get there. I were careful never to lock the boxes. She's not trapped, not anymore. When she lands, she'll be worlds away from London."

Horror had spread like a plague across our faces, Lestrade standing with a hand over his mouth and Dr. Watson and I staring as if somehow the force of our sympathy could undo what had been done. Only Mr. Holmes remained impassive, his skin marble white and his eyes positively metallic.

"Did anyone notice you?" he asked in the same hypnotic tone. "Packing the boxes, or perhaps carrying them?"

"Not I. I went by night down to the river steps."

"Hopkins, run and fetch us a constable," Lestrade commanded with uncharacteristic gruffness.

"No, not on my life!" Mr. Holmes growled fiercely.

"Can you be serious?" Dr. Watson cried.

"Now who's theorizing in advance of facts?" Lestrade snapped, brushing an angry hand over his face. "Get this Arlie lad to his feet, come with me, and we'll find a cab. Hopkins here is about to report that an abandoned building has been broken into. Aren't you, Hopkins?" he added meaningfully.

"Yes, sir," I answered with some passion.

"What of the bloodied hatchet?" Dr. Watson wondered as he and Mr. Holmes together helped the emaciated youth to stand.

"They had just killed a hare for supper when they suddenly vanished," I supplied at once. "It's a great mystery as to where they went. I daresay it's possible they left a letter of intent somewhere, however, and I daresay I can bring it to the constable's notice."

"Right, that's settled." Lestrade shook his head in despair. "Lord have mercy. Doctor, can you find him a temporary place?"

"I've a friend with a thriving practice for neurotics in the Kent countryside." Dr. Watson sighed. "I'll wire him at once. Arlie, we're taking you to our home in Baker Street where you'll have a bath and a warm meal, all right?"

Arlie made no sound, but leaned on the doctor and nodded his tangled head.

"Good," my senior approved. "Gentlemen, are we all in complete agreement?"

After a pause, Mr. Holmes said, "Poe referred to the Thames as the River of Silence. Ever since reading that, I've thought of it so."

"Very well," said Inspector Lestrade. "Let no more words be spoken on the subject, then. *Ever.* Inspector Hopkins, I regret to say that your first case remains unsolved in truth, though let's see if we can fabricate something for you."

So my first case was a failure twice over, and I am glad of it. I didn't solve it, Mr. Holmes did, and to boot the facts will never come to light.

It was the right thing to do. It was the only thing to do, and the best thing to do.

Yet my heart has been tugged in so many directions today that I feel all unravelled, regarding pieces of myself drifting away downriver.

Letter sent from Inspector Stanley Michael Hopkins to Mrs. Leticia Elizabeth Hopkins, Saturday, May 5th, 1894:

Dearest Mum,

My first case, once so bright in its promise of removing a villain from our streets, turns out to be the basest of hoaxes. A rogue medical student was guilty of chopping a body into seven parts and setting them adrift. Women of your constitution don't shirk at such macabre news, yet I loathe telling you, for it means after all that there is nothing of importance to tell. I am none the less weary for this having turned out to be a prank, however, and so will write you properly tomorrow or the next day. The bubble and squeak turns out to travel very well indeed in wax paper, and will serve as my breakfast.

Exhausted but hale,

Your Stanley

Entry in the diary of Stanley Michael Hopkins, Tuesday, October 9th, 1894:

Six months after the business of the false Chinese box, three cases total logged working with the incomparable Sherlock Holmes (and the estimable Dr. Watson), and today I received the shock of my life when he arrived at the Yard with fresh evidence for Inspector Bradstreet. Mr. Holmes never vacillates once a course is set, sails ahead like a schooner with an aquiline prow. But he paused before my alcove as if he'd expected to find me there.

"A word when I'm through, if you please, Inspector Hopkins," he decreed, whisking off without awaiting a reply.

I'd no notion of whether to feel excitement or anxiety and settled on a queasy combination by default. Meantime, I had need of a file and thought a brief dash to the archives might settle me. It would have worked, too, had Sherlock Holmes not been seated in my chair when I returned, his fingers steepled and his stork's legs crossed in front of him. Greeting him as cheerily as I could, I dropped the papers and leaned against my cubby's dividing wall.

"Can I help, Mr. Holmes?"

Inspecting me with hooded grey eyes, the detective considered. "That depends entirely upon your response to a query of mine. Three possible outcomes present themselves. Either you'll give me a satisfactory answer, an unsatisfactory answer, or you'll refuse to answer altogether, as I've no right to wonder what I've been wondering of late."

"You may ask me anything, Mr. Holmes."

"In that case, I wonder that you didn't try for another profession," he observed idly.

"By George, I don't . . . why . . . what do you mean by that, sir?" The effort not to appear slighted was excruciating.

"Dear me, no, put the thought from your head. You've a natural talent for police work." Mr. Holmes made a lazy figure eight of dismissal with his forefinger. "It's the income, you see. Detection doesn't pay the official force well, not when they're honest, which you are, and rewards are rare—maybe more so than you'd hoped. You could easily have been a City clerk with your acumen and risen accordingly, but instead you live week to week, probably because you are forced to support someone who is not in your immediate family but is nevertheless dear to you, following a tragedy which affected that person gravely."

Someone who's never spoken with Mr. Holmes might think they'd anticipate his omniscience, maybe even expect he's about to throw open the curtains of their lives and survey the mess in broad daylight. Well, I record it here for posterity: no one save Dr. Watson himself fares any better than I did.

"Heavens, lad, sit down!" Mr. Holmes tugged me towards my own chair, pivoting so his lean body rested against my desk. "Upon my word, I didn't imagine you'd react so strongly. The brandy flask I once observed in your top left drawer—"

"No, thank you." I chuckled weakly as Sherlock Holmes of Baker Street offered me both my own chair and my own brandy. "I'm surprised at myself. Forgive me."

"Pray don't ask such a thing. It's hardly the first time I've staggered a stout fellow. Recently, at that. I must add such to my list of talents." He glanced away, an unreadable look briefly warping his perfect suavity. "I did you a disservice. Let us abandon the topic in favour of—"

"Not a bit of it!" I exclaimed, recovering. "Now you must explain how you knew. I shall catalogue every detail."

Mr. Holmes did not smile, but his wintry eyes warmed. "There were a number of small indications, so many that I must take a moment to sort them. Yes, first I noted that the button on your left ulster sleeve is cheaper than that on the right, and mended by a man unversed in the art of tailoring. Clearly, that man is you, and while you are impeccably neat, you neither bothered to match the expense of your lost button, which was made of polished horn like its brethren, nor to match the thread colour, using instead whatever you had to hand. That you are a bachelor would have been obvious from your hat brim, but your financial straits speak more clearly through your buttonhole."

"I'll have to be more meticulous in future. Why need there have been a tragedy?"

Mr. Holmes jutted his bold chin at my torso as he lit a cigarette. "Your watch chain is an old family heirloom, but the type of locket hanging from it with the scalloped edge was in fashion some five years ago, before I met my untimely demise."

"Thankfully very untimely indeed!"

"Your servant. The locket is a memento, and five years is approximately the amount of time it takes to lose a well-sewn button and for one's hat colour to pass out of style. No offence intended."

I shrugged. "None taken. So I have financial problems, and you say they point to a tragedy. Supposing I merely had onerous debts?"

"You'd have pawned the locket or the watch chain or simply the watch to ease your path."

"What if they were all too dear to me?"

"After having gifted your beloved late father's Bible to a cousin? Please. You aren't a man driven by foolish sentiment, and your high expenses haunt you monthly, which is why you know better than to squander your keepsakes at a jerryshop. Economy is the only solution. Your mother mails you dinner, for heaven's sake, or at least so the writing on your many savoury smelling packages indicates. No, don't ask, it's too obvious and I've glimpsed the addresses—you write a male version of her penmanship."

Despite my distress, I smiled. "The tragically afflicted—you said not a family member? It might be my sister."

"If your sister were impoverished or afflicted, she would live with you and reattach your buttons, or live with your mother and eat her mince pies," Mr. Holmes said so smoothly that his tone might nearly have been called kind.

"Quite so." I cleared my throat. "Mr. Holmes, what is this about?"

Sherlock Holmes's head swiveled to regard me fully, a bird of prey ruminating over a hapless mammal.

"You joined H Division at the age of twenty-five in the immediate wake of the Ripper murders," he said with clinical detachment. "Eighteen eighty-nine. More than that, H Division was the Whitechapel force *investigating* it. I ought to know, I was there. Why? That was madness. Men spit at the uniformed constables in the streets, women refused to look at them, I was acquainted with canines that wouldn't so much as bark in a bobby's direction. You are intelligent, active, and approachable, and even if you'd no desire to be a clergyman, the world was still your oyster, and you chose to join an institution which had been hung out to dry. Pray refrain from telling me it was all thanks to the *Strand*, though the doctor has every right to be flattered some good has come out of his melodramas. There is another, darker reason, and if I am to rely upon your sober judgement, as I wish to do in future, I request you tell me what it is."

Despite my reluctance to reveal the source of my heartache, there is nothing quite so persuasive as Sherlock Holmes urging a man to prove himself trustworthy. I straightened my shoulders, tugged down my waistcoat, and set to.

"I was engaged to be married in eighteen eighty-eight to a Miss Lilla Dunton. She was—is—a woman of finest character, and I'd known her if only peripherally since childhood. The towns in southeast London aren't populous, Mr. Holmes, and she attended my father's congregation. I regret to say that her family life was not a happy one. Her father was born in West Africa to colonial parents and saw much hatred and degradation along the Gold Coast and as a young man in Freetown.

"Mr. Dunton told Lilla tales, even as a little girl, which invested her with waking nightmares, and as her mother died in childbirth, there was no one at home to offset this morbidity save a doddering old nurse. When the Ripper crimes commenced, she was merely appalled, as we all were, but when they continued, she was reminded of brutal stories she never dreamed would be brought to life here in England. Tribal massacres, soldiers ruthlessly quashing native unrest—things no one could bear to imagine, blood-soaked images which had tortured Lilla since childhood. By the time Mary Jane Kelly was left in shreds," I finished hoarsely, "her mind was in a similar state."

It's obvious from Dr. Watson's writing that the aloof Mr. Holmes is affected by misfortune and grief—dashed if I hadn't already seen it myself, on our very first case together, when we encountered Arlie in Limehouse. On this occasion, his iron expression did not harden so much as it melted before snapping back into that perfect equilibrium he so famously maintains.

"My dear fellow. What steps did you take?" he asked softly.

"Lilla lives at an asylum in the Sussex countryside—a humane and peaceable one, much lauded by both locals and professionals. It's quite lovely there, actually, I try to visit whenever I can. The expense is . . . significant. I split it with her father, who is by this time a broken man. My locket containing a miniature silhouette is all I have left of her, though I often dream she'll write me one day. Despite our geographical proximity, during our engagement, we used to exchange love letters absurdly often. I'd still give anything to see her handwriting in my post. Meanwhile, I promised myself I'd do everything possible to prevent such a monster ever desecrating our streets again."

"You may yet hear from her," he observed as if making a remark about the weather.

My answering smile was one of thanks and not joy. "That's past praying for, I fear, Mr. Holmes. Highly improbable."

"But not impossible." The sleuth stood fully, gathering up the hat and gloves he had laid upon my desk. "Thank you for the candour of your reply. Mr. Hopkins, I intend to make a detective of you."

"I . . . just a moment, you . . ." I trailed off, reduced again to a blithering neophyte, as appears to be my natural state when in the presence of Sherlock Holmes.

"One cannot help but agree that you would make an execrable clergyman, and so we must see what we can do about making you a crack investigator." He winked, and for the first time I was granted a glimpse of the impish good humour Dr. Watson has so often recorded.

"Do you really mean it?" I whispered in awe. "You'll, I can't believe it, you'll share your methods, allow me to ask questions, that sort of thing?"

"I'll teach you the whole art of detection myself only supposing you have mercy on my sensibilities and don't mistake wheelbarrow tracks for bicycle tracks again as you did last—"

The unfortunate Mr. Holmes was interrupted, for I was wringing his hand so hard he must have been in some pain.

"And if you don't break my fingers, Hopkins, I need them. All right, all *right*," he gasped, laughing. "I ask a single favour in return, mind."

"Name it, please," I urged, half-delirious with happiness. "Anything you like. I am yours to command. I was before, anyhow."

"The name of this bucolic hospital in Sussex. Tut, tut! This is not about your former fiancée, whose health I hope improves by the hour—I've been struck by a sudden inspiration, one the doctor will enjoy tremendously, and keeping Watson in good spirits has direct bearing upon the quality of my living arrangements."

Deeply puzzled, I wrote down the address. "It has nothing to do with me, then?"

"I did not say that either," Mr. Holmes chided, declining to meet my questioning eyes. He took the paper with a flourish. "Good day, Inspector Hopkins. Until you have need of me. Which you will."

Dunce that I am, it took me all evening to work it out. What an ass I've been, and what a worthy hero I've chosen to guide me on my chosen path. As mired in penury as Mr. Holmes and Dr. Watson were in *A Study in Scarlet*, now they are internationally celebrated and sought after—and wealthy to boot.

Of course his asking after the asylum had nothing to do with my poor, precious Lilla.

It had everything to do with Arlie, however.

I find that I could never have written down an account of what transpired between Mr. Holmes and myself without this new practice of recording what people actually say! This dialogue experiment has been a decided success. My descriptions of our meeting would have been overly long and still inadequate, dry where speaking with Sherlock Holmes is only ever the most riveting experience. Already I find that I listen more attentively and with better recollection. It is the second most gratifying thing to happen to me recently. The first is still not quite to be believed. Sherlock Holmes offering to mentor me is a dream, and I'll wake up at any moment. This, though, is tangible and entirely mine.

I'll be the Dr. John Watson of Scotland Yard! And Mr. Holmes will make a detective of me. And we'll solve crimes, and save lives, and right wrongs, and even though all is not well, nor never can be, I'll be just about the happiest man walking the streets of London.

Telegram from GREAT SCOTLAND YARD, WHITEHALL to BEXLEY, Tuesday, October 9th, 1894:

INCREDIBLE NEWS **STOP** AM TO TUTOR WITH THE GREAT DETECTIVE SHERLOCK HOLMES **STOP** WHO KNOWS BUT THAT YOUR BOY MIGHT NOT FIND HIMSELF IN THE STRAND ONE DAY **STOP** WILL BE HOME FOR SUPPER TOMORROW WITH CHAMPAGNE—STANLEY

THE GOSPEL OF SHEBA

(A. Davenport Lomax)

Letter sent from Mrs. Colette Lomax to Mr. A. Davenport Lomax, Wednesday,
September 3rd, 1902

My only darling,

You cannot possibly comprehend the level of incompetence to which I
was subjected today.

You know full well I *never* demand a private dressing room when sta-
tionary, as the very notion implies a callous disrespect for the sensitivities
of other artists. However, it cannot pass my notice when I am engaged in a
second-class chamber en route from Reims to Strasbourg. The porter assured
me that private cars were simply not available on so small a railway line
as our company was forced to book—and yet, I feel justified in suspecting
the managers have hoaxed their "rising star" once again. The reek of soup
from the dining car's proximity alone would depress my spirits, even were
my ankles not confined one atop the other in a padlock-like fashion.

I do so loathe *krautsuppe*. Hell, I assure you, my love, simmers with the
aroma of softening cabbage.

The little towns with their sloping roofs and single church spires whir
past whilst I write to you as if they were so many picture postcards. It's
dreadfully tedious. Loss of privacy for my vocal exercises notwithstanding,
my usual transitory repose is impaired by the snores of a typist en route to
a new position as well as a mother whose infant does us the discourtesy

of weeping infinitely. Bless fair fortune that our Grace has already grown to be guiltless of such alarming impositions—though as you often remind me, I am not present at our home often enough to state so with scientific certitude. The fact that you are right pains me more than I can express. Please pull our daughter close and know in the meanwhile that I have never been more revoltingly ungrateful to be engaged in an operatic tour.

How have your colleagues responded to your request for a more appropriate wage as sublibrarian? The Librarian in particular? I cannot imagine a more worthy candidate than you for promotion, and thus live in hope that you have been celebrating so ardently that you simply neglected to inform your wife of the good news.

All my love, infinitely,

Mrs. Colette Lomax

Note pasted in the commonplace book of Mr. A. Davenport Lomax, Wednesday, September 3rd, 1902:

Papa,

This morning after chasing butterflys in the back area with the net you gav me I was asked by Miss church if I wanted to go inside and record the shapes of their wings as I remembered them, I wanted to but more than that thought if there are butterflys why not faeries? You've allways said they don't exist apart from our imaginashuns but I know we must use the sientific method to find out for certain and maybe they are real after all. I tried to find proof they *weren't* real and didn't manage it.

Love, Grace

Excerpt from the private journal of Mr. A. Davenport Lomax, Wednesday, September 3rd, 1902:

I have been pondering imponderables of late.

How comes it, for instance, that within mortal viruses like anthrax and rabies, potions can be extracted from poisons, and a doctor the caliber of

Pasteur can create a vaccine from the disease itself? How comes it that my wife, Lettie, who apparently loves me "infinitely," accepts operatic contracts removing her from my presence for the foreseeable future? How comes it that a sublibrarian constantly assured of the value of his scholarship cannot so much as afford to keep his own carriage, let alone an automobile, and more often than not travels via Underground?

I've always adored paradoxes, but admittedly some are far more tedious than others.

Take this contradiction, for example: compliments, at least insofar as my position at the London Library is concerned, have become a decided blight. The moment I accept a semipublic compliment from the Librarian—a press of his withered hand to my shoulder as we pass amidst the stacks, a wet and fibrous cough of approval when he is within earshot of my advice to our members—I am automatically consulted upon count-less further topics. Last week it was rare species of maidenhair ferns, this week the principles of bridge engineering. Next week, I brace myself to field queries upon monophonic chants and perhaps the dietary habits of the domestic black pig.

The life of a sublibrarian surely wasn't intended to be quite this difficult? Walking through St. James's Square towards the queerly narrow building, the fog's perennial grime painting a thin veneer upon the Portland stone and the many windowpanes distorting movements of blurred, faceless strangers within, I feel worn after merely setting boot upon the Library's foyer rug. By the time I've hung my overcoat in the cloakroom, I've practi-cally exhausted myself. I adore learning of all types, but one cannot imagine that Sisyphean labour was countenanced in Carlyle's day.

Or perhaps it was, and the sublibrarians present wisely elected not to record their woes.

To boot, Lettie's travels leave me the indisputable guardian of little Grace's heart and mind. I find myself fretting over this critical task more often than is remotely necessary, given that 1) I am a scholar of some note, and an intellectual omnivore, and thus should act with confidence, 2) Grace is a singularly apt and gentle child, and 3) Lettie has not been at home for longer than a fortnight in six months' time, so I ought to be accustomed to this by now.

Her absence is far more wearing than her presence is costly. Mind, I knew when we wed that her tastes ran more to champagne and cracked oysters than beer and peanut shells. But Lettie is brilliant in her own whimsical fashion, and back when I rhapsodised more over lights flickering across her hair arrangements than what was beneath the tiara, we hadn't a daughter demanding to know whether moonbeams possess the quality of weight. Lacking Lettie, who would have delivered a wonderfully silly answer, I found myself at an absurd crossroads this morning between wanting to assure Grace that one could feel the weight of a moonbeam if sensitive enough and to tell her that, according to recent postulations, velocity is much more relevant to the subject than density.

Well, never mind Lettie. I ever want to think of her as happy, and I've told her so numberless times, and she is happiest when singing. Therefore the rest of us will toddle along on our own and no one the worse for it. I shall think of Lettie with her golden hair piled atop her head, smiling in a sly, knowing fashion over the footlights, and be content.

After all, I find myself effortlessly contented when with Grace. And she with me, shockingly. All is watercolours and learning to whistle, and nothing extraneous to distract us from the immediate bright sun of the rear yard or the cheerful green ivy paper of the nursery walls. Arrogantly, I suspect spending more time with Grace will prove a benefit to her. I trust that Miss Church does her best, but she is neither a close reasoner nor an artist, and thus as a governess cannot be expected to shape a child into anything other than a prosaic mouse.

Earlier today, speaking of mice, I enjoyed a bizarre appointment with one at the London Library. Mr. Theodore Grange entered my little office with the stated purpose of consulting me upon the subject of ceremonial magic, but he could as easily have wondered where the best cheese rinds were to be found (either way, I am armed with sufficient books to oblige him). His thin lips twitched following every pronouncement, his eyes were dull and brown, his hair without shine, his blinks frequent, the skin beneath his eyes too loose, his aspect altogether melancholy.

"I was sent to you upon the very *best* recommendation, Mr. Lomax," he squeaked, mopping the sweat from his upper lip though it is quite frigid in the library for September, and the light through the windows tinged coolly blue. "It's imperative you tell me everything you know about black magic—and at once."

"In that case, I shall," I answered hesitantly, this request being without precedent. "Mr. . . . ?"

"Grange, sir, Mr. Theodore Grange. Thank heaven," he exhaled. "I feared lest you hadn't the time. I have it from the head Librarian himself that you are positively encyclopedic in your studies, sir!"

"Do you," I sighed.

"Indeed so! You are my last and best hope—the Brotherhood of Solomon may not exist in a year, sir, without your expert support. We are tearing apart as a society! Ripping at the very seams, and even as its newest member, my heart breaks at the prospect."

"Then we cannot allow such a thing to happen," I said dubiously, leading him through tall byways of polished wood shelves and worn leather binding to the appropriate stacks.

Whilst eager folk demanding I tell them definitively whether faeries or dragons or succubi exist are often fanciful simpletons (leaving aside little Grace, who ought to be asking such things), I found myself feeling strangely sympathetic towards Mr. Grange. The man seems fragile as antique paper, and I lent him a friendly ear as we went, our boots singing softly against the wrought iron stairs. Specifically, Mr. Grange is interested in grimoires and their efficacy. I felt nearly as delicate in telling him their efficacy was negligible as I would discrediting Father Christmas to Grace, so determined not to press the issue. We've several occult texts within the collection which ought to suit him admirably well.

"With your expert help, I can now prove or disprove the validity of *The Gospel of Sheba* once and for all!" he proclaimed, shaking my hand.

"I should like nothing better," I assured him, as in the dark as previous and increasingly amused by the fact.

Mr. Theodore Grange lingers in my memory still, brandy in hand and feet stretched towards the hearth as Grace flips through my astronomical charts. I admit my preoccupation strange, for I cannot know whether I shall exchange words with him again at all; I lent him our most reliable books upon the dubious topic of dark magic, and I may not be present when he returns them to the collection. My curiosity over the man is likely to go unslaked. In any case, I must assist Grace in constructing a mobile of the solar system at her request and then pen a reply to Lettie. Mr. Grange's intentions are by no means the business of a sublibrarian after his duty has been executed.

Unsettling, the way a man's mind can wander from subject to subject. I sit here adoring every aspect of Grace which makes her unmistakably Lettie's this evening—pale skin pearlescent in the firelight, the nearly stubborn pout of her lip, the green-tinged blue of her eye—while simultaneously experiencing a joy akin to relief that she owns copious soft brown curls like mine, that her hands are steady and deft as mine are, and that her chin is square and without cleft.

What an altogether unworthy observation, though I suppose a predictably paternal one. Who the devil else should Grace look like? I shall make every effort never to repeat such a brutish study and consider the subject well closed.

Letter sent from Mrs. Colette Lomax to Mr. A. Davenport Lomax, Monday, September 8th, 1902:

My only darling,

Have just attempted to rectify a ghastly nightmare in which my production company saw fit to house me in a dwelling which could rock the scientific community were mould studies a lucrative exploit. (Are they, love? Hasten to me and capitalise upon a fresh source of riches!) In lieu of longer explanation, I shall state that the colour of the bedclothes were not typical and leave the remainder to your fertile imagination.

How is Grace faring? The picture she sent of the star system you were studying through your telescope was such a comfort to me. Shortly before

I come down with fatal pneumonia—as seems inevitable when I allow myself to study the state of this place in any detail—I'll mark down the constellations I can see from my thin little window and request you quiz her on the subject.

Performing Massenet's *Sapho* in a European pretension of a city is not the activity I wish to be engaged in during my final days, alas. Think of me fondly, and know that I suffered for my art.

All my love,

Mrs. Colette Lomax

Excerpt from the private journal of Mr. A. Davenport Lomax, Tuesday, September 9th, 1902:

"It's absolutely no good, Mr. Lomax!" Mr. Theodore Grange piped shrilly this morning, reappearing after an absence of six days and dropping the magical texts I'd recommended upon a table from emphatic height. "This grimoire of Mr. Sebastian Scovil's is the genuine article. I have researched extensively along the lines which you suggested and am forced to conclude that a hitherto undiscovered demonic text of great power and possibly greater malevolence has been unearthed!"

Looking up while removing my set of half-spectacles, I took a moment to goggle at the poor fellow. He'd discovered me in the reading and periodicals room. I'd tucked myself out of immediate sight under one of the tall white pillars in a commodious leather armchair, subtly hiding from the Librarian as I studied ancient Celtic coins on behalf of a member. Mr. Grange landed in the chair opposite, the hearth's glow illuminating the unhealthy sweat upon his brow.

"Your friend Mr. Scovil is likewise interested in occult studies?" I hazarded, glad to see him again in spite of my preoccupation.

He waved an unsteady hand before his face. "All of us are, to a man—the Brotherhood of Solomon exists to study the supernatural. I am its newest member, as I told you, and thus less tutored than my fellows in what ignorant folk term the dark arts. The club is a small one, and consists of influential men of business, you understand. My firm invests in a wide variety of securities, and thus cultivating acquaintances with such people is essential to me—and really, what is the difference between forming friendships over whiskey and cigars at a horse race versus whiskey and cigars hunched over magical manuscripts?"

There seemed to me to be quite a bit of difference, but I neglected to point this out.

"I was a skeptic, I'll admit as much," Mr. Grange said hoarsely, shuddering. "A grimoire which poisons all who dare to study it, save for those with the purest of intentions and keenest skills? Preposterous. And yet, I am convinced. *The Gospel of Sheba* is a text of extraordinary power, and a power Mr. Scovil alone can wield."

Tapping my spectacles against my lip, I pondered. Grimoires are paradoxes after my own heart. They tend to contain explicit instructions as to the rituals necessary to summon demons and, having summoned them, bind them to the magician's will. Ceremonial magic to an enormous extent, however, is said to depend upon the virtue of the sorcerer—his altruism in calling upon angels or their fallen brethren to do his bidding—and by definition, to my mind, a chap whistling for Beelzebub is likely to be up to no good.

"A book which poisons those who study it?" I repeated, fascinated. "Surely that is impossible."

Mr. Grange shook his head, pulling a small square of silk from his pocket and mopping the back of his neck. His appearance was, if anything, more unhealthy than the man I'd met six days previous. An ashen quality dulled the limp folds of his throat, and his eyes reflected steady pain.

"I am myself suffering from the effects of reading *The Gospel of Sheba*," he assured me. "After reaching the conclusion thanks to the volumes you lent me that its provenance is undoubtedly genuine, I lost no time in returning the wretched thing to Mr. Scovil. He is a great scholar of the esoteric, the discoverer of the gospel, and the one man who suffers no ill effects from it."

A numismatist, perhaps, would have absorbed this madness with aplomb and returned to the study of the lyrical golden images stamped upon the coinage of the Parisii. I am not a numismatist, however, and thus closed the volume on Celtic coinage and begged Mr. Grange to tell me more. The poor man seemed eager to unburden himself. He shifted in his chair, darting glances along the sparsely populated reading room as if he feared being overheard.

"It's been two months since I joined the Brotherhood of Solomon," he murmured. "An acquaintance of mine, a Mr. Cornelius Pyatt, recommended it to me as a worthy hobby—one followed by men of intellect and character and means. I attended a meeting and found the company and the wine cellar both to my liking, and the subject to be of considerable interest. Are you familiar with the types of ceremonial magic? I confess I was not, and have since grown quite obsessed, sir."

"Somewhat familiar," I owned, wiping my half-spectacles upon my sleeve. "Spellcasting is divided in the broadest sense into white magic and black magic, which differ less in execution than in intention. White magic attempts to summon good spirits, and to a good purpose—black magic evil spirits, and to a wicked purpose. Other categorical distinctions are regional, of course. One would find different instructions in a text of Parisian diabolism than in the Hebrew Kabalah, but all are paths to mastery of the spirit realm. Or so they claim."

"Just so!" he approved. "Just so, sir, and the Brotherhood of Solomon's express purpose is to explore the sacred mysteries recorded by the legendarily wise Biblical King Solomon."

A less than comfortable thrill wormed its way through my belly. "You study S. Liddell Mathers's 1888 English translation of *The Key of Solomon the King*, in that case. I read it with interest when I was at university."

"Did you indeed? Wonderful! What drew you to it?"

"I felt I needed to see for myself what the fuss was about, probably because all types of knowledge interest me and that one seemed marvellously forbidden. I'm sorry to tell you I didn't find much sense in it."

The Key of Solomon the King is the monarch of all the grimoires, the eldest surviving copies dating from the Italian Renaissance, though its purported author was the great Hebrew ruler himself. The Latin codex translated by

Mathers resides at the British Museum. It's full of orations, conjurations, invocations, and recitations, some of them for the purpose of summoning spirits and others for tricking one's enemies or for finding lost objects. I never went so far as to write anything out in bat's blood, but I do recall, as a more than half-humourous experiment, searching for a lost penknife by means of reciting:

> O *Almighty Father and Lord, Who regardest the Heavens, the Earth, and the Abyss, mercifully grant unto me by Thy Holy Name written with four letters, YOD, HE, VAU, HE, that by this exorcism I may obtain virtue, Thou Who art IAH, IAH, IAH, grant that by Thy power these Spirits may discover that which we require and which we hope to find, and may they show and declare unto us the persons who have committed the theft, and where they are to be found.*

The penknife never turned up, but I felt suitably irreligious afterwards that despite owning no very strong godly passions, I plunged myself into a study of the early Christian martyrs until I felt that some balance had been restored to my soul. And Lettie, upon being told the tale when we were courting, had a heartily fond laugh over my foolishness.

"The Brotherhood of Solomon revere his teachings above all others." Mr. Grange loosened his necktie. He seemed feverish, a bright red flush adorning his cheeks. "We've all been thrown into *such* disarray since Mr. Scovil found the Sheba text. Our meetings generally consist of debate over particular ceremonies found in *The Key of Solomon the King*—whether incenses and perfumes are of any tangible efficacy when enacting spells, study of the Order of the Pentacles, the proper preparation of virgin parchment and whether blood sacrifice is truly evil if enacted for a noble purpose, that sort of thing."

Fighting not to laugh, I gestured with the spectacles in my hand to continue.

"But then Mr. Scovil announced that a secret library had been found within his very own townhouse in Pall Mall, and that it was full of magical texts, and that one of them—*The Gospel of Sheba*—was an unprecedented find. Mr. Sebastian Scovil is from a very long line of esoteric scholars, Mr. Lomax, so we greeted his discovery with ardent interest. But the book itself is cursed, I assure you, sir! There is no other explanation."

"A little slower," I requested. "As a bibliophile, not to mention a lover of conundrums, your story is terribly interesting. Let me be certain I understand you?"

"By all means, Mr. Lomax."

"First, speaking historically, King Solomon was renowned for his great wisdom, and for his closeness to God, and the hopes of those studying grimoires ascribed to him are that his words remain largely intact. The Queen of Sheba was the monarch of a lost African kingdom who appears in the Koran as well as the Bible and travelled to meet with King Solomon after tales of his great wealth and wisdom reached her people. Have I got the proper context?"

"As concise as any encyclopedia and as accurate, sir! The gospel purports to be written in her hand, revealing ceremonial rites more powerful than any King Solomon developed before meeting her. Apparently the King and the Queen were lovers, Mr. Lomax, and brought the study of ceremonial magic to new heights."

"The text is in Hebrew?"

"The text is in Latin, sir, transcribed by a sixteenth century monk, we believe."

"And you claim it has made you physically *ill*?" I demanded, awed.

Mr. Theodore Grange did, to give him credit, look very ill indeed. Even were his colour not similar to candle wax and his limbs all a-quiver, he seemed to have shrunk somehow in the six days since I'd seen him, his skin shrugged on as if a child were wrapped in its father's coat. His navy-blue suit was likewise too large, twiglike wrists obscenely thrusting out from gaping cuffs.

"Not just me!" he protested. "First my friend Cornelius Pyatt took the volume home to study, and he fell ill almost instantly. Then Huggins had a crack at it, and we're all three in the same sad straits. No, I tell you, that gospel is the genuine article and Mr. Sebastian Scovil is the single man worthy of its powers."

"Oh, there you are, Mr. Lomax, at last I've found you."

The gentle, rasping tones of the Librarian startled me out of my rapt attention. My head shifted upwards to take in his bowed back, the genial tufts of hair about his ears, the air of absentminded benevolence that wafts about with him like the aroma of his sweet pipe smoke, and prayed that I would not be complimented.

"Apologies, sir, did you want me?" I asked.

"Oh, no, no, my boy, you appear engaged. But Mr. Sullivan, I should tell you, was *most* pleased by your assistance with his geological studies. He claimed that you identified a book which shed all manner of light upon his research into sedimentary facies. You are to be congratulated again, Mr. Lomax."

There is a many-paned window at the end of the periodicals room, and reflected in its glass I could see Mr. Grange and the Librarian, my own slender seated figure with its mop of wildly curling brown hair, and the six or seven members who had perked up and were now eyeing me with interest, wondering what arcane knowledge I could gift them before teatime.

"Thank you, sir," I said, rubbing at my eyes. "I did my best."

"Quite right, quite right. Carry on, then! You do us credit, Mr. Lomax, and I don't care who knows it."

Chuckling in resignation, my eyes drifted back to the volume I'd abandoned when Mr. Grange arrived. It was nearly lunch hour and time for a hastily procured sandwich or at least the apple in my greatcoat pocket; I didn't know nearly enough about Celtic coinage to assist Mr. McGraw yet, and he was due at the Library at one o'clock sharp. Outside, a thin patter of rain had commenced, darkening the paving stones of St. James's Square and quickening the steps of the shivering pedestrians below.

"Mr. Grange, I should love to hear more about *The Gospel of Sheba*, truly, but my mind is spoken for at the moment." Rising, I gathered the magical volumes he'd returned, meaning to check them in. "When is the next meeting of the Brotherhood of Solomon? Might a stray bibliophile be welcome in your company?"

"Oh, undoubtedly, Mr. Lomax!" Mr. Theodore Grange cried, mirroring me. Grasping my hand in his palsied one, he shook it. "I was about to propose the very thing. Tuesday next is our regular gathering. We dine at the Savile Club in Piccadilly. The works of scholarship you were kind enough to lend me introduced no doubts in my mind as to the authenticity of *The Gospel of Sheba*, but I would greatly value a fresh pair of eyes. We have been at one another's throats over this discovery, and two chaps have quit the club entirely, claiming outright Satanic influence at work regarding our sudden poor health. I shall look forward to seeing you at eight o'clock sharp, Mr. Lomax, and in the meanwhile wish you a very good week."

Frowning as I watched Mr. Grange depart, I went to check in his returns, placing them upon a cart to be shelved. A book possessed of such occult power that it worked upon the reader like a disease? Impossible.

And yet, I had witnessed the decline of Mr. Grange myself. The man appeared to be shriveling before my very eyes into a grey husk.

Could poison be at work here? Something more pedestrian but no less sinister than demonic influence?

The very question is unnerving. I am not callow enough to suppose that books are not powerful—on the contrary, a book is the most delicious of paradoxes, an inert collection of symbols that are capable of changing the universe when once the cover is opened. Imagine what the world would look like had the Book of John never been written, or *On the Revolutions of Heavenly Spheres*, or *Romeo and Juliet*? One day I attended the opera and was captivated by a beautiful blonde soprano with a mocking blue eye and a milk-white neck with the loveliest smooth hollows, but I fell in love with Colette when she admitted to me that she couldn't read Petrarch's poems to Laura without weeping and had never bothered over being ashamed of the fact.

I look forward to Tuesday with the greatest interest. Meanwhile, Celtic currency calls to me and I've a new set of picture books to bring home to Grace this evening.

Excerpt from the private journal of Mr. A. Davenport Lomax, Monday, September 15th, 1902:

What a ghastly day this was.

My friend Dr. John Watson stopped by the London Library in need of my assistance late in the evening, looking battlefield grim. All the newspapers have been screaming that his friend Mr. Sherlock Holmes was attacked by men armed with sticks outside the Café Royal a week ago today and is languishing at the door of death. Whatever they were investigating, they still seem to be in the thick of it. I berated myself at once for not having wired asking after Watson's well-being. He little considers the topic himself.

"My God, Watson, how are you?" I whipped my half-spectacles off when the doctor came into sight cresting a spiralling staircase. Lost in thought in a peculiarly narrow Library byway, I stood seeking out a book on native Esquimaux art for a member. "More to the point, how is Mr. Holmes?"

Watson smiled, a sincerely meant expression that nevertheless failed to meet his eyes. As a collector of dichotomies, I am rather fascinated by Watson. I met him four years ago, before being hired at the London Library, when I used to frequent his club. We share an interest in cricket, and I think the kaleidoscopic quality of my studies amuses him. Watson is a doctor and a soldier, about two decades my senior but no less hearty for that, and the man is so utterly decent that he ought to be the most appalling bore in Christendom. The fact he is just the opposite is therefore rather baffling. He is well-built and sturdy, a bit shorter than I am, with a neatly groomed brown moustache and an air of rapt attention when he is listening to you. But this evening he looked exhausted, a solid line etched between his brows and his hat clutched a bit too hard in his fingers.

And no wonder too. Anyone with a copy of the *Strand Magazine* and the ability to read its text can tell that Watson has devoted the lion's share of his time and energies to Sherlock Holmes ever since meeting him. If I were to go so far as to make a "deduction" myself, that indicates Sherlock Holmes is indeed a worthy individual.

"Between the two of us, Lomax, Holmes is better than can be expected, which . . . frankly is still not well at all," he sighed, shaking my hand. "I'm to lay it on thick for the papers, but I trust in your discretion. He'll make a full recovery, thank God."

Feeling rather inexplicably relieved, I nodded. I have never been introduced to Sherlock Holmes, but like the rest of London and possibly the world am deeply intrigued by Watson's accounts of his exploits. And it simply doesn't seem right to me that there should be a world without Sherlock Holmes in it. There was, of course, for three years' time, but now? After all this while and so many daring exploits and feats of intellect? He feels like a permanent fixture.

"His attackers are known to you?"

Watson's determined jaw tightened as he nodded once. "The case is a complex one, with the safety of a lady at stake, or I should have horsewhipped them by this time."

"Naturally. Can I do anything?"

"As a matter of fact, you can. I'm to spend the next twenty-four hours in an intensive study of Chinese pottery."

"To what purpose?"

The smallest hint of mystified good humour entered his blue eyes. "Surely you know better than to ask. I haven't the smallest notion."

Laughing, I waved the doctor farther into the labyrinthine stacks. He left with a mighty book under his arm, making promises of an evening of billiards. Watson has a brisk military stride, and I could not help but compliment myself that it appeared more buoyant as he exited than when he'd first appeared.

I saw the two of them once, outside of a tobacconist's in Regent Street. I'd have known Mr. Holmes from his likeness in the newspapers, not to mention the *Strand Magazine,* but when Watson appeared in his wake, I was sure of myself. Sherlock Holmes and John Watson were exiting with replenished cigarette cases, Dr. Watson casting about for a cab, and they were so complete together. Wanting no other company save themselves. Watson, just as their hansom slowed, stopped to flip a coin to a crippled veteran by the side of the road—and Mr. Holmes, who cannot be a patient man at the best of times, rather than pull a face, simply called out to the driver to ensure they kept their cab. They reminded me of my wife alongside her cohorts at the end of a lengthy curtain call, air reeking of hothouse roses and the heat sending trickles of sweat down the faces of worshipful spectators—and all the while, the performers in perfect, casual tune.

They are just as Grace and I are together, I've decided. The harmony. The friendship, the complete ease. Mr. Holmes's genius seems the icy sort, all edges and angles, but despite his legendary prickliness, he is most certainly held in the highest esteem. I don't like to think of how Watson looked this afternoon.

When I said that there ought not be a world without Sherlock Holmes, that was a firmly believed but abstract concept, like thinking that the British flag ought to consist of red, white, and blue. When I think of a Dr. John Watson without Sherlock Holmes, however, I experience a much firmer twist of feeling.

I must turn the lamp down and retire shortly. What odd connections we make as we pass through life—old friends, new ones, perhaps if we're lucky even ones we've brought into being. But why do I remain so pensive over such a happy topic? I must confess, though camaraderie of the highest level is deeply satisfying and fatherhood still more so, I miss Lettie terribly. The romance that so bafflingly visited a bookish scholar's life has departed, leaving bare halls with traces of magic swept away under carpeting. It has been so long since the early days of our marriage, when we lay entwined with the windows open, breakfasting upon stale bread and returning hastily to mussed bedclothes, hours lost in poetry and skin.

It has been so very long since Lettie chose to *stay*.

Tomorrow at least I shall have the distraction of the Brotherhood of Solomon. What on earth can the matter be with these people and their accursed new acquisition? I've been dying to discover the truth, and I don't mind admitting it. One hopes that the morrow will reveal all.

Letter sent from Mrs. Colette Lomax to Mr. A. Davenport Lomax, Tuesday, September 16th, 1902:

Dearest,

I fear that I write with as much speed as affection today. The sudden epidemic of stupidity which appears to have beset our company managers has led to our being double-booked: both at the theatre where we are paid to sing, and at the country home of a Bavarian duke who has decided that I am a better English interpreter of Germanic music than many of my predecessors, where we *are not paid to sing.*

You can imagine I am both flattered and furious. But the Duke himself is charming enough despite being pasty and made all appropriate apologies for my being forced to attend a champagne fete when in a state of such exhaustion, so I suppose complaints are unworthy of me. The repast was admittedly beyond reproach—I haven't tasted caviar this fine in a twelve-month or more.

More anon, love, and kiss Grace for me,

Mrs. Colette Lomax

Excerpt from the private journal of Mr. A. Davenport Lomax, Tuesday, September 16th, 1902:

I've emerged victorious, with a terribly queer book upon my desk. But I shall tell it in order, I suppose, or never recall it correctly.

Not having been there previous, I noted that the Savile Club is done in the traditional style, its walls teeming with textural flourishes and a quiet pomp in the mouldings accenting its ivory ceilings. Art abounds, as does crystal, as does the sort of furniture inviting terribly expensive trousers to be seated. There was quite a grand fire in the dining room we occupied, and the requisite set of picture-windows—all the details one expects when one comes from old money, not actually possessing any. But that is the lot of having a great many brothers, I suppose, and when one is younger, and a natural scientist, one is trusted to do well on one's own. I arrived at ten minutes to eight, rather at a loss over introductions after handing away my coat. But I was prevented any awkwardness by Mr. Grange, who charged (well, made weak haste, anyhow) towards me within seconds.

"Mr. Lomax!" he cried. His complexion, previously grey, had gained a slight touch of pink in the week we were apart, though his appetite clearly had not returned and his upper lip twitched tremulously. "Just the man we wanted—here, may I present my friend Mr. Cornelius Pyatt, another investor like myself and the one who introduced me to the Brotherhood of Solomon."

As I entered the dining room fully, I shook hands with a sallow man of perhaps forty years with a calculating expression and a crow's sable hair. Mr. Pyatt, according to Mr. Grange, likewise suffered the ghastly effects of *The Gospel of Sheba*, but he seems to have made a full recovery if so. His handshake was certainly firm enough, and his aspect one of clear, cutting focus.

"Delighted to meet you, Mr. Lomax," he professed. "I hear you've consented to get to the bottom of this business. And high time, too, though I am by now convinced we are dealing with mighty supernatural forces. I was quite prostrate with the effects of studying this volume some weeks ago."

"So I have heard. I'm happy to see you are well again," I answered. Another man stepped forward from the depths of the carpeted dining room, and I stepped aside to include him. "But I cannot understand how such a thing could be possible outside the realm of ghost stories. The best sort of ghost stories, of course."

"I thought precisely as you did, Mr. Lomax," admitted the newcomer. "Especially since I failed to suffer the symptoms associated with exposure to the book myself. It all seemed the merest coincidence, or else an especially grim fairy tale. But as the evidence mounts, I grow ever more convinced that my find was a monumental one. Mr. Sebastian Scovil, at your service, and eager to hear your conclusions."

If I come from old money which leaked away from the Lomax family in small but steady trickles, surely Mr. Scovil's funding commenced with the pharaohs and built its way upward from there. He was a small man, very quietly dressed in grey, with every seam and tuck so perfectly tailored in the finest traditional taste that you could have made a model of the chap based solely upon his clothing and not the other way round. His brown eyes twinkled, his apple cheeks shone with cheer, and the pocket watch he consulted after shaking my hand cost a hundred quid if it cost a shilling. Which it probably hadn't, since the initials etched upon it ended duly in *S.* An inheritance, no doubt, to the diminutive yet decisive heir apparent. Mr. Sebastian Scovil was so very small, as a matter of fact, and so very wealthy in appearance, that he brought to mind a Lilliputian dignitary.

"I am eager to see it, as I've dedicated my life to books of all sorts," I owned, my pulse quickening.

"Come, come sir!" Mr. Grange exclaimed. "I told Mr. Scovil as much, and you shall examine it at once! Right this way."

We passed farther into the dining area, towards a table where several well-to-do fellows stood muttering—some angrily, some raptly—over a cloth-veiled object. They were successful businessmen on the clubbable model, warm when it came to handshakes and ruthless when it came to figures. The fact they didn't suppose consorting with the devil to be any particular blemish so long as the chequebook balanced at the end of the day failed to shock me; the acquisition of money is a high virtue indeed in some circles.

I was such a man myself once, at university. For a month after I was given to understand there would be a small allowance but no inheritance from the Lomax estate, I studied with the deliberate intent of becoming a tycoon. Then a fellow cricketer left a book upon Persian stonemasonry lying about and I was lost to the world for days save for the classes I could not miss. After coming out of my trance by means of finishing the final page, I realised that I didn't actually desire the rare objects money could procure me—I only wanted to know all about them. I told Lettie that tale, on one of her tours when I scandalously joined her in Paris before we were wed, and she smirked and reached in all her bare glory for her wineglass and said it was all right, we could have the smallest house in the West End.

"But *in the West End*, mind," she'd added mock-sternly, pulling her fingertips down the planes of my chest.

"Mr. Lomax is here as an impartial expert!" Mr. Grange squeaked. "Please, gentlemen, step aside and allow him to view *The Gospel of Sheba* uninhibited. Your questions and comments will be answered in due course."

"It's not much to look at," Mr. Scovil said ruefully as the Brotherhood parted and he flipped aside the black velvet wrapping. A pair of white cotton gloves rested next to the shabby volume he uncovered, and I donned them after sliding my half-spectacles up my nose. "Which to my way of thinking—as a connoisseur and never a professional, mind—stands in its favour. I've a wretchedly old townhouse the family expects me to care for, eighteenth century you know, impossible to heat, and I discovered this in a secret room behind a sliding panel along with many other books of esoteric medicine and alchemy. Here is *The Gospel of Sheba*, Mr. Lomax, make what you will of it. Apparently I'm the only chap it's taken a liking to thus far."

Leaning down with pale gloves hovering, I eased back the cover. The Brotherhood of Solomon behind me engaged in muttered speculations—questions as to my presence, accusations of the book's fraudulence, warnings over the dangers in dabbling with ancient vice.

The Gospel of Sheba certainly looked like a sixteenth-century document to me. It still does, here upon my desk, while Grace slumbers down the hall with her stuffed rabbit clutched to her neck. It was re-bound around two hundred years ago, I believe, with crackling blue animal hide stamped in black, but the paper seemed very old indeed and the penmanship typically cramped and mesmerizing. Books can own a curiously hypnotic draw, and this is one of them, whatsoever its occult capacities may be.

Conscious of many eyes boring into me, I moved with care through the pages, noting esoteric symbols paired with line drawings of recognizably African beasts, and recalled that the Queen of Sheba was the all-powerful ruler of her Ethiope empire. There was something electrifying about thinking it possible—that here were her occult studies, combined with King Solomon's over the sort of giddy intimacy Lettie and I used to share, preserved by an obscure Christian monk without a name or a legacy many centuries later. I said as much.

"Yes, precisely!" cried one of the Brotherhood. "It's the most important discovery since *The Key of Solomon the King* itself."

"It's a bloody hoax," sighed a bearded banker.

"It's evil made manifest, Mr. Jenkins, and you ought *not* to be playing with such fire," whimpered a third man, who kept himself well away from proceedings and had poured himself a very large glass of claret. "We are scholars, mystics, men who seek the ancient insights of a Biblical king—we are not *sorcerers*, scheming to unleash the furies of hell upon our enemies."

"I can think of one or two enemies I'd not mind lending that book to, as a matter of fact, if it weren't a fraud," quipped the banker called Jenkins, and several chuckled.

"Stop *touching* it, I tell you. No purity of soul could withstand the summoning of the creatures listed in that blasphemous thing."

"It's a little thick, don't you think, Huggins, whinging over blasphemy at this point?" drawled a City type with a waxed moustache. "By Jove, next he'll be trying to wring spells out of the Sermon on the Mount. I say let a scientist study it rather than we financial types—it isn't as if we have any clue what we're talking about in the forensical sense."

To tell the truth, neither do I. I am a student of all disciplines, a kite upon the wind of the rare and the beautiful. I only know that something in me loved this book from the beginning, wanted to peel back its feather-soft pages and lose myself in the gentle curlicues of its embellished borders. I confess I am doing so now between jotting down these notes, my amber lamplight lost eternally the instant it hits the void-like black of *The Gospel of Sheba*'s ink. The Latin is lyrical enough never to be tedious, and I just translated:

> *Come further into the night, O spirit longing to serve me, O Many-Eyed, Hairy-Tongued Beast of Burden. Come further. Come into me*

with your seven furred tongues and your single hand beckoning, place your hand in my darkest place and be made flesh among the living, as you were living, as you are dead, as you were gone, as you are returned, as you are summoned, as you are MINE TO COMMAND.

It isn't Shakespeare exactly, but it gets the point across.

At the Savile Club earlier, after I'd completed a cursory examination, I closed the book and glanced over my shoulder. Hunger must have burned in my gaze, for Mr. Scovil behind me winked a single genteel eye and gestured at the book, tilting a shoulder in question to Mr. Pyatt. Mr. Pyatt, his black head cocked at me like a magpie's, grinned suddenly and called out to the small assembly.

"Mr. Huggins, it seems your fears will soon be tested against the facts," he announced, proffering Mr. Scovil a flute from a waiter's champagne tray and taking another for himself. "Our visiting scholar is having a turn with the blasted thing. You'll see for yourself, as I promised you, Mr. Jenkins—there is an otherworldly presence in this book, and Mr. Lomax will prove it to you. Is not electricity a real, if unseen, force? Is not magnetism, is not gravity? Does not the earth travel round the sun despite our inability to sense the fact, and are these not universally acknowledged to be ancient and wholesome laws of nature?"

"I think Galileo would have words with you on that subject, were he here," I observed, earning a few appreciative grunts.

"Just so!" Mr. Pyatt nodded sagely, his inky hair gleaming. "We men of mettle cannot allow ourselves to be hampered by outdated morals and petty superstitions. It seems this book has chosen a master for itself, and if that is the case, well, we must have Mr. Scovil upon our side in the future. That's all I can say upon the subject. In fact, let none of us argue any further and come to regret it before our impartial judge has returned with an assessment."

Understanding I was allowed to take *The Gospel of Sheba* home for study, I wrapped the gloves within the covering and placed all in a leather satchel I'd carried thither in hopes of just such an event. Mr. Grange hobbled on unsteady legs towards me, breathing heavily.

"I am most grateful," he whispered as the others turned to more usual talk of business and of ritual. "You'll save us yet, sir, deliver us the hard *facts*, and we'll make a judgement accordingly. All this political bickering will be a thing of the past."

"Bickering can be ruinous to any club, I quite under—wait, did you say *political?*" I questioned, a bit bemused. But Mr. Grange had already teetered off to herald the cold pheasant's arrival.

"Bickering aplenty. He means the role of the book and its potential spiritual dangers, obviously, but he also refers to my possible election as president of the club." Mr. Scovil appeared at my elbow, passing me a frothing glass of champagne. "There are whispers. We've never had one previous, you see. I don't want any such thing, I'll tell them *no* outright if they force me, but it would be rather piggish of me to decline a position I haven't been offered yet."

Taking the drink, I nodded. I don't have to employ many words for men of his type to peg me. *Old money, bit of a poet, younger son, has to make his own way.* They can read it all in my manner and clothing, likely spy reflections of silver spoons in my disordered hair follicles even as my mended kerchief screams penury.

"Frankly, it's a rotten situation to be placed in." He took a discreet pull of sparkling liquid, his eyes dancing—an aristocrat, yes, but one who exuded affability. "I can't explain why the book doesn't hurt me, no more than I can explain why Mr. Grange has been so pallid since he studied it. Nor why Mr. Huggins developed severe heart palpitations, nor why Mr. Pyatt fell so dreadfully ill. It wasn't even *my* idea to lend the book out after I'd presented it to the company. Oh, you'll take every care with it, won't you? If nothing else, it's an antique curiosity as well as an esoteric wonder. I'm pleased to have found the thing no matter what sort of trouble it causes. I'm mad for such treasures. Isn't it beautiful, in a simple way?"

"Yes," I said, thinking of calmly drawn letters in perfect horizontal lines, the hours spent making words appear by hand and will. "Yes, I agree with you."

Prior to dinner, I enquired as to the health problems suffered by each of *The Gospel of Sheba*'s borrowers chronologically—Mr. Pyatt first, then Mr. Huggins, and finally Mr. Grange. Each reported identical symptoms: freakish numbness, chest pains, the virulent inability to digest foodstuffs. But I am no doctor, so such details meant little to me. After dinner and talk of stocks, banks, acquisitions, and rites enacted within sacred circles chalked by holy madmen, I made my goodbyes. As I departed, I passed Mr. Scovil and paused to ask him the question that had been nagging me.

"Why this hobby, Mr. Scovil?" I enquired. "You've the means to explore any field you desire, and then add more—form Arctic expeditions, excavate tombs. Why dark magic?"

He shrugged in the fashion very rich people do, when the slight flex of a muscle is pleasing to their own bodies.

"It's in the family, as it were. Anyway, why art?" he replied, smiling. "Why hospitals? Why battle and conquest? Why patronage or charity? A man has to have something to work for, doesn't he, besides money?"

I thought so too. I think so now. And yet . . .

I want to know whether Lettie believed me when I told her we would never be well off all those years ago. Is it reasonable to wonder if perhaps she imagined me overly modest, or afraid of designing females, or simply a liar? She may have thought me the branch of a great tree which would flower in its due course, showering her with perfumed blossoms that glimmered in the sun.

When in fact, as is becoming heartrendingly clear, I am only a sublibrarian.

Note pasted in the commonplace book of Mr. A. Davenport Lomax, Wednesday, September 17th, 1902:

Papa,

I wonder if you could say when mother is coming home I only ask becaz Miss church wants me to pick new clothes for spring and when mother is heer it's a lark. If you tell me, Ill paste it in my small calendur she sent from Florents.

Love, Grace

Excerpt from the private journal of Mr. A. Davenport Lomax, Thursday, September 18th, 1902:

My life has taken a stark turn towards madness.

The Librarian approached me in the stacks today, exuding pipe smoke and benevolence, and I seized my opportunity.

My wife is beautiful, and she is kind, and she is witty. She deserves better than cold meat picnics in Regent's Park. So does Grace, for that matter, even if she is quite content when in the company of bread and ducks. Is it humiliating for a man of my breeding to *ask* for money? Exceedingly. But I cannot always be sending Lettie accounts of new research projects and old books, not when she is art to be held up and wondered over and praised by dukes and even kings—sometimes, I must write to her of victories. Even of *salary increases.*

The Librarian opened his mouth to compliment me, and I mine to request a larger wage, one Lettie might consider livable and may even bring her home, when suddenly he stopped.

"Are you all right, Mr. Lomax?" he asked. "You seem very pale, my dear boy, and your expression . . . I've never seen it before. Are you resting quite enough?"

Standing there, dumb, I found he was correct. I was wearing a look painted by an unknown artist—and I found it singularly difficult to adjust my features into my usual warm if somewhat harried expression. My heart was racing for no earthly reason, and my fingertips had gone decidedly numb.

The Librarian clucked sympathetically. "I fear my great enthusiasm for my most admirable sublibrarian has led to overwork on your part. Go home, Mr. Lomax, and leave a list of your appointments upon my desk. I shall see to everything."

I obeyed him and, after returning home and resting for an hour, drew out *The Gospel of Sheba* and returned to studying it, translating the Latin as I went into a separate notebook:

When summoning the Nameless Crone who Birthed the Five Pale Ones, suffer a virgin lamb to be drugged but not killed. And after calling unto the Crone, take up the iron needle you have forged, and sew into the live lamb's flesh the words . . .

To my shock, I grew dizzy midway through my third paragraph. I tore my half-spectacles off my face, panting. My heart leapt like a fish on a glad summer's day. The nausea I have been feeling and ascribed to purposely cheap meals and poor cuts of meat increased.

Is an ancient tome to cause my demise? Can such an object actually send evil through its ink into my person? It would prove ironic, I grant, for a lover of books to be murdered by one—and yet, stranger things have happened. I study paradoxes, after all.

Abandoning the project, gasping for air, I threw open a window in my study and hid *The Gospel of Sheba* in its dark cloth. There must be a scientific explanation for this phenomenon. There simply must, for the two remaining options are quite untenable: either I am a lunatic, or the world's delicate mechanism has smashed to pieces before my eyes.

Meanwhile, the relations between the Brotherhood of Solomon were rather peculiar, I think. Their conversation nags at me just before sleeping, when usually I am dreaming of Lettie's rare guileless smile or of Grace's belly-shaking laugh.

The pressure in my chest, a sensation I'd attributed to the sudden steep fall in London temperatures, tightened to a bone-crushing ache just now, as if an iron crowbar had struck my heart.

Perhaps I ought to seek a doctor after all. Or barring that, some sort of priest.

Letter sent from Mrs. Colette Lomax to Mr. A. Davenport Lomax, Friday, September 19th, 1902:

Darling,

It is horrible, it is unfair to you, but I cannot write at any length just now. Forgive me. There are no canals in Strasbourg, and you know how the sight of water always calms me when I am distressed, and I am engaged yet again to be paraded like a show pony before the Duke. I long so for home, and a good pint of bitters though you know I cannot palate beer generally, and for a little stillness.

Love,

Mrs. Colette Lomax

Excerpt from the private journal of Mr. A. Davenport Lomax, Friday, September 19th, 1902:

The numbness in my hands is increasing. Every time I pick up *The Gospel of Sheba*, it sinks into my veins and spreads outward like bad liquor in the gut.

I cannot bring myself to care. There, I have set it down at last, hours after I should have done. The post arrived this morning as usual, I sorted my correspondence, we sat down to dinner, I read *One Thousand and One Nights* to Grace, I worked at the translation, and finally I have opened my journal and hereby admit that I cannot *care* whether I am being poisoned by a blighted book of spells. I want to fight, desperately. It shames me, this lack of will, this *sorrow*. Grace is beginning to notice, and Grace deserves none of this. Who is meant to shield her from such things if not her father?

I hope most ardently that Grace will never be exposed to a document as wicked as *The Gospel of Sheba*. Nor learn after I have read her mother's latest letter to us aloud that there are in fact plentiful canals in Strasbourg.

Where in the world has my wife taken herself?

Excerpt from the private journal of Mr. A. Davenport Lomax, Saturday, September 20th, 1902:

A light glimmers, though a dim one, and one which gives no appreciable warmth. Casting my mind back throughout the day, I recalled every nuance of conversation I could glean from the gathering of the Brotherhood of Solomon, and I believe an answer may be close to hand. The Librarian commented again upon my haggard looks, but I blamed it on the dagger-like turn in the weather and my wife's extended absence.

The latter cause of my symptoms, I will confess here if only here, is not far from the honest truth.

Excerpt from the private journal of Mr. A. Davenport Lomax, Sunday, September 21st, 1902:

Casual herbalism and knowledge of where to find the best books on the subject within my intellectual anthill of a workplace has never served me so well as today, which already makes this date worthy of note. And this evening for the first time—which must be of some significance, if only to me personally—I consulted the celebrated Mr. Sherlock Holmes of 221B Baker Street.

To my great happiness, after ringing the bell and being shown upstairs by a porcelain figure of a snowy-haired old woman, I found Watson occupying the rooms. Indeed, it was he who opened the door to the first floor flat, just as Mr. Holmes was chuckling, "No, it's a positive crime you weren't there, I tell you that Lestrade couldn't breathe for laughter and Hopkins will never look at a pennywhistle the same way again in his life."

Into this easy merriment I intruded, just as Watson was laughing his fullest. Despite my devastating circumstances, I could not help but smile at him in return as I clasped his hand. I was right, then, when I saw them in the street together. Sherlock Holmes is not merely the champion of his city; he makes Watson happy.

"You've solved it, then?" I said to the doctor. "The . . . Chinese pottery matter?"

"Lomax! I'd meant to wire you on the subject—we have indeed, and no small thanks to you, my good man. Am I already delinquent in returning your book? Well, well, that's all right, then, I didn't suppose you lot made house calls. Come in at once, it's ghastly out there. Take the chair nearer the fire," Watson greeted me, shutting the sitting room door.

"Thank you."

"Did you see the results of the Kent match last night?"

"I've been terribly occupied, I'm afraid," I admitted, entering the room in a sort of numb daze.

Their hearth was roaring like a chained beast, and the gleefully untidy parlour smelled of tobacco and the remnants of a curry supper. Mr. Holmes was stretched full out upon the settee, his head thickly bandaged, only trousers with white shirtsleeves and a dressing gown covering his gaunt frame. If Mr. Holmes is a bit of a scarecrow, I grant he is an impressive one—a wiry, hawk-nosed giant with a queerly abrupt grace in his movements. His hands are particularly arresting. When making a point, he either does so with subtle flicks and flitters, or else performs the sort of extravagant gesture my wife employs, so that it can be seen equally as well from the back row. Seeing me, his smile dimmed but failed to disappear.

"Mr. Arthur Davenport Lomax of the London Library," he drawled, taking a pull from the cigarette in his hand. He is a tenor, I noted. Should I ever see my spouse again, she will surely ask me, and I shall tell her. Closing his eyes, he settled further back into the furnishings, careful of the cloth bound over his brow. "Watson's friend the sublibrarian. Cambridge, I think, cricketer, economical, genteel, bearing an object of some import—probably a book—and suffering from hyperopia, of all the vexing ailments for a bibliophile. Do sit down."

Watson, moustache twitching in amusement, took my coat. Then his face adopted a darker cast. "By George, Lomax, have you fallen ill?"

"I think not," I said carefully, "but that is for Mr. Holmes to determine."

My friend took no offence, for I meant none. "I am at your service should you want me. You truly don't need a doctor?"

"I need a detective. More specifically, a detective who is also a chemist."

Mr. Holmes half-opened one eye as I sat across from him in an arm-chair. I learned then that it is a quirk of his to feign boredom, for that is the best way to draw some subjects out. I had the man's full attention—from the slight quirk of his pale brow to his naked toes. I never once imagined that when I met the most famous crime solver, I would be greeted by the man's bare feet. Seeing my thought, he smirked, and slid them into a pair of house slippers on the carpet, tucking himself back in cozily. He raised his dark eyebrows, expectant.

"Cambridge, cricketer, economical, bearing an important object, and hyperopia I can work out myself based on the way Watson just greeted me and the physical clues I present," I remarked. "I read the *Strand*, everyone does. The last is the most venturesome, and even when I'm not wearing my spectacles, their imprint is probably on my nose. Why genteel? We've never had a conversation."

Whatever else I expected the great detective to do, I did not expect him to dissolve into helpless laughter, wincing at his injured ribs. Somehow managing to bow to me from a fully supine position using only the stub of a cigarette, he cast a glance at Watson as the doctor passed me a generous spill of brandy. Sherlock Holmes would have been famous, or perhaps infamous, in any field he chose, I think. His eyes are positive razors. Briefly, I wondered what sort of criminal he would have made, or alternately prime minister, and concluded that he could have been the mastermind behind the world's most feared underground organization, or ruler of a midsize nation, taking his pick.

"My dear fellow, what *have* you brought into our establishment?" he asked without desiring an answer. His gaze returned to me. "Of course you're genteel, Watson thoroughly enjoys your company."

This was flattering, and since he had no reason to flatter me, I took it for sincerity. "The same to you, I'm sure, Mr. Holmes."

"Out with it, then. You are being poisoned. How and by whom?"

Watson's jaw dropped in dismay as he settled into his chair with his own glass, having refilled the sleuth's en route. "Good heavens. Is this true, Lomax? What on earth can have happened?"

I told them. Watson sat, eyes bright, nodding at my every pause, mouth twisting in muted but obvious sympathy at twists in the plot. Mr. Holmes reclined, motionless, carved into his own ivory statue, his fingertips steepled before his closed eyes and his bare ankles demurely crossed at the other end of the sofa. When I reached the end, he placed one arm under his head and rolled to face the room. Tapping his free fist against his lips a few times in thought, he digested the tale. It was obvious to me that he had reached a conclusion—or several—but did not know quite what to make of them yet.

"I am at your service, Mr. Lomax, but you must tell me," he said in a slightly theatrical whisper, "what you would have me do to bring about resolution? Take this to the Yard? Impractical, not to say rather out of the question. Decide my own penances? Effective, but presumptuous on my part. Watch those involved for greater misdeeds and take no action yet, only to pounce at a later date? Safe, but unsatisfying. Justice lies in your hands, you know."

"Holmes," Watson chided, shifting in his chair as if it were a very old argument.

"Watson," the detective returned, eyebrow quirked.

"It's a serious matter."

The detective looked insulted. "I am treating it seriously."

"No, you are playing at judge, jury, and executioner, and it's not even October yet. He gets this way in winter, especially close to Christmas, but not usually so early," Watson added to me, shifting a rueful hand across his moustache.

"My dear fellow, I am hardly some sort of despot hearing cases laid out before his throne and unilaterally meting out justice. To hear you talk, you'd think I was King Solomon and had just suggested chopping a baby in half. Anyway, I was putting the matter in your friend Mr. Lomax's hands just now!"

The doctor did not so much as glance at Mr. Holmes during this small tirade, continuing to address me. "He just ruined a wedding by breaking and entering followed by theft, and I confess I'd hoped it might hold him for a week."

"You were every particle as dead set against that wedding as I was, and a fully apprised participant in the charade!" Mr. Holmes exclaimed in either real or pretended outrage. I confess I could not quite tell, but it was riveting either way.

"Chinese pottery," Watson explained to me on a sigh. "I was to be a decoy, a distraction. Terribly flattering. Fully apprised, Holmes? No, that is not quite right, something sounds amiss about your phrasing . . . ah, yes, the word *fully*. And also the word *apprised*."

"You have never previously shrunk from such tactics. Why grow squeamish over feigning an expertise in Chinese pottery of all things?" his friend retorted, pushing himself up a bit further. It seemed he had already reached his limit, however, because he collapsed almost immediately back again onto his arm. I took a great deal of care not to smile.

"Because, Holmes, such enterprises on our part do not usually dissolve into utter chaos. Usually, when I am assisting you at housebreaking, you are not badly injured and subsequently questioned by the police on the topic, having allowed the man of the house to discover you in the act of stealing his lust diary."

"I knew perfectly well all of that was potentially going to happen, Watson, and was prepared to face the consequences, deeming them light when compared with the results," Mr. Holmes snapped.

Watson did not quite roll his eyes, but he pinched the bridge of his nose. "Of course you did. And let me remind you that the only reason Baron Gruner failed to shoot us both is that he was the *victim of a vitriol throwing enacted by your accomplice Miss Winter.* I've been shot before, you know, and should prefer not to repeat the experience if it's all the same to you. It was unpleasant. And I should vastly prefer that you never have to experience it at all. No! No, not a single word from you about my lack of aptitude when impersonating a lover of Oriental antiquities, I haven't the stomach at present."

Mr. Holmes had the grace to look, if not chastened, then magnanimously sympathetic regarding his friend's chaotic whims. "As if I would allow you to be shot."

Watson did roll his eyes then, but they remained fixed on the ceiling as he laughed in disbelief. *"Allow* me? Yes, yes, of course, my being shot or not depends entirely upon what you'll allow. How is your head feeling, by the by? And your ribs? I heard a rumour that they took a near-fatal thrashing recently, but I'm sure that it's only because you allowed it. Go on, then. Just carry on playing God, and I'll watch."

Frowning, Holmes splayed his fingers across his breast in an unconvincing but nevertheless droll protestation of innocence. "I am not playing at judge, jury, and executioner. I am asking your friend Mr. Lomax to do so—he solved the crime, he knows best what's to be done about it."

"No, he doesn't!" Watson exclaimed, waving his brandy glass. "And you're just doing what you always do, only vicariously this time! No offence, Lomax, there's a good fellow."

"None taken." Despite my dark circumstances, it was impossible not to be highly amused by this display. As much as they had seemed to be in each other's pockets, as the saying goes, when I saw them together, hearing them argue was enough to set up a pair of armchairs on a stage, adjust the lighting to suit, and sell music hall tickets.

"You aren't following me. If he's right about this crime, which he is, which I shall determine once and for all tonight, I presume, or else why would he be here, none of it can be proven in court," Mr. Holmes protested, a scowl distorting his lean features.

Watson sat forward, moustache bristling. "Why the devil can't it be? Attempted murder I should think would do nicely. Any one of these four men—Pyatt, Huggins, Grange, and now Lomax—could easily have been killed over this dirty business."

"Not Pyatt," I suggested, sipping at the brandy. Its pleasant burn distracted me from other, deeper aches.

"No, I rather think not," Mr. Holmes agreed, his thin mouth quirking.

"Why . . ." Watson began, and then his eyes lost themselves in the crackling flames. "Oh!" he said softly, glancing back at Mr. Holmes. "The swiftness of Pyatt's recovery. The dismissive attitude Scovil evinced towards presidency of the Brotherhood of Solomon. Yes, I see."

"Do you really, or shall your sublibrarian friend explain it?" Mr. Holmes asked pettishly. "Go on, Mr. Lomax, I believe your reasoning is quite sound. Put it in order, and tell me whether you think a jury would swallow it."

Hesitating, I turned to Watson, who sat with his head angled in expectation. If he was piqued by the detective's remark, he failed to show it in any frustration that extended to me personally, for which I was grateful. Watson seemed, as always, entirely genial. I did not like to take sides in this fracas just yet and so determined to speak only what I believed to be factual.

"Scovil really did discover a centuries-old grimoire hidden in a secret room in his family manse and saw a rare opportunity," I said slowly. "The book itself is genuine. I honestly don't think he believes in ritual magic himself—it's a pastime, not an art. If he could introduce his grimoire to the Brotherhood and then insinuate that he was the only mage righteous and disciplined enough to wield it, however, they'd naturally desire him for their leader. So he picked the right toxin and sent the book off with his comrades one by one, poisoning them. But lest he be suspected of a power grab, and lest he create an obvious motive for himself which would be noticed should a death occur, he brought Pyatt into his scheme. Scovil would shun the presidency as a true holy priest might—but Pyatt, who had believed in him, would be chosen in his stead. Pyatt claimed to have suffered the same symptoms when he studied *The Gospel of Sheba*, but he was probably shamming all along, spreading rumours so the club would be primed when Huggins fell ill. Pyatt and Scovil meant to rule that club with an iron fist."

"To what specific object, I wonder, though I doubt not you are right," Mr. Holmes mused, rolling carefully from his side to his back and tapping his index fingers together.

"Would you like my friend the sublibrarian to explain it to you?" Watson asked in a tone dryer than their fireplace.

Mr. Holmes's head drew back fractionally. It appeared that since they were old hands at needling each other, it was as clear as achroite tourmaline crystals when they had gone too far. Silence stretched for a few seconds, but not uncomfortably so. The detective caved first, to my surprise.

"Yes, do go on, Mr. Lomax," he suggested. "I am all attention."

I knew it a peace offering, for all that the entire exchange had been encoded. I speak the tongue fluently myself. I know that when Grace is moody and cross over going to bed, it is because she has missed me, and that I must absolutely put my foot down and leave the building on time if not early the next day. I know that when she asks me to brush her hair, she instead misses her mother. Apparently, my friend Watson and Mr. Holmes are likewise fluent in a two-person dialect, and it always gladdens me to see such a thing. I am a voracious student of all subjects, and obscure languages are no exception.

Watson smiled briefly at his friend, which translated into *all is forgiven*, before returning his attention back to me. "Go on then, Lomax. What was the motive?"

"Money," I said. I twisted my shoulders in apology for my class. "There are some for whom it is a religion. More money, always more. Scovil was of the type who hide the avocation well—outwardly open, inwardly grasping. He loved treasures, he told me, and such objects have their price. Pyatt was more obviously greedy, but no matter; Scovil's mask was complete enough that they could milk the Brotherhood for all they liked. It was always more of a businessmen's club than an occult academy. As for potential challengers, well, send *The Gospel of Sheba* home with any upstarts and they would at once fall ill and surrender. Frankly, though, Mr. Holmes, I agree with Watson—I don't see why they shouldn't be prosecuted for poisoning their supposed friends."

The sleuth waved his hand in the air bonelessly. "Watson does, though, now you've stated the case so clear. Explain the legal difficulties to your friend the sublibrarian, there's a good fellow."

Watson's face gave the oddest twitch imaginable as he stifled a laugh. "I am afraid," he confessed when the fond exasperation had passed, "that no one can say when or where the poison itself was introduced. The book was discovered, the book was presented to the group, and later the book was lent out. Therefore, among the Brotherhood—"

"Everyone touched it, thus everyone is a suspect," I realised, wincing. "After all, they are convinced Pyatt likewise was sickened by the text.

And Scovil professed to abhor the notion of presidency to me, but later, he could simply claim he failed to study his find altogether due to business obligations or some such, and thus escaped unscathed. Nothing ties him to the poison directly. Therefore, a jury would be about as useful for us as would a pod of whales."

"When did you suspect him first?" Mr. Holmes enquired, head listing towards me as he pulled a cigarette case from behind a settee cushion. "You've a keen eye and a wit to match, but you're no detective. As a fellow man of science, I can understand your hesitancy to believe a supernatural agency at work, but what led you to decide Scovil was the mastermind?"

It was gratifying indeed for Mr. Holmes to so easily refer to me as a fellow scientist. I had always imagined from Watson's stories that he would be a highly difficult, if not impossible, man with whom to ingratiate one-self. But it seems that if you are already friends with Watson, he is rather more willing to shrug and accept you without question. Genteel, he had called me, and now a fellow scientist. Of all the receptions I had expected to receive from Mr. Holmes when I called at Baker Street, affability had decidedly not been one of them.

"Scovil warned me to handle the book with care explicitly when he lent it to me," I recalled. "I found it . . . superfluous. I'm a bibliophile and a sublibrarian. It was a nonsensical thing to say."

Nodding, Mr. Holmes pulled matches from the pocket of his dressing gown and lit a fresh cigarette, watching the smoke spiral upwards. Watson crossed his legs, cogitating. We were quiet briefly.

"There's something else troubling you, Mr. Lomax," Mr. Holmes said after several long seconds. "Can I help?"

"Not unless you can remove all the canals from Strasbourg."

"Pardon?"

"No," I said hoarsely. "You can't."

A quicksilver flash was all it was, without any movement of his pale profile, but the famous detective glanced at me. There was a great deal in that peripheral stare—catlike curiosity, intellectual interest—but also sincere goodwill, which confirmed what I had long suspected as a reader.

Dr. Watson tolerates the company of Mr. Holmes not because they are very different and thus complementary, but because they are at heart very similar.

A disquieting thought occurred. I would have to like Mr. Holmes, in that case, I realised. To my further shock, I already did. The strange phenomenon had started about twenty minutes previous. There is a very great difference between being a good person and a likeable person, and it seems that Sherlock Holmes despite his quirks is actually both. And he has quirks aplenty. I'd have to like him despite his theatrics, his glib remarks, and his almost childlike demand that all attention be riveted upon him perennially, achieved alternately by fluid, frenetic movement and by absolute stillness. I'll confess the prospect was a little daunting. But having already fallen into the practice of liking the man, keeping it up would hardly be taxing, I thought.

"Never mind, then," Mr. Holmes said, half-stifling a yawn with the back of his hand, and once again it was a cryptic message. He did not mean he was disinterested; he meant that I need not speak of what pained me. Again, in code, but a polite one which he knew I would understand. Almost at once, I relaxed my brittle bearing.

"Watson, are you yet convinced we are clearly the law of the land in this matter?" the detective continued in a more grave tone. "I ask for efficiency's sake as much as anything. Do we pass judgement ourselves, or do we tie up the courts with aristocrats who'll be declared innocent after all of three minutes of jury deliberation? I leave the matter to you and the sublibrarian."

The appellation "the sublibrarian" was ostensibly dismissive, of course. But it was not an empty compliment, as I have so often experienced. It was instead a tribute disguised as a dismissal. It was, I realised in a flash of understanding, something akin to a nickname. Despite myself, I laughed. Neither noticed me. Or they pretended not to. Mr. Holmes resumed contemplating the ceiling as he smoked while Watson rubbed at his brow with his knuckles.

"All right," Watson said, finishing the last of his brandy. "Holmes, you'll test Lomax's assertions tonight?"

"Oh, supposing he wants me to," Mr. Holmes said airily, which was code for *of course I will.*

"Supposing he wants you to, and supposing he is right, might I suggest the following courses of action?"

"By all means," I prodded.

"You know I follow you in these matters as much as the converse is true," the sleuth said nearly under his breath.

"First," Watson declaimed, holding up a finger, "we inform Mycroft Holmes—my friend here's brother, who moves in very high circles indeed—to keep an eye on Mr. Sebastian Scovil and to hamper him whensoever he sees fit."

A tiny grin flashed to life on the detective's face, which at lightning speed returned to composed neutrality. He appeared to quite relish this idea.

"Second," Watson continued, adding another digit, "while we cannot see Pyatt gets quite what he deserves, perhaps an inspector might visit the next meeting of the Brotherhood of Solomon following an anonymous complaint? This inspector would know all the true facts of the case and be instructed to make a very public show of believing Pyatt poisoned his comrades. Dark hints would surface, apt accusations. If nothing else, it would be humiliating. There would be a . . . lessening of trust among the brothers towards Pyatt, and in business, trust is everything. I say make a deal of noise at the Savile Club, maybe even clap a pair of derbies on the scoundrel, and thoroughly trounce his reputation. Might even scare a confession out of him, but it doesn't matter if we don't. The horse will already have fled the barn."

"Bravo!" Mr. Holmes exclaimed, a wide smile crinkling his eyes as he raised himself up on one elbow. "I hadn't thought of that, but it would prove a most effective stopgap measure."

"Well, one can't think of *everything*," Watson returned mildly.

Standing, I approached the settee with the object in question. I passed it to Mr. Holmes, who covered his bare hand with the kerchief stuffed in his dressing gown pocket before accepting my evidence. He consigned it to the side table behind him. When he turned back to me, his grey eyes were pinched worriedly at the corners. I knew what he was about to ask, and dreaded it.

"You want me to test this for poison tonight?" he asked softly. I nodded. "The symptoms you recorded and, I fear, suffer from, speak clearly enough—you want me to confirm aconitine?"

"I consulted a book upon herbaceous poisons this afternoon so as not to waste your time, and yes, that was my amateur conclusion, Mr. Holmes," I agreed.

"Aconitine!" Watson said, gasping. "Lomax—"

"I was . . . not very long exposed," I half-lied.

"But my dear chap—"

"He's young and vigourous and sturdy of constitution, Watson," the detective pronounced as if blessed with the authority to decide such things. As if I was not *allowed* to succumb to poisoning, just as Watson was not allowed to be shot. It was both maddening and rather endearing at once. "Why, he must be twenty years our junior. How old are you, Mr. Lomax?"

"Twenty-nine," I allowed.

"Ha! You see?" Mr. Holmes demanded, as if a point had been scored. He jerked his thumb at Watson. "The doctor here was twenty-nine when we met, and after a bullet on the battlefield didn't manage to kill him, enteric fever couldn't finish the rogue off either. I've every expectation of your full recovery, Mr. Lomax. When you are twenty-nine, you are invincible."

"A fact I have multiple times stressed when making a different point entirely," Watson muttered with a harried glance at the detective's bandaging.

Laughing, I gave them a small wave. "I appreciate the vote of confidence, gentlemen. As well as the assistance."

"Won't you stay for another brandy?" Watson asked in a measured tone as I donned my coat.

He wanted only to cheer and reassure me, but I didn't find myself in a very expansive humour any longer despite his gracious intentions. For of course, there is no cure whatsoever for aconitine poisoning. There is only rest, and will, and perhaps fate.

"I must be getting home—my daughter will be worried," I said.

"It was a pleasure," said Mr. Holmes. Again, the warmth was unexpected but not jarring. I hoped in fact that I would live to get used to it. "Get some rest, my good man, and I shall see to the remainder."

I took my leave of the pair, and—living in the West End a very short distance from Baker Street indeed—chose to walk home. As I strolled, I thought of the architects who had built the houses I passed. The impressive stone facades, the careful masonry, the uniformity of the scarlet bricks. Did those paying to erect the grand townhouses, I wondered, spare any thought towards the actual makers? The men with rock-steady grips and calloused fingers? Did capitalists of Scovil's sort see beauty in work and skill, or was everything denuded into pounds and pence? If the latter, how could they live that way?

Not that I'd any sound advice to offer regarding how to live life, apparently.

Constructing a house is a craft, I concluded as I walked, one boot before the other, in a sort of trance. Constructing a life, meanwhile, is an art, and one I'd apparently lost the knack of. And could I countenance shaping a *human*—a living, breathing human called Grace, who'd survived an acute bout of croup at age two thanks only to her mother's ferocity and my mute, terrified assistance—alongside someone who clearly didn't love me and had perhaps never intended to do so?

The biting wind filled my nostrils with an ephemeral bitterness, and the occasional harmless raindrop all but lashed against my skin. I was in a vicious mood, I recognise now, and a dangerous one.

For the first time in my life, I wanted to hurt somebody.

So, as any sublibrarian would do, I categorised the sensation.

What sort of hurt was I after, exactly? A senseless public house brawl soon forgotten? A rash act harming my own person? A delicious personal revenge?

Then the word *divorce* hit me like a physical slap.

An ugly event, divorce—a rare one, and still uglier for being so rare. Were more people officially divided, one might not be so very shamed by it. I could never put Lettie through such a trial, I comprehended in that moment. I was still in love with her, after all. Her sideways smile understood my jokes too well, and her top notes were too pure for me to throw her out upon the unpoetic streets.

No, I realised. That premise was grossly incomplete. I would never put *Grace* through such a thing. No matter who her mother was, or where for that matter.

An arrangement will have to be made.

I've just arrived home, and all the house is asleep. For some reason, I've pulled *The Gospel of Sheba* out of its covering and brought it with me as I retire to bed. The spells are absurd, the propositions either dreadful or ridiculous despite the elegance of the Latin used, and ceremonial magic is all comprehensive nonsense anyhow.

Nevertheless. The book is a marvel. It is a very old copy of very old spells made by a long-dead scholar, even if the Queen of Sheba had nothing to do with its provenance.

But what if she had? What if an African queen, arrayed in scarlet and purple and orange silks, skin oiled until it shone brighter than the gold dripping from her every appendage, heard a rumour of another monarch far away who loved knowledge the way other men loved gemstones? What if she scried him in a polished quartz and saw in him her double, though they ruled two distant lands, and knew she had to meet with him or regret his absence forever? And what if, when she came before Solomon's throne, divinity crackled like thunder in the air between them, and they set about recording their sinister secrets?

The Gospel of Sheba resides upon Lettie's pillow now, but I shall find a safer resting place for it on the morrow. I hate to think of returning it.

Exhaustion claims me even as I pen this, and my body revolts against the poison saturating it. Whether I will awaken after sleep takes me tonight is by no means a certainty. If I do, I must live better henceforth, of that much I am certain. I have caught glimpses of true happiness—in Lettie, who expanded my dreams; in Grace, for whom I can live to see hers be realised if I am lucky. But just now my heart dully throbs, pumping naught but cinders and grief, and I must consign myself to oblivion hoping I land in the proper sphere.

If I fail to wake on Earth, pray God Lettie never sees this. I did so desire ever to see her happy, and always told her so from the beginning.

Telegram from BAKER STREET to LISSON GROVE, Monday, September 22nd, 1902, marked URGENT:

EXAMINED WHITE PROTECTIVE GLOVES FOUND HIGH CONCENTRATION OF MONKSHOOD THEREIN **STOP** ACONITINE NEED NOT BE INGESTED, ABSORBED THROUGH TOUCH PARTICULARLY HANDS THUS ALL YOUR THEORIES CONFIRMED **STOP** INSIDIOUS BUT YOU MUST ADMIT VERY CLEVER **STOP** HAS YOUR CONDITION IMPROVED? **STOP** GLOVES WILL RETURN TO YOU BY AFTERNOON POST, ADVISE WHEN YOU MEAN TO RETURN ALL TO BROTHERHOOD AND I SHALL HAVE AN INSPECTOR AT THE READY PER WATSON'S PLAN—SH

Telegram from STRASBOURG, GERMANY to LISSON GROVE, Monday, September 22nd, 1902, marked URGENT:

SIR WE REGRET TO INFORM YOU OF SERIOUS EMERGENCY OVERSIGHT **STOP** YOUR WIFE MRS. COLETTE LOMAX HAS BEEN FOR NEARLY TWO WEEKS LYING ILL WITH PNEUMONIA IN STRASBOURG **STOP** SHE ASSURED US THE ISSUE WAS FATIGUE AND VOCAL OVERWORK **STOP** PLEASE PROCEED WITH HASTE TO THE HOTEL JOSEPHINE, AS SHE IS UNABLE TO TRAVEL ALONE, OR WIRE FUNDS FOR AN ESCORT—MDW, ESQ, COMPANY MANAGER

Letter sent from Mrs. Colette Lomax to Mr. A. Davenport Lomax, Monday, September 22nd, 1902:

Oh my Arthur,

I've lied to you, which is absolutely horrid, and forces me to see myself as I am—a woman who would rather invent a duke than admit to sleeping in mould. By this time even lifting a pen is a challenge, so I must confess quickly: I am really sincerely unwell, to my honest dismay. I haven't so much as set foot in Strasbourg proper yet, only hidden in this rathole of a hotel they booked for me, but I so hope that you will take me to see the sights when you come. If you do come.

Forgive me, I beg you. You said you only wanted me to be happy, you see, and I turned it into something false and dreadful, imaging you wanted a meadowlark in a cage and not a free songbird. At any rate, I've invented an entire duke at this point to stop you from fretting and I cannot continue in this vein any longer. A bit of pride was at work as well. I know you didn't wish for me to accept this tour, but I so wanted to feel valued in my profession, and I couldn't admit that you were right, and a better-organised engagement would have come along sooner or later. Even if you are angry, which you've every right to be, please take me away from this small corner of hell.

Always,

Mrs. Colette Lomax

Excerpt from the private journal of Mr. A. Davenport Lomax, Monday, September 22nd, 1902:

I fairly ran through the tiny spaces between the stacks today, breathless and dizzy, having been told by a new hire that my governess wanted to see me urgently in the foyer (Miss Church not being a member). Subtle iron finials were subjected to brutal treatment upon my part as I raced to what was certainly—I imagined—more unhappy news, this time involving my little girl.

Seeing Grace safe and quiet and clutching her doll next to Miss Church, my heart commenced beating in the usual manner again. Well, not quite usual, yet suffering from aconitine poisoning absorbed through monkshood-laced gloves and all. Still, closer to hale than its condition the night before. While weak and willowy, I find myself harder to kill than I'd imagined, if not nearly so hard to kill as Watson.

"What the devil has happened?" I exclaimed, advancing towards Miss Church's ruddy, slightly obstinate countenance.

"You can read, I think, or do y'want the likes of me to open your mail?" she desired to know. It was a fair answer to a stupid question. "These said *urgent*. What's happened, then? Where's the missus?"

I read my correspondence, hardly daring to breathe.

I gasped aloud.

After making arrangements with Miss Church to tend Grace for the next few days without me, and kissing my darling girl goodbye, I rushed for the exit. I was stopped by an elderly gentleman returning from lunch with several equally grey peers. The Librarian's hair curled invitingly, his merry brown eyes sparked, and he held out a hand as if preparing to compliment me before his cronies.

I was having none of it. There are more important things in this world—though not very many—than a position at the London Library. I surged ahead. But the Librarian was surrounded by men I now recognised as donors, and the group blocked my path.

"Are you all right, Mr. Lomax?" the Librarian questioned.

Laughing, I nodded. "Yes, everything's marvellous! My wife is very ill, you see. I'm to fetch her home from Strasbourg."

"Ah," he answered, eyes wide. "I am sorry to hear it."

"Don't be sorry, I'm alive this afternoon to go to her, and she has been bedridden for a week, so things really couldn't be going any better," I assured him. "I'll be back in three or four days, sir. Farewell!"

"But I mean to speak with you!" the Librarian called after me as I edged past baffled patrons.

"No time!"

"But I mean to increase your wage, given your unprecedented work ethic, Mr. Lomax! Allow me to make you an offer at least."

"I accept!" I cried happily as I reached the door, throwing my arms wide.

"Marvellous!" exclaimed the Librarian. We were really making far too much noise for the foyer of the London Library, for arriving members were turning to stare in dismay alongside the shocked donors. "Magnificent! I shall adjust your figures accordingly and enter them in the books. Strasbourg, you say? Godspeed, Mr. Lomax!"

I write this from a second-class train, retracing Lettie's path. My fingertips are still numb, and thus clumsy, but I have never cared less for penmanship. The little towns with their church spires do resemble picture postcards, just as my wife said, and upon viewing them I know they bored her dreadfully. How tedious her travels must have been, and still worse her confinement to unhygienic chambers. If Lettie insists upon one thing, it is absolute cleanliness.

Details continue to flood back to me as I draw closer to her—the tiny gap in my wife's front teeth, the faint spice to her skin, the fact that if she wishes to raise a single eyebrow, it will assuredly be the left one. So many of her aspects are unusual. She is as vain as any artist, and yet ferociously protective of her fellow singers, and refuses to put on any airs they are not likewise entitled to. She is gleefully dismissive of works others deem important and she thinks trite. She is nearly always ruminating over food and drink and luxurious surroundings, and she reads Shakespeare when in the dumps. She doesn't want more children, asked me, "But darling, how much toll to you expect my body to *take*?" but would tear apart a wolf with her bare hands if it threatened Grace. She is absent, but she loves me.

I honestly cannot conceive how I could have forgotten: when it comes to studying complex subjects, Colette has always been the most satisfying paradox of them all.

A LIFE WELL LIVED

(Martha Hudson)

For Market (Julia, have a care with the eggs!)
  —butter
  —cress (if very fresh)
  —endive
  —parsley
  —lettuce (likewise very fresh)
  —1 chicken (check shortness of leg for better flavour)
  —cucumber
  —12 eggs, unbroken

Entry in the diary of Mrs. Martha Rose Hudson, Friday, April 10th, 1903:

It was unseasonably warm this afternoon, for which these old bones are increasingly grateful. Daily I thank goodness for my health, because just imagining what the cold would feel like *with* a chill if it feels like this when I'm fit as an ox gives me a little shiver. February was a trial, March scarce better. I'd ask Dr. Watson about it, but even I know that there's no cure for the passage of years.

Ha, there I've made myself smile—the *cure* for the passage of years is something I'm only too close to contemplating. And I want nothing to do with it. Thank you very much.

Julia seems to be settling in well, both in the household and with Mary Jane. While I'm only happy that Providence sent Henrietta such a charming young man in the form of our dear postman, it's always a fuss to train new help. Well, I should say former postman. What a beautiful surprise that Henrietta's beau has an uncle who was only waiting for the sound of wedding bells as a signal to pounce, promptly retiring from that dry goods store in Leeds to leave it all in his nephew's capable hands. I picture them as being very well situated domestically.

Now I'm smiling again—to think of the sweet looks exchanged, hearty food on the table, a warm hearth, *children*. Henrietta can't cook very well yet as she's only twenty-one, though I taught her a number of simple dishes. In cookery, practice means everything. But it was a joy during a lull in the afternoon to carefully explain the finer points of a mutton stew, or how best to scale a perch. I shall miss her, as I miss so many things. More and more things with the passage of time, naturally.

I shall miss Henrietta very much, for all she was only here for three years.

Points in Julia's favour: she's quick to take on tasks, doesn't dally in the midst of them, and seems bright, kindly, and good-natured. She sings folk ballads and harmless music-hall ditties while she works in a clear, light voice. It's rather charming. She is economical with the stove fire. And she saw me suffering visibly from the minor aches brought on by the weather last week and started bringing me perfectly-brewed tea without being asked. I might have thought it a bit of a liberty. The *very* miserly would have thought it stealing tea. But I'm well past such nonsense in household management and thought it quite considerate. She was only being kind. Kindness goes a long way, as far as I am concerned.

Points against Julia: she breaks eggs and is extremely pretty. She is quite *round* in all the places men appreciate, has a thick head of nearly blonde hair, and a sweet snub nose. Julia may well make off with our *new* postman, who is just as engaging as the last young fellow, only dark where the former was fair. I shouldn't be a whit surprised and only hope Providence sees fit to let her stay for a while first.

Speaking of engaging fellows, Mr. Hoxsey was here this morning. Well, of course he was, he's here every day saving Sunday, but he came inside for a moment. It's so nice to have a regular caller of my own age to talk to. I'm constantly impressed that he can tolerate the rigours of being a milkman at all. But then again, driving a cart isn't very difficult, nor is carrying a jug or two at a time. So I suppose it's not so very staggering, since he keeps in such fine training. He claims that active work *keeps* him in training, and many believe in the merit of this opinion. Mr. Holmes would say the same. So would I, when stirring a pot or lifting a sack of potatoes. Thank the Lord that Mr. Hoxsey, like me, has his health.

"Mrs. Hudson," he said warmly, sweeping his cap off his hairless head. "And how are you faring this morning?"

"Very well indeed, thank you, Mr. Hoxsey, and yourself? Do come inside."

"Sure, and any day I get to look into the bluest eyes I've ever seen is bound to be a good day." He winked. "Where shall I set this for you?"

Mr. Hoxsey is a shameless flirt. But he is always the perfect gentleman about it. He is also very nearly as English as they come, but he once told me —after proud presentation of a four-leaf clover which I pressed dry and keep in my *Mrs. Beeton's*—that he was born in Belfast. His accent is thoroughly English to my own ear, but the phrase "sure, and" seems to have stuck. I wonder if Mr. Holmes could tell he was from Belfast by that unaccented tic alone? Probably. No, almost assuredly. How it happens that he came from Ireland I can't imagine. My curiosity is piqued, though. I wonder what profession his father practised. I'd invite Mr. Hoxsey in for longer, a cuppa and chat, but I fear it would disrupt his rounds. Would it be rude of me? Even asking to delay him makes me slightly uncomfortable.

Maybe I'll extend the invitation anyhow. He can always decline.

Mr. Holmes is in one of his funks again. I ache for the poor dear when he gets like this, but it does grow trying. He hasn't changed out of one dressing gown or other for three days, not even for an *earl*. And I *told* him it was an earl, there was the card and all as the nobility shuffled his feet by the coat rack, and my lodger said, "Unless it's His Majesty wanting me to find the lost mate to a pair of his royal cufflinks, this will do nicely, since it's a perfectly regal purple. Send him straight up, Mrs. Hudson."

Lord forgive me, I know it's not his fault, but there are times when I do very briefly picture taking Sherlock Holmes by his shoulders and gently *shaking*. Especially when the doctor is away.

He won't eat again, either. And I repeat, *again*. My suppers have nearly run the full spectrum already. I've tried a rich and tempting dish, wine-braised oxtail with roasted parsnips. I've tried a simple and delicate dish, a macaroni and leek soup with my best veal broth. Both came back untouched—obviously so, utensils clean and lying perfectly parallel on the tray and napkin still folded, so that I felt no twinge of conscience when I sighed and gave each to Mary Jane and Julia to share. I'd already served them simpler meals, roast potatoes with thick slices of ham, but I do my best for Sherlock Holmes, Lord help me. He deserves it even when he doesn't deserve it, if that makes sense.

The entire city owes him in one way or another.

Which means I don't suppose my help have ever tasted anything of the kind, not intending to flatter myself. A long time ago, Dr. Watson wrote that Mr. Holmes had referred to my cuisine as "a little limited." Well, *that* certainly lit a fire under me all those years back! Without realizing it, I was still cooking all of my darling Matthew's favourite dishes. Mr. Holmes had been here eight years by then, but he had no way of knowing how much grief I still carried when he and Dr. Watson arrived in 1881. I'd never had lodgers before them. It never occurred to me to vary the menu.

In a way, I suppose I was still in mourning yet. Still am, a little. I suppose I'll feel it every day.

I promptly set out, bought my beloved copy of *Mrs. Beeton's*, and now I only cook roasted lamb shoulder on Matthew's birthday. Well, what would have been dearest Matthew's birthday. Mr. Holmes has been here twenty-two years now and while he never complains—I like to think he hasn't any cause to—occasionally I get compliments like "Mrs. Hudson, you have outdone yourself!" or even, wonder of wonders, an entirely empty plate.

They mean the same thing. I receive them as identical praise.

For supper tomorrow I've decided I'll fry up a batch of oysters with a dish of stewed mushrooms. When oysters don't sway Sherlock Holmes, all hope is lost and I must simply weather the storm, and anyway they're only in peak through the end of the month. It would be a waste not to take advantage. At least he is on a case at the moment, I believe, seeing he is out at all hours, which ought to put him in a better humour.

Lemons for the lemon peel strips are already in the pantry, as is the ketchup I made last week, and *unbroken* eggs, and I've plenty of lard for frying, so all I need else is parsley. With nutmeg in the flour or without? A hint, I think. Bread crumbs too. Every tool at my disposal. May the good Lord send me the very freshest shellfish when I do the shopping myself tomorrow morning despite its being the end of their season, for I myself am at the end of my *wits* over my lodger.

And not for the first time, either. Not even in this journal volume, which is barely a third full. I hope Dr. Watson will be back from Queen Anne Street soon.

I do pray that his business there is going well. It has still been too painful for me to *write* about his business there, but I feel I must, and very soon. That it would be healing to set it down, not to mention cowardly to avoid the topic. If there is one vice we do not tolerate in this household, neither upstairs nor downstairs, it is cowardice. I learned that about Sherlock Holmes and John Watson decades ago—I don't intend to shirk them by shying away from my own diary.

OYSTERS FRIED IN BATTER

INGREDIENTS: 2 pints oysters, 2 eggs, pint milk, enough flour to form the batter, bread crumbs; salt, pepper, and nutmeg to taste; hot lard for frying.

MODE: Beard the oysters. Drain the liquor from them, boil it, and use it to scald them. Lay them on a dry cloth to drain. Heat the lard to frying temperature in a deep pan. Mix the eggs, milk, flour, and seasoning to form the batter. Scatter the breadcrumbs on a plate. After laying out a napkin, dip the oysters one at a time with a skewer, first in the batter, then in the crumbs, then in the hot lard until the crust is golden and crisp, laying them on the napkin when done.

Entry in the diary of Mrs. Martha Rose Hudson, Saturday, April 11th, 1903:

I give up. Unless the oysters later today work, I wave the white flag.

I roasted a very fine duck yesterday, the skin crisp, the flesh tender. Of course, Mr. Holmes treated it like river sludge, though I caught Julia licking her fingers. Ah, well. It's very suitable for a fine duck hash, which may yet be of use. It's much easier to have something ready to hand to place alongside some toast on a tray supposing Mr. Holmes decides to eat lunch on a whim than it is to make a new dish altogether.

Not that Sherlock Holmes expects one. But for threefold reasons, I consider it my Providence-gifted duty. First, I now take pride in and enjoy my cooking, and I've too many times glimpsed the silly man dashing out my front door with something resembling a sandwich half-sticking out of his pocket (whether he looked like himself at the time or no). Who on earth puts sandwiches in their pocket? Second, he pays me an absurd sum of money for the upstairs rooms. *Both* of them. So he deserves good meals. Tempting ones, when he isn't is the spirits for them.

What with Dr. Watson temporarily living in Queen Anne Street (I venture to hope *very* temporarily), things are even *worse.* Shrieking violin at all hours that even I in my comfortable downstairs apartment can hear, when Mr. Holmes is usually considerate of volume if not pitch; trays returned merely picked at for days at a time; heavy sacks under his eyes. I am anxious for his friend's return.

Not that I imagine all will be peaceable at first, when the doctor arrives with his bags. I have history to back my belief. Doubtless they will debate over arrangements again. There was that whole horrible business with the waterfall, for example—I still shudder to think of it—when the doctor returned, they had quite the argument over rent. It would shame me to even consider eavesdropping on my tenants. However, Sherlock Holmes decided to involve me directly, which was considerate and rude and rather terrifying all at once. He can certainly be rather terrifying when he pleases to be. I'd gone in to clear away their dinner dishes and met with the most impassioned row.

"But I tell you, I've the means once I do a little juggling!" Dr. Watson protested. He gripped the greying hair at the back of his neck in frustration. I think Mr. Holmes caused some of those strands, what with the dying and all, and I also think he knows it, and it disturbs him. He often makes me feel the same way. But thankfully, my hair went snowy white long ago over my own affairs. "We can carry on just as before, splitting it evenly!"

"We shall do nothing of the kind," Mr. Holmes decreed with that god-like air he assumes. "It's my own fault. I'm completely remiss. I ought to have been paying you this entire time, sharing rewards, the lot of it. You won't accept any sort of actual funds from me, I know you too well to even dream of it, so this is the perfect solution. Forgive me for being so thoughtless, pack your things, and consider your part of the rent nil."

"Holmes, not only is this overbearing, it's none of your business what shape my finances are in."

"Says the man who first took diggings with me here because we were both perfectly candid with one another about *having no finances to spare*."

"I won't do it, Holmes."

"You're going to have to if we go back to the system of your chequebook being locked in my drawer. Because even if I accept the first payment, I won't take any subsequent ones."

I don't think I've ever documented this particular situation. At the time, it's because everything was too terribly unbalanced and delicate in the immediate wake of Sherlock Holmes's miraculous resurrection, and afterwards, it's because I was reminded of the embarrassing scene whenever I tried to write about it. Personally, I was tremendously off my kilter. Mr. Mycroft Holmes had been paying me rent for three years to dust the furnishings, air the rooms fortnightly, live my life, and do nothing else. My house was like a shrine to Sherlock Holmes without any pilgrims. It was most disconcerting. I thought the man quite mad, and yet I had neither the affrontery to challenge him nor familiarity enough with the elder brother to sit down and share my tears and sympathies over his lost sibling. If there is one thing I can commiserate over, it is unbearable loss. And yet I was intimidated enough by the younger Holmes without attempting intimacy with the elder. I could only trust in Providence that all would be healed in due season.

And now here Mr. Sherlock Holmes was in the flesh! It really was a bit much, taken all in all. Sherlock Holmes is always a bit much.

"If you truly want me back here after . . . after everything, it's on my terms, my dear fellow," Dr. Watson seethed.

"Fine. Then you'll take half my reward earnings?"

"Of course I won't. The mind solving the cases isn't mine."

"The revolver and the aim are, though."

"Are you hiring me as a bodyguard or asking me to come home?"

There was a long pause. "The latter, my dear Watson." Mr. Holmes sounded steely, but he'd gone even a shade paler.

"Then do stop pressing the point."

"So long as you stop pressing half the rent on me, there's a good fellow."

"I have clients at my residence too, you know."

"Not ones you find half as interesting as mine!"

"You aren't the only expert in your field."

"Watson, I've no doubt but that you *are* an expert general practitioner, but in the realm of expertise, allow me to claim—"

"Be that as it may," the doctor growled, "my clients don't argue over me paying my own way in the world, and their company is seeming more agreeable by the minute!"

"Mrs. Hudson!"

Mr. Holmes has a very odd ability to shout without standing up, without dropping his jaw, without really doing any of the things I associate with actual shouting. It's as if suddenly his throat has a megaphone lodged inside, as Mr. Edison would have it, and one second he's speaking, the next he's shouting. Despite how close we are, he cows me a bit during the best of times, so the silverware I was gathering clattered to the tray. Bracing myself for a rant about being somehow underfoot, I straightened.

"Holmes, *really*," huffed Dr. Watson. "Are you all right, Mrs. Hudson?"

Sherlock Holmes closed his oddly pale eyes briefly, sucked air through his nostrils, and released it through his lips. He looked at me.

"My sincere apologies. Mrs. Hudson, tell me something. If I didn't pay you for these rooms and this very fine fare you are good enough to take such care over, would you provide it gratis?"

"Oh, for heaven's sake," the doctor groaned.

Hesitating, I worried over how best to resolve this for them. "No, sir, I'm afraid I couldn't manage to do such a thing. I'd have to find another tenant."

Mr. Holmes shot a smug look at his smoldering medical friend. "I thought so, my dear lady. And if I asked you to help me with my cases, throw yourself into dangerous situations, encounter all manner of unpleasantness, would you perform that much more arduous task free of charge?"

"Yes, sir, in a heartbeat. I already have done."

While that bold jaw might not have dropped while he was shouting, it did then. In utter bafflement. Dr. John Watson released a bark of laughter much more characteristic of his friend than of the evenly spoken doctor.

"I—excuse me?" the detective managed.

Giving him a motherly smile, I explained, "You don't see me sending you a bill for crawling on hand and knee to change the position of your bust in the window every fifteen minutes, do you? Even though Colonel Moran's entire goal was to shoot it with an air rifle?"

Dr. Watson flashed a triumphant grin at me and started clapping politely. I knew better than to respond other than a simple nod. They would hash it out between them. I took the dishes and left the room. Whatever they decided that day in 1894, my rent was always prompt and (as usual) from Mr. Holmes's cheques, so I never knew the verdict.

I've noticed of late that more and more often, my diary is becoming a repository of significant stories I didn't know how to set down when they happened, rather than the straightforward events of the day. But I don't find that I mind it. There's something soothing about unpicking past dramas, now that I know more fully how the stitches were sewn. Now that I am old enough and therefore bold enough to write them down.

Today, then! A curious thing did happen. Julia came up to me around midday with an unmarked little cardboard box in her hand.

"Found it sitting outside the service door, mum," she said, handing it to me. I cannot justly reproduce the way Julia speaks, a thick Cockney cant she seems to have worked hard excising the slang from, but it is quite charming to my ear. "Must be for you? Or . . . who can say till it's open, I suppose?"

Eyebrows raised in confusion, I shook the little parcel extremely gently. Whatever lay within was muffled by straw.

"I shall see to this, dear," I told Julia. "Would you stir the onions and make certain they don't brown?"

"Yes, mum."

Slowly, I made my way up the staircase. It's more slowly every passing year, but it's not a bit difficult yet, and I don't mind taking my time. A false step and a tumble at my age would hardly be advisable.

But this trek to see my lodger was an established rule of the household. Ever since that wretched box from Dr. Culverton Smith, when Mr. Holmes—well, never mind that horrid affair now, I shall address it someday—was sent the poison-tipped spring, unless I know the sender *and* the sender's handwriting, it's Sherlock Holmes who opens the mail. I can see the value in the precaution, obviously; he feels safer about me, I feel safer about everyone, and unmarked mail is almost always for him anyhow. I can also see the value in climbing stairs at all, as it's excellent for my health. Invigorates my constitution.

The door was swung half open, but I tapped anyhow. As usual pipe smoke filled the air, and that vaguely harsh aroma left over from a chemical experiment. Mr. Holmes was in his armchair, today in the blue dressing gown, his remarkable face cleanly shaved but his hair carelessly done. A piece of mingled black and silver was falling towards one grey eye.

I sighed, stepping over the threshold while praying in the restorative power of oysters. Providence had blessed me with remarkably fat ones this morning. They were waiting in a salt brine to be rendered juicy, tender, and crisp.

"Ah, Mrs. Hudson." Mr. Holmes has a high, cultured, clipped voice—by turns very lazy, quite bland, or shockingly rapid. "I don't think I rang."

"You didn't, sir." He knew he had not, but he prefers that sort of remark to outright asking what I'm doing there. Mr. Holmes does very few things directly.

"Then to what do I owe this pleasure?" he sighed.

He is still so out of sorts that the question was only empty courtesy mingled with distantly felt affection. *Not* genuine curiosity. But I appreciated it anyway, because it wasn't being shouted at, which I have studiously learned to ignore. Mr. Holmes looked up from nothing whatsoever, pretending to be interested in whatever I had to say. Sherlock Holmes has not changed so very much in over two decades; he is wiry and pale, but then he was always wiry and pale. His hairline comes to a point above his nose with sweeping indentations above each eye; but then it always did. The only difference is that thick patches above each ear are almost entirely silver. His stone-coloured eyes are often half-lidded; but then they always were. In the sense that he is courteous, snappish, active, indolent, friendly, aloof, and at the end of the day utterly changeable, he's rather a fixed point in my life.

"A box was left at the servants' entrance, Mr. Holmes."

Sherlock Holmes granted an upwards jerk of his chin, but no spoken words. We don't really require them at this point, between us. I went to his armchair and handed over the box.

"Mrs. Hudson, I've a multiplex knife on the right-hand side of the mantelpiece. Would you mind terribly bringing it here?"

Fetching it for him, I reflected on my habit of instantly obeying Sherlock Holmes within the confines of my own home. It's an eccentric practice for an experienced woman. But the habit serves multiple purposes. For one, I learned early that the sleuth is almost always right when he issues commands. There was the very vividly remembered occasion, for instance, when he suddenly shouted at me to get down (which I did without fuss) and then threw his entire body over me onto the bearskin rug, which had been a very choice wedding gift, as three gunshots shattered my window (which caused much more inclination to fuss on my part). Second, I've learned that villainous types tend to focus all their attention on my lodger and none on the white-haired landlady, so it's best I follow his lead.

Third, having his commands followed makes the poor fellow *much* more agreeable. I've met a few other men like this, but not to the extent Sherlock Holmes carries it. He can be very masterful when not being extremely lazy.

"Well, well, well, what have we here," he wondered aloud. Mr. Holmes has a strange tendency towards self-narration when the doctor isn't present to do it for him. "And where did this come from?"

"It was left outside, Mr. Holmes. I thought it best you take a look first."

"Very right of you too."

Lifting the little multiplex knife, he cut into the package with considerable care. At first, it revealed only straw. Gradually, as he continued, a trio of bonny blue eggs revealed themselves. Which was quite baffling—for the both of us, for once.

"My dear Mrs. Hudson, I take it that these were not ordered from the grocer by you?"

"No, not at all. How remarkable."

One of the reasons that Sherlock Holmes pays me a ridiculous amount for his rooms is that there is no knowing whether or when someone is trying to kill him. Therefore, we are both very careful, I am very accommodating about the risk, and he is very generous in his rent. Now I consider it, there is nearly always someone trying to kill him.

"They're quite pretty, aren't they?" I mused.

"Yes, but many deadly things are pretty."

"What do you have so far?"

"Not much," he admitted. "A male, I think, a local, takes his daily news from the *St. James's*, someone who makes regular rounds at deliveries."

This is an old dance, but he's always rather thrilling when he explains. "How so?"

"A woman who knows how to purchase comestibles would never buy *three* eggs. It's a terribly impractical amount—two or six or a dozen, certainly, but not three. It's not as if they go stale immediately. He's a local because these distinctive blue eggs are from a charming little shop not a quarter mile from here—I've seen them in passing and one can never tell when such information could be useful. And since he managed to drop them off unnoticed by any of the servants, I imagine deliveries are not an unknown task for him."

"How on earth can you know he takes the *St. James's*, Mr. Holmes?"

"What do you observe?"

The detective theatrically turned his hand over, placing the box on his flattened palm a little distance under my nose. At first, all I could see was the straw. But gradually, I glimpsed underneath that hints of crumpled newsprint making a nest for the eggs, and saw that only the sides were lined with straw.

"You can truly see that's a page from the *St. James's*?" I exclaimed, laughing.

"Doubtless only due to my more youthful eyesight," he teased. "And the fact that I think I have spent a bit more time than you have making a study of ink and of typeface. You may well have noticed that it is something of a preoccupation with me."

Clucking, I shot him a genuinely fond look indicating that sometimes I could not even see the sitting room for the abundance of scattered newsprint. With a smile, he drew back his arm.

"Well really, Mrs. Hudson, I have helped eleven men escape the gallows and caught twenty-eight murderers with the stuff. You cannot deny its use. Watson doesn't even try anymore, poor soul."

"Mmm. Do you think they're dangerous?"

"Mrs. Hudson, I truly don't know. May I keep one of these eggs to examine?"

So that was that. He kept one, and when I brought his dinner, he said he could find absolutely nothing chemically wrong with it. Thus, it would be fine for me to eat the other two.

I don't know what to make of any of it. But then again, that is a familiar feeling around Sherlock Holmes.

Entry in the diary of Mrs. Martha Rose Hudson, Sunday, April 12th, 1903:

He is going to drive me to distraction, utterly.

And it's not just the fits of pique—though admittedly, my irritation is tempered greatly by gratitude. Even though I'm sure it's his fault, and they are meant for Sherlock Holmes, another box appeared, and he is treating it with the utmost care and caution. This box contained a small jug of perfectly clotted cream. My tenant is performing chemical analyses on it. A bit of it is simmering amongst his chemistry apparatus. Though this seems outwardly ridiculous, since I have not the slightest idea what to do about these items, I am duly grateful. Only, I am still annoyed that I can cook a perfect fillet of haddock with leeks and duchess potatoes and have the dish returned after dinner entirely untouched. Not so much as a bite taken.

Dr. Watson, may you return with the greatest of haste.

Which leads me to the reason Dr. Watson is living in Queen Anne Street at all. Dr. Watson, who thought himself completely alone insofar as relations went, was mistaken. He had a cousin, a Mr. Edward Watson, who turned up about a month ago. When I answered the door, I assumed him a client—but I had a sneaking intuition that something was amiss, and it was only in retrospect that I understood I had been recognising a family resemblance. The same square jaw and proud neck, the handsome features, though his eyes were brown and the doctor's are blue. Mr. Edward Watson weighed fully two stone less than he ought to have. His skin was pale as if cold in the sweet July sunshine, but sickly sweat dotted his brow. His hands were palsied and twitching. He clutched the handrail as if about to fall.

"Oh sir, are you all right? Are you here to see Sherlock Holmes?" I asked at once.

"N-no," he gasped, looking as if he might be ill all over my steps. "But is Dr. Watson in? I need to speak with *him* most urgently."

"Right this way. You may lean on me if you like, sir. I'm much stronger than I look."

He took my arm with an air of desperation and we made our slow way up the stairs. I hugged the wall so that he might use both me and the bannister.

When we arrived upstairs, the door was already cracked open. It often is. I knocked anyhow, and as I led the unexpected visitor inside, Dr. Watson's face displayed blatant shock.

"Edward?" he exclaimed, startled onto his feet.

Mr. Holmes, as ever when something unexpected happens involving the doctor, looked suddenly as if fire bells had just started clanging. Few would have recognised it, but I can. Easily. There's an unmistakable fluttering of eyelashes as he tries to work out what's happening.

"Is this a relation of yours, my dear fellow?" he asked blandly. "Of course it is. There's no mistaking that jawline, or quite the contour of those ears. My dear sir, to what do we owe the pleasure? Do sit down."

"My name is Edward Watson," the man gasped. "I'm sorry . . . so sorry, that you find me in such a state, but there are designs upon my life. The pair of you—oh, I'd be so grateful for your help. Someone is after me, and I don't know who."

"Edward, how is that possible?" Dr. Watson demanded, incredulous.

"Please *sit down*, Mr. Watson," Sherlock Holmes said suavely. "It's a delight to meet anyone associated with my associate, as it were. You shall tell me all about it and I will then put it right."

The doctor was glaring daggers at his cousin by that time. And yes, the cousin was . . . very much impaired.

Dr. Watson does not suffer from the same illness as his late brother did, poor soul. And his cousin, apparently. When I encounter him coming home from his club, he's often the smallest bit blurred, but happy. And I once arrived upstairs with breakfast only to find all of Mr. Holmes's limbs impossibly folded into his armchair, Dr. Watson splayed full length on the settee with its blanket pulled over him, and an empty bottle of cognac between them, as they'd apparently been out doing something ungodly dangerous all night long. Both were fast asleep enough for it to be almost amusing. Leaving the breakfast tray quietly, I surveyed the teapot with skepticism and returned downstairs for a second pot, this time of coffee. My medical tenant had a splitting headache all afternoon, and I don't think he touched spirits for a week afterwards if the spent glassware I collected could speak.

This condition, though—Mr. Edward Watson, like the good doctor's long-passed sibling? This afflication is something much darker.

And yet, in a way I think, the doctor does have the same illness. There are the horse races, many of them. Rugby matches. Cricket. And his cheque book is resolutely locked in Mr. Holmes's desk. May the Lord help any such people, feeling such compulsions. My heart breaks when I think of my poor dashing Matthew—so kind, so quick-witted, so strong in the face of absolutely everything else Providence delivered us—with his head in his hands one day when we were both twenty-nine.

"Never again, Martha," he said from behind his fingers. "Never again. I'll never pick up a hand of cards again, nor so much as look at a pack."

"How much was it this time?" I asked, heart in my throat.

"Twenty pounds," he whispered.

Somehow, I fed us. Our clothing grew quite worn. But I fed us.

On the one hand, his transgression mattered very much. Matthew came from a well-established family, and they had helped us to buy our beautiful Baker Street home outright. By the same token, the Hudsons helped Matthew's career along in what small nudges they could. He was a banker at Barclay's—it should not have been my responsibility to scrimp and save because something about a Jack of Diamonds or a Queen of Hearts captivated his kindly eye like nothing else could. Not even me. On the other hand, his folly mattered not at all.

I was desperately in love with my husband.

Dr. Watson is one of the most decent people I've ever met. And Mr. Holmes, long ago, used to be a very different man when his spirits were depressed. Lax at some times and frenetic at others; through both moods uncaring, glassy-eyed, altogether *absent*. Something—I never understood quite what—was very wrong with him. He, too, comprehends, I believe, that desire to escape the world's troubles while still living in it. But his friend took it as his sworn duty to put a stop to all that business. Successfully. Mr. Holmes in turn put a lock on his desk that hadn't been there before and, when he fetched his key out of his waistcoat pocket, smiled carefully at the doctor whenever asked for access to the chequebook shut within.

And so, when Mr. Edward Watson turned up desperately ailing, it wasn't any wonder to me that, three days later, I interrupted another impassioned battle over housing arrangements between my tenants. As it happened, there were property documents I needed from the safe, and the safe is in the sitting room behind the doctor's portrait of General Gordon.

The trouble was that I kept rummaging and rummaging and could not for life or death find them. I could have sworn they were in the bottom third of the stack.

"Edward's life isn't being threatened, that's pure paranoia," Dr. Watson was arguing, "but he needs help and apparently I have one living relation, so I'm going to provide it."

"That is most generous of you," Mr. Holmes said icily in return. "Do wire me occasionally to let me know how it goes."

"For heaven's sake, Holmes."

"And why the devil is Queen Anne Street necessary, may I ask?"

"Holmes, we've already been through this. He doesn't need a detective; he's delusional. Edward requires a *doctor*. I am a doctor."

"As I am aware."

I made as if to go. This was all becoming entirely too personal.

"No, don't allow our little quarrel to distress you, Mrs. Hudson," Dr. Watson said in some exhaustion.

And it was a simple gambit, too. At times, the sleuth's temper may be cooled by my continued third-party observation. Anyway, it had worked in the past.

"Oh yes, Mrs. Hudson, pray don't mind us, I observe you're still empty-handed," Mr. Holmes drawled.

This time, it didn't seem to be working.

"He only needs to dry out, my dear fellow," Dr. Watson argued, "and he has every hope of being all right again. And to accomplish that, to quash this absurd paranoia, somebody must see that Edward does right by himself. I am free to do so. It's not as if I'm running a practice at the moment. But if I take a set of small rooms in Queen Anne Street and stay with him until he's in less danger—"

"What, and simply leave everything?" Mr. Holmes made an expansive gesture around him in exasperation.

"Holmes," Dr. Watson said warningly. "If I am to care for Edward for even a few weeks' time, it cannot be here, surely you realise as much. You see your clients here. Where am I to put the man, hm? Behind my bedpost upstairs? Be reasonable."

"Your cousin intruded into the middle of your life and you're dropping everything over it. Mind, I'm sure you would have done the same for your brother."

"I would have, for Henry, had I been able," the doctor said through his teeth. "Yes, I would have done a very great deal."

"Including abdicate your role as physician and turn nursemaid?"

I winced into the safe where the pair could not see me.

"I've done it before, haven't I?" Dr. Watson volleyed back.

At last I had my fingers on the paperwork I needed. As quickly as possible, I shut the safe, replaced the painting, and turned to leave. Both men, when I turned, looked more than usually miserable.

"Never mind me, my dear fellow," Mr. Holmes said quietly as he rose to stoke the fire, his brownish dressing gown billowing. "I was being most uncharitable. I only wonder what toll it will take on *you*."

This is all very distressing. When those two are at odds, my entire household goes topsy-turvy. Other than my maids, there are only three of us in it, after all.

Dr. Watson will be back very soon indeed. Any day now, in fact. Meanwhile, I must try to distract myself.

Thus, I roasted a brace of chickens today, and there's plentiful ham left, so I can make potted fowl out of the leftovers. It's much easier to put a pot and some toast on a tray supposing Mr. Holmes decides to eat lunch on a whim than it is to make a curry.

POTTED FOWL

INGREDIENTS: The remains of a cold roast chicken; for every lb. of meat, ¼ lb. fresh butter, 2–3 slices of ham, salt and cayenne to taste, 1 tsp. pounded mace, ½ tsp small ground nutmeg.

MODE: Strip the meat from the bird and remove any skin and gristle. Weigh out the above proportions. Cut the meat including the ham into very small pieces and pound it into the butter, gradually sprinkling in the spices. Continue pounding until a smooth paste forms. Place in potting-pots to serve, covering with ¼ inch of clarified butter. Keep in a cool, dry place and serve for breakfast or luncheon with toasted bread.

Entry in the diary of Mrs. Martha Rose Hudson, Monday, April 13th, 1903:

Another box at the doorstep, another visit to Mr. Holmes. This is so very, very mysterious. Which, of course, is a word which encompasses one's entire life when associated with Sherlock Holmes.

Mr. Holmes has quite deft hands which are always highly careful with packages, so it's rather interesting just to watch him open them. As he did, I could see him delicately sniffing the air, running his scarred fingers over textures, and shifting around like an excited puppy. He was obviously trying to pretend he was only distressed over the situation when in fact he also loved it. The distraction of the chase, the game being played—whatever it was. He at times forgets that I'm old enough to be his mother, and that I can read him like the *Strand Magazine.*

"Mrs. Hudson, this is most peculiar." He frowned, a sharp line forming over that very impressive nose. "Blue eggs and clotted cream and now Turkish delight?"

Staring at the package, my mouth dropped a bit open. What on earth was going on?

"Needless to say, you are not allowed to actually consume any of these comestibles."

"No, I expected that," I admitted.

"Mrs. Hudson, I fear I must ask an indelicate question."

"Oh?"

"Mmh. Have you ever, to your knowledge, incurred any . . . enemies?"

"No, Mr. Holmes, but *you* have."

"Indeed," he said after a pause. "Touché."

"I didn't mean it like that."

"Naturally not, Mrs. Hudson. But would you honour me with the broad sketch of your story before we met? It may help."

I nodded. And I trust Sherlock Holmes. So I told him much more than I thought I would. He also can put on a rapt air of captivity when someone else is talking. Just as he can put on a blank air of utter boredom. In this case, thankfully, it was the former.

"I married my husband, Matthew, when I was twenty," I told him. "Never was I able to bear children, but it was a happy union nonetheless, and we had this home here in Baker Street. I learned to cook, he learned to cultivate plants to cheer the house. I loved him very much, but he did have his . . . flaws."

"What sort, my dear Mrs. Hudson?"

"Ah . . . the very same sort which I believe affect your friend the doctor."

"The doctor?" For a moment, Mr. Holmes looked frankly baffled. "What possible . . . oh. *Oh.*"

"Yes, it was mainly cards and not horses, but . . . It led to financial distress."

"Of a serious nature?"

"I was able to avoid that, in the main."

"So we are not looking at a situation in which you are haunted by old enemies or creditors. This is almost definitely my fault."

"So it would seem."

Mr. Holmes's grey eyes lost their focus. I have always found it odd that when the man is thinking the hardest, he looks least like he is thinking at all. When Sherlock Holmes is thinking very *very* hard, he looks asleep. His long fingers started drumming an odd little beat on his armchair. Then he reached for one of his pipes on a nearby side table and lit whatever was left in it.

"It's most vexing that Watson won't be back until the day after tomorrow," he observed. "Speaking aloud to him greatly clarifies my mental processes. Granted, I could be speaking to the fireplace for all the insight he provides me. But—"

"But you miss him," I provided with a surge of boldness. "I know. I'm going to make beef brisket tonight, unless there's something else you request, and then find the fattest, freshest fish in the marketplace the day after tomorrow for you and the doctor to celebrate. I'd appreciate it if you *ate* some. And I'm sure you'll work out this odd business with the packages."

Sherlock Holmes stared at me, momentarily shocked, before his features settled back into neutrality. Then he cleared his throat.

"Yes, Mrs. Hudson, that would be most agreeable. And your oysters were, as always, a delight. I am sorry Watson missed them."

"I am too, sir," I said kindly. "Now, as to the brisket. Seven o'clock?"

"Dear me, ah . . . please do make it eight thirty; Lestrade will be arriving to consult over something, and he always appreciates your skills."

I smiled. "Eight-thirty it is."

BRISKET OF BEEF A LA FLAMANDE

INGREDIENTS: 6 lbs. brisket of beef, 8 slices of bacon, 2 carrots, 2 large onions, a bunch of savoury herbs to hand, salt and pepper to taste, 6 cloves, 4 whole allspice, 2 blades of mace.

MODE: Trim the gristle from the brisket and wrap it with the bacon slices before putting it in a stewpan. Add the vegetables (chopped rough), herbs, spices, and seasoning, and cover with basic meat or vegetable stock, whichever available. Close stewpan as tightly as possible and simmer for at least 4 hours. Strain the liquor; reserve a portion for sauce, boiling remainder over a very hot fire until reduced to a glaze, which will glaze the meat. Thicken and season the liquor reserved for the sauce, pour it round the meat, and serve. Garnish this dish with cooked turnips, artichoke bottoms, glazed onions, cabbage, or carrots as available.

Entry in the diary of Mrs. Martha Rose Hudson, Tuesday, April 14th, 1903:

What a pleasant day I've just passed!

Mr. Hoxsey paused to chat, bald pate gleaming in the spring sunshine when he swept his red and grey cloth cap off his head. He has very gentle eyes—green ones—that seem so at home surrounded by the frantic blossoming of April's new growth, for all his advanced age. We were at the service entrance, naturally, and my tulip bed was a riot of pinks and yellows and purples above the green.

"Sure and we've much to be thankful for this morning, do we not, Mrs. Hudson?" he asked.

"Always, Mr. Hoxsey," I agreed with a warm smile.

"I do take your point, but it's easier to really feel it on a day like today, isn't it?"

"Well, there are aspects of a good sparkling frost I like too." I took the milk.

"I couldn't agree more!" He flapped his cap back on. "Makes the bulbs bloom, doesn't it?"

"My own mother used to say so too."

Mr. Hoxsey wagged his index finger at the full jar I held. "Be good now," he admonished the milk. "If I hear tell that Mrs. Hudson's tea was anything short of perfect today, you'll catch it from *me*, d'you hear?"

Laughing at his surprisingly jaunty back as he walked away whistling, my lungs took in the morning air and I thought about what a strange home I lived in, where bullets flew past my head and street urchins came pounding up my stairs and waxen busts must be crawled to over the bearskin and boxes must needs be checked against tropical disease embedded on sharpened springs, and I laughed even harder.

"Are you all right, missus?" Julia asked as she came up to take the milk from my hands.

"Very much so," I replied, meaning it. "Come along, now, we're making kippers for ourselves and the boys,"

"Just the one boy at the moment, missus," Julia noted, showing the gap in her teeth prettily as she grinned.

"Oh, yes, of course, you're right. Silly of me." I took her arm chummily as we went inside. "But the other will be back tomorrow. He'll be back."

Later that night, at eight-thirty, I served brisket of beef and found myself smiling again as I made my careful way down the stairs. I could hear the clatter of serving utensils and the high buzz of conversation between the unofficial detective and the official detective and the sudden bark of a laugh.

I quite like that Inspector Lestrade fellow and always have. That's for a number of reasons, I imagine. For one thing, it's pleasant to be acquainted with someone who so unerringly knows how to irritate Sherlock Holmes. For another, the irritation is all quite harmless. He seems unimpeachably loyal. And the lot of them can be up half the night laughing over some case they just concluded, all three of the boys very, very happy indeed. I don't see what there is to laugh over when someone was just aiming bullets at you, but apparently *they do*.

For yet another, that makes at least two of them who actually *eat* the cooking I produce. And thank me at the end of the meal.

Entry in the diary of Mrs. Martha Rose Hudson, Wednesday, April 15th, 1903:

All right, enough is enough.

This time the package I brought Mr. Holmes was decorated. It was still cardboard but with its top and sides inlaid with baby shells poking through in a lovely swirling pattern, the whorled kind of shell with the conical tops. Seeing from a distance that today's mystery item was potentially much sharper than the usual, my lodger flew out of his chair.

"Mrs. Hudson!" he snapped. "You are being the most dreadful impediment to my investigation. Haven't you some form of Scottish swill to try to foist on my palate? Do not *touch this*."

In his brash way, the rudeness was amusing. Obviously, it was protective. And the Scotswoman portion is a longstanding joke. He detected a tiny trace of it in my accent after he and the doctor took the rooms, but I've never so much as been to Scotland. My mother was born there, which explains the almost inaudible lilt, and he knows this full well. He still teases me about everything I do being Scottish, staring down at the most delicate breakfasts and morosely asking if it's to be ham and eggs with curried fowl *again*. Granted, he teases everyone he knows with everything he can get away with, but I am not a Scotswoman. It's enough of a permanent jest at Baker Street that Dr. Watson put it in a story about a government treaty just to see the expression on my face and Mr. Holmes's when it was published, and then laughed himself to tears.

"Mr. Holmes, you know full well I am not Scottish," I said with admirable patience.

His dark brows twitched as he instantly turned more agreeable.

"My dear Mrs. Hudson, of course you are not. May I?"

I handed over the box, and he quickly laid hands on a magnifying glass.

"All right," he announced. "This . . . correspondent is probably located in Marylebone as we are, smokes fairly refined tobacco, owns a cat."

I allowed my eyes to be question marks since the words weren't needed. We both knew that this was a shockingly poor showing for the likes of Sherlock Holmes.

"As to living here in Marylebone, there's no postmark, so this was dropped off. We had already postulated about deliveries, but these were not hand-collected. They are commercially grown, which is why one may obtain so many identical ones at a low price, and one such seller has his shop very near to here, in Blandford Street. The tobacco I can smell in the packaging. It's too delicate a blend for me to quite make out; however, nothing like the sort of swill I and the doctor favour—though I'd put money on its being from India. And finally, surely I don't need to explain to you the significance of a cat hair."

He did not. Really. The very idea.

"But aren't you going to open it?" I urged.

Using the multiplex knife, he ever so delicately wedged open the cardboard. Inside lay a carved shell brooch, nestled on newsprint and cradled by straw. It was a bonny thing, shades of peach and pink and orange. But I saw Mr. Holmes's mind—make a few harmless offerings over several days and then sharpen two or three of the small decorative shells and dip them in what you will. People had gone to far greater lengths, with far more outlandish ideas, to kill Sherlock Holmes.

"Are we in danger?" I asked, bypassing the rest of his showmanship.

"Mrs. Hudson, I don't *know*," he replied with some asperity. "I have to examine each of these individually."

"How so?"

"I'll take swabs of them. It shouldn't be more than a couple of hours."

The door opened behind us, and I only had to see Sherlock Holmes's face settle into a small, satisfied smile to know who it was.

He has a very particular smile for every occasion. I'll list a few of them. There's the comforting a client in distress smile. The comforting a frightened *female* client in distress smile. Another for Inspector Lestrade. Another for members of the aristocracy soliciting his help whom he doesn't like. That one has knives in it. Another for children, mainly those impossible Irregulars. He has one for me, as well, and it's quite gracious. Then there's the smile he has for Dr. Watson.

"How nice to find you both here at once!" the doctor exclaimed.

"How nice to be found," the detective said smoothly. "How is your cousin?"

"Ah, well," the doctor prevaricated. He seemed worn down. "Better, but not entirely well, shall we say. I can do nothing more, really, save hope that actual nutrition, hydration, and sleep will provoke continued abstinence. But I have done what I could, and it was the right and proper thing to do."

Mr. Holmes had rested the box on his chemistry table.

"What do you have there?"

"We have been receiving some potentially rather distressing anonymous correspondence since your departure. Then again, perhaps not. Still."

"Still, an extremely large percentage of the anonymous missives you receive have been intended with your funeral in mind."

"You put it well, Doctor. I cannot help but be cautious. It doesn't behoove me to dwell upon what could have happened over Culverton Smith had, God forbid, one of you opened that cursed box. You very nearly *did* do so, and since then anonymous correspondence has carried with it an eighty-three percent chance of proving vengeful in nature." Mr. Holmes sighed, shaking his head. "Thirty-eight times, might I add."

Dr. Watson instantly sprang into action—asking questions, goading, being gently silent at times as he listened to the tale unfold. Somehow, he always knows just what to do. They bickered happily and for a few minutes, I stayed lest Mr. Holmes have any more questions or suggestions.

Often—not all the time, but often—our home together is a very contented one.

Entry in the diary of Mrs. Martha Rose Hudson, Thursday, April 16th, 1903:

Today, like a pendulum, my glad mood was replaced with a singularly glum one to that of yesterday. I think it must have been the mention of Culverton Smith Mr. Holmes made.

I dislike writing of things I cannot change, I discover. Like Mr. Holmes, I much prefer to have some agency. Ironic, in a diarist, for I know perfectly well that I cannot alter the past at all. The past is written in ink, not in pencil. Matthew will never come back to me. The weather will always have been unseasonably fine on that fateful occasion. So he will always have chosen to walk home through Marylebone on that day rather than taking a hansom. He will always have found himself on Gloucester Place.

There will always have been a spooked horse there, and they will always have fatally collided.

Ruining the present carries every chance with it of ruining the immediate future, Lord forbid. But there is nothing wrong with due diligence either. And I can see Mr. Holmes twitching and sweating and mewling in his bed, wracked with pain and fever, as clearly as if I had only five minutes ago bolted out of 221 to fetch Dr. Watson with the Reaper once again at my heels. It was one of the worst moments of my life, for all that it wasn't real.

Then he really did die, in Switzerland. Dr. Watson could not bear to come here often afterwards. He was heartbroken. And I was alone again.

I'd thought I understood what Mycroft Holmes was doing all those years ago in preserving his brother's rooms. I'd already done the same thing with my cooking, after all. No, regarding our mail with suspicion and disbelief is a small price to pay if it helps to keep the boys safe. With people, it is so very different—I can see their eyes, hear their voices. I've an uncanny knack for it, actually, my friends have always told me.

I trust people, or I don't trust them. I trust none of Mr. Holmes's mail.

Entry in the diary of Mrs. Martha Rose Hudson, Thursday, April 16th, 1903:

Oh, no. Oh, dear. I've solved it.

Mr. Hoxsey came with the milk. He winked at me. And then I knew it was him. From the moment he handed over the jug. He has been leaving me gifts. Small, harmless gifts.

And the surprising part is. . . I welcome them. Entirely. It's very sentimental for a woman of my years, but I cannot very well help myself.

Yesterday's cloud dissolved as if under a bright sun.

I brought up some ham and mustard and fresh bread for luncheon, not knowing whether Sherlock Holmes and John Watson would be there at all and intending to leave it on the sideboard. Instead, there they both were,

Mr. Holmes with his pipe between his lips as he read the newspaper, Dr. Watson sprawled at his ease on my settee with a yellow-backed novel. His face brightened when he saw me.

"Mrs. Hudson!" the doctor exclaimed. "And how are you? We did not speak for long yesterday."

"Much better now that you've returned to us, Dr. Watson," I said with wry affection, shooting a dark glance at Sherlock Holmes.

He took it in the teasing spirit it was intended, eyes floating above the newspaper. "Why, Mrs. Hudson, is not my company enough for you?"

"It can be *more* than enough at times, sir, that is the problem."

Dr. Watson stifled a laugh as a small snort of derision rattled the newspaper.

"Doctor, how are affairs with your cousin?" I asked. "I overheard you say he was not completely recovered."

"He will not ever be, though he can be completely relapsed, I suppose." Dr. Watson brushed at his moustache. "There's no climbing back from some moral retrogressions. And I shall continue to assist all I can, but the lion's share of the work is his and I may have forgotten that in my enthusiasm. Due to prior experience."

The newspaper released an emphatic puff.

"You see, Doctor?" said I. "You did all that was humanly possible."

"Well," he replied, looking a bit abashed, "it seems that in one respect I myself was in the wrong."

"Oh? And what was that?"

Mr. Holmes fluidly interjected, "Someone actually was trying to kill Edward Watson."

"No!" I gasped. "They were? Truly?"

"Most assuredly." Mr. Holmes released another stream of pipe smoke. "From the moment of his arrival here, I thought it best to take due precautions. It was obvious to me at once that alcohol was not his sole vice. He'd just a hint of the sort of tickets one collects betting on the horses or dog races creeping out of his shirt pocket, his knuckles were bruised faintly from some sort of fight or other, and naturally there was the impaired mental judgement incurred by strong drink to consider. Such men rarely lead perfectly peaceable lives."

"To think I chalked it all up to some sort of mania," Dr. Watson moaned.

"Come now, it is my profession to seek out what is sinister where others see what is harmless," Mr. Holmes replied amiably. The man himself at last materialised from the news of the day, dropping it to the floor, gesturing with his pipe stem. "It only required a bit of research on my part to discover his most serious infraction to date, a large debt over cards to a Whitechapel ruffian of very ill repute and even worse temper. When our good Inspector Lestrade was here the other night, it was at my behest, and I suggested in the strongest terms that he arrest this unpleasant fellow on any number of provable charges, thus neatly avoiding tragedy where the Watson family is concerned. It's much more difficult to pummel a man to death from inside a Black Maria, or a gaol cell, I find. The confinement creates certain impediments to fisticuffs. Or knives or guns, for that matter. Prior to that, the good doctor here never left Edward Watson's side, so he was quite safe."

He flashed a quick smile at Dr. Watson, who returned it with a longer one. I found myself helplessly smiling too.

"Well, that is very good news," I offered. "Mr. Holmes, I have further . . . good news. I've solved the matter of the packages."

"Did you really?" he exclaimed, spine straightening. "I confess I've made scant progress over them still. The newest is on the mantelpiece just there, Mrs. Hudson. It's quite safe to the touch."

"Yes, these mightily intrigue me. Enumerate the items again, Mrs. Hudson?" Dr. Watson requested.

Instead, Mr. Holmes counted on his fingers. "Three blue eggs, a jar of clotted cream, Turkish delight, and now this curious box with its intricate carving. I've begun to suspect it's not a trap but rather a code I'm meant to decipher."

I would have liked to have listed them myself, of course. But Dr. Watson was only just returned to us, and if there is one thing Sherlock Holmes enjoys nearly as much as chasing a criminal, it is telling a story. The man really can be ridiculously endearing when he isn't nudging me ever closer and closer to Bedlam.

"And I cannot report the finale of this tale, because apparently, it's Mrs. Hudson who solved it," he concluded. "So pray do tell us, my dear woman, what is your conclusion?"

"All the packages were for me," I admitted, blushing. "I've a . . . secret admirer. In the form of our milkman."

Sherlock Holmes sat frozen for a moment before he burst out laughing, covering his pale eyes with his hand. The poor fellow is so melancholy at times that it is quite wonderful to see him thoroughly at his ease. And I could not possibly be offended; I had thought the notion quite as absurd and self-flattering as he did. Certainly I could never have gone so far as to propose such an idea as a theory. It is not that I mean to disparage my own attributes, for I do not; I merely mean it would take someone who belonged in an asylum to put up with Sherlock Holmes for this long, and I should have thought that degree of madness rendered my companionship a moot point.

"Oh, Mrs. Hudson," he gasped. "Do please forgive me. I never meant to cast any aspersions on your considerable charms by failing to consider this. The milkman, you say? The hairless fellow who was born in Belfast?"

Smiling indulgently, I admitted, "I thought you might be able to tell. And I'm not Scottish. Where else has he lived?"

"Dublin, Waterford, Cork, Manchester, Twickenham, and now here in Marylebone. I cannot with *absolute* certitude tell you the order, but it's a safe balance of odds that the family made their way south-eastward in such a manner, supposing they never backtracked but meant to emigrate. How charming. I've encountered him once or twice as I was coming back from some late-night affair or other. I asked him whether one could tell where a cow had pastured from the quality of its milk and he assured me that one could. I'd have made a study of it, but was engaged in a very taxing case regarding a bloodied glove at the time. Mr. Hoxsey, I think? He seems an upstanding gentleman."

Dr. Watson's eyes twinkled with mirth. "I seem to have missed a great deal in my absence. I shall never leave again. And if you don't mind my asking, Mrs. Hudson, what do you intend to do about this?"

Considering, I paused. I thought of Matthew and of the children we'd attempted to create. I thought of his bright wit and his ready laugh and his narrow chin. I thought of purchasing this home in Baker Street, and of the accident which felled him, and of the pair of absolutely remarkable lodgers who have enabled me to live in so much comfort—and danger too, but never mind that. I'm accustomed to it now. I recalled how lonesome I was before these madmen arrived here, and how I could have had a string of tenants, always advertising for more, never growing attached, instead of these brave boys as permanent fixtures. I thought of all the other pathways my life could have taken and concluded that I'd never gotten anywhere in my life by saying *no*, only *yes*.

"My dear Doctor, she is obviously considering the courtship." Mr. Holmes smirked. "That blush isn't from rouge as she is quite above cosmetics, I've not seen her do her hair in quite this style a single time previously, that lovely green dress I last witnessed six years ago, at Christmas, she has her hands clasped in front of her as she does when she's thinking, and since my olfactory senses are very highly honed indeed, I can catch a small trace of perfume from across the room. As I said, she is at least considering it."

At times, it is annoying to be dissected by Sherlock Holmes. But this was not one of them. Dr. Watson fairly beamed at me. I smoothed my palms over the dress in question.

"Far be it from me to contradict the great consulting detective," I answered coyly.

They both fairly howled with laughter. But it was not mocking, all felt warm and solid and *right*. After a few more minutes of easy banter, I left them to their conversation and their noxious pipe smoke.

I am going to cook guinea hens tomorrow, with buttered parsnips. And when Mr. Hoxsey arrives, there will be a package wrapped with brown paper containing a luncheon awaiting him. How better to express myself than with my cooking? I will doubtless think of my darling Matthew often as I go about this. But if my life's lessons have taught me one thing—my husband's sad demise, my own recovery from it, Mr. Holmes's death and resurrection, Dr. Watson's return to Baker Street—life must be lived moment to moment, neither in the past nor in the future. Mr. Holmes, for all his fits of melancholy, lives very fully. Dr. Watson seems entirely unable to help throwing himself wholeheartedly into any subject which interests him, and for many years that subject has been Sherlock Holmes. I know both men well enough to know they have both experienced serious hardships, the doctor with the Afghan War and the detective with his own mind.

But they carry on, and they have each other, and I have them, and that is a very great balm indeed.

I think I will ask young Julia to accompany me to market. If I were wise, I would set her to cleaning the kitchen hearth while I'm gone. But instead, I will point out to Julia how to select the very best poultry, and which stalls have the plumpest vegetables. She will need to know these things someday, and I am only a foolish old woman, after all.

ABOUT THE CONTRIBUTORS

IRENE ADLER
"The Adventure of the Stopped Clocks"

To Sherlock Holmes, Irene Adler is always "the" woman; to John Watson, she is of more dubious and questionable memory, although it's possible to detect hints of the doctor protesting too much. Most of his first passage devoted to Irene Adler in "A Scandal in Bohemia" has naught to do with Adler and much more to do with the doctor's utter bafflement that Holmes—a presumed walking abacus or ambulatory microscope—could ever be charmed by a brilliant, beautiful prima donna contralto in the first place. And yet, there we have it: Holmes is charmed flat into the cobblestones, with seeming no distress to his aloof personage. All this despite the fact she appears in but a single story, though her untimely demise is mentioned later.

As for the adventuress Adler herself, we know little of her and see still less. She hails from New Jersey. She is kind and cunning. She feels threatened by the hereditary King of Bohemia, with whom she once had a dalliance, though she quickly marries the much more dashing solicitor

Godfrey Norton. The king desires an incriminating photo of his majesty and the chanteuse returned; Adler desires nothing of the sort. A game of cloak and dagger ensues which, once the king has been trounced enough times, calls for Sherlock Holmes to settle the whole royal mess. Cue smoke rockets, disguises, brave damsels, and daring escapes—surely a guaranteed list of things likely to charm Mr. Sherlock Holmes.

HENRY WIGGINS
"The Song of a Want"

Wiggins is the commander of the "Baker Street Irregulars," the network of destitute street urchins Sherlock Holmes employs when he wishes to act absolutely in secret; penniless children are all but invisible to the denizens of London. Wiggins is taller and older than the rest of the gang, with a nonchalant superiority Watson finds amusing in a shoeless ragamuffin. Holmes trusts Wiggins enough for the younger scamps to report to Wiggins, and Wiggins thence back to Holmes, and for Wiggins to distribute their wages as well. One easily pictures the lad's chest puffing with pride at the fact he is of such tangible service.

An unquestionable rapport exists between the unlikely friends. It seems one that could only have sprung up under the most extraordinary of circumstances—and in Wiggins' case, before meeting Holmes, his situation could not possibly have been other than cruelly bleak. As for Holmes, he was living in Montague Street, studying subjects he thought might prove useful to detective work at the British Library. Their meeting, as will be seen, was indeed an extraordinary one.

There are those who find themselves puzzled when the decidedly unfussy Holmes accepts exorbitant rewards from aristocrats he despises—but surely we need look no further than Wiggins and his ilk to discover the sleuth's motives. Holmes would not take talent under his wing and then leave it to flounder unsupported; we know as much from the fact Wiggins himself compiled this remarkable volume.

GEOFFREY LESTRADE
"Our Common Correspondent"

Regarding friends, Sherlock Holmes famously likes to claim to Watson that the doctor himself is his sole companion: those of us who pay attention to what the sleuth actually does rather than how he describes himself know he is an inveterate liar on the subject of one Mr. Sherlock Holmes, particularly as regards his friendship with that unimaginative but utterly beloved comrade, Inspector Lestrade. It's difficult to imagine Holmes inviting anyone other than his old friend Lestrade to best Colonel Moran and help resurrect the sleuth from the maw of a deadly Swiss waterfall. Who but Lestrade would Holmes trust when he needs another gun to bring down the gruesome hound of the Baskervilles? Above all, who save Lestrade could bring Holmes practically to tears when the inspector explains that they are not jealous of him down at Scotland Yard—no, no, he assures the astonished detective, "we are very proud of you . . ." The declaration moves Holmes to such depth of feeling that he seems to consider for a moment simply hiding in the broom closet.

Descriptions of the trio's tete-a-tetes are no less engaging. Watson claims Lestrade drops by for supper, they sit by the fire and smoke, and talk of crime. Well, they also talk about police headquarters gossip, recent newspaper reports, and—of all things—the weather. These are not men forced to endure each other's company. These are brothers in arms, which could only have come about in a highly dramatic fashion.

STANLEY HOPKINS
"The River of Silence"

At the outset of these beloved accounts, who could ever have imagined Sherlock Holmes with a protégé? He is revered, yes. He is famous—even infamous—admittedly. He grants hints and writes international correspondence. It's remotely possible to picture an eighteen-year-old Roundsman Wiggins being clapped on the back and pointed in the right direction. Such may well have happened, in fact. But a genuine Scotland Yard inspector with a true case of hero worship? Enter Stanley Hopkins.

While it is an irrefutable fact Sherlock Holmes loves teasing people, it's charming to picture him really ribbing Hopkins, because Inspector Hopkins is so utterly and innocently sincere. Of course, he isn't unused to the evils of London, or of humanity at large, but he is such a good-natured fellow, and one who so effortlessly wants to right wrongs as opposed to advance in ranks, that it's easy to discern that in spite of—no, because of—the teasing, Holmes genuinely likes the chap. Holmes claims that he's taken Hopkins under his wing because he shows remarkable aptitude for a Yarder; it's a dubious statement. Lestrade owns manifestly better instincts, there are hundreds we don't know, and even Bradstreet seems to be an eminently capable man when it comes to observation and inference. Inspector Hopkins is no protégé of Sherlock Holmes because he is gifted. He is taken under the sleuth's wing because he is good, and Holmes knows that protectors with nobility and sincerity are what London truly needs.

A. DAVENPORT LOMAX
"The Gospel of Sheba"

It's easy to think of Sherlock Holmes himself as the greatest mystery of the Sherlock Holmes canon—did he spring fully formed from the head of Zeus? Other than Watson and his brother Mycroft, who were his attachments? Was he ever the victim of a tragic love affair? Did he really manage to convince a doctor that snakes drink milk? The evidence is compelling, and yet, another candidate for utmost inscrutability presents himself: Dr. Watson is opaque in an entirely differently fashion. And what better way of proving this than discussing the charming physician's friends?

Schoolmates with Stamford at St. Bart's. Lifelong partner of Sherlock Holmes. Chummy with his clubmates. All this makes eminent sense, but how on earth did he encounter a sub-librarian named Lomax at the London Library and come to be on such intimate terms with the fellow that he essentially said, "Lomax, I must become an expert on Chinese pottery," and Lomax indicated right this way. Watson gives every appearance of relying on Lomax the way Holmes relies on the British Library, which is entirely appropriate as regards scale: Watson is an intelligent man who consults a brilliant one when conducting researches, and Holmes is a genius who consults an entire library when doing the same. Lomax seems as if he must be an intelligent, genteel fellow, though we never hear him utter a word in the canon. The matter is still obvious: any friend of Watson's is a friend to all.

MARTHA HUDSON
"A Life Well Lived"

221 Baker Street (flat B in particular) is many things to many people. To John Watson, it is a haven of hope following a grim war. To Sherlock Holmes it is the comfort of a life no longer lived in grim solitude. To the postman, it is a very popular address, to the plants it is a greenhouse, to the cats it is a hearth.

To Mrs. Hudson, it is a vocation.

Mrs. Hudson has been many things to many people. When she was sixteen, she had two beaus (at once!). She wed at the age of twenty-three, just at the cusp of being an old maid in those days. But he swept her off her slippers, and that night as a bride she nearly danced the soles off them too, and they had seven happy years together, and then that was that. Martha Hudson had a broken heart, a pair of cracked slippers she still kept in a cedar box, and she had 221 Baker Street. She had no idea what was about to become of flat B.

Would it have shocked her to learn what it would mean to so many? How many it would save? How it would save her? Even her lodgers? Would she one day learn that 221 wasn't simply a street address, but a haven?

Possibly. But in the main, to Martha Hudson, 221 Baker Street is her calling.